SF:

THE

OTHER

SIDE

OF

REALISM

Essays On
Modern Fantasy
And
Science Fiction

SF:
THE OTHER SIDE OF REALISM

ESSAYS ON
MODERN FANTASY
AND
SCIENCE FICTION

Edited by

THOMAS D. CLARESON

Bowling Green University Popular Press
Bowling Green, Ohio 43403

The pictures reproduce illustrations from John A. Mitchell's novel,
Drowsy (1917), reprinted with the permission of the Executors of
the Mitchell Estate.

ESPECIALLY

FOR

ALICE

AND

TOMMY

It has always seemed to me that if there were such a thing as "mainstream," science fiction should belong, at least marginally, to it, for everyone who writes, whatever he may write, does so within the parameters of a literary tradition that has evolved, developed and changed through the years. And the effort to disassociate fantasy (which is pretty much an undefinable term) and science fiction (which is perhaps as much so) arises from the intricate business of arguing how many angels can dance on the head of a pin. I don't think that we should attempt to distinguish between the two, and that the writer, especially, should disregard any artificial line that exists between them. The best stories, it seems to me, are fantasies, whether they be based on solid scientific extrapolation, or on engineering concepts carried to an ultimate point, or on something else.

Clifford D. Simak
December, 1969

CONTENTS

CONTENTS

INTRODUCTION:
THE
CRITICAL RECEPTION
OF
SCIENCE FICTION

At the MLA Forum on Science Fiction in 1968, Fred Pohl, the veteran editor and writer, suggested that it did not matter what had been or was being written in the field of science fiction. The real difficulty in obtaining a critical hearing—particularly among librarians and teachers at all levels—lay in that from 1926, when Hugo Gernsback founded *Amazing Stories,* the first pulp devoted exclusively to the genre, until the 1940's at least, sf had lived "amid garish covers and poor print and rough edges" so that "you usually carried them home under your coat because you didn't want anyone to know what you were reading."[1] The "Bug-Eyed-Monsters" ("BEM's") and lithe Martian princesses or harem-like spacegirls have largely surrendered the covers of the specialist magazines. Within the past decade or so science fiction has gained a narrow critical and academic respectability because of its concern with utopian-dystopian themes. But "modern" science fiction has never completely overcome its popular origins in dime pulps featuring such titles as *Thrilling Wonder Stories, Astounding, Startling,* or *Super-Science Stories.* Because it has been confined to such magazines and their successors, there has grown up that short-sighted perspective which speaks of the genre only in terms of what has been published originally in those pulps. In February, 1970, for example, a blurb from the Science Fiction Book Club advertized a volume, *Science Fiction Hall of Fame,* containing "26 'very best' short stories in all, spanning four decades . . . the best there've been to date. The stories' appearance in one book constitutes a rare publishing achievement. Arranged by order of original publication, they are, in effect, a record of the genre's development."[2] Although its editor, Robert Silverberg, is among the first to acknowledge that limiting the genre to the specialist magazines confines it historically and critically, many of its aficionados do date its beginning from 1926, arguing that Gernsback coined the term "science fiction." (Actually, he first spoke of "scientifiction.") They will agree that, of course, such men as Jules Verne and H. G. Wells wrote sf, but they also frequently dismiss such writers as hopelessly old-fashioned and unreadable or as mere forerunners of the form which has reached its full maturity only within the past generation. In the instance of some editors and writers whose careers go back into the 1940's or 1930's, this turning in upon themselves is understandable. They are the men who have created "modern" science fiction, and they guard it proudly; it is their baby. On the other hand, a few, like Kurt Vonnegut, Jr., who have achieved a degree of critical recognition beyond the working circle, have sometimes denied that their work should be included in the category of science fiction, although, if nothing else, the republication of their early works shows their indebtedness to the specialist magazines as a starting place.[3]

One cause of this introversion or denial stems from the failure of the critics, both of the popular press and of academe, to afford sf even the small recognition given to the western story and the detective novel as forms of popular literature. This is not to say that it has received no attention prior to the last ten or fifteen years; indeed not, but from the first, that interest, often with tongue-in-cheek, focused upon ideas, dismissing any consideration of it as literature. Although as early as 1930 Edward Shanks, in the *New Statesman,* did think it a phenomenon worthy of study,[4] in 1936 Clemence Dane called it "nothing in the world but America's fairy stories" and regarded it as so much "nonsense."[5] Three years later Bernard DeVoto could do little but deplore what he considered its uniformly pessimistic view of the future.[6] The first spate of criticism came in the early 1950's under the cloud of Hiroshima. In 1953, J. B. Priestley found one type of story worth attention: the "future nightmare" as typified by Ray Bradbury.[7] J. Donald Adams thought it to be a literature "deeply concerned with mankind's present plight and its problematical future."[8] A number of critics insisted that it be judged on its literary merit, but they themselves did not do so. Some scientists wondered why scientists read it; Bentley Glass preferred the treatment such a writer as Sinclair Lewis gave science and scientists in *Arrowsmith,* although he thought that in literature generally there did not "appear to be any profound understanding of science itself," let alone the scientist.[9] Essentially, however, the critics seem to have looked for a simplistic answer to what had happened at Hiroshima and what might now happen any day. When they did not find that magic explanation, they turned to the genre's most fantastic "gadgets" and ideas; often the fiction was virtually dragged in as an after-thought to a bemused discussion of the latest monsters and special effects used in movies or TV series. To read many of the articles in *Life, Newsweek,* and, on occasion, *The Saturday Review,* for example, is to feel that one is reading the same thin file.

To such appraisal came a few answers. Among them, Ray Bradbury felt that science fiction is the only form of literature in which philosophy, sociology, psychology, and history can be "played with" without ruining the work as literature; it creates "outsize images" of the problems that face society.[10] John W. Campbell wanted it to be judged as a literature of prophecy, for its "fundamental purpose" is "to make accurately loose prophecies of general trends."[11] Isaac Asimov and Fletcher Pratt also stressed the importance of prophecy.[12] August Derleth, in *The English Journal,* was one of the few who suggested that the genre "embraces all imaginary fiction which grows out of scientific concepts."[13] Yet open hostility never ceased completely. On 22 February 1970, in a review of Ira Levin's dystopian novel, *This Perfect Day,* the writer for the Cleveland *Plain Dealer* exclaimed: "Because of the basic subject matter the science fiction set will do its best to cuddle *This Perfect Day* to its steely, electronic bosom. They have already claimed *Brave New World* and *1984* not to mention *Alice* and *The Wizard of Oz* and about half the stories of Saki. I will thank them to keep their tinny little hands off Mr. Levin."[14]

Even now, although academic courses devoted to some phase of science fiction have increased in number in the last few years—

one is tempted to say semesters—the teachers, too, often wary of the opinions of their colleagues, have remained most careful.[15] Among numerous letters to *Extrapolation* within the past year announcing or inquiring about such courses, some still cautiously name Wells, Huxley, Bellamy, Orwell, and Bradbury, and then ask for additional titles "which appear, by some sort of consensus, to be classics of science fiction."

The response over the years to such critical and academic reception should come as no surprise. Although most editors and writers have most graciously and enthusiastically cooperated with the MLA Seminar on Science Fiction, for example, there remain a few devotees who regard as unnecessary the belated academic interest in the genre which has developed *primarily* during the 1960's. They argue that the academic world—and critics in general —knows little about the contemporary field and therefore limits its discussion to such classic figures as Verne and Wells, as well as to certain themes only, ignoring the rest of the field. There is some justice in their reaction.

As a group, science fiction enthusiasts—editors, writers, and the hardcore of readers—have withdrawn to themselves. (At various times they have been accused of being cultish or defensive.) In doing so, they have created one of the most colorful sub-cultures, not only in the United States and Canada, but in Australia and New Zealand, Great Britain, and throughout continental Europe, for science fiction has become as popular in the East as the West.

Although they tend to remain apart as a sub-culture, they make themselves known through their frequent conferences and conventions—regionally, nationally, internationally. Over the Labor Day week end, 1969, some 1800 people gathered in St. Louis for the 27th "World Science Fiction Convention." In August, 1970, they met in Heidelberg, West Germany. They make themselves heard not only through the professional magazines, but also through the hundreds of periodicals published by enthusiasts —the so-called "fanzines," many of which have had long runs and contain materials that would be invaluable to the study of the genre. Many of the young writers and artists entering the field come up through the fanzines. Although these often publish original fiction and poetry and can be given over to personal and letter columns, the majority of the criticism of science fiction, usually in the form of book reviews, has thus far been published either in them or the professional magazines. On occasion these reviews have been collected, added to, and published by specialist houses. Although August Derleth's Arkham House has devoted some thirty years to the fiction and papers of H. P. Lovecraft, as well as the circle developing around him, the most influential at the moment seems to be Advent Publishers, which has issued a number of studies written especially for them. Individuals like Donald B. Day or the MIT Society have done valuable work in bibliography and in indexing the professional magazines. One fanzine, published during the 1960's, deserving attention is Leland Sapiro's *Riverside Quarterly*, now included in the *PMLA* annual bibliography. If the work of one man deserves singling out, he is Sam Moskowitz, certainly one of the foremost bibliophiles in the field. His surveys have done much to introduce a wider audience to the genre, but because of his extensive knowledge as a collector, his most valuable work continues to be such specialized studies as *Science Fiction by Gaslight: A History and Anthology of Science Fiction in the Popular Magazines, 1891-1911* (1968) and *Under the Moons of Mars: A History and Anthology of 'The Scientific Romance' in the Munsey Magazines, 1912-1920* (1970). Nor should one overlook Everett F. Bleiler's *The Checklist of Fantastic Literature* (1948). Most often, however, the editions of the critical works have been small, sometimes only a few hundred copies privately printed, so that much has been irretrievably lost. Perhaps equally important, aficionado has written for aficionado. Under such circumstances, criticism can become personality-centered and, of course, contribute to the idea that the period from 1926 or so is somehow unique and science fiction separate from the larger body of literature.

When academic attention came to sf in any quantity, it focused primarily upon the utopian-dystopian themes, as noted, and in the United States has not moved far beyond that parochial interest, unless it has been to examine the genre, recently, as a source of myth. Dorothy Scarborough gave attention to Wells and others in a chapter, "Supernatural Science," in *The Supernatural in Modern English Fiction* (1917), but J. O. Bailey's *Pilgrims Through Space and Time* (1947) provides a landmark as the first academic study of the genre as a whole. Philip Babcock Gove's investigation of *The Imaginary Voyage in Prose Fiction* (1941) had preceded it, while Marjorie Nicolson's *Voyages to the Moon* (1948) followed it. Yet not until Kingsley Amis's *New Maps of Hell* (1960), can one say that the academic "boom" started in the United States. Since then, many journals and little magazines have included the occasional article on science fiction, but too often the apparent editorial policy of one article has made them seem a dutiful gesture to a topical interest.[16]

Although in recent years several conferences that promise to continue have sprung up, and although a research association is in the process of forming, during the past decade the Modern Language Association itself has provided the focal point for continuing academic interest in the genre.[17] In 1958, primarily through the efforts of the late Professor Scott Osborn (Mississippi State University), the MLA scheduled the first Conference on Science Fiction at its New York meetings. I had the privilege of chairing that first Conference. Now the Seminar on Science Fiction, it has met annually since 1958 and is one of the two oldest continuing Seminars of the MLA. Such scholars in the field as J. O. Bailey (North Carolina University), Mark Hillegas (Southern Illinois University), and Bruce Franklin (Stanford University) have served as chairmen of subsequent meetings. In 1968, at the request of members of the Seminar, the MLA Executive Committe recognized the now-permanent interest in this peculiarly modern genre when it gave over one of its special Forums to the topic, "Science Fiction: the New Mythology." Professor Franklin moderated a panel made up of Isaac Asimov, Fred Pohl, and Professor Darko Suvin of the University of Montreal. Judith Merril had planned to take part but was unfortunately ill at the time.

Extrapolation was first published in December, 1959, to act as the Newsletter of the Seminar. It functioned at first to print the papers derived from the annual meeting, to provide working bibliographies and annotated checklists, and to include various notes, several no more than a page long and few longer than a thousand words. Its growing reliance upon more extended essays may serve as one index of the increasing scholarly interest in the field of science fiction, as may the reprinting of its first ten volumes by Johnson Reprint Corporation. Happily, it has also provided a meeting ground for the academic and science fiction communities, not only here in the United States and Canada, but throughout he United Kingdom and continental Europe, both East and West.

Since science fiction, obviously, is not the domain of any one group or one nation, I have tried to bring together a sampling of essays and notes, primarily but not exclusively, from the 1960's and from academic, pop lar, and specialist sources in order to indicate the diversity with which the genre may be approached. Of course this volume wishes to celebrate the first decade of the Seminar and the Newsletter, but far more important it wishes to celebrate the world-wide community of scholars, professionals, and enthusiasts who have made science fiction their interest. All contribute their perspectives to "the other side of realism."

The College of Wooster
October, 1970

NOTES

[1]"The MLA Forum: Science Fiction: The New Mythology," *Extrapolation*, 10 (May 1969), 99.

[2]*Things to Come* (May 1970), p. 2: This four page circular is put out by the Doubleday Science Fiction Book Club to announce each selection. This month the cover reads: "In one great collection—*all* of the best science fiction short stories of this century!"

[3]J. Michael Crichton, "Sci-Fi and Vonnegut," *The New Republic*, 26 April 1969, pp. 33-35. In addition to identifying Vonnegut with science fiction, he makes such observations as "It is still as pulpy, and as awful, as ever." p. 33.

[4]Edward Shanks, "Other Worlds Than Ours," *The New Statesman*, 14 June 1930, pp. 305-306.

[5]Clemence Dane, "American Fairy Tale," *North American Review*, 242 (Autumn 1936), 143-152.

[6]Bernard DeVoto, "Doom Beyond Jupiter," *Harpers*, 179 (September 1939), 445-448.

[7]J. B. Priestley, "They Came from Inner Space," *New Statesman and Nation*, 5 December 1953, pp. 712-714.

[8]J. Donald Adams, "Speaking of Books," The New York *Times Book Review*, 13 September 1953, p. 2.

[9]Bentley Glass, "The Scientist in Contemporary Fiction," *The Scientific Monthly*, 85 (December 1957), 288-293.

[10]Ray Bradbury, "Day After Tomorrow: Why Science Fiction?" *Nation*, 2 May 1953, pp. 364-367.

[11]John W. Campbell, Jr., "Science Fiction and the Opinion of the Unwise," *The Saturday Review*, 12 May 1956, pp. 9-10.

[12]Fletcher Pratt, "Science Fiction and Fantasy—1949," *The Saturday Review of Literature*, 24 December 1949, pp. 7-9; Isaac Asimov, "The MLA Forum: Science Fiction: The New Mythology," *Extrapolation*, 10 (May 1969), 81-85.

[13]August Derleth, "Contemporary Science Fiction," *The English Journal*, 61 (January 1952), 1-8.

[14]Eugenia Thornton, "After 'Rosemary's Baby'—Uni-Comp," The Cleveland *Plain Dealer*, 22 January 1970.

[15]Mark Hillegas, "The Course in Science Fiction: A Hope Deferred," *Extrapolation*, 9 (December 1967), 19-21.

[16]The most comprehensive bibliographical account of the field remains: R. Neil Barron, "Anatomy of Wonder: A Bibliographic Guide to Science Fiction," *Choice*, 6 (January 1970), 1537-1545.

[17]For two years in a row Professor Ivor Rogers has chaired "The Secondary Universe Conference": 1968, University of Wisconsin, Milwaukee; 1969, University of Wisconsin, Green Bay. In March, 1969, Fred Lerner organized the first Science Fiction Bibliographical Conference at Columbia University.

Fall, 1970, the third of the "Secondary Universe" Conferences was held at Queensborough Community College, Bayside, L.I., New York, organized by Professor Virginia Carew. It served as the first conference of the new, international Science Fiction Research Association (SFRA). I have the privilege of serving as chairman of that organization.

In addition, Fred Pohl has suggested that the United States sponsor a truly international conference of sf scholars, such as that held in Japan during the summer of 1970.

THOMAS D. CLARESON

THE OTHER SIDE OF REALISM

I do not recall where or when I first heard the explicit distinction made between "mainstream" fiction and science fiction, with some of its most ardent enthusiasts muttering that some day, some day science fiction *would* replace the mainstream.[1] They talked about it some at the British Science Fiction Association meeting at Oxford during Easter week, 1969, reporting that in *Stand on Zanzibar*, John Brunner had advanced the cause by "pulling a Dos Passos." Few said that to Brunner himself, who turned purple at the compliment. Certainly it reveals a deep personal bias to think, even to hope, that "realistic" fiction will not always obtain an audience. More widespread, perhaps especially in the academic interest in the genre, is the feeling that science fiction merits consideration because it has created a new mythology.

At the MLA Forum, Lester del Rey, veteran editor and writer, spoke truly when he said that science fiction "is the myth-making principle of human nature today." He didn't stop there. "Previously," he continued, "we had backward-looking myths. They always looked back to a golden age. They looked back to demons also. Now science, knowledge, experience have largely destroyed those myths. The 'New Wave' in science fiction is crying busily about the lack of those myths and saying that man is a degraded and indecent animal, doomed to failure against the utter evil of the Cosmos. It is, in other words, naturalism transferred to science fiction, where it doesn't fit very well."[2] By the "New Wave" he referred to the theories and practices of many of the

1

younger writers whose careers have begun within the last decade or so. One such individual felt that by stressing ideological content of the genre, del Rey did not adequately emphasize that the so-called "New Wave" has been essentially a revolution in style and technique more than anything else. On the other hand, one young woman declared that del Rey could not be more correct; she wrote science fiction, she explained, to escape "writing about adultery in the suburbs."

The discussion turned, as it usually does, to what has always remained the central, running debate in sf circles: the didactic theory of literature. Many see science fiction as a unique kind of story whose purpose is to teach and prophesy. For that reason it concerns itself with the future. Who cares how the story is told so long as the reader has teaching and preaching and prophesying? Yet even those who hold most firmly to this view will agree that while sf has been long on prediction, it has been short on accurate detail in its predictions.3

Since the didactic element is thematic and can therefore be infused into any story, then if the most valid way of judging the genre is as story that promotes a certain kind of idea, simply by naming some of the genre's more common plot motifs—stories—one should be able to discover the uniqueness of science fiction, to find something that no other form of fiction can do. For example:

1. The protagonist, an alien creature, invades and struggles to survive amid a hostile society which dominates the planet—as in *The Invisible Man* by Ralph Ellison.

2. The protagonist exists amid multiple dimensions and has no way to hold himself at any one point in time or space—as in *Remembrance of Things Past* by Marcel Proust.

3. The protagonist suffers in a fearsomely dystopian world which would destroy him—as in *An American Tragedy* by Theodore Dreiser.

4. The protagonist finds the remnant of a noble, once-powerful race living in an essentially unknown quarter of the globe, now caught up in a fierce battle for its very existence—as in *The Last of the Mohicans* by James Fenimore Cooper.

5. Or, to change the pace: the protagonist reveals in detail the problems of plant management—as in *Player Piano* by Kurt Vonnegut, Jr.

Apparently by naming the plot motif, one gets at nothing essential because the same old story can be told in a number of ways. Someone may already have protested that the foregoing examples are not valid because they do not begin: *"In the future the protagonist . . ."* But science fiction contains motifs such as parallel universes, time travel from the present into the past, even impending invasion or catastrophe (from World War III to onrushing asteroids, to virulent new diseases, to aliens already on earth in the shape of man, or some such). These have been discovered last week, yesterday, today, tomorrow, this week, this month: in short, *now*—and such a timing often increases the dramatic impact of the story. Perhaps the emphasis upon the future is no more than a convenient and widely used convention which gets to the essence of science fiction little more than does the naming of stories. Perhaps, to some extent at least, the emphasis upon the future has contributed to the short-sighted perspective governing so much criticism of the genre.

As such critics as Harry Levin have underscored, all literature forms a continuum which the writers of each generation manipulate in their own idiom and manner to reflect those ideas and focus upon those areas of human experience which most concern them. Fantasy—the other side of realism, of which science fiction is the latest expression—has existed side by side with what has come to be called the mainstream—the "realistic," the representational—throughout literature and certainly throughout the history of modern fiction. More important, because any writer, however bizarre his imagined world, has had to make that world sufficiently representational to be acceptable by his readers, the two parallel traditions have frequently intertwined, fused together. One cannot but think of the lavish, representational description of Arthur's Yuletide banquet before the Green Knight intrudes. Finally, many writers dealing with science fiction have said that it more than any other literary form reflects the impact of modern scientific thought upon the literary imagination. But why say that of sf any more than of literary realism or literary naturalism? The same forces and concerns which created modern realistic-naturalistic fiction created science fiction—and subjected it, in its own way, to the same kind of limitations.

At the risk that summary must incur: modern prose fiction

originated in the eighteenth century when not only the intellec-
tuals but the literate society in general turned from mysticism to
rationalism, from the City of God to the Town of Man, a change
begun, of course, in the Renaissance. The same new interest in
natural science that brought about the formation of the Royal
Society, to which so many of the literary men belonged, created a
new literary form: the modern novel. It originated in the impulse
of its writers to observe and record—to represent the world about
them. Thus a small group of characters were brought together and
"watched" as their actions and conversations were reported or
dramatized, or they were "listened to" as their letters were read.
Simultaneously, however, the continued great interest in exploration led to the emphasis of the imaginary voyage motif, whether
to show that the common sense of an Englishman could overcome
his environment, even if it were a desert island, or to invent a
grotesque Brobdingnagian world with which to decry common
sense and castigate the grossness of man.

The Gothic intervened. Although its pages are cluttered by
dungeons, giantism, and high emotion, its enduring core grew out
of the disquieting debate of the psychological empiricists. Man,
the solitary, was immersed in a vast, brooding nature which one
could not be certain was "reality." Left with that problem, man
became isolated amid the myriad impressions of his mind, but, of
course, he could not be certain that his mind functioned properly
or perceived "reality." And so the Gothic reawakened the demon-
ic and irrational. In doing so, it created the first enduring modern
myth, that of a monster given life by a science that trespassed
beyond those limits set for man. Simultaneously, even in the
figure of Dr. Frankenstein, it explored the abnormal state of mind
—madness—which at the hands of Edgar Allan Poe achieved an
unmatched artistry. At his best he employed the convention of
the first-person narrator, to the effect that his readers, as well as
his narrator, entered an horrific nightmare that *must not* be
reality, but might well be, as in *The Narrative of A. Gordon Pym.*[4]

Yet because for the moment some men could transcend the
possibility of a distorted Gothic world and assure Divinity Schools
that "Nature is the opposite of the soul, answering to it part for
part" in a divinely-ordered, benevolent Cosmos, the energies of the
Gothic seemed to dissipate by mid-century. It never disappeared,

of course, but by and large in England particularly it contented itself with the traditional ghost story and demons out of folklore. It called attention to itself as something more than atmospheric paraphenalia only in such a story as FitzJames O'Brien's "The Diamond Lens," while its central vision persisted, as illustrated by Mark Twain's recently-published "The Great Dark."[5] In addition, the imaginary voyage motif continued popular. But the mid-century novel, with its social concerns, continued to examine society. It was at this point that fantasy seemed to disengage itself from what has been termed the mainstream of realistic fiction.

About mid-century, through such sources as "local color," both in the U. S. and abroad, there began to arise one of the great delusions of the last century: the concept of literary realism. Its rise reflected the intellectual history of its times, for it was the child of scientific materialism. In *Modern Science and Modern Man,* when James B. Conant discusses what "some might call the eighteenth- and nineteenth-century misconceptions of the nature of scientific investigations," he makes an analogy between the scientists of the period and "the early explorers and map makers":

> . . . by a series of successive approximations, so to speak, maps and descriptions of distant lands were becoming closer and closer *to accurate descriptions of reality.* Why should not the labors of those who worked in the laboratories have the same outcome? No one doubted that there were real rivers, mountains, trees, bays with tides, rainfall, snowfall, glaciers; one could doubt any particular map or description, of course, but given time and patience, *it was assumed the truth would be ascertained.* By the same token there must be *a truth* about the nature of heat, light, and matter.[6]

In capping his assertion of the weakness of the "in principle" theory, Conant sets up "an island surrounded by reefs that made direct access out of the question except with special equipment."[7] The geographer-sea captain who came upon the island could gaze at it lovingly with his telescope and make certain approximations; he knew that when he returned with the necessary equipment, he would reach the island, map every foot of its surface, and learn all that could be known of it. He would know it in its fullest reality. (Should it sink before he returned, he was certain that "in principle" he could have known it.)

If the sea captain and the worker in the laboratory, why not the artist, too?   For example, in "Novel-Writing and Novel-Reading" (1899)[8] William Dean Howells admired the romance because it had "as great purity of intention as the novel," but thought it inferior because it dealt "with life allegorically and not representatively." He denounced the "romanticistic novel" as the lowest order of fiction because it seeks "effect rather than truth; and endeavors to hide in a cloud of incident the deformity and ar-tificiality of its creations.   It revels in the extravagant, the unusual and bizarre.   The worst examples of it are to be found in the fictions of two very great men: Charles Dickens and Victor Hugo."[9] On the other hand, he understood the novel proper "to be the sincere and conscientious endeavor to picture life as it is, to deal with character as we witness it in living people, and to record the incidents that grow out of character." If this is done, no sub-ject matter can "corrupt" or "deprave," for the novelist, as did Howells himself, has made "truth the prime test of a novel. If I do not find that it is like life, then it does not exist for me as art. It is ugly, it is ludicrous, it is impossible." But if it is true, it will pro-duce beauty: that is, "the truth which is the only beauty . . . truth to human experience."[10]

The novels to which he gave highest praise "all rely for their moral effect simply and solely upon their truth to nature." Several times he emphasized the morality of fiction. In short, implicitly or explicitly, it taught. Technically, he insisted, "The old superstition of a dramatic situation as the supreme representa-tion of life must be discarded." Instead the novelist must "try to give the general resemblance which can come only from the most devoted fidelity to particulars."[11]   By this line of reasoning, he assigned a function to the novel and gave a significant role to the novelist:

> . . . truth to life is the supreme office of the novel, in whatever form. . . . the business of the novelist is to make you under-stand the real world through his faithful effigy to it.[12]

The novelist with his faithful, representational effigy; the sci-entist with his inexorable physical analysis: and so they described the reality of the world. Howells, of course, was not alone. Two of his contemporaries, Charles Reade in England and Emile Zola in France, researched their topics so that in writing they would not stray from fact, from truth to life. In England many critics damned Reade for a harsh realism and laughed at his countless blue books. In France, in *Le Roman Experimental* (1884) Zola compared himself with the scientist and declared that he sought the great laws of heredity and sociology upon which a just ethic could be based. With his characters as his specimens in the test tubes of his fiction, he decided that "A" would show a tendency toward alcoholism; "B," an inclination toward blood lust; "C," a propensity toward nymphomania. Then he would subject the test tubes to the variable pressures and temperatures of the Second Empire, shake well, and wait for the basis of a just ethic to precipitate. That, at least, was the theory. He forgot, of course, that a scientist does not arbitrarily decide upon the characteristics of the specimens he must work with.

But Zola appealed to the only source that could speak with authority to him and many of his contemporaries. For literary realism and the subsequent naturalism arose amid the ruins of traditional values. A Louis Agassiz might argue for the immutability of the species, and a John Fiske might find a reconciliation in a *Cosmic Philosophy,* but the closed, essentially benevolent system—whether appealed to through reason, imagination, or faith —which had so long nurtured western man staggered before the impact of ideals like determinism. As such scholars as Robert E. Spiller have stressed, once that collapse began, the entire critical and technical battleground of late nineteenth and twentieth century literature focused upon the attempts of writers and critics to find a new center, a new rationale with which to justify their art.

Although the letters of men like Twain and Howells record their increasing, despairing pessimism in the face of possible meaninglessness, Howells, at least, in enunciating the theory of literary realism, propounded a center for the novelist's art in the empirical method of the scientist. The convention of representational detail was elevated to a principle that should define and determine the function and nature of the novel. Let no one "suppose," wrote Howells, that "this fidelity to life can be carried too far."[13] In the theory, if not the practice, lay the delusion.

George Gissing also voiced it: "The world is for me a collection of phenomena, which are to be studied and reproduced artistically."[14]   Change a word or two and the statement might well be that of one of his contemporaries who worked in a laboratory. The literary realists came to believe that by reproducing phenomena, by erecting careful, representational effigies of the world, they captured the singular reality of the world. In short, art could deal meaningfully with life, because it was "as like life" as possible; thus could it serve a useful, hopefully moral, purpose in a scientifically-oriented, secular society. This is the basic source for that later, dissenting criticism which has complained that literary realism deals only with surfaces.

Fuse together the method of the realists and the disconcerting concept of meaninglessness: the result is that literary naturalism to which Lester del Rey referred at the MLA Forum, saying that it "did not fit well" into science fiction. Realism-naturalism had deprived itself of a mythic base, for the forces leading to it had largely destroyed the authority of the systems from which the myths came. It had, in fact, forced itself into a *cul-de-sac*. It had trapped itself in the here-and-now. It had committed itself to an examination of everyday life. On the one hand, it could portray a character's outward actions in society; on the other, it could probe his "conscious sensibility." But it had trapped him in the here-and-now.

This does *not* ignore or dismiss the finest accomplishments of the mode. From the first, however, those novelists who escaped the *cul-de-sac* somehow transcended the general theory and thus have led twentieth century fiction through those many distortions producing what may now be called, perhaps most simply, the grotesque.

Similarly, all of the critical concern for such matters as perspective and point-of-view may well have resulted, consciously or unconsciously, from attempts to escape the dilemma. For however much one may expostulate about morality and sensibility, literary realism-naturalism either immersed animal-man into the hostile environment of a meaningless nature (an "alien universe"), or it isolated him in the meaningless flux of his own mind. Howells declared that the imagination could "work only with the stuff of experience. It can absolutely create nothing; it can only compose,"[15] while Zola announced that he had returned the brain to its proper place as an organ of the body. (Freudian theory, of course, reinstated the imagination as well as giving new viability to myth. Small wonder that critics and writers cling to Freud a generation after psychologists have dethroned him.) The product of the scientific ideas and procedures of its times, the realistic-naturalistic "mainstream" might just as well be called science fiction as anything else. But it is not.

Instead that name has been given to a kind of fantasy which took shape as a diverse, recognizable genre during the same period which saw the rise of literary realism, 1870-1910.[16] It made use of such established conventions as the imaginary voyage and the utopia, and had seen earlier expression in the works of such authors as Mary Shelley and Poe, but it did not coalesce into a distinctly separate, modern fantasy until the last decades of the nineteenth century. Jules Verne and H. G. Wells have been saluted as seminal figures, as they should be, but to think of them as isolated figures or the outstanding representatives of some minute group of writers is to ignore that the new fantasy existed, quantitatively, in fiction at least to the same extent as did realism.[17] It was truly the other side of realism, the companion response to the new age of science. The essential difference between the parallel streams of literary response lay in this: whereas realism-naturalism reacted to the threat of nihilism incipient in the newly-emphasized concept of a mechanistic universe, science fiction reacted to the headlines, to the more obvious accomplishments of the age.

Much has been said of the topicality of science fiction. It was so from the first. To read such periodicals as *Atlantic Monthly, Cosmopolitan,* and *Popular Science* is to discover the sources of much of its "scientific" content. For example, in 1873 the *Atlantic* published an article which argued the feasibility of Symmes's theory of the hollow earth,[18] an idea advanced in Captain Adam Seaborn's *Symzonia* (1820) and employed so successfully by Poe. From then on, a polar setting—either Arctic or Antarctic, whether a hidden valley heated, successively, by hot springs, electricity, or a mother lode of radium, or some inner Symzonian world—became one of the most frequent settings for the utopian and "lost-race" motifs. As did South and Central America: the exploration of the last corners of the world fed the imaginations of the writers of fantasy as well as those of the reading public. In 1877 the Italian astronomer, Giovanni Schiaparelli, precipitated one of the most heated controversies of the period when he announced that he had observed "canali" on Mars. Percival Lowell entered the fray. During the oppositions of Mars in 1892 and 1909, Harvard and the Lowell Observatory financed separate expeditions to confirm the sightings. Nicola Tesla got into it by announcing that he had received electrical impulses that could have emanated only from Mars. Each phase of the debate was seized upon by the fiction, and at least one spaceship departed for Mars on the night of the 1909 opposition. It also provided Wells with his point of departure in *War of the Worlds* (1897). Such of those as the Theosophists who had seized upon the concept of parallel evolution as the unifying principle of the Cosmos grasped eagerly at these first "scientific" hints of a Martian civilization; indeed, they helped to establish *The Certainty of a Future Life on Mars,* the title Louis Gratacap gave his 1905 novel.

In 1882 Ignatius Donnelly argued on the basis of what he thought the best scientific evidence available for the existence of *Atlantis: The Antediluvian World.* At the time this was no mythic dream. It gave local habitation and a name to that civilization that existed during the Golden Age from which we had so long ago fallen and only now clambered toward again. Moreover, such a central civilization was absolutely necessary to the theory of diffusion, the only possible way to explain why both the Mayans and Egyptians had the pyramid, to say nothing of the Mayans' extraordinary knowledge of astronomy. They *must* be the colonies of a mother civilization. (When Atlantis in these terms was no longer viable, Lemuria—"Mother Mu"—rose out of the ancient Pacific.) Geology, archeology, and paleontology fascinated the period; they were used to fit all of earth's past history into a linear reality that culminated, of course, in the present age, for this was the period that gave *popular* enshrinement to the doctrine of inevitable progress.

Still another motif grew out of the fascination for prehistory and evolution. At the turn of the century scientific speculation saw man's mental capacity—quite literally the size of his brain—as the key in the transition from "ape" to modern man. (This permitted acceptance of the Piltdown hoax, for his brain was of the crucial size although his "face" was that of an ape; similarly, it caused the rejection of *Pithecanthropus* despite his pelvis and thumb, for his brainpan was scarcely larger than that of an ape.) Such novels as Stanley Waterloo's *The Story of Ab: A Tale of the Cavemen* (1897) and Jack London's *Before Adam* (1906) dramatized the transition in terms of a single protagonist, whose larger brain told him that he must tame fire, invent weapons and the dugout canoe, and feel something akin to brotherhood toward man and love toward a single woman. Racial memory entered these novels as a convention which allowed a "modern" man to dream his way through previous incarnations, thereby making the account of prehistory more credible.

Hardly had the Franco-Prussian War ended than, as I. F. Clarke has shown so well,[19] the armaments race, the political realignment, and the fear of a forthcoming war created the "future war" motif, portraying always a world-wide conflict that occurred sometime within a generation. It found an audience in America, too, from the 1890's onward, as the monthly periodicals began to battle with such menaces as "the yellow peril." In giving attention to the great battles to come, the novelists tried to give thorough descriptions of the latest—or newly proposed—"hardware." They were little but chauvanistic propaganda, although they increasingly gave attention to the scientist.

The most popular motif, however, portrayed the remnant of some "lost race" surviving in an as yet unexplored corner of the world. It could become the vehicle for diagramming a utopia, or at least praising the virtues of some primitive or classical civilization that had not known the fever of modern times. Or it could content itself with the exciting account of exploration and discovery. The pattern of the motif may be seen in one of the earliest and best-known American titles, *A Strange Manuscript Found in a Copper Cylinder* (1888) by James DeMille. The bulk of the novel is narrated by a shipwrecked English sailor, Thomas More, who tells of being swept into a Symzonian world, encountering prehistoric beasts, and finding a society antipodal in its customs and beliefs to modern western society. Men aboard a becalmed yacht have found the manuscript and read it to pass the time; within this frame, they interrupt at will in order to authenticate the account of the marvelous adventures by references to such early explorers of the Antarctic as Wilkes and Ross, to identify the very species of dinosaur described, and finally to decide that the "lost race" is made up of the children of Shem, somehow deposited where they are by the Ark. They perform a test to verify that the story-teller has made use of papyrus. These intrusions are to be regarded as scientific discussions and make use of much contemporary data.

The "lost race" motif, however, achieved its final form only at the hand of H. Rider Haggard: a love story between some intrepid naval lieutenant or an explorer and the princess or priestess of a lost city—against a backdrop of abundant descriptions of the local flora and fauna, natives, and geography. Against this background of exotic primitivism, Haggard evoked what must be regarded as the erotic dream of the end of the century: that of the bewitchingly beautiful temptress who could never be possessed, Ayesha, "She Who Must Be Obeyed."[20]

Such stories may seem so dated as to provoke at least a smile, just as, inevitably, such figures as 007 and the current legion of spies and private detectives will one day provoke at least a smile. Yet these motifs, and others, measure the diversity of the imaginative response to the science of the late nineteenth century. Perhaps the most telling evaluation of them all was made in an 1872 review of Jules Verne's *A Journey to the Center of the Earth*: "There is a good deal of scientific information scattered through the book."[21] By 1877, in *Men of Mark*, while sketching Verne's career, the writer could say: "[He] now hit on the happy idea of presenting to the public, in a series of fantastic romances and marvelous travels, the results of the wonderful discoveries and theories of modern men of science."[22]

Yet at one end of the spectrum, the genre fused realism and fantasy so thoroughly that the stories have been absorbed into the so-called mainstream and, often, are not spoken of as fantasy, let alone science fiction. For example, in Frank Norris's *Vandover and the Brute*, regarded as one of the early naturalistic studies of degeneration, the protagonist suffers from lycanthropy. Ambrose Bierce and Henry James transformed the traditional ghost story into a study of fear—of "an anxious state of mind." In the collection of short stories, *Questionable Shapes* (1903), Howells himself introduced a psychologist, Wanhope, who explained away the ghost stories of his dinner companions in terms of the psychological theories of the day, although confiding to them at one point that "all psychology is in a manner dealing with the occult."[23] In "The Damned Thing," one of his finest stories, Ambrose Bierce dramatized—somewhat sardonically—the verdict of a coroner's jury that the dead man had been killed by a mountain lion rather than by an invisible creature, as an eyewitness reported to them. Only in the last section of the story did Bierce introduce a diary verifying the eye-witness's account and concluding:

'There are sounds we cannot hear. . . .

'As with sounds, so with colors.   At each end of the solar spectrum the chemist can detect the presence of what are known as 'actinic' rays.   They represent colors—integral colors in the composition of light—which we are unable to discern.   The human eye is an imperfect instrument; its range is but a few scales of the real 'chromatic scale.'   I am not mad; there are colors that we cannot see.

'And, God help me!   The Damned Thing is of such a color.'[24]

As in so many of his stories, Bierce dwelt upon the horror that can engulf everyday life. In doing so, he intimated the world of Gothic distortion more than any of his contemporaries, and here he heightened the effect by appealing to scientific facts which are still acceptable, thereby throwing a new and distinctly modern perspective upon that Gothic world. In contrast, Jack London appealed to no authority in "The Red One" (1916); its protagonist, an American naturalist dying of fever amidst headhunters, becomes obsessed with a desire to see their god, whom he has heard described as "the Star-Born." When he sees it, he realizes that it is an alien spaceship fallen to earth—whether ages ago or within recent generations he cannot ascertain. Its presence permits him to wonder whether brotherhood or natural selection is the law of the universe.   And one is tempted to recall how thoroughly the Frankenstein myth was absorbed into Stephen Crane's parable of man's fear and inhumanity, *The Monster*.

At the other end of the genre's spectrum gathered those writers who could not accept, emotionally or intellectually, a deterministic universe. They explored the occult *sciences* in an attempt to re-establish the old traditions in an acceptable idiom. Among them Theosophy reigned, and her commandment was parallel evolution. As a group they tried either to establish a new metaphysics or to interpret the scientific discoveries and theories in such a way as to preserve the old Mosaic cosmogony. As noted, they seized particularly, though not exclusively, upon the imaginary voyage and Atlantean motifs. One example may illustrate how they yoked science and mysticism. The first half of Mark Wicks' *To Mars Via the Moon* (1911) presents little more than a series of discussions of such phenomena as the sun and moon seen from outer space, the size and chemical composition of the sun, and the nature and origin of the Milky Way. In a prefatory note he hoped that "the book may be referred to with as much confidence as any ordinary textbook."[25] No sooner does the protagonist land on Mars, however, than he encounters a young boy who is the reincarnation of his deceased son. Personal immortality will out! Mars is heaven! And the remainder of the book becomes a discussion of cosmic unity, from which the protagonist somehow learns the "great lesson" that the Martian civilization has to teach: "Onward . . . Upward. . . . The possibilities of the human race in the ages yet to come are so vast as to be beyond our conception."[26] As in the case of Bellamy's *Looking Backward,* the quality of human experience is totally ignored in favor of grand ideas. But these are the two extremes of the spectrum.

There is a hardcore of science fiction devotees who remain unwilling to accept any of the motifs or stories cited into their definition of science fiction. In the introduction to a 1949 anthology, Melvin Korshak asserted that "In the past there were several types of stories that were based on imaginative science, although they were not unified into any single body of literature." He explained that "The importance of these earlier usages of imaginative science in literature was not only that they pointed out new themes for the use of the writer of fiction, but also they proved that a reading public, for the sake of the story, would accept a fantastic premise in fiction."[27] First, of course, one might note that, for the sake of the story, audiences have been accepting fantastic premises as long as narrative has existed. Shall one begin the examples with the parting of the Red Sea, Polyphemus, Beowulf's fight with Grendel, Faustus, Gulliver? Secondly, if these stories involving imaginary science were not unified into a single body of literature, why weren't they, since they dealt with a common subject? In like manner, the editors of a privately-printed annotated checklist relegated the "lost race" motif to fantasy, even while acknowledging that it had been created by the "fascinating lure which archeology holds for us . . ."[28] If these judgments seem somewhat arbitrary, it is that some devotees of science fiction will admit to the genre only those motifs which have celebrated science. It is, moreover, a matter of ideology. These writers and this audience have been the optimists, enthralled by the transformations being brought about in everyday life by a vibrant technology. They were the ones who believed when, in 1908, *Cosmopolitan* published a featured article, "Man's Machine-Made Millenium."[29]

In *Progress and Power,* Carl Becker pointed out that the imagination of man throughout history has focused upon three major dreams: that of a Golden Age from which we have fallen; that of the City of God, unattainable in this life; and from the Renaissance onward, though it reached its greatest popularity at the end of the nineteenth century, that of Utopia, the Earthly Paradise, begotten by socialism on the body of science.

Along with Buffalo Bill and Nick Carter, the scientist—or more properly, the inventor-technician devoted to the physical sciences—became one of the standard heroes not only of the dime novels and hardback science fiction, but of realistic fiction as well. "The admiration for the scientist," wrote Everett Carter, "became a commonplace of realistic fiction. As the clear-eyed observor, he was portrayed as seeing through sentimentality to the truth."[30] If he were a hero because he saw the truth, how much more of a hero he was if he were the one to transform the world! Gradually some of the utopian novels cast farther into the future to allow the fullest technological development, as in Chauncey Thomas's *The Crystal Button* (1891), which mirrored the forty-seventh century. But the debate over socialism waxed too hot for the majority of the utopian novels to give more than cursory attention to the forthcoming technological perfection or to the scientist himself.

But he was everywhere else. Some may still conjure with the name Tom Swift, but he was a latecomer, for as early as the 1880's

Frank Reade, Jr., already used his inventions for a moral purpose, as when he employed his electric tricycle to break up the slave trade of Nigeria.[31] His fraternity grew crowded and featured such a boy as "Frank Edison, nephew of a noted scientific savant," who graced the juvenile fiction of J. Weldon Cobb. On occasion, he was "mad," as in William Henry Rhodes's "The Case of Summerfield" (1871) or Stewart Edward White's *The Sign at Six* (1912); but most often as an adult he triumphantly pursued the "ultimate metal" or the "ultimate energy" or the "ultimate weapon." Hardly had Wells's *The War of the Worlds* run in *Cosmopolitan* before Garrett P. Serviss, who wrote a newspaper column on astronomy, produced a sequel, *Edison's Conquest of Mars,* serialized in the New York *Evening Journal* in 1898.[32]

Especially in the juveniles did the scientist-inventor's home grounds remain the "wonderful invention" motif. For the most part he easily improved upon the "gadgets" already on the drawing boards or projected by the engineers. In the "future war" motif, emerging from his industrial or academic laboratory, he either saved the United States from threatened invasion, or with newly-discovered energies at his command, conquered the nations of Europe in order to establish a world state where scientists, as well as science, ruled. A molecular scientist from Harvard did so in Simon Newcomb's *His Wisdom, the Defender* (1900), while the protagonist (Edelstone!) of J. Stewart Barney's *L.P.M.: The End of the Great War* (1915) established a government by "the Aristocracy of the Mind," to be conducted like the Boards of Directors of "the great American corporations."[33] By 1910 the first scientific detective appeared, and the adventures of the most famous, Arthur B. Reeve's Craig Kennedy, occurred monthly in *Cosmopolitan* from 1911 to 1915. His reference to "psychanalysis" [*sic*] may well be the first explicit mention of Freudian theory in American popular fiction.

A brief incident in Roy Norton's *The Vanishing Fleets* (1908), one of the best-known American future war novels, seems to have captured much of the magic which the scientist-inventor held for the public and literary imaginations. An admiral, "fascinated by the mystery of science," watches a scientist and his daughter-technician release the electrical forces which create an antigravity field:

. . . as if endowed with a soul, the lights once more flashed here and there, glaring at them with sinister contempt—Frankensteins under control.[34]

Frankensteins under control! The present generation, surfeited with technological development, may not comprehend the degree to which society was "so quickly and so profoundly transformed in its external aspects by matter-of-fact scientific knowledge" in the years between, say, 1870 and 1920. In writing of the discrepancy between man's social and material progress, Carl Becker emphasizes the emergence of "a new class of learned men . . . whose function is to increase rather than to preserve knowledge." These have been the "exceptional few" who could "move with assurance and live at ease in an infinitely expanded time-and-space world." They were, in Becker's eyes, the scientists and technicians who had little or nothing in common with the "undistinguished many," who could not comprehend the universe into which they had been thrust.[35] If Becker could say this in 1932, when the sciences had become an established part of the curriculum, what then must have been the attitudes of the "undistinguished many" during the early stages of the transformation? Truly, the scientist-inventor must have seemed a magician.

In its diverse motifs science fiction made up a literary romanticism which celebrated the reality and future of progress, choosing, obviously, the scientist as its hero. It paid him its accolade in what has been termed the "catastrophe" motif, in which some man-made or, more often, natural disaster threatened to destroy the world. For example, in Garrett P. Serviss's *The Second Deluge* (1912), when a watery nebula approaches the earth, the scoffed-at scientist, Cosmos Versal, builds an ark and acts as the sole judge to choose who shall board her; he begins "with the men of science. They are the true leaders."[36] (He excludes all lawyers.) Although a geological phenomenon allows others to survive, Versal founds an enduring new society based upon "the principles of genetics" and deeply "implanted" with the "seeds of science."[37] In George Allan England's trilogy, *Darkness and Dawn* (1914), centuries after a natural disaster has ripped the American continent and poisoned the earth's atmosphere, one man and one woman awaken from suspended animation to begin rebuilding civilization. "Something drove [the protagonist] inexorably, for he was an engineer—and an American." Theirs would be "a kinder and saner world this time. No misery, no war, no poverty, woe, strife, creeds, oppression, tears—for we are wiser than those other folk, and there shall be no error."[38]

Thus did the "catastrophe" motif approach mythic statement. Unless one assigns an archetypal value to Haggard's Ayesha —The eternal temptress? A poor piece of eroticism to fulfill such a value—only the scientist in the "future war" and "catastrophe" motifs achieved anything like mythic proportion. That the myth seems naive and dated, perhaps was so even as it was verbalized, has occurred because even before the 1920's—after Verdun and Passenchendale—had come the first glimpses of an earthly hell.

Much has been made of science fiction writers themselves being scientists, sometimes said in such a way as to suggest that that fact alone explained any want of "literary" merit in their stories. Beyond its obvious snobbishness, such emphasis has overlooked the greatest importance of their scientific backgrounds. The men who created and continued the specialist magazines through the 1930's at least—writers and editors—were, by and large, enthusiasts of science. They, too, believed that science, technology in particular, gave men the tools with which to remedy the ills of society and advance it toward some (ever-more-distant?) perfection. They spoke affirmatively for the scientific ethos. It was their faith, their creed, and if anything, it was strengthened by the experience of the Depression. As late as 1937 when John Campbell, Jr., began his influential editorship of *Astounding Stories,* his "message remained clear," according to Sam Moskowitz: "the machine is *not* the enemy and ruination of man; it is his friend and protector."[39]

The view was epitomized in the work and influence of Hugo Gernsback. Fifteen years before he founded *Amazing Stories,* Gernsback, an electrical engineer who edited *Modern Electric,* serialized his own novel, *Ralph 124C 41+: A Romance of the Year 2660,* in 1911. The tale of a scientist-inventor so great that he belonged not to himself but to the world, it is a love story, involving a Martian as the other man and ending only after Ralph brings his beloved back to life following the accident in which she was killed; to do this, he manufactures in his laboratory—in six hours—

a new gas needed to preserve human tissue. Presumably they lived happily ever-after despite her six hours' oxygen-starvation. But the story line—the quality of human experience—is submerged amid lengthy descriptions of the "gadgets" that flourish in the society. In the preface to its 1950 edition, Fletcher Pratt declared that its method, "that of supplying the people of the future with *technical inventions which are the logical outgrowths of those currently in use or logically developed from currently accepted theories*" has proved "fundamental" to science fiction.[40] He continued:

> [Gernsback] founded the school of fiction in which *the technical plausibility of the surroundings is at least as important as the literary plausibility of the characters.* For that matter, the reader is besought to show some interest in what can be done for us by the chemist, the inventor, the electrician, and even the meteorologist.[41]

Although Gernsback did not long remain an active editor or publisher during the 1930's, he did have a forceful personality. In 1943, *New Yorker*, for one, called him, "The Father of Science Fiction";[42] for the 1952 World Convention in Chicago, he himself wrote an introduction to a brief bibliographical study in which he accepted the title;[43] and as late as 1963, *Life*, in referring to him as "the Barnum of the Space Age," retained the title and nominated *Ralph 124C 41+* as the prototype of the genre, nevertheless noting that his insistence upon plausibility "is known among dissenters in the trade as the 'Gernsback Delusion.' "[44] There can be no doubt of his influence. Such magazines as *All Story* and *Argosy* included science fiction titles as late as the 1920's and 1930's, but by creating the specialist magazine, Gernsback found a medium through which a greater quantity of sf could reach a larger audience more regularly. On the other hand, by restricting itself more and more to the specialist magazines, science fiction separated itself from the general body of popular magazine fiction and created a specialist audience, ostensibly of readers who shared a basic enthusiasm for science. Nor can one doubt that Gernsback's emphasis upon plausibility and advanced gadgetry provided one of the important sources of the view that the function of the genre is to predict future developments—to prophesy affirmatively. For it has been largely the writers and editors who came into the field in the 1930's and 1940's and shared Gernsback's faith in science and technology, who have stressed the prophetic role of science fiction.

This unwavering belief in science and the scientific spirit of men led the genre toward a *cul-de-sac* much like that in which literary realism-naturalism found itself. One might suggest that the enormous attention given to "surroundings" sacrificed much of the potential of the genre to a kind of "local color." More important, by insisting upon plausibility and extrapolation from "inventions which are the logical outgrowths of those currently in use or logically developed from currently accepted theories"— (May one say, "Truth to life?")—Gernsback and his followers restricted science fiction to prediction along a linear reality. That is to say, whether the world portrayed in a story were 2660 or the forty-seventh century, whether 2000 or 22,000, the future was very much seen in terms of the present. No matter how many empires rose and fell, no matter what dangers faced man, no discontinuity severed the future from the present, for man would be triumphant, leaving a dying earth if necessary, and science would lead him onward. For science dealt with truth, with reality, and man had only to be guided by her. Indeed, even so fine a work as H. G. Wells's *The Time Machine* (1895) had travelled the same linear reality, for the Morlocks and Eloi were but the final result of Marxian economic determinism.

Thus, at a time when the main impulse of twentieth century fiction tried to achieve a symbolic level or turned inward to search for order in the human mind, Gernsback and his followers prescribed a thin story line that disregarded the quality of human experience in order to propagandize for technology, although Wells, Jack London, E. M. Forster, and Aldous Huxley had glimpsed dystopia and questioned the concept of inevitable progress. The result was to divorce science fiction further from the *Geist* of the period.

When such writers as E. E. Smith and John Campbell threw open the galactic stage, man conquered the stars. The formula demanding plausibility continued. One has only to turn to the indignant letters of readers who felt that so-and-so had not been true to such-and-such a theory or had not bothered to include suf-

ficient detail regarding his newest planet or space-drive to realize
how important attention to "surroundings" remained. These
"gadgets" bring the snickers, and these stories became the much-
derided "space opera." But they were the logical extension of the
scientist as hero, and in their own way they reached for the epic,
the heroic, vision of man triumphant in a hostile universe.

In "Image of the Scientist in Science Fiction [1926-
1950],"[45] published in 1958, in which he several times refers to
his findings "in terms of 'reflection' of reality," Walter Hirsch
reported a steady decrease in the frequency with which the natural
scientist was portrayed as hero. "The naive adulation of the omni-
potent and omniscient scientist is no longer a feature of the genre
as it had been in its childhood."[46] Furthermore, he continued,
instead of superman or villain, the scientist had become more
human, "facing moral dilemmas" and recognizing that "science
alone is not an adequate guide" for the decisions man must
make.[47] Any re-humanizing of the scientist arose from a variety
of reasons, for, as might be expected, the writers of the 1940's
spoke with their own voices. Such a veteran as Jack Williamson
had questioned the cost of progress. One of the most notable
stories in that it became something of a prototype, Murray Leinster's "First Contact" (1942) threw a new perspective upon the
encounter in deep space between an earth ship and that of aliens.
Afraid that the other ship might follow them home and destroy
their planets, the crews exchange ships, hoping to gain knowledge
and establish friendship between their races. The greatest single
influence came from John Campbell, editor of Astounding, who
encouraged sociological or anthropological emphasis in stories
submitted to him so that instead of super-adventure, the genre
might explore the impact of science upon the individual and the
culture. This proved a key shift. Nevertheless, although one of his
own last stories, "The Idealists" (1954), acknowledges that "a
high degree of technical development does not necessarily carry
with it maturity in dealing with different cultures,"[48] one of the
now-legendary heights of his career and that of Astounding came
when government officials thought there had been a security leak
just a few months before Hiroshima because a story had described,
with technical virtuosity, the dropping of an atom bomb.[49] The
basic confidence in science had not palled. Man would conquer
the stars.

Hiroshima ended that. The cloud brought with it a flood of stories in which, for example, the writers foresaw a world where mutation ran wild, or described a last fire-storm which they could not judge an Armageddon. Suddenly, as it were, science fiction foresaw dystopia everywhere, although others had previously mapped its geography: Wells and Forster, Zamiatin and Capek, Huxley and Orwell. Once American science fiction glimpsed the anti-utopia, it grew fascinated with the probability of an earthly hell, just as half a century earlier it had grown fascinated with the probability of an earthly paradise. Man might not conquer the stars. Just as philosophical determinism had reduced man to animal existence, so now the mushrooming technology might reduce him to a robot existence, if it did not anihilate him. By its concern for the anti-utopia, the genre ended a largely self-imposed exile by moving toward the essentially anti-scientific mood and themes of the main body of twentieth century literature. Ironically, only in doing so, did it begin to receive belated critical and academic attention, as witnessed by recent titles.[50]

More important, perhaps, the concern for anti-utopia gave the genre a new vitality. Once again it became an important medium for social and political criticism. (Its devotees may not exaggerate too much when they say that in the McCarthy era, science fiction was the only literary form that could criticize government policies because the politicians either did not read or could not understand the stories.) The discovery of dystopia, however, did not of itself free science fiction from its linear reality. A thinly disguised essay in which the quality of human experience is submerged by grand ideas remains an essay, whether it diagrams heaven or hell.

In describing the revolution in modern physics, Conant reminded his readers that the physicist no longer pretends that he is dealing with reality, but accepts instead that he works with interlocking conceptual schemes—with models—that are productive for a time but are constantly modified. As with the physicist, so with the writer. Few, if any, writers would now insist that their fictional worlds reproduce reality. Instead the writer creates a model, an imitation, a symbolic construct through which he tries to capture the quality of human experience. He clothes that world with the sensuous language of perception so that the reader can see, hear, smell, taste, feel what it is to live in that imagined place at that imagined time and share that imagined experience with those imagined characters. Obviously in the light of twentieth century critical thinking, this is to say nothing new; but it is to stress that in this fusion of language and imagination lies the source of so-called "literary" quality.

If the writer represents what seems to be the familiar every-day life, he moves toward what has been labelled realism; if he creates a less familiar world requiring a greater suspension of disbelief, he moves toward fantasy. In either case, using the flesh and blood of characters acting in a time and a place, he reveals obliquely how he perceives the human condition. But whichever its mode, the best fiction escapes the literal and moves toward metaphor, toward symbol.

For example, critics have long worried over Mark Twain's *The Adventures of Huckleberry Finn,* lamenting Huck's failure to retain the moral insight he has gained during his odyssey, or calling the last third of the novel—concerned with the grotesque escape through which Tom puts Jim—a flaw in tone and structure. One recalls the impoverished symbolism of the river (good) and the shore (bad) despite the presence of the King and Duke aboard the raft. Yet if one were to read *Huckleberry Finn* as Twain's meta-phor of despair—despair that no value system, whether derived from nature and the heart or from inherited tradition, proved adequate to face the brutality of the Mississippi valley-world—then these critical questions might be laid aside and the novel truly recognized as one of the finest achievements of the "realistic" movement because it rose above the theoretical limitations of the movement. Dreiser has been soundly condemned for his repre-sentational paraphenalia, every brick and sign post of it, yet in *An American Tragedy* he created a symbolic action that well revealed the agony of being young and impoverished in a laissez-faire soci-ety. Hemingway's *A Farewell to Arms,* with its rain-soaked war, and Dos Passos' *Manhattan Transfer,* with its kaleidoscopic city: what better symbols has the representational-"realistic" mode achieved to evoke the chaotic world that man himself has brought about? In the twilight of Victorian fiction Thomas Hardy conjured up the kingdom of Wessex, while more recently William Faulkner gave incarnation to Yoknapatopha County. Such works as these must remain, ultimately, the finest expression of the representational mode just in proportion to their movement from the literal through the distorted and grotesque toward symbol and myth. —And all of these were written before science fiction had firmly established itself in the specialist magazines.

In the world of the late nineteenth century, where neither Odysseus and Beowulf, nor Adam and Arthur, could walk with authority; in a world where the first two dreams named by Becker lay waste, science fiction emerged as the newest form of fantasy to give expression to yet a third dream. For Arthur and Adam, it substituted Frankenstein and the Scientist as Saviour. The latter, too, is now untenable, for at least one of those figures can no longer walk the earth.

At the BSFA meeting in Oxford during the Easter weekend, 1969, J. G. Ballard, one of the promising young English writers, suggested that realism and naturalism had been the responses of the nineteenth century to the new world of science, while science fiction might well prove the most valid expression of the twentieth century response to science. As noted, the failure of the representational mode to achieve an audience seems wishful-thinking; and Ballard also seemed to forget momentarily that the genre was also a nineteenth century response: the romantic response. But there is in his speculation a provocative challenge.

One has to look only as far as Kurt Vonnegut, Jr., Anthony Burgess, or Michael Crichton's *The Andromeda Strain,* despite its casual ending, to see that writers outside the specialist group continue to make use of science fiction motifs, although some, for whatever reason, may not wish their work to be identified with it. One has to look only as far as John Hersey's *The Child Buyer,* William Golding's *The Inheritors,* or such of Arthur C. Clarke's stories as "The Sentinel" or "If I Forget Thee, O Earth," to find fiction in which the two traditions have fused themselves into one.

If science fiction has now released itself from the simplistic conviction that it must prophesy the diagrams of heaven or hell, then it may provide writers of the late twentieth century with the vehicle that has the greatest freedom to seek for metaphors that can speak to the condition of man. Fantasy has always had the greatest freedom to expand man's perception of himself; one need only to look at Kafka's *Metamorphosis* or Lagerkvist's *The Hang-*

man or "The Children's Campaign" for modern examples of the power of fantasy. Just as the Gothic caught the heart of the Romantic dilemma; just as the hallucinated imaginations of the French symbolists rejected a too parochial "reality" and thereby proved a seminal influence leading twentieth century literature toward the symbolic and grotesque, so now science fiction, with its freedom to create unearthly worlds as well as to explore and distort time and space, may give new vitality to the dream of human experience.

NOTES

[1]Isaac Asimov made the distinction when he asserted that some science fiction is as "well written as many 'mainstream' novels." See: *Bulletin of the Atomic Scientists,* 13 (May 1957) inside back cover. Asimov had replied in a letter to A. S. Barron's "Why Do Scientists Read Science Fiction?" *BAS,* 13 (Feb. 1957), 62-65.

[2]"The MLA Forum: Science Fiction: The New Mythology," *Extrapolation,* 10 (May 1969), 102.

[3]L. W. Michaelson, "Science Fiction and the Rate of Social Change," *Extrapolation,* 11 (Dec. 1969), 25-27. This is the latest of several of his articles on the topic.

[4]I have cited *The Narrative of A. Gordon Pym* rather than one of Poe's shorter, less controversial stories because *Pym* proved especially attractive to writers at the end of the century. No one knows how many "lost race" novelists tried to complete his adventures. They were, of course, more Haggard than Poe. A typical representative was Charles Romyn Dake, *A Strange Discovery* (NY: H. J. Kimball, 1899).

[5]Including "The Great Dark" in *Letters from the Earth* (1962), the editor, Bernard DeVoto, specifically denied the influence of O'Brien's "The Diamond Lens" on Twain—quite correctly.

[6]James B. Conant, *Modern Science and Modern Man* (NY: Columbia University Press, 1952), p. 55.

[7]*Ibid.,* p. 56.

[8]William Dean Howells, "Novel-Writing and Novel-Reading. An Impersonal Explanation," *Howells and James: A Double Billing,* edited by William M. Gibson (NY: New York Public Library, 1958), pp. 7-24. To anyone who may think I have been at fault for basing so much of my argument on the single article, I cite Gibson: ". . . it is the fullest, most detailed, most penetrating analysis of the novelist's craft that Howells ever wrote, and it therefore takes its place . . ." p. 7.

[9]Howells, p. 10.

[10]*Ibid.,* p. 9.

[11]*Ibid.*, p. 21.

[12]*Ibid.*, p. 24.

[13]*Ibid.*, p. 15.

[14]George Gissing, letter to Algernon Gissing, 18 July 1883, quoted in Jacob Korg, *George Gissing: A Critical Biography* (Seattle: University of Washington Press, 1963), p. 71.

[15]Howells, p. 15.

[16]These dates are those of the journal *American Literary Realism* 1870-1910, edited by Professor Clayton L. Eichelberger, University of Texas at Arlington. I. F. Clarke has also stressed the importance of the early 1870's: *Voices Prophesying War* (Oxford, 1966).

[17]Everett F. Bleiler, editor, *The Checklist of Fantastic Literature* (Chicago: Shasta Publishers, 1948); I. F. Clarke, editor, *The Tale of the Future* (London: The   Library   Association,   1961);   Thomas D. Clareson, "An Annotated Checklist of American Science Fiction 1880-1915," *Extrapolation*, 1 (Dec. 1959), 5-20. There has been no definitive listing of hardbacks, and Sam Moskowitz is the only one who has begun to work with the fiction in the popular magazines.

[18]P. Clarke, "Symmes Theory of the Earth," *The Atlantic Monthly,* 31 (April 1873), 471-480.

[19]I. F. Clarke, *Voices Prophesying War* (London: The Oxford University Press, 1966), pp. 1-63.

[20]Within a year of *She* (1887), no less than five parodies had been published of that novel or *King Solomon's Mines* (1885). See Bleiler, pp. 435-436. *He* was attributed to Andrew Lang and W. H. Pollock. The title page of Munro's edition of *He* (1887) reads: "By the author of the following works contained in Munro's Twenty-five Cent Edition: 721- *He*, a companion to *She*; 726- *It*; 733- *Pa*; 734- *Ma*; 736- *King Solomon's Wives*; 737- *King Solomon's Treasures*; 739- *Bess*, a companion to *Jess*." Only copies of *Pa* and *Ma* are unknown at this time.

[21]*The Illustrated Review*, 16 December 1872, pp. 373-374.

[22]*Men of Mark* (London: 1877); Verne is number 24.

[23]William Dean Howells, *Questionable Shapes* (NY and London: Harper Brothers, 1903), p. 215.

[24]Ambrose Bierce, "The Damned Thing," *Can Such Things Be? Complete Works* (NY and Washington: The Neale Publishing Company, 1910), III, 296.

[25]Mark Wicks, *To Mars Via the Moon* (Philadelphia: J. B. Lippincott Company, 1911), pp. ix-x.

[26]*Ibid.*, p. 301.

[27]Melvin Korshak, "Introduction," *Best Science Fiction: 1949* (NY: Frederick Fell, 1949), pp. xi-xii.

[28]*333: A Bibliography of the Science-Fantasy Novel,* edited by Joseph H. Crawford *et. al.* (Providence, Rhode Island: The Grandon Company, 1953), p. 3.

[29]Hudson Maxim, "Man's Machine-Made Millenium," *Cosmopolitan*, 45 (November 1908), 569-576.

[30]Everett Carter, *Howells and the Age of Realism* (Philadelphia: J. B. Lippincott Company), p. 92.

[31]J. O. Bailey, *Pilgrims Through Space and Time* (NY: Argus Books, 1947), p. 98. Somehow this use of the electric tricycle has always seemed the epitome of the "moral technology" being created in the novels. Interestingly, perhaps significantly, the Bodelian Library, Oxford, has what seems to be a complete run of the Frank Reade, Jr., stories.

[32]Garrett P. Serviss, *Edison's Conquest of Mars*, with an introduction by A. Langley Searles (Los Angeles: Carcosa House, 1947), p. xiv. This was the first hardback edition.

[33]J. Stewart Barney, *L.P.M.: The End of the Great War* (NY: G. P. Putnam's Sons, 1915), pp. 414-416.

[34]Roy Norton, *The Vanishing Fleets* (NY: D. Appleton and Company, 1908), pp. 210-211.

[35]Carl Becker, *Progress and Power* (NY: Alfred A. Knopf, 1963), pp. 106-108.

[36]Garrett P. Serviss, "The Second Deluge," *Fantastic Novels Magazine*, II (July 1948), 30.

[37]*Ibid.*, II:125.

[38]George Allan England, *Darkness and Dawn* (Boston: Small, Maynard, and Company, 1914), pp. 80, 164.

[39]Sam Moskowitz, "John W. Campbell," *Seekers of Tomorrow: Masters of Modern Science Fiction* (Cleveland and NY: The World Publishing Company, 1966), p. 40.

[40]Hugo Gernsback, *Ralph 124C 41+: A Romance of the Year 2660*, forewords by Lee De Forest and Fletcher Pratt (NY: Frederick Fell, Inc., 1950), pp. 19-20.

[41]*Ibid.*, pp. 20-21.

[42]"Onward & Upward With the Arts/Inertium, Netronium, Chromaloy, P-P-P-Proot!" *The New Yorker*, 13 February 1943, pp. 42-53.

[43]Hugo Gernsback, *Evolution of Modern Science Fiction*, 12 pp. mimeographed pamphlet, privately printed for the World Science Fiction Convention: Chicago, 1952.

[44]"The Amazing Hugo Gernsback: Barnum of the Space Age," *Life*, 26 July 1963, p. 66.

[45]Walter Hirsch, "Image of the Scientist in Science Fiction [1926-1950]," *The American Journal of Sociology*, LXIII (March 1958), 506-512.

[46]*Ibid.*, LXIII, 610.

[47]*Ibid.*, LXIII, 512.

[48]Moskowitz, p. 46.

[49]Cleve Cartmill, "Deadline," *Astounding Science Fiction* (March 1944).

[50]Ignoring the titles from the periodicals, chief among these would be the following: Kingsley Amis, *New Maps of Hell* (1960); Chad Walsh, *From Utopia to Nightmare* (1962); and Mark Hillegas, *The Future as Nightmare: H. G. Wells and the Anti-Utopians* (1967).

I have, incidentally, intentionally omitted from this entire discussion the works of H. P. Lovecraft and that circle of writers who gathered about him in *Weird Tales* and Arkham House. His own title, *Supernatural Horror in Fiction* (NY: Ben Abramson, 1947), perhaps gives the most succinct indication of why I have excluded him. Although a few of his stories, "The Colour Out of Space," for example, are science fiction, he specialized in horror fantasy.

JULIUS KAGARLITSKI

REALISM
AND
FANTASY

Hegel compared fantasy to inlaid work. This image contains a strikingly true notion. Fantasy, a child of the new age, came into being only with the destruction of syncretic thought, wherein the real and the imaginary, the rational and the spiritual are inseparable. Fantasy begins to take shape only from the moment when the original unity is destroyed and disintegrates into a mosaic of the probable and the improbable. A myth is believed in too much for it to be fantasy. When disbelief arises side by side with belief, fantasy comes into being.

All fantasy is "scientific" in the sense that it is engendered by that type of thinking whose mission it was to determine the real natural laws of the world and to transform it. And in this sense, all fantasy is, in its own way, contemporary.

Still, let us try to confine ourselves to narrower limits. To be sure, the history of fantasy is a very long one. Lucian, Rabelais, Swift, and Voltaire can be named among its representatives. However, fantasy became an independent field of literature only a short while ago.

Several distinct forms of fantasy, soon called romantic, were already evident in the last third of the 18th century. Thus, in France in the 1770's and the 1780's there was published a series of "fantastic journeys, dreams, visions and cabalistic novels" numbering several dozens of volumes. Realistic fantasy emerged considerably later, in the 60's and 70's of the last century, and is indebted for its formation, first and foremost, to Jules Verne. Today we call this fantasy, "scientific" fantasy.

29

Jules Verne himself did not use this term. He entitled his cycle of novels *Extraordinary Journeys*, but in his correspondence he sometimes used the term "novels about science." The present Russian term "scientific fantasy" (*nauřnaja fantastika*), although inaccurate, is far more appropriate than the English "science fiction" (*naučnaja belletristika*), which was first used by Hugo Gernsback in the magazine, *Science Wonder Stories;* however, up until then he still sometimes used the similar term "scientifiction." Be that as it may, this term was aptly applied to the work of Jules Verne. The connection between science and fantasy was expressed very directly in his work. In addition, the very effort to find a definition for realistic fantasy indicated that it was conceived of as a separate branch of literature.

But wan't it too separate?

Henceforth, fantasy had its own group of authors, its own circle of readers, its own favorite themes. It was capable of "living on its own." But a definite danger was concealed in this. The separateness so necessary for the development of its particular continuity could at any moment take a bad turn. Fantasy was threatened by the danger of finding itself cut off from the basic flow of literature.

The history of fantasy attests to the fact that this danger did become a reality several times. At times fantasy reached the reader possessed of a well-developed aesthetic perception and sense of contemporaneity, but at times it moved extraordinarily far away from him. To a certain extent this danger was perceptible from the very beginning.

In courses of literary history written in France toward the end of the last century, the name of Jules Verne was simply not mentioned. This fact can be cited as one of the most striking examples of the blindness of contemporaries. For the writer who did so much for the future, there was no place in books filled with scores of names having absolutely no significance for us. But Jules Verne was considered not to be contemporary—not only because he belonged to the future, but also because he belonged to the past.

The great European realism of the 19th century, critical realism, as it is customarily called, arose as the result of an extraordinarily complex dialectic process, in the course of which the realism of the enlightenment enriched itself by everything of epoch-making importance discovered by the romantics, and as a result, changed into a realism of a completely new type.

This did not occur in fantasy. Realistic fantasy developed not by assimilating but by rejecting the purely romantic element which it found in romantic fantasy. Jules Verne mechanically separated the "material fantasy" (*material 'naja fantasticňost,'* according to the term of Dostoevsky) of Edgar Allan Poe and other American romanticists from the sinister and the unknowable, and having made use of the former, he rejected or reinterpreted the latter in a directly realistic spirit. Jules Verne was by no means a critical realist in his own creative method. In the 60's he was, as before, extraordinarily dependent upon the realism of the enlightenment and although that realism, as it is easily surmised, was renewed and adapted also for the fulfillment of the specific goals "of the novel about science," it was by no means subject to any fundamental reorganization. He, if one is to say the worst about him, is inflexible, non-dialectical; he is ill adept at analysis of the complex social contradictions which arose in the "age of science" being described.

The positivist convictions of Jules Verne did not appear here underestimated. In the positivist system, science occupies the supreme position, and it could not but attract such an adherent of progress as Jules Verne. However, the conception of the positivists as to the character and course of progress is extremely non-dialectic. Although clearly distinguishing moral progress and material progress, they see no contradiction between them. The progress of morality moves, according to the positivists, along with the progress of civilization, at times falling back only slightly from it. Material progress in the framework of bourgeois society seems to them the most reliable condition for moral progress, and by the same token, the most reliable for the social perfection of mankind. Romanticism, imbued with an awareness of the discord in a world full of passion and tragedy, had nothing in common with this bland and optimistic doctrine.

In the 70's the positivist conception of "guaranteed progress" —"moral progress together with the progress of civilization"— encountered opposition. At the very beginning of this period, there appeared almost simultaneously *The Coming Race* by Bulwer

Lytton and *Erewhon* by Samuel Butler—works which mentioned the danger hidden in material progress. In 1895 Wells's *The Time Machine* appeared. A quarter of a century proved sufficient for the problem to mature and for a new view of things to be expressed completely and without compromise. Here there was no mention of "moral progress together with the progress of civilization." On the contrary, Wells, with all the ardour of youth, contended that a materialistic civilization, developing within the framework of an unjust society, would lead to the destruction of mankind.

The future history of civilization acquired, by the same token, unprecedented drama. Nature itself no longer seemed an affectionate godfather of man, ready to return his efforts a hundredfold. Beginning with the 1880's, there is increasing affirmation of Thomas Huxley's theory, according to which the universe and man are in a state of continuous struggle. Nature is determined, subject to cause-and-effect relations, cruel and inhuman. Man, on the contrary, lives by moral concepts unknown to nature, and the more the system of moral values prevails in him, the more he becomes a man. The task of nature is to suppress the human in man, to subordinate him again to animal instincts, and to destroy—either by cold or rain or earthquake—the work of his hands. The task of man is to vindicate himself and the creation of his hands.

From then on it was not only the future which harboured unknown dangers. Every segment of history turned out to be a field of battle between the past, which did not wish to release man, and the future, as it should be. This struggle could take place in the expanses of the universe and in the soul of individual man. The world encompassed by the eye of the artist acquired both exceptional length in time and space and exceptional depth.

In this world, as dramatic and boundless as can be, romanticism inevitably had to return to life. It was helped by everything, even those tendencies of the time, which, it would seem, should have been harmful to it.

In January, 1902, H. G. Wells, who had already managed in his thirty-five years to earn the status of a classic, gave a short lecture, "The Discovery of the Future." In it he attempted to determine both whether or not we can obtain knowledge of the future and what the nature of this knowledge would be. As a point of departure, Wells proposed to ponder another question—

the question of penetration into the past.

For contemporary man, said Wells, three forms of the past exist. The first of them—"the personal past"—is extracted from our recollections. One should not expect great authenticity here, of course, but in return, this past is emotionally colored, transformed by us, and is therefore closest of all to that conception of the world which literature creates. Another past he called "historical." It is more extensive. It consists of the recollections not only of one man, but of mankind. The degree of personal access to this past, however, is less. The third past Wells called the "scientific" past. It is given to us by a science capable of penetrating to times not only when there were no people, but when there was no organic life at all. But with this the subjective, emotional, artistic elements completely disappear. And so, continued Wells, inasmuch as none of us has been in the future, it is possible to investigate it only by the scientific method. Soon science would undertake a systematic investigation of the future.

As is generally known, this did occur. In the 20th century a new science came into being—futurology, which engaged in precisely that systematic investigation of the future. But did not Wells say something highly distressing? Does it not follow from his words, that fantasy is condemned to have a very weak involvement with literature? In fact, does not fantasy concern itself with the future, and does not this concern with the future cut us off from everything subjective, emotional, artistic?

There is a degree of truth in this in relation to the fantasy of the previous centuries. It looks into the future more and more and inevitably draws from prognostication a certain share of its abstractness. The fantasy of Francis Bacon (*The New Atlantis*) consists completely of prognostication. Prognostication comprises the major interest of many of Jules Verne's novels. Subsequently, the personal interest of humanity and of fantasy in the future did not diminish, but rather increased. Does it not follow from this, if one is to be strictly logical, that fantasy as artistic prose is soon to perish? And has it not fallen into a hopeless situation: science, which had opened to fantasy areas inaccessible to other forms of literature, and, by the same token, made fantasy particularly contemporary—that very same science threatened to destroy it.

It is obvious that it was necessary, while preserving that great stimulus which science had given to fantasy, somehow "to fence oneself off" from it, to save oneself from its levelling influence, There was one solution—to return to the fantastic imaginativeness lost by Jules Verne, but preserved by the romantics. Science itself helped romanticism to return to fantasy. It is true that in this process romanticism was faced with somehow coming to terms with science. Romanticism had returned not in order to triumph over its old rival, realism, but in order to aid it.

Young Wells was aware of this. The style of the new fantasy was already essentially developed in his early works. In 1888 he wrote his first science fiction tale, *The Chronic Argonauts*. This was a romantic piece. In the process of revising, which took seven years, *The Argonauts* became a realistic work, although the romantic bases of this new realism were not forgotten; they were transformed. In the last version everything was changed—even the title. *The Argonauts* was now called *The Time Machine*. The history of the new fantasy begins from the moment of the publication of this novel.

The fantasy of Jules Verne was, if one may phrase it thus, a fantasy of "objects." Verne gave his heroes unusually advanced (and in this sense fantastic) machines and devices, and owing to this, placed them in unusual (fantastic) situations. Wells used many of the devices of Verne's fantasy, but the aesthetic basis of his fantasy differed. He operated with fantastic images which had their roots in the soil of romanticism. Under the pen of Wells, they were transformed in a realistic spirit.

This dual nature of Wells's fantasy becomes quite apparent in *The Time Machine*. First of all—in the image of the "underground world" discovered by the Traveler through time in 802,701, when mankind had deteriorated into Morlock and Eloi. The whitish, bent figures of the Morlocks, their predatory habits, and their eyes glowing red in the dark compel us to remember all the infernal beings which folk fantasy had given birth to; and the place of their habitation—Hell. Along with this, it is an "industrial" hell, with its "hell's kitchen," where machines of incomprehensible complexity rumble in the darkness, and with its "hell's dining room," where Morlocks devour human meat placed on zinc tables—as in an operating theater. This was a romantic image deeply rooted in folk consciousness and folklore, but also completely devoid of the elements of the ancient and sacred provincial tradition. This hell was more than half recreated from contemporary details. Yet it was precisely the romantic which gave a general coloration to the picture, thereby enabling all these details to combine into a single fantastic image.

Thus was laid the foundation of the fantastic literature of the 20th century. In the last years of the 19th century and the first of the 20th, this new fantasy was taking shape in the works of Wells himself. Subsequently the baton was passed on to younger writers.

As a matter of fact, Wells played the same essential role for fantasy that Balzac and Dickens had in their time for non-fantastic literature. Although with appreciable lateness, a process was completed in fantasy identical to the process which had taken place in non-fantastic literature a half a century before: the tendencies of the realism of the enlightenment and romanticism merged, were subject to reciprocal influence, were transformed, and yielded a new form.

One may continue this train of thought and point to the fact that it was essentially through the works of Wells that the creation of the method of critical realism was completed—it now spread to that area of literature in which, up to then, the old, didactic realism had reigned supreme. It is more important, however, to notice another fact: Wells's method was already being formed in the 90's of the last century. If Wells did "repeat the experiment" of his predecessors (and he, as a scientist, well knew that repetition of the experiment serves as a guarantee of its reliability), he did it in another time, under different circumstances. His method was not absolutely equivalent to the critical realism of the middle of the century; it was not a simple transferal of it into the sphere of fantasy. On it were imprinted, although in a distinctive form mediated through fantasy, some features of the realism of the 20th century, and first of all, the ability to look at the present from the point of view of the future. The end of the last century gave birth to a feeling of a great transition to something new, uncertain, alluring, and frightening. At that time it was not only the fantasist who judged the present from the point of view of the future. If the critical realists of the 19th century succeeded in seeing the new in its relationship to the old, with Wells the very meaning of the historical approach to the contemporary changed—today

itself became "the old." What are *Forsyte Saga, Jean Christophe,
Les Thibault* but historical novels about the contemporary? To
these magnificent realistic epics there has been given a new quality,
a sense of the present as a passing moment of history. H. G. Wells
conveyed this constant co-presence of the future in its most open
form. Even the fantastic image which had become the artistic core
of Wells's novel was created under the influence of the time: in a
moment of transition—and the world was experiencing precisely
such a period—a situation frequently does not lend itself so much
to description as to images which do not coincide with the real,
images containing in themselves something greater than reality.

And in yet another respect Wells was by no means late in
completing his discovery. At present the idea is becoming more
and more accepted that "in a certain sense the romantic sensibility
and all the more the romantic technique, enter into the amalgam
of the new realism of the 20th century."[1] This lack in the romantic sensibility and technique was already felt by literature in a
period when the foundations of the new realism were just being
laid. To this, one must suppose, the neo-romantics are indebted to
an appreciable degree for their existence. This, in a paradoxical
manner, affected the development of form for the naturalists, who
had rejected the romantic method and, at the same time, everything
which critical realism had assimilated from it.

As is generally known, the naturalists of the end of the 19th
century at times felt very sharply the lack of complexity in the
images created by them. These images lacked the expansiveness of
a Balzac; the vulgar appeared as simply vulgar, and not as "grandi-
ose vulgar." And then they created symbolic pictures. The symbol
came to the aid of a reality brought down to the everyday level. It
was, in certain instances, an attempt to go beyond the boundaries
of a harshly depicted reality. Thus, Frank Norris, in *The Octopus,*
having shown capitalistic rapaciousness, nevertheless wishes somehow to express his hope that the reign of the octopi is not eternal.
In the denouement of the novel, therefore, the streams of grain
stolen from the farmers flood and suffocate the chief predator in
the hold of the ship.

The fantasy of Wells was an attempt to return to the image
multiplicity of meaning, to raise it by the force of its internal
possibilities to the level of a generality. In order to accomplish

this task, he turned both to the romanticism scornfully slighted by the naturalists and to the everyday, familiar reality the neo-romantics were turning away from.

These two factors—the primary inherent duality of 20th century fantasy and the peculiar "defenselessness" of 20th century literature as a whole against romanticism—lead to the fact that the romantic in contemporary fantasy is easily isolated. One might cite many examples.

In Sir Walter Scott's novel, *The Fair Maid of Perth* (1828), an ancient custom, "ordeal by fire," is described, in which rite a person suspected of murder must stand by the coffin of the murdered person and swear "by all that was created in seven days and seven nights, by heaven, by hell, by his part of paradise, and by the God and author of all, that he was free and sackless of the bloody deed done upon the corpse before which he stood, and on whose breast he made the sign of the cross."[2] In the rite the corpse then attested to his guilt or innocence: if the murderer approached the corpse, from the body of the victim blood oozed forth. In the book of the American popularizer Bernard Siemon, *The River of Life* (1961), numerous cases in which this belief helped to reveal a criminal are presented: convinced that the corpse was actually capable of producing its own evidence, the criminal would refuse to approach it.[3]

In the novel by the modern Japanese writer Kobo Abé, *Inter Ice Age 4*, a corpse also gives witness against its murderer. But this time the procedure of exposing the criminal is far more romantic than in Walter Scott. A "stimulation" of the corpse (described in detail) takes place, whereupon the personality of the deceased is transferred to a machine which, feeling itself to be the person in whose name it speaks, converses with the investigator.[4] Thus, rather than being antagonistic to the romantic tradition, the machine has helped it to manifest itself.

In Stanislaw Lem's *Solaris*, phantoms of flesh and blood appear to the workers of a scientific station situated on an alien planet: these phantoms are unique copies of people who had existed at one time and are re-created by the thinking ocean—the sole "inhabitant" of the planet. The ocean extracted them from the consciousness of those persons to whom they appear. *Solaris* is one of the most romantic works of modern science fiction.

Nevertheless, the basis of the event bears a scientific character (in the sense, of course, in which the word is used in science fiction). Having told a story of crime and repentance, having forced his heroes to suffer in private with the unrelenting recollections which had materialized, Lem also wished to warn the reader that, in connection with the beginning of the era of space flight, "among the stars the Unknown awaits us."[5] In another of Lem's stories, "The Formula of Limfater," the hero, using purely scientific methods, creates a machine which has all the attributes of personality and possesses practical omnipotence.

Thomas Henry Huxley had foretold similar developments. In 1892 he wrote: "Without stepping beyond the analogy of that which is known, it is easy to people the cosmos with entities, in ascending scale, until we reach something practically indistinguishable from omnipotence, omnipresence, and omniscience." He continued: "If evidence that a thing may be, were equivalent to proof that it is, analogy might justify the construction of a naturalistic theology and demonology not less wonderful than the current supernatural; just as it might justify the peopling of Mars, or of Jupiter, with living forms to which terrestrial biology offers no parallel."[6]

There is much similar to "the naturalistic theology and demonology" in contemporary fantasy. H. G. Wells opened the way to this. At the height of Jules Verne's literary career, he believed that all the fundamental principles had already been clarified so that all that remained was to work out the details and to find the best technical application for the well-known and indisputable scientific truths. In contrast, Wells thought that in the course of progress scientific principles themselves change. If so, today's miracle could prove to be an everyday concept tomorrow. Science had discovered the practically eternal possibility for the existence of mankind, and therefore also the possibility for a practically eternal, ever-quickening progress extending over millions of years. If so, fantasists have a right to resort to the peculiar "logic of the miraculous." Now, according to the apt expression of Isaac Asimov, any myth can be turned into a fantastic story by substituting the intervention of science for the intervention of the gods. Fantasists eagerly take advantage of this possibility. Thus a story furnished with devices and machines—even those which have not yet come into mass production—may seem old-fashioned to us. The story of a miracle, however, is completely contemporary. Technology grows old; magic does not, for with the help of science, it acquires a unique place in a world from which all supernatural forces are excluded.

Some fantasists are particularly devoted to "naturalistic demonology." Robert Sheckley, for example, while remaining a science fiction writer, considers it proper to write about genies who appear on command to the owner of a magic lamp—provided that he also writes about tele-transportation, that process, theoretically substantiated by Norbert Wiener, of transmitting material bodies by radio, telephone, or any other yet unknown channel of communication. In speaking of genies, he simply transfers things which are absolutely real and known to everyone to a humorous plane. Just as scientifically substantiated (although on the strictly theoretical level) is the possibility of the appearance of a double. In 1951 John von Neiman, one of the greatest mathematicians of modern times, proved the possibility of creating a machine capable of reproducing any other machine, including itself. The double thus received the sanction of science. The paradox of time, which has so caught the fancy of contemporary fantasy, also brought the double to life. Returning to some period of time, a man could, without difficulty, meet himself—only, let's say, not as a forty-year-old, but as a thirty-year-old. As a result, the double has made himself so at home in contemporary fantasy that he has had the time to provide himself with a double—in humorous fantasy. Its heroes encounter many comic adventures and misunderstandings (in Lem's work, for example) as the result of an unexpected meeting with doubles.

Have we not here run into still another paradox, this time one involving literary history? If the words "science fiction" are no more than a designation of contemporary realistic fantasy, then does it not seem strange that science, at a certain point, begins to undermine the rights of realism and to help romanticism?

It would appear, nonetheless, that it is not so. Modern science actually undermines the rights of realism, but not all kinds of realism, only that of the Jules Verne variety. It does this both because of the reasons just stated, and also because science itself is ceasing to be that rigid, logical system which it was when it was

called "simply developed common sense." Statistics and probability take root in it more and more; increasingly it breaks with
common sense as the settled view of the past. All this makes
realism of the Jules Verne variety unacceptable by reason of its
very spirit. But not realism as a whole. And if science helps
romanticism to penetrate into modern fantasy, then it is in the
interests of realism—but only of modern realism.

The proximity of the romantic to the scientific is not of itself
a product of recent years. We find an example of similar kind in
Mary Shelley's *Frankenstein*. If in our time this process has
intensified, then the principal reason is that the constant presence
of romanticism is vitally necessary to modern fantasy. No matter
how paradoxical it may sound, it is precisely romanticism which is
helping contemporary fantasy to remain realistic fantasy.

The Time Machine, in its realistic quality, found its continua-
tion, as was said, first of all in the work of Wells himself. After
The Time Machine the pendulum of his work swung to romanticism (*The Island of Doctor Moreau*), then to everyday realism
(*The Invisible Man*), and finally stopped at *The War of the Worlds*
—a work which expresses to the fullest degree the peculiarities of
20th century realistic fantasy. However, the synthesis which
seemed to have been achieved in *The War of the Worlds* proved to
be fragile. In the next novel, *When the Sleeper Wakes*, a certain
aesthetic double layering is already clearly evident. The city of
the 21st century described by Wells is depicted with naturalistic concreteness and with a single meaning. In contrast, a certain
symbolic colouring in the spirit of Christian socialism is attached
to the image of the Sleeper. The fantastic image has disappeared.
Its place has been taken by naturalistic descriptions and a symbol
charged with the task of compensating for the singleness of meaning of the description. *The First Men in the Moon* returns us for
an instant to the synthesis (although not to the complete one of
The War of the Worlds). In *The Food of the Gods*, however, this
synthesis is again ready to disintegrate.

The fantasy of the 20th century, as has been said, draws its
realistic quality from a multiply-significant image full of the force
of generalization, such as the Morlocks and Eloi, the Martians and
Selenites of Wells. This image is genetically related to romanticism.
On the other hand, as time has shown, this image is threatened by

the danger of breaking down into concrete description and abstract, artificial symbol. The constant injection of romanticism is indispensable to it: it increases its stability.

In this regard one should also note another fact as well: the romanticism which makes up part of the atmosphere in which realistic fantasy exists is qualitatively distinct from several other phenomena, which in form and origin are similar to it in many respects. This romanticism, one of the elements of a dynamic whole called realistic fantasy, may become isolated, but it remains in the field of attraction of this fantasy and is at any moment capable of again combining with it. Here the forces of attraction are always in operation.

In other cases there are in operation, of course, the forces of repulsion.

The fantastic (real or apparent) is peculiar not only to the literary phenomena under discussion, but also to some forms of contemporary modernism. However, although modernistic fantasy proceeds from the same reality as realistic fantasy and for that reason may somewhat resemble it, it is essentially distinct from it.

Here much depends on the position of the artist in relation to the world as a whole. He may attempt to examine the universe, using the expression of I. Becher, as "chaos from the point of view of chaos." He may, on the other hand, attempt to gain a foothold outside this chaos, and then, behind the irregular "Brownian movement" of the particles of the universe, try to describe the complete picture. He may, in fear of the world which has been set in motion, imagine it as senseless turmoil; on the other hand, no matter how difficult the task, he may strive to see the real motion of the present universe which is expanding to unimaginable dimensions.

Modern realistic fantasy in the West rightly calls itself scientific. In this is expressed not necessarily the obligation "to state the achievements of science in literary form," but something different and immeasurably greater. The connection of modern realistic fantasy with science is expressed first of all in the fact that it proceeds from a system of thought sometimes called "scientific humanism"—in other words, from the modern adaptation of the Enlightenment. It is precisely in this that it finds a foothold "outside of chaos."

Eckermann cites an interesting conversation between Goethe and Hegel regarding the nature of the dialectic. In answer to Goethe's hope that it was not misused to make the false true and the true false, Hegel replied that such "happens . . . only with people who are mentally diseased."

"I therefore congratulate myself," said Goethe, "upon the study of nature, which preserves me from such a disease. For here we have to deal with the infinitely and eternally true, which throws off as incapable everyone who does not proceed purely and honestly with the treatment and observation of his subject. I am also certain that many a dialectic disease would find a wholesome remedy in the study of nature."[7]

This is also the meaning that science has for modern realistic fantasy in the West. This fantasy adopts the name "science fiction" because, in spite of all the inauthenticity of particular scientific suppositions utilized in science fiction, science serves as the guarantee of the authenticity of its general view of the world. True, not one of its suppositions possesses the merits of absolute truth, but it is precisely the development of scientific knowledge which has brought us to understand truth's unattainability. Moreover—and this is extremely important for fantasy—the thesis of the unattainability of absolute truth implies the existence of many, and at times contradictory, concepts of natural science.

Critical realism set as its goal the portrayal of man through society, society through man. The formula of science fiction is also a twofold one, but is different: "The world through man, man through the universe." According to Wells, in order to portray man, one must begin from the creation of the world and end with his expectations of eternity. Such a scale could not be more appropriate in an epoch when the activity of man has attained global dimensions and humanity has entered into the cosmic phase of its evolution.

Modern fantasy of the romantic variety attempts to see the world in this very scale. In no lesser, and possibly even greater measure than realistic fantasy, it pretends to embrace all of life, and its pretensions are the more valid, because it has in this regard quite a deep and firm tradition. In this it does not always hold to its old forms. It no longer has need of the Old Testament devil. He has long ago turned into the Department in Charge of Horns.

and Hooves, his accustomed attributes. Nonetheless, its cardinal feature is its difference from realistic fantasy.

Modern romantic fantasy of the traditional type, in its attempt to embrace all of life, ascertains that in the world there are two types of life, that it has two faces. These two forms of life, the material and the spiritual, are in essence incompatible, and a person to whom the other life has been revealed must make a choice. In the real world, if he does not wish to sacrifice his spirituality, he is condemned to solitude. Access to the other world is most fully realized through death.

There are few examples of such fantasy today, but they draw attention to themselves. Behind them is an enormous tradition frequently connected with the entire complex of humane concepts mediated by religious myth—which in the course of human history has absorbed a great number of man's hopes and disillusionments. Therefore, to call this fantasy "religious fantasy," as is usually done in the West in reference to its most outstanding example, the trilogy (*Out of the Silent Planet, Perelandra, That Hideous Strength*) of Clive Staples Lewis, the Cambridge professor who died in 1963, does not at all mean that the question has been exhausted. Essentially we are dealing here with a contemporary modification of romantic fantasy.

The aesthetics of such fantasy are quite markedly different from realistic fantasy.

The realistic fantasy of the 19th and 29th centuries took shape as a fantasy based on a single premise. In such a work, the foundation of the plot usually consists of a single fantastic assumption, "the truth" of which is established in its elaboration by every available means. This fantastic assumption makes it possible to develop a chain of events and thoughts, and the latter in their turn, insofar as they follow the logic of the basic premise, "train" the reader to use the premise, and by the same token, provide its justification.

Walter Scott had already approached the idea that the principle of the single premise draws a distinct boundary between the different forms of fantasy. In his article on Hoffmann, he emphasized that although in *Frankenstein* "the creation of a thinking and feeling being with the aid of a technical invention must be ascribed to the realm of fantasy, nevertheless, the main interest is directed not to the miraculous creation of Frankenstein, but to the experiences and feelings which should be naturally present in this monster, if indeed such a word as natural is applicable to a hero so unnatural in his origin and way of life."[8] To fantasy of such type Walter Scott juxtaposed another which "does not bind itself at all by such a condition, and [whose] sole aim is to astonish its audience solely by its wonders. But the reader is deceived and led astray by the odd phantoms whose tricks, devoid of rhyme and reason, find their justification only in their strangeness."[9]

By no means can it be said that Walter Scott understood the artistic principles of Mary Shelley and Hoffmann very deeply. In his treatment of them, which occupies some fifty pages of the printed text, there is much that is naive. But he did grasp the significance of the principle of the single or multiple premise as a distinguishing principle.

More than a hundred years later, H. G. Wells again emphasized the meaning of the principle of a single premise. In the introduction to his collection, *Seven Famous Novels*, he wrote: "Anyone can think up inside out people, antigravity, or worlds in the shape of dumbbells. Interest arises when all of this is conveyed in everyday language and all the other marvels are simply swept away. . . . Where anything can happen, nothing is interesting. The reader must accept the rules of the game, and the author, insofar as tact permits, must exert every effort so that the reader can 'feel at home' with his fantastic hypothesis. With the help of a probable supposition he must compel in the reader a wholehearted concession and continue the story as long as the illusion is maintained. . . . He must take the details from everyday reality . . . in order to preserve the strict truth of the initial fantastic premise, for any superfluous invention going beyond its boundaries gives to the whole work an aura of senseless contrivance."[10]

The principle of the single premise seemed to Wells the only possible one for fantasy as a whole. The fantastic world, "where anything can happen," seemed to him (as it did before him to Walter Scott) simply uninteresting and foolish, therefore having no right to existence. But justified or not, such a world does exist. It was created by the pre-romantics in England and in France, the romantics in Germany, and then given new life by the school of the absurd.

Yet is it really true that "anything can happen" in this world? Of course not. Any absurdity is subordinate to its particular logic. But the dualism of the pre-romantics and the relativism emphasized by the absurdists dictate another aesthetic principle to them —the principle of multiple premises. If the concept of multiplicity does not correspond with the concept of limitlessness, and even the very right to any number of premises is utilized at times quite modestly, this has no particular meaning. The important fact is that here the principle of the single premise is nullified, a principle going back to the Enlightenment.

The meaning of this principle is by no means limited to the sphere of aesthetics. It is based on the desire of the man of the Enlightenment to find a single sensual interpretation of the world. The need of many premises in fantasy was a reaction to the Enlightenment. Realistic fantasy explains the diversity of the forms of life which it exhibits with such pleasure in terms of the boundless riches of nature alone; romantic fantasy—by the fact that there are in operation in the world many conflicting laws and that the world lacks unity. This universe knows only one general law—lawlessness.

One may see to what extent a reliance on one or the other of these two principles produces a different artistic effect by the fact that even the works of one and the same author, trying his hand in turn in both manners, may prove to be quite different from one another. Mihail Bulgakov provides a clear example.

The Master and Margarita, it seems to us, represents an attempt to unite the traditions of realistic and romantic fantasy, underpinning them with the single moral conception of the world so natural for a Russian writer. Much has been achieved by Bulgakov along this line. Nevertheless, the different nature of various scenes is very much felt, creating at times (though not too often) a sense of stylistic strip-farming.

Actually, before *The Master and Margarita* two completely different tendencies were discernible in the work of Bulgakov. The first of them might be called the Wellsian tendency. Like many other men of letters of the 20's, Bulgakov experienced a constant interest in the work of Wells, as shown very markedly in the story *The Fatal Eggs* (1923), in which the plot combines elements of *The Food of the Gods* (directly mentioned by Bulgakov) and *The War of the Worlds*. The role of the "food" is played in this instance by the "red ray," discovered by Professor Persikov. This ray phenomenally increases the rate of reproduction and the quantity of animals. Persikov decides to conduct the first experiments on chickens. By mistake, however, snake eggs (needed for Persikov's laboratory) are sent to the *sovhoz* where the experiments are to take place, whereas he needed—chicken eggs. Thus, as in *The War of the Worlds*, where the Martians march on London, so in *The Fatal Eggs* giant reptiles crawl on Moscow, sweeping away everything in their path. They perish as did the Martians, of themselves—this time, to be sure, not because of microbes, but because of an eighteen degree frost.

The Deviliad (1926) expresses the other tendency. Here we have before us Hoffmann refracted through Gogol. This is a story of how a clerk of the *Glavcentrobazspimat* (Main Central Base for Match Materials) loses his mind, being unable to endure the fact that salaries are paid in matches or that a man named Kal'soner (who had, in addition, a bearded twin brother) has been appointed manager; in general, the clerk cannot endure the institutional way of life of the 20's. A similar plot might have been chosen by Ilf and Petrov, but Bulgakov does not write satire, but phantasmagoria, the real bases of which are hardly discernible. The author of *The Deviliad* speaks not about the disorders of life, but about its complete absurdity.

The desire to unite these two tendencies so evident in *The Master and Margarita* has, to be sure, sufficiently deep roots in the internal dynamics of Mihail Bulgakov's creative work. However, one must suppose that here, a definite dynamic of form in general was making itself felt. Bulgakov felt earlier than others that "Wellsian" fantasy, no matter how it broadened possibilities for the writer in comparison to fantasy of the Jules Verne variety, nonetheless set definite limits for him. Many years after Bulgakov, when the seeds sown by Wells had had time to produce luxuriant offshoots and the "fantasy boom" of the 40's and 50's had ended, many others, usually the most talented writers, also felt this. Is it not in this way that we may explain the evolution of the brothers Strugatsky from *The Land of the Crimson Clouds* through *It Is Difficult to Be God* to *The Helix on the Slope*?

The fact is that science fiction has a very complex relationship to other forms of art. It may very emphatically express one or another tendency of the art of its time. This capability is in its very nature. According to information theory, the greatest quantity of information is carried by unexpected communication, and the communication of fantasy is indeed "unexpected" in relation to life in its usual forms. However, for this very reason, fantasy has less need of the renewal of its devices; it is less subject to the general dynamic of style. At times, in the literary sense, it turns out to be quite conservative. Having once expressed a complex of ideas formulated by the epoch and having found for itself the requisite form, fantasy then begins to mark time, re-working these ideas and combining them in new ways. Here the combinatory capabilities of the intellect are employed and no others. Nevertheless, for fantasy, as long as it remains literature, knowledge must be the same as for any other type of literature—artistic knowledge; and this is connected with the movement of style.

But "the single premise" obligatory for Wellsian fantasy noticeably sets it off from traditional non-fantastic literature. "The single premise" is the most important formative element of the work. Having freely made some fantastic assumption, the writer is no longer in command of his own novel. The more fantastic the premise (and it must be as fantastic as possible, for it is this which determines its suitability in a fantastic novel), the more difficult it is to provide a basis for it. The more difficult it is to provide a basis for it, the more every aspect of the novel must serve this aim.

The possibilities are quite great. A distinct indication of the "reality" of a fantastic premise may be provided by a plot which is tense and calculated with mathematical precision. It is all the more appropriate in works of this type since the detective story has several features in common with fantasy. Both fantasy and the detective story are based on a particular "aesthetic of extreme circumstances." Adventure literature, the detective story in particular, shows a person "at the limit" of his intellectual and physical capacities, and places life itself at the limit of the possible. The extrapolating of fantasy also reveals the limit of modern tendencies noted in society or in men, only shown realized in time.

Fantasy, as does the detective story, also possesses a peculiar emphasis, a "purity" of method, an appeal to the combinatory and logical abilities of the reader's mind. This is also connected, one would have to think, with the peculiar "objectivity" of both methods. Fantasy tries to base itself on the objectivity of scientific knowledge, the detective story on a faith in abstract justice. The detective story is based on a patriarchal consciousness and this bestows on it a moral definiteness.[11] Of course the possibilities which make fantasy similar to the detective genre are certainly not always utilized to the good. Fantasy strives to overstep abruptly the boundaries of the accustomed. But some writers do not have the ability, the qualities as thinker and fantasist, to make the transition; thus they merely borrow similar devices from the related genre. In such works adventures do not serve so much as the foundation of the fantasy as a substitute for it. But the majority of science fiction writers have used the adventure plot as the basis of their fantasy with success.

Authenticity of everyday detail is also a very widespread and successful method for giving a realistic foundation to a fantastic premise. There are also other means to convince the reader of the authenticity of the improbable, but the "highest" of these, without question, is "foundation through man." Nothing serves so well for the authenticity of fantasy as the authenticity of human reactions to the events. It is in this direction that fantasy has achieved its greatest artistic successes. Yurij Oleša noted with admiration the complete "authenticity" of several episodes of The First Men in the Moon, the basis of which is in the truthfulness of the reactions of the heroes. One could say the same also of The Invisible Man and of many other works written by Wells and after Wells.

Here, however, at this very point, when it would seem that single premise fantasy had come closest to non-fantastic literature, there may be observed most clearly the cardinal difference between them. In fantasy of the single premise no matter how lofty the position occupied by the hero, nonetheless one will always feel that it is not he who is the chief element, for the basic formative element is the fantastic premise, and everything serves it, including the hero. In the genuinely realistic novel the situation is completely different. There the formative element is the hero himself; everything serves him; it is he who subjects the novel to the logic of his own character.

Meanwhile, fantasy in general, from decade to decade, has been showing more and more interest in man, for it would be illogical in defining the place of man in the modern world to forget about man himself. And it must be said that in fantasy's approach to man there are noticeable advantages. In order to describe modern man in a revealing way, it is often necessary to place him in an unusual situation. He has already displayed accustomed reactions in almost every conceivably possible normal situation. Fantasy possesses the enormous ability to create the most improbable of situations. By this very fact it enables people to be revealed in most unexpected ways. In this connection we refer not only to satire, but also to the most sensitive portrayals of men, as, for example, in Wells's story "The Door in the Wall" or Priestley's story "Another Place." The heroes of these works, feeling themselves to be in a fairy-tale world where nothing binds them, reveal themselves in their best qualities because of that very circumstance.

(Is it not for this reason, incidentally, that in modern literature in the West and in the U.S.A.—literature not necessarily satirical—there is such a strong attraction toward a certain "displacement of reality?")

However, the more thoroughly the author wishes to elaborate the image of man, the more he is compelled to "soften" the principle of the single premise, to attach a wider significance to it. To a certain degree it is possible to do this without losing the principle itself. An excellent example of this is Wells's *The Invisible Man*. But the further the process goes, the more the primary fantastic supposition loses the significance of a "single premise." In the stories of Wells and Priestley just mentioned, the fantastic transition from our reality into another fantastic reality is not a "single premise" because it demands no proof at all: it is simply a miracle. Earlier the hero served as the basis for the "single premise"—at times so zealously that he had no time to be occupied with himself. Now, in order to allow the hero to reveal himself genuinely, he is freed from any obligations with regard to the premise. And the premise itself is no longer a premise but rather an arbitrary authorial act. Incidentally, the heroes of Wells and Priestley, according to the method of the "single premise," could not have confirmed the reality of the other world by their own actions, no matter how much they desired to do so. There are two reasons for this: first, this world does not even attempt to appear real, and second, the hero is not present there: only his "better self" is found there.

In any case, the basic fantastic assumption is quite easily formalized, which fact leads to the complete renunciation of the principle of the "single premise." But let us remember that the principle of the single premise was the main principle of fantasy tending toward realism! It was through this very principle that there was expressed in the aesthetic sphere a conception of the unity of the world!

And what is most surprising is that this principle was destroyed not under the influence of tendencies hostile to realism, but by a striving to reveal man in the fullest way possible. The limitation of the principle destroyed it more truly than the intrigues of its enemies.

H. G. Wells, in whose works there is roughly outlined a portion of the path which confronted fantastic literature as a whole, showed that fantasy, having renounced the principle of the "single premise," may cease to be fantasy at all. After "The Door in the Wall" he did not write fantasy in the old sense of the word. His initial fantastic assumption was thoroughly formalized, and in such novels as *The Dream*, we have what is essentially ordinary realistic literature. A work which employs a conditional fantastic device is far from always being a work of fantasy.

But another path is possible. If the basic fantastic assumption does not fully determine the aesthetic nature of the work, then the fantastic quality must be attained by some other means, by the help of some supplementary devices, sometimes very weakly connected with the primary premise. In this case the initial premise may be thoroughly scientific and realistic and the fantastic "supplement" of the work quite unscientific and unrealistic. Thus, in the novel by C. S. Lewis, *Out of the Silent Planet*, which was mentioned as a model of modern romantic fantasy having a pronounced religious inclination, the heroes get to Mars in an interplanetary rocket constructed by the physicist villain.

In this case, a case of formalization of the initial premise, no scientific quality serves as a guarantee of realism. Here science is quite capable of taking on the role of a doorkeeper opening the way into a world where "everything is possible," where "there is only one general law—lawlessness"; in other words, a world of romantic fantasy. The question of the realistic or, conditionally expressing it, the romantic nature of a work of contemporary fantasy is thus still further complicated.

Aesthetic strip-farming in modern fantasy is constantly increasing. The harmony of the old principles has been destroyed. And the system which will supplant the declining one will be far from a rigid one such as Jules Verne's and even more flexible than that of Wells. The post-Wellsian system, one must think, will provide a dynamic equilibrium of some sort. At any rate, it is in this direction that everything is moving.

Of course it is impossible to say how this new fantastic realism will look in its concrete embodiments. Few have been successful in literary prognosis. But in any case, it is clear that the exhaustion (or, let us assume, the generally recognized exhaustion) of the principle of the single premise does not mean that realism has exhausted itself. We are simply unable to predict the forms of this new realism.

NOTES

[1]D. Zatonskij, "The Career Novel and the 20th Century," *Voprosy Literatury*, No. 9 (1968), p. 156.

[2]Sir Walter Scott, "The Fair Maid of Perth," *Works: International Limited Edition* (Boston: Estes and Laureat, 1894), 42:89; note, 342-346.

[3]Bernard Sieman, *The River of Life* (New York: W. W. Norton, 1961), pp. 49-54.

[4]Kobo Abe, *Inter Ice Age 4* (New York: Alfred A. Knopf, 1970), pp. 53-58.

[5]Stanislaw Lem, "Author's Preface," *Solaris*, in *The Library of Fantasy and Travel* (Moscow: Molodaja Gvardija, 1965), p. 8. [Ed. note: the "Preface" was not included in the American edition issued by Walker & Company, 1970.]

[6]Thomas H. Huxley, "Prologue [Controverted Questions, 1892]," *Science and the Christian Tradition* (New York: D. Appleton and Company, 1896), pp. 39-40.

[7]Eckermann, *Conversations with Goethe* (London: J. M. Dent; New York: E. P. Dutton, 1930, 1951), p. 244.

[8]Sir Walter Scott, *Critical and Miscellaneous Essays* (Philadelphia: Carey & Hart, 1841), II, 24.

[9]*Ibid.*, II, 24.

[10]H. G. Wells, "Preface," *Seven Famous Novels* (New York: Alfred A. Knopf, 1934), p. viii.

[11]L. Zonina clearly felt this in her article, "The Myth Named Inspector Maigrat." She wrote: "The detective story . . . is the most dialectical genre of prose. In it are exposed and made concrete concepts of what is right and criminal, just and base . . . . In the myth of a man nobly defending the humble there are deep folk roots." *Novyj Mir*, No. 5 (1967), p. 258.

Translated by Milda Carroll

JUDITH MERRIL

WHAT DO YOU MEAN:
SCIENCE?
FICTION?

I used to know what "science" meant: at least I understood the word well enough to believe that a statement like, "A revolution is occurring in science," made clear sense. At that time, the distinctions between "physical sciences" and "biological sciences," "theory" and "application," "research" and "engineering," "experimental" and "clinical," seemed perfectly obvious.

I also used to know what "fiction" meant. I knew the difference between a novel, a novella, a novelette, a short story, and a vignette; between "subjective" and "objective" narrative styles; between "psychological fiction" and the "adventure story;" between "realism" and "fantasy."

I never did know just what "science fiction" meant: in all the nights I stayed awake till dawn debating definitions, I do not recall one that stood up unflinchingly to the light of day. They all relied, in any case, on certain axiomatic assumptions about the meanings of "science" and "fiction."

Actually, when I first became involved in such debates—about twenty-five years ago—there was already a fair amount of honest confusion (among scientists) about the meaning of 'science' in the 20th century. As dedicated—*addicted*—s-f readers, we had some awareness of the upheaval in process in scientific philosophy, following on the work of Heisenberg and Schroedinger, Bridgman

Originally published in two installments in *Extrapolation*, 7 (May 1966), 30-46; 8 (December 1966), 2-19. Reprinted by permission of the author.

and de Broglie; but as dedicated—*addicted*—s-f readers, we also made a complete, unconscious adjustment when we talked stories instead of concepts—"science" in "science fiction" meant (and for most readers—and writers—still does mean—"technology."

What is viable in "science fiction" (whatever *that* may mean) today is coming from a comparatively small group of serious writers—in and out of the specialty field—who are applying the traditions of the genre and the techniques of contemporary literature to the concepts of 20th century science. The first results are already barely discernible. Science fiction is catching up with science. And the genre is returning from its forty years of self-imposed wandering away from the wellsprings of literature.

The two events could only be simultaneous. Art at any time can achieve validity only if it is rooted in the accumulated human experience of its day, and touches somewhere on the nerve center of the culture from which it springs. The literature of the mid-20th century can be meaningful only in so far as it perceives, and relates itself to, the central reality of our culture: the revolution in scientific thought which has replaced mechanics with dynamics, classification with integration, positivism with relativity, certainties with statistical probabilities, dualism with parity.

If it seems I am saying that there is no adequate literature in existence now—I am. If it further seems I am claiming a special literary validity for science fiction—I would be, except that as it achieves that validity, it ceases to be 'science fiction' and becomes simply contemporary literature instead.

I must pause here to establish my lack of credentials. Although, as fellow science fiction readers, our knowledge of scientific history, and contemporary scientific concepts, is probably roughly equatable, and (for many of you at least) arrived at in rather the same manner (elementary courses at school, and wide and presumably intelligent reading since), our knowledge of literature is neither equal nor similar. I learned my definitions of "fiction" from pulp writers and editors initially: their rules were hard-and-fast, and the penalty for breaking them was hunger; or worse yet, working for a living instead of selling stories.

So when I say I knew what fiction was, I mean I really *knew*. Things like: a short story is limited to one main character, who must be involved in a conflict which is resolved before the end of the story; it can be told from only one viewpoint, which must not shift during the story. A novelette is still primarily about one character, though it is possible to develop one or even two subsidiary characters to some degree—the main distinction is that there can be more than one or two incidents involved in developing the conflict before the resolution: if you get good enough, you can occasionally shift viewpoints in a novelette without killing the sale. Things like that.

I found out by a combination of my own dissatisfaction with the rule-book, and by a very slow and extremely erratic catching-up process (still far from complete) in my reading that the rules I had learned were not only not universal, but not particularly applicable to anything I wanted to do—except *sell*. I also found out that in the upper literary strata, it was possible to break them and sell; and in the way-out literary strata (where nobody gets paid for anything) it was almost required to break them.

I didn't find the rules in other areas any improvement; at least, I kept on enjoying *reading* s-f more than other contemporary work—until a few years ago. What happened, or started to happen, a few years ago, I will come back to. Meantime, let me tell you about my great discoveries, and try to see them through the eyes of a genuine discoverer. Bear with me if I sometimes state the obvious; it was not so to me. And if some things I say are obviously *not* so—remember, I claim no authority: I am speaking only of my own experiences and discoveries.

It is not the Bomb or the Pill (or miracle drugs or synthetic materials or space travel) that are forcing us to re-think the meaning of "science": these, after all, are comparatively mechanical, *technological,* applications of what I have been calling 20th century scientific concepts—although they of course began in the 19th. The reverberations of that conceptual revolution have by now shaken every branch of scientific investigation and human life. Indeed the failure of entrenched, established academic Humanism to comprehend the meaning of the rumblings from cross-campus (the "two-culture" phenomenon) was probably due in part to preoccupation with the local effects of the same conceptual explosion in the arts and social sciences.

It was not James Joyce or Henry Miller or Jack Kerouac or William Burroughs who made it necessary to re-examine the idea of "fiction." They were simply pioneers in the process of re-examination. The seeds of the upheaval, as in the case of the scientific revolution, appeared at the height of Victorian formalist-mechanist complacency—the beginning of modern social science (Darwin, Freud, Boas, Veblen . . .) with a focus on human motivations, rather than surface behavior.

What happened in the various sciences had its almost exact counterpart in literature, and most markedly so in "fiction," that curious prose form which, like physics and chemistry, anthropology and psychology (and their numerous and hybrid offspring) came into existence as a distinct area of human endeavor during the Great Crackup of the 17th century. I will not attempt here to argue the causes. I am inclined to the notion that the voyages of exploration and discovery of America, and the printing press, with its attendant revolution in communications, were major factors. Whatever the chain of causation, the result was as though a figurative planet composed of man's intellect, suddenly acquired so much additional mass, or velocity (or both?) that it flew out of orbit, breaking up and fragmenting under the strain. (Perhaps the settlement of America enlarged the "subjective mass" of the planet in men's minds? Or possibly just the first accumulation of the sheer bulk of paper under which we are nowadays likely to be buried . . .)

One might carry the metaphor further, and assume that the reduced planet, and its severed chunks, would have settled, eventually, into new orbits closer to the source of energy. Some bits would have been drawn into the sun and lost entirely: Divine Right went that way (and with it a substantial part of the certainty of divinity). Other pieces, the largest ones, would have been drawn back into the parent body very quickly, and become attached as discrete territories, no longer part of the amorphous whole: one might conceive of the establishment of national sovereignties this way, or of the broad demarcations of not-yet-'scientific' disciplines as they first appeared—naturalist, mathematician-astronomer, philosopher, and so forth. The intermediate chunks, settling into orbits somewhat closer to the sun at first, absorbed more energy perhaps, and *grew,* moving back closer to the parent body with each increment of mass and velocity.

Take the fancy one bit farther, and picture the return of the pieces (rather as Planetarium lecturers are fond of presenting the image of an eventual falling-back of the Moon). At least one of the first returning bodies would have landed with tremendous impact—Newtonian physics, the laws of motion, gravitation, and the Calculus, containing within them (if anyone had thought to notice, or had energy to spare to think it through) a clear explanatory warning of descents yet to come.

The new literary form, fiction, may be considered to have made its (far less impactful) return as a clearly formed body somewhere about the middle of the 18th century. (Even fancifullier, one might postulate that the date went unnoticed, and is still argued, because it landed in the tropic sea of some enchanted voyage of exploration—quite possibly just out of sight of Alexander Selkirk's lonely island—and that it was in the nourishing warmth of these waters that the solid mass broke somewhat apart, and eventually attached itself to the land mass again as the full-blown novel and incipient short story.)

\- \- \-

All metaphors aside, I believe it is significant that the fiction form took shape and name in the same intellectual-cultural upheaval from which the familiar "scientific disciplines" emerged— that it achieved a discernible form and popularity just about half way between the beginnings of physics and anthropology, and that its later history shows so many parallels with those of nineteenth-century science.

We tend to think of the 19th century in terms of its own popular image of itself: a time of complacency and classification, of rationality, mechanistic philosophy, scientific certainties, technological, literary and artistic polish rather than innovation. Actually, there seem almost to have been two parallel 19th centuries: some things about the *other* one we are still finding out. But we do know that the groundwork for modern mathematics—the non-Euclidean geometries of Gauss, Lobachevsky, and Riemann, as well as Boolean algebra and the basis of symbolic logic, had already been worked out in 1850—when Kierkegaard wars writing the first Existential works, and Baudelaire was setting forth the principles of the Symbolist movement—all before either the publication of *The Descent of Man,* or the organization of the Periodic Table.

Fifty years later—just at the turn of the century, while Victoria still reigned, and Teddy Roosevelt brandished his Big Stick—Freud and Pavolv, Lorentz and Fitzgerald, Buber and Heidegger laid the foundations for thought control, space-time cosmology, and even the Ecumenical Council.

The first confused wave of reaction against these innovations came in the form of reinforced mechanism and increasingly "discrete" and complicated "classification"; perhaps it was not so much *reaction* as an honest effort on the part of people trained in the formalisms of the nineteenth century to cope with the fascinating, staggering, new integrations while still using the familiar methods of separation and analysis.

Thus, the twentieth century opened to a compartmentation and fragmentation of knowledge unprecedented in scope, and probably in attitude. Within the physical sciences, separate but traditional disciplines were splitting and resplitting: chemists became organic or inorganic chemists—then bio-chemists or physical chemists, etc. They devoted themselves to theory or to application. In the "social sciences," the same phenomenon occurred. In both areas, the engineers took over—at least in popular esteem.

The reasons for this are both obvious and subtle, and it would require, I think, a complete separate essay to examine them satisfactorily. All that matters for purposes of this retrospection, is that two completely separate—and for a time increasingly separating—streams of intellectual endeavor proceeded, in dialectical fashion, from the origins of modern thought in the last half of the nineteenth century. The most obvious, and most comprehensible of these was for some time the essentially engineering-type application of bits and pieces of new conceptual discoveries by the best of the old-school mechanicians: the flood of electronic, aeronautic, and biochemical inventions; the sensational discoveries of the behaviorists and early cultural anthropologists; the economic determinists in politics and sociology; and the school of twentieth-century "realism" in fiction.

I cannot define science fiction, but I can locate it, philosophically and historically:

There is a body of writing of whose general outlines the readers of *Extrapolation* are, by common consent, already aware: that is to say, the "classical antecedents" from Lucian and Plato through, approximately, Kepler and de Bergerac; the "borderline" (both of acceptability and between periods) instances of *Don Quixote* and *Robinson Crusoe,* terminating probably (in general acceptability) with *Gulliver's Travels* and *Micromegas*; the "Gothic" vein which characterizes the first half, or two-thirds, of the nineteenth century, and continues as a major element well into the twentieth; the period generally considered as "modern," beginning with Verne, and achieving general popularity in the last two decades of the nineteenth century; and the specific area of American specialty science fiction starting in the pulp adventure magazines of the 1910's, and being consolidated by Hugo Gernsback as a discrete phenomenon in his specialty publications during the 1920's.

Assuming this to represent some general area of agreement on what we mean when we talk about "science fiction," I believe it is possible to distinguish within the broad area certain distinct and more reasonably definable forms:

1) "Teaching stories": the dramatized essay or disguised treatise, in which the fiction form is utilized to present a new scientific idea, sometimes (as with the *Somnium,* or the works of "John Taine" and other pseudonymous scientists) because of social, political, religious, or academic pressures operating against a direct presentation; sometimes (as with the typical Gernsbackian story, and a fair proportion of late nineteenth-century work) as a means of "popularizing" scientific information or theories, or (hopefully) sugarcoating an educational pill. (This is what used to be called by literary snobs, "pseudoscience," and should have been called "pseudofiction"—although in the hands of an expert it can become reasonably good fiction: Arthur C. Clarke manages it occasionally, although his best work—*Childhood's End,* for instance—is not of this type.)

2) "Preaching stories": primarily allegories and satires— morality pieces, prophecies, visions, and warnings, more concerned with the conduct of human society than with its techniques. These are the true "pseudoscience" stories: they utilize science (or

technology), or a plausible semblance of science (or technology), or at least the language and atmosphere, in just the same way that the scientific treatise in disguise utilizes fiction. And let me point out again (rather more enthusiastically than before) that some first-rate writing has emerged from this sort of forced marriage. (Perhaps the difference between the work of a marriage broker and a shotgun wedding?) Stapledon's *Star Maker* falls into this group, as well as Ray Bradbury's (specifically) science fiction and a large proportion of both Utopian and anti-Utopian novels up through the turn of the century.

3) Speculative fiction: stories whose objective is to explore, to discover, to *learn*, by means of projection, extrapolation, analogue, hypothesis-and-paper-experimentation, something about the nature of the universe, of man, of "reality." Obviously, all fiction worth considering is "speculative" in the sense that it endeavors to reach, or to expose, some aspect of Truth. But it is equally true—and irrelevant—to say that all fiction is imaginative or all fiction is fantasy. I use the term "speculative fiction" here specifically to describe the mode which makes use of the traditional "scientific method" (observation, hypothesis, experimentation) to examine some postulated approximation of reality, by introducing a given set of changes—imaginary or inventive—into the common background of "known facts," creating an environment in which the responses and perceptions of the characters will reveal something about the inventions, the characters, or both.

It is in this last area that the essence of science fiction resides; it covers a great deal of territory, shading at either end into the first two categories. Clearly, there is hybridization all through the groups—as for instance in satire (such as *The Child Buyer*, or *Player Piano*) whose main devil actually is some specific aspect of science or technology.

For purposes of this discussion, I am not considering the space adventure story, the transplanted western or historical, as science fiction at all.

- - -

In his introduction to *Future Perfect*, H. Bruce Franklin points out: "There was no major nineteenth-century American writer of fiction, and indeed few in the second rank, who did not write some science fiction or at least one Utopian romance."

I doubt that a statement quite so all-embracing could be made for all of Western literature, but if you take fiction, for the moment, to include *all* forms of story-telling (other than the documented reportorial), and allow science its broadest (and I think truest) meaning—the conscientious seeking after knowledge of the nature of the universe, the nature of man, and the nature of "reality"—then I believe Franklin's statement can be applied with few exceptions to the major story-tellers of Western civilization, at almost all times in almost all countries.

One of the exceptional times-and-countries was America of the first half of the 20th century. (There is, frankly, some question in my mind as to whether this period can claim any "major" writers. But within its own framework, it had accepted "greats"— and almost to a man, they shunned anything resembling either science fiction or fantasy—except such fantasy as clearly existed only in the mind of a character.)

My contention is that "realistic" fiction, rather than speculative or science fiction, was the transient oddity—as grotesque a product of nineteenth-century super-rationalism and mechanistic philosophy as Watson babies and the Stakhanovite movement. For nearly a half century, American writers were somehow impelled to choose, not only one *field* of writing (poetry, essays, journalism, drama, fiction, biography), but—within fiction at least—one *area*. "Serious" fiction writers wrote realistic fiction (with Cabell as the exception). "Slick writers" wrote "realistic" stereotypes for the glossy magazines; "pulp writers," for the pulps. (They at least had some variety of subject, if not style, open to them.) Offhand, I can think of four notable names other than Cabell who broke the rules: Philip Wylie, Conrad Aiken, William Saroyan, and Stephen Vincent Benet. (When Santayana published *The Last Puritan*, he added an epilogue explaining that it was really a work of philosophy more than a novel.) But the Name Novelists—with the notable exception of Sinclair Lewis in *It Can't Happen Here*—stuck to realism exclusively; or if they didn't, their realistic work was all we saw. (I used a science-fiction satire of Farrell's in a recent anthology, and met astonishment everywhere; the truth is, Farrell wrote the story almost fifteen years ago, and *wasn't able to sell it:*

it wasn't "Farrell!") Men of scientific or academic or professional
standing who suffered from a compulsion to write fiction did so
under pen names. Eventually, even the pulp adventure magazines
broke up into "categories": detective, western, sea, sports, science
fiction, fantasy.

This was the unique—indeed, baroque—situation, when the
first magazines devoted exclusively to fantasy and science fiction
were published here in the mid-twenties. It was a time for
extremes and bizarre combinations. The richest country in the
world was enjoying its richest years—in the cities—while mortgages
foreclosed and the Big Depression gained its first beachhead on the
farms. These were the years of prohibition and gangsterism, Bix
Beiderbecke and Isadora Duncan; the Scopes Trial in Tennessee
and psychoanalysis in New York; bottle babies and "back to
normalcy." Heisenberg published his theories on quantum
matrices the year after Coolidge's election, and announced his
"uncertainty" principle the year before the Model A replaced the
Model T. Alfred Korzybski's first book had been published here
in 1921; Ruth Benedict and Margaret Mead were working with
Franz Boas in the new field of cultural anthropology; Eugene
O'Neill's *The Hairy Ape* and T. S. Eliot's *The Wasteland* had
appeared in 1922, as had *Ulysses,* and the big American novel that
year was *Babbitt.* In 1926, the "new criticism" was gaining adherents here, but Dali and Surrealism were still almost unknown on
this side of the ocean; Goddard tested his first successful liquid
fuel rocket; while Lindbergh prepared for his non-stop flight to
Paris; Rudolph Valentino died, and the first sound film was made;
Hemingway (in Paris) published *The Sun Also Rises,* and became
an important writer overnight.

The War to End All War had ended a way of life in Europe;
here, we were still clinging desperately to certainties where we
could find them, flinging out wildly when we lost hold. If Darwin,
Freud, and Einstein had made Our Trust in God less than certain,
Edison, Ford, and Marconi had given us back something *solid.* We
did our speculating on the stock market—not in our fiction.

"Scientification" in its beginnings was a pure extension of the
most mechanistic realism: tomorrow's machines today. The early
Gernsback magazines were confined almost entirely to the Teaching school of science fiction, and were further confined almost

exclusively to technology in particular rather than science in general. (The exceptions tended to be pseudonymous works by scholars and scientists who had no other outlet, in the rigid framework of the academic Establishment, for speculation outside the sharply defined range of their own specialties.) John Taine (Eric Temple Bell) affords perhaps the best, though not only, example.

The others, such as *Amazing,* seem, in retrospect, to have contained endless expositions of technical, technological, technophiliac, and Technocratic ideas, set forth in ponderous prose, illustrated with cardboard figures spouting wooden dialogue—yet at the time, it was exciting stuff indeed. Perhaps it gave us only more hardware, and gave it dressed in olive drab—but it was *tomorrow's* hardware, and it was knowledgeably projected. There was vast scope of the reader's own imagination to operate in the cities and spaceships and satellites and time machines of the World of Science (Technology) and Progress to Come.

And of course, "scientification" was not the only game in town. For those who craved madder music and gaudier lights, there was always *Weird Tales* (established in 1923), where amid warlocks and werewolves one could still find a good supply of mad scientists, mutant plants, Unidentified Alien Objects, mysterious islands, hollow planets, hypnotized beauties, shambling neo-frankensteins, lost civilizations, and all the rest of the gorgeous panoply of Gothic romance—perhaps a bit worn from a century's heavy use by Hawthorne, Poe, Mary Shelley, Wilkie Collins, Stevenson, Doyle, Haggard, Wells, *et al.* At times this Gothicism hardly showed the shabby spots at all in the bright purple and muted mauve lighting effects preferred by Lovecraft and Clark Ashton Smith—and was perhaps no less powerful in its symbolism than when it was first used.

Weird ran heavily to the Preaching school—allegory and fable, not satire—with the idea content almost exclusively limited to the Battle between Good and Evil. Technological or scientific novelties introduced were usually fully exploited by the author; they left comparatively little to the reader's imagination. *But* the rare story (and they were probably no less rare in the fantasy magazines than in science fiction) that did contain some genuine speculative content was much more likely to be equipped with movable-joint characters and appropriate imagery in the background—plus a considerably more colorful and complex prose style. (When they were good they were really quite good, but when they were bad, they were Gothic *awful*.)

What I have described is of course an extreme differentiating characteristic, not so much of two specific magazines as of the prevailing atmospheres   associated with "scientification" and "weird"   as sub-categories of the magazine specialty field of science fiction: Gernsback and Lovecraft (who dominated *Weird Tales,* though he did not edit it) as they look forty years after.

Actually, the near-total polarization imputed here was effective, if at all, only at the starting-point. Science fiction and fantasy of all sorts were still appearing regularly in a number of "all-story" pulp magazines in the twenties, particularly what one might call (absurdly) the "prestige pulps" (*Golden Book, Argosy, Blue Book*). And by 1930, there were two more specialty magazines: Street & Smith's *Astounding,* and Gernsback's *Wonder* (first *Air Wonder* and *Science Wonder;* later, combined in the single title; later yet, *Thrilling Wonder*).   In the decade following the first issue of *Amazing,* the admixture of story types, and overlap of authors— and readers—was considerable.   Although *Weird* retained its own distinctive flavor, several of its authors (Carl Jacobi, Clark Ashton Smith, C. L. Moore, for instance) adapting their styles somewhat, began to appear in the other magazines; other writers from the general pulp field, like Leinster and Williamson, made themselves at home, particularly in *Astounding* under Tremaine's editorship; and new writers, science fiction specialists from the beginning, established themselves (John W. Campbell, Jr., Harry Bates, and Clifford D. Simak and, from England, John Beynon Harris—now John Wyndham—and Eric Frank Russell).

In the thirties, or more precisely in October 1929, it became abruptly apparent, even to the most dedicated believers in Progress as embodied in Free Enterprise and the Survival of the Fittest, that all was not necessarily for the best in this most solid of all possible worlds.   Yet inside science fiction, there was no serious questioning of the virtue inherent in machines, or of the inevitability of the accelerated growth of the super-technological civilization.   (However blind the first viewpoint may have been, the second was absolutely clear-sighted.)   The net effect was simply to soften the Technocratic tone, and make the evangelical aspect less obvious. The problem-story took over from the treatise: how to *use* the machine, how to *apply* the techniques.

- - -

When John W. Campbell, Jr., took over the editorship of *Astounding* at the end of 1937, the field in general, and *Astounding* in particular, had acquired a solid nucleus of steady contributors of true speculative science fiction: and I do mean "nucleus." The number of thinkers capable of new ideas is never large; the number of those with even those rudimentary insights into human behavior and the story-telling knack that constitute the bare minimum capability of a writer of fiction is much smaller. There has never been any likelihood of *much* genuine speculative science fiction at any time: less so in a low-paid and low-prestige isolated enclave of literature. The *astounding* thing is not that the quantity was small, but that there was any noticeable quantity at all. Much more astounding was the rapid growth of that nucleus during Campbell's first five years of editorship.

The list of new names in *Astounding* and *Unknown* in 1938 and 1939 alone contains more than half the important bylines of the first book publishing boom of the early 50's; Asimov, De Camp, del Rey, Gold, Heinlein, Hubbard, Jameson, Kuttner, Leiber, Sturgeon, van Vogt. (Boucher, Frederic Brown, Hal Clement, George O. Smith and James H. Schmitz came along in 1941-3.)

Thus the field gained strength; yet John Campbell has taken a good deal of criticism these past years, from fans, writers, and critics inside the field; recently he has been subject to what might better be called abuse, mostly from people too new to the field, or too uninformed (i.e., Amis' churlish comments in *New Maps of Hell*), to comprehend Campbell's role as writer and editor in the decade 1935-1945—or how much of what has happened since derived from his impact at that time. If he has been a damaging influence on some writers in recent years, the evil he has done is still far outweighed by the good—and one cannot but suspect, particularly considering Campbell's working habits—that those writers who have been trapped in the *Analog* Formula these last years (or intellectually raped by Campbell's enthusiasms) solicited the economic haven of the trap, and offered up their thematic honor more eagerly than otherwise. Since 1948, it has been easy for any writer who cared to, to resist Campbell's pressure; before that, *Astounding* dominated the market so completely that a case might be made against the man for literary despoilage at that time —if anyone cared to. Certainly it is true that Asimov, Sturgeon, Heinlein, Leiber, were revivified by the emergence of new and more literarily demanding markets in the fifties. But it is hardly reasonable to condemn Campbell for not improving things *enough*; the fact is, when he took over *Astounding*, the time was ripe for the qualitative, and quantitative, explosion that occurred. But it is equally true that Campbell was the right man for the right time— and perhaps as true that his peculiar limitations were as useful as his considerable abilities.

After the 1965 Science Fiction Convention in London, the *London Sunday Times Magazine* published a thoughtful profile of Campbell, by Pat Williams, who suggested:

> . . . Life to Campbell is a gigantic experiment in form, and earth the forcing-house—an impeccable vision, but one not warmed (in his theories, that is) by a feeling for the pain or personal potential of the individuals in the experiment. That kind of gentleness in expression seemed to disappear with Don A. Stuart.

> So that, ironically, as SF becomes increasingly respectable, John Campbell, its acknowledged father-figure, can't really claim his throne. He provides the continuity, he shaped much of the thought, he made many reputations. SF narrowed from the vastness of space to the greater complexity of "sociological" SF with him presiding.

> But now it is narrowing towards the highly-focused, upside-down detail of "inner space." The tone is personal and subjective, the quality of expression important. . . . None of this is Campbell's style.

I think Mrs. Williams was exceptionally perceptive in her interviewing, and intelligent in her assessment; if she missed a stage between Campbell and "inner space," it is understandable, because British science fiction has not gone through exactly the same development. It was never effectively cut off, as the specialty field was here, from the main streams of literature and scientific philosophy. In England, they had Priestley, Huxley, Collier, Stapledon, Lewis, Heard, Kersh, Russell, through the thirties and forties. Here, we had Campbell—and eventually, Anthony Boucher and H. L. Gold.

It may seem self-contradictory to say that Campbell is the "sociological science fiction" editor, and add that his great limitation is his essentially *engineering* frame of mind: but this is precisely the "useful" limitation I referred to earlier. In the deepest sense, Campbell was the linear and logical successor to Gernsback. He was as technology-minded and application-oriented as the rest of the field in the thirties, with this difference: that he had a broader concept of the scope of "science" (technology and *engineering*); he wanted to explore the effects of the new technological world on *people*. Cultural anthropology, social psychology, cybernetics, communications, sociology, education, psychometrics—all these, and a dozen intermediate points, were thrown open for examination.

There were two immediately noticeable effects: better stories and more and better speculative development. A third effect came inevitably on their heels: one I do not believe Campbell was looking for, and may not have noticed when it arrived—better writing.

The thinking improved not only because there were vast unworked areas to explore, but because these particular areas attracted writers of somewhat more flexible intellectual inclination—and most of all, because the editor *wanted* clear thinking; he was honestly (at the beginning) interested in learning about human behavior; he genuinely lacked (as yet) any preconceptions, or even strong opinions, about how the answers should look.

The stories improved because they were required to be about things that happened to people, rather than just to have people in them. (Nor could they be *inside* people—and as the "mainstream" has painfully learned, psychiatric introspections make little good fiction.)

The writing gradually improved because the essence of good writing is clear observation, and you cannot project human responses accurately without observing some humans closely first. It also improved, I think, through hybridization: "scientification" had been pro-machine; the Lovecraft school, generally anti-machine. There had been some overlapping before, but now there was fluent admixture of those writers from both areas who were least satisfied with their own sub-genre patterns. Treatise Drab and Poe Purple studied each other with interest, and adapted toward a common center. The general result was not anything that could properly be called literary style; but it approximated a tolerable narrative prose—determinedly matter-of-fact, slangy, colloquial with a fair balance of color and economy.

There was even the beginning of characterization. In Asimov's robot stories an individual grew out of a prototype: Dr. Susan Calvin became more complex and believable in each story. And of course the robots were individuals: in fact, characterization for aliens, elves, androids and others hit the field awhile before living breathing humans arrived. Some of Leiber's too-true witches may have marked the transition. Del Rey began to generate character in his protagonists. Simak was perhaps the first to do so with any consistency (in the *City* series). Sturgeon, at that stage, was creating memorable puppets: his characters were cut from no stock on which other authors drew, but the Sturgeon whole-cloth was no more genuine—just brighter colored and better designed.

In those first few years of Campbell's domination of the field, the basic pattern was set for the next twenty years: the application of technological development to human problems; the application of human development to technology.

And, my God, how the stories rolled out! *Beyond This Horizon, Gather Darkness,* Asimov's robots, "Microcosmic God," "The Gnarly Man," "Elsewhen," "Helen O'Loy," "Mimsy Were the Borogroves," *Slan,* "Pride," "Smoke Ghost," the *City* stories, "First Contact," *Universe,* "Etaoin Shrdlu," "Nightfall," "Killdozer!," "Opposites—React!," "No Woman Born," "Nerves," "Adam and no Eve". . . One could go on and on, and the sad fact is that with all but a few, remembering them is better than rereading them.

It was in those bright days—in 1941, to be precise—that I discovered the science fiction magazines. Ten years later, I could still re-read every story I've mentioned here, and a good many more, with almost undiminished renewal of experience: I *know* this, because I had cause to reread them, critically, when I began editing "theme anthologies" in 1952 (reading for reprint, you do not allow rosy memories to haze over the actual words). And by that time, there was some impressive new work to compare it with—some of it by the same authors, some by the next flood of new names of the early fifties—generally so much better *written* as to place great strain on the acceptability of the earlier work.

The stories I have mentioned did stand up to—*that*—re-examination. I tried some of them again recently, and will probably not do so again. They were every bit as good as I remembered—but it was not the prose (however good it looked by comparison at the time) or the characters; it was the ideas that were vivid and memorable—and they remain so; re-reading adds nothing. (There is not much of what we now consider good characterization in *Beowulf*, either. Idea-fiction, like pure myth, seems to work as well with solidly constructed prototypes—and there *is* a difference between a player's mask and a cardboard cutout, between Everyman and no-one-at-all. But when did you last *re*-read *Beowulf*?)

By comparison with the new work of the early fifties, the best of the 1940-period stories survived; they still do—on their own terms. But their terms have no more to do with today's science fiction than—let us say, *The Red Badge of Courage* has to do with *Gone With the Wind*.

- - -

I said earlier that Campbell's specific limitation was his "engineering mind," and that I thought this had been useful to him and to s-f. I think it was useful—indeed essential—for the role he played in his first years as editor; I think it was almost as useful—to the field as a whole, though not to his own position in the field—in its second phase.

A few months ago, I participated in a late night radio talk-program, on which John Campbell and two professors of physics from local schools were co-panelists. To everyone's surprise (particularly the M.C.'s) we got into a hot-and-heavy discussion of objective-vs.-subjective reality. In the course of one exchange, I accused Campbell of confusing logic with hardware. He replied that there *is* no logic without hardware.

I do *not* believe Campbell would have said this twenty years ago. And I offer it here, not in definition of what I mean by "engineering mind," but of what happened to Campbell's attitude —and thus to American science fiction, which, in the late forties, he dominated almost entirely.

An engineer is a man who converts scientific reasoning into functioning technology. (If the word "technology" confuses anyone if applied to the social sciences, I offer my apologies—but I know no more appropriate term. I do *not* mean machines, and *I* do not mean "hardware"—artifacts. I mean useful constructs derived from scientific concepts, but not requiring scientific training or understanding to use. Geometry is part of our technology, and so is algebra—and so is symbolic logic, and so are the "tools" of psychometrics—and the generally less tangible tools of psychoanalysis. Learning theory is part of the body of scientific knowledge and inquiry; teachers' colleges offer education courses consisting of the *technology,* the techniques, and the catalog of materiel, which apply learning theory to the teaching process. It is irrelevant whether the theory is sound or the technology is well-designed; the definitions are the same.)

The way a good engineer works is first to absorb the theory applicable to his job; then to investigate the technology already available for the purpose; determine what is useful to him, and what he needs, to design specifically for the job; try out (as much as possible on paper or in his mind—perhaps in model form) as many ideas as possible *to find out what will work best to do the job*—what offers the best combination of economy, durability, adherence to specifications, ease of operation, etc.; and then construct a pilot model embodying the most of the best of what he has learned. His objective is not learning-for-learning's sake, but the accomplishment of a particular utilitarian goal.

There is today a field called "human engineering," and when the first School of Human Engineering is opened, John W. Campbell will be entitled to the deanship; I doubt that the full extent of his influence, once or twice removed (through his own writing and that of the authors he attracted to what amounted to a "movement" in those early years of *Astounding*-and-*Unknown*), will ever be fully tabulated. Campbell did not originate the ideas; he did not stimulate the emergence of the field; he was one of its earliest and most productive engineers.

And as it happens, the first phases of an engineering job are almost indistinguishable from scientific research; the only significant difference is that side-tracks are less likely to be followed for any length. There may be something interesting at the end of one or another of the by-lanes, but as soon as it becomes apparent that what lies that way does not concern this *particular* job, it is set aside, or referred to the man who is working on that aspect.

Because Campbell thought like an engineer, because there was a specific kind of information he was after, rather than knowledge-in-general, he was able to give shape and direction to the science fiction of the forties, and it was precisely the shape and direction it most needed. Because he was a *good* engineer, he kept his mind entirely open about the nature of the answers he would find, except that he wanted things that *would work in practice*.

Problem: Human nature is such that it has changed the natural environment of humans and is continuing to do so at an accelerating pace. How to adapt human nature to its new environment?

It was when Campbell began to think he had found the answers that the "Golden Age" of *Astounding* was over. [I think, in retrospect, that Dianetics was the line of demarcation. There have been several other Answers since then, but from (at least somewhere about) that time, he has been in the second phase of the engineering job.] He stopped asking questions and examining the available equipment, and started making designs and building models. *Astounding,* quite appropriately, eventually became *Analog*; but long before that, Campbell had lost his real impact on the field. He remains the honored Senior Editor; most of the "big name" s-f writers of today started by selling, or trying to sell, to Campbell. Most of the younger writers, in America at least, grew up on *Astounding* and *Unknown,* and on the reject-overflow into Other magazines. Mrs. Williams' characterization of John Campbell as "father-figure" is, I think, exact and precise.

But there is beginning to be—there already is, in England—a body of writers at work who are conscious of no debt at all to Campbell—indeed, know him only as the didactic and "increasingly magisterial" (Mrs. Williams' phrase) figure of the past ten or fifteen years. It is these writers, on the whole, who are making the new science fiction of the sixties, and what they are doing will prove, I think, a more radical and more exciting—intellectually *and* artistically—departure than anything up till now.

What *they* "grew up on" was the specialty s-f of the fifties, and the increasing bulk of s-f writing from "outside" sources.

At the end of World War II, *Astounding* was the only monthly in the field; *Amazing, Fantastic, Weird,* and *Famous Fantastic Mysteries* were bi-monthlies; *Planet, Startling,* and *Thrilling Wonder Stories,* quarterlies—four magazines a month altogether.

Bit by bit, the paper—and author—shortage came to an end. By the summer of 1949, *Amazing* and *Fantastic* were monthly, *Startling* and *TWS* bi-monthly. There were three new titles: *Fantastic Novels* (bi-monthly), *Avon Fantasy Reader* (three issues a year), and Forrest J. Ackerman's "semi-pro" *Fantasy Book* (once or twice a year)—seven magazines a month.

Then the Boom began. It seems appropriate to date it from the first issue of *Fantasy and Science Fiction* (Fall, 1949); (as *The Magazine of Fantasy*—bi-monthly from January, 1951; monthly in August, 1952). *Galaxy* started one year later, a monthly from the beginning.

Other Worlds came November, 1949; *Imagination*, October, 1950. *If, Infinity* and *Science Fiction Stories* followed shortly. Through the first half of the decade, new titles kept appearing, old-new ones dropping out. Publishing schedules fluctuated wildly on the second-string regulars; it worked out to between eight and ten magazines a month, on the average. (There were now four s-f magazines in England.)

But the American specialty magazines were no longer an index of the health or popularity of the field. Science fiction was appearing, infrequently, but regularly, in such places as *Colliers, The Saturday Evening Post, Esquire, Bluebook, Good Housekeeping, Ellery Queen.* Above all, there were books.

Before 1948, there were six anthologies of science fiction in print, all published during the forties: Phil Strong's *Other Worlds,* Wollheim's *Pocket Book of Science Fiction* and *Viking Portable Novels of Science Fiction,* Julius Fast's paperback, *Out of This World,* the Healy-McComas *Adventures in Time and Space,* and Conklin's *The Best of Science Fiction.* In 1948-49, there were six more, including the first of the Bleiler-Dikty *Best Science*

Fiction Stories annuals. There were at least another six in 1950. 1951 was when the Book Boom began. (22 anthologies alone, if memory serves.) The same thing was happening with novels and short story collections. By 1950 or 1951, Doubleday, Simon and Schuster, Pellegrini and Cudahy, as well as most of the paperback houses, were all firmly in the science fiction business, and there were half a dozen specialty houses.

Those were the surface manifestations of a transformation inside s-f which was, within a few years, to make the genre, in the special form in which it had existed for thirty years, moribund.

II

I started reading science fiction in the early Campbell years, but my first science fiction story was published in June, 1948. I was living in New York then, working at Bantam Books; my first anthology (*Shot in the Dark,* because that's the way Bantam felt about it) came out in 1950; and I was active in the semi-official s-f professional group, The Hydra Club, all through its first hectic years from 1948 until 1952. Which is to say, I came into the center of professional activity just as the Big Boom was building up.

The qualitative changes in science fiction at that time may have been evident to people outside—the still-small, but growing, fringe audience—but those of us working in the field were dazzled at first by the sudden proliferation of markets. When we began to notice the literary improvement, we tended to attribute it to the Boom: more markets with more money, demanding better work, more room for a range of editorial taste and personality. And all this, of course, was true—once it got started. As to what started it . . .

The Bomb did not produce the Boom. If anything, the anti-egghead reaction damaged the field—although there was a powerful indirect stimulus in the flood of "Preaching story," atom-doom writing, during the militant days of the atomic scientists' *Bulletin,* the United World Federalists and Garry Davis' World Citizen movement. Everyone got into that act—Philip Wylie, Leo Szilard, Pat Frank, an unknown writer named Judith Merril; but most of it was not labeled "science fiction" and did little to interest new readers in other kinds of s-f. What it did do was bring new writers into the field and break the ice with some book publishers and a few editors of national magazines.

The most important secondary effect of the Bomb was not felt until the height of the McCarthy era, when science fiction became, for a time, virtually the only vehicle of political dissent; but that was later, when the Boom was well under way.

More significant in 1947-1948 was the beginning of serious, official interest in space flight and satellites. We were trained sign-readers, remember; we knew the government was getting interested when (1) the Hayden Planetarium started its space symposium series, (2) *Colliers* worked the material into a glossy spread filling half the magazine, (3) *Destination Moon* was produced as a major film, (4) Viking brought out the first beautiful Bonestell-Ley volume, *The Conquest of Space,* and Wernher von Braun's name kept popping up in the papers. (That was 1948; I think the IGY satellite projects were actually announced in 1950 or 1951.)

- - -

A prophet can be honored in his own land; it all depends on the kind of news he brings. As prophet-in-chief of the Atom Age, John Campbell got nothing but trouble; whatever good the Bomb did for s-f occurred in books and national magazines. As prophet-in-chief of the Space Age, Campbell came into his own in the outside world. *Astounding* prospered, Campbell's own work went into books, and instead of (or in addition to) stealing his best authors, the big magazines interviewed and consulted him. (All this may have had something to do with his phase-change, too; it is difficult to be an open-minded expert.)

What part of *Astounding,* and later *Analog,* was not devoted to the successive Campbell Enthusiasms (Dianetics, Psionics, et al.), or the exposition of his hypotheses on education, religion, social organization, etc., remained (and remains) open to one highly developed type of speculative story, the so-called "new map" extrapolation, primarily as it relates to space flight and the technology associated with it.

"New map" stories are those that offer a detailed, sometimes highly technical, often very knowledgeable, explication of some as-yet unfilled-in area in a territory recently explored by the "concept" and "research" people, but open now to settlement and building-up by the "engineering" and "applications" men. It was to this kind of science fiction more than any other that the new readers of the Boom turned. Space was the trigger that turned them, but a thousand other frontiers of the Post War World held them.

All these factors, at least, and probably others I have overlooked, acted both on each other and on the reading public to produce the Boom phenomenon, and to improve the quality of the stories as the market spread. But the qualitative transformation had actually started before the Boom and had its roots essentially in the same ground that produced the infant space industry.

One of the more intriguing and less resolvable philosophic puzzles concerns the role a prophecy may play in its own fulfillment. There is no doubt that the prophets of modern science fiction acted directly on the chain of events simply by voicing their predictions. They were a significant conditioning factor on the acceptance threshold of society in general and of the scientific/technical segment in particular. How much of the work in the engineering phases of space flight and atomics, for instance, has developed along the lines of prevailing s-f views because that work is a logical development? How much because the work is being done by engineers and technicians who devoured *Astounding* and *Amazing* with their breakfast Wheaties, twenty, thirty, forty years ago, and knew roughly how it would all work before they got their first slide rules? Or how many of them started reading science fiction because of a previous technical orientation—and how many were oriented toward science-and-engineering by science fiction? One can only speculate.

Viewed historically, I believe that American science fiction functioned between the mid-twenties and 1950 as an *Encyclopedie* of the Space Age. The early "scientifictionists" were markedly evangelical: in 1925 they already knew that space flight, atomic power, servo-mechanisms, efficient world-wide video-audio communication, hydroponic farming and chemical synthesis of needed materials, *could* and *would* be achieved. The basic theories already existed; the engineering potential was already available. Only two things were lacking: financial incentive and public acceptance. By the time the (not precisely financial) incentive for crash programs on rocketry and atomics materialized during World War II, science fiction had already made the *idea* of such possibilities public property; and a thousand-and-one specific ideas for development had been tried out on paper and in fan-talk bull sessions.

At the end of World War II, there were few people outside the ranks of science fiction fans and rocket experts who "believed in" space flight—or so they said. Yet there had already been enough belief in 1938 to panic the State of New Jersey when Orson Welles did his famous *War of the Worlds* broadcast. (Nobody "believed" *Buck Rogers* or *Flash Gordon* or *Superman* either; but everybody *read* them.) In 1950, a small percentage of *Colliers'* readers had joined the ranks of Believers; the overwhelming majority still regarded the whole business, overtly, as anything from "crazy comic strip stuff" to "neurotic escapism" and "phallic symbolism." But the soil had been spaded, and the seeds were already swollen; it took less than two years of an official information campaign to convince the world that *Sputnik* was neither a hoax nor an obvious impossibility.

There is a rich field for future literary-sociological scholars in the chicken-egg argument implicit here, but it is certain that the publicity given to atomic power, space flight, and servo-mechanisms by science fiction, before the fact, was fully reciprocated by the publicity the developing facts gave science fiction in the late forties and fifties. (Often enough, the same people were involved as working scientists, popular science writers, and/or science fictionists: Willy Ley, Arthur Clarke, Isaac Asimov, John Pierce, Norbert Wiener, Harry Stine. . . .) Or, egg-chicken-wise, the boost these developments gave to the Boom of the fifties was a feedback from the preceding twenty years of "scientifiction" and its successors.

That much we understood, at least vaguely, even at the time. The other feedback circuits operating inside publishing were less obvious.

First of all, those five great years of *Astounding* (and *Unknown*) had attracted not only new writers, but new readers—and continued to attract them, even after Campbell's own focus had shifted. Those were the same stories, that (*before* the Boom) filled the first two big anthologies, *Adventures in Time and Space* and *The Best of Science Fiction,* and made a whole new audience of book-buyers aware of s-f as something other than a successor to Tom Swift and Edgar Rice Burroughs.

When Campbell's personal interest and editorial influence moved from the exploratory to the analog-building phase, the magazine did not suffer. (By that time there were a lot more technicians than there had been ten years earlier; Oak Ridge was one of *Astounding*'s hottest sales areas.) But the "fringe" readers did suffer. Campbell had, in effect, created an audience for new speculative idea fiction, which his own magazine was no longer supplying. The Healy-McComas and Conklin anthologies renewed those readers' interest, while swelling their ranks.

At this point, the Campbell feedback circuit joined another one, in book publishing. Science fiction book publishing in the U. S. all but disappeared in the thirties. We had *It Can't Happen Here* and Stephen Vincent Benet, plus some superlative peripheral work—William Sloane's memorable speculative-fantasy novels; Thorne Smith; some of Don Marquis; Philip Wylie's bits-and-pieces scattered through other books; Stewart's *Fire* and *Storm.* In the early forties there was Fearing's *Clark Gifford's Body,* and McHugh's *I Am Thinking of My Darling.*

In England, however, it was different. *Brave New World, The Shape of Things to Come,* John Collier's *Green Thoughts,* Olaf Stapledon's *Last and First Men* and *Last Men in London* had all appeared between 1931-1934; the next year, there were *Odd John* and *The Star Maker,* Susan Ertz's *Woman Alive,* and E. C. Large's *Sugar in the Air.* In the forties (with Huxley, Collier, and Stapledon still going strong) came J. B. Priestley, C. S. Lewis and Gerald Kersh, as well as the books edging curiously in-and-out of the boundaries of science fiction by such writers as Nevil Shute, H. F. Heard, Nigel Balchin, Dennis Wheatley, David Garnett, Alfred Noyes, R. C. Sherriff, Rex Warner, Graham Greene, and a whole crew usually associated with the detective story—Agatha Christie, Dorothy Sayers, John Dickson Carr, Philip MacDonald, Marjorie Allingham, Leslie Charteris, Eric Linklater, etc. Then came Orwell.

Of course we had had some of the British stuff here all along —Huxley, Priestley, later Collier. (British books, then as now, were available here if you knew what to look for; I am talking about what was actually *written* and/or *published* here.) Between these and the comics and radio and the specialty field, science fiction was a recognized and accepted part of American culture in the mid-forties: it just wasn't a respectable part—not something a serious American writer would do, whether it was art or money he was serious about.

With the end of the war, and the run of atom-doom stories from Big-Name mainstream writers and scientists, the strands began to combine and the (not-yet-quite-Boom) book break-through began here: the two big anthologies, *Mr. Adam, The Big Eye, The Big Ball of Wax,* and Ward Moore's exciting *Greener Than You Think.* America discovered Kafka and Graham Greene. *Charm* and *Mademoiselle* discovered Kuttner and Bradbury. *Colliers* published Wylie's "Blunder" in 1946, and Will Jenkins' "Symbiosis" in 1947—the same year the *Post* adopted Heinlein, and introduced Gerald Kersh to American readers.

And then came Orwell.

1984 was ponderous. It was obvious. It was somewhat less than original. But it had some good catchy phrases, and it was eminently respectable, both literarily and politically. (Even Joe McCarthy had to approve—a wonderful joke with no one to laugh at it, because American readers were no more aware than Big Joe himself that the author of this great anti-Communist document was himself a leading British Socialist.) Above all, it was a best-seller.

When the *New Yorker* published a Roald Dahl science fiction story in 1949, and E. B. White himself wrote one the next year (while Paul Gallico tried his hand at it in the *Post*), the break-through was complete.

The new crop of American science fiction writers—the people who began in *Astounding* between 1946-48, and the new names everywhere in 1949-50—no longer had to think of themselves as literary Untouchables—or even resign themselves to a choice of poverty or part-time, insofar as s-f was concerned. Nobody—except perhaps Orwell, Huxley, and Wylie—was making money on the stuff yet; but it was already possible to write with one eye on the slicks and the other on book publication, knowing the special-ty magazines were there to catch everything that missed.

Once again, the right man came along at the right time. Until Boucher and McComas started *Fantasy and Science Fiction,* in

1949, the Campbell-dominated specialty field had no place in it for the kind of stories Beaumont, Budrys, Clingerman, Cogswell, Dick, Henderson, Matheson, Miller, MacDonald, Moore, Nourse, Pangborn, Tenn, Vance, Vonnegut, and a score of others began to produce—as did Asimov, Bester, Leiber, Wyndham, and others, many of whom had virtually stopped writing until the necessary new magazine came along.

- - -

Anthony Boucher's role in the emergence of American science fiction from its self-made ghetto has never, I think, been fully appreciated—except among the authors writing for him at the time.

Boucher was neither scientist, worldsaver, or prophet. He was a man of enormous erudition, catholic interests, discriminating tastes, overweening curiosity, and rich humour—a humanist in the best and widest sense, one of the most civilized human beings it has ever been my pleasure to know. He brought literary standards and literary status, both, into the specialty field. Already well established as author and critic in the then far more respectable neighboring field of mystery and detection, he was able to attract a large segment of new readers, including a fair sprinkling of intrigued writers, publishers, influential critics, and educators. He approached his editorship with a revolutionary concept: the idea that science-fantasy (as he preferred to call the whole field of rational-imaginative-speculative fiction) *could be well-written.*

Boucher carried this to an unheard-of extreme. He would not buy a story just for the idea; he had to like the writing. And unlike most earlier editors, he was not style-deaf.

Neither was Horace Gold, the first editor of *Galaxy,* which began publication the following year (1950), but he was more deeply rooted in the traditions of the field. (Both men, by the way, first entered the field through Campbell's *Unknown.* And here is another curious bypath for those scholars-to-come: the re-emergence of the author-editor in s-f, at a time when the phenomenon had virtually disappeared from publishing.) Gold would not buy for idea *alone,* but he would settle for just-competent writing when the idea appealed enough (or do some heavy rewriting himself—one of the factors that eventually lost a number of *Galaxy* names to *F&SF*). What appealed to Gold was important, because it provided a counterweight to Campbell's restrictions. *Galaxy* wanted psychiatric stories and social satires: no one could have written "Baby is Three" (the core of *More Than Human*), for instance, or *The Demolished Man,* or *The Space Merchants,* for *Astounding.*

Galaxy was an immediate favorite among science fiction fans. It had Sturgeon, Heinlein, Leiber, and Bester almost exclusively for several years, and among the newer writers, Tenn, Pangborn, Kornbluth and Pohl. But what at first seemed marvelous freedom turned out to be as limiting (from the opposite end) as writing for Campbell. More and more, writers with fresh ideas and serious intentions turned to *F&SF*: there was one unbelievable period when Boucher, paying exactly half the word-rate of either of the other Big Three, was getting first submissions from a sizeable majority of the top names in the field.

Possibly the most significant thing about Boucher (equivalent to the importance of the word "engineer" applied to Campbell) was his respect for the manifold meanings of "literature": the history and traditions, the exercise of the craft, the working body of authors. His literary requirements were as powerful an attraction to writers as his sensitive critiques. (It was a not-quite-joke among writers that Boucher's letters of rejection could be more encouraging than another editor's checks.) And the writers, new and old, s-f specialists and names from all over, responded. (Most startling were people like Mack Reynolds, Philip Jose Farmer, Chad Oliver, Mark Clifton—idea-men, "Teacher-story" writers, who could not be bothered, elsewhere, with more than putting their thoughts down in competent language; when they published in *F&SF* it turned out they could *write,* too.)

Boucher's function as book reviewer was no less important than as editor. He had, at least part of the time, brilliant competition. For many fans, Damon Knight was the preferred critic; for others, William Atheling. But for the writers, it was Boucher's accolade that counted, and for thousands of new readers of s-f books, it was Boucher's guidance they trusted.

I said earlier that science fiction today is catching up with science; Anthony Boucher was the dominant force in the fifties when science fiction began to catch up with fiction.

Then, as had been true with Campbell, Boucher's special qualification became his limiting factor. He was the first editor in the field—perhaps the only one in this country who understood the specialty field as a phenomenon in the history of literature. Even in the first few years of *F&SF*, at the height of the magazine boom (there were more than thirty magazine titles in 1952) with his own publication the ackowledged prestige leader, Boucher had few illusions about the viability of the specialty field, or of the magazines in particular. His views on "The Publishing of Science Fiction" are on record, along with those of John W. Campbell and several other distinguished persons, in a symposium, *Modern Science Fiction*, edited by Reginald Bretnor (Coward-McCann, 1953).

Boucher anticipated a dropping-off of magazine popularity in favor of books, and a gradual re-union of the side-stream with the main-stream of literature. He saw the relationship of the category to the large body of fiction as an almost exact parallel with another category, detective fiction, whose development and specialized audience were in many ways similar. His blind spot was in his failure to recognize the essential element of opposition in the two fields.

As humanist and true aficionado of literature, Boucher was also something of a classicist; the forms and styles of fiction delighted him for their own sake. His emphasis was as much on sci-ence-*fiction,* as Campbell's was on *science-*(technology)-fiction. (By my way of thinking, Boucher had more comprehension of science, in the modern sense, than Campbell did—but it was less important to him. On the form/content seesaw, he counterbalanced Gold: Boucher would always settle for just-adequate thinking if the writing was good enough.) From the beginning *F&SF* suffered somewhat from a tendency to select for the elegant and stylistic (and occasionally precious) rather than the vigorous.

This emphasis was desperately needed in 1950. It was what made Boucher the right man at the right time. And it is what makes his influence, fifteen years later, almost as restrictive in its way as Campbell's. Boucher or Boucher-as-was, is probably still the dominating influence on the specialty field here. What might have happened had he stayed with the magazine is hard to tell: I rather doubt that Boucher (1966) would be exerting the same subtly retarding force that the still-honored image of Boucher (1956) does today. But—with all due respect to some excellent editors since then (notably Robert P. Mills, Cele Goldsmith Lalli, Fred Pohl, and increasingly now, Ed Ferman)—there has been no sustained influence of equal intensity in this country since Anthony Boucher retired, and his editorial ghost is by now not an unrestricted asset.

- - -

The Boom, as such, broke in 1955. Book titles dropped off, but not all the way, and not for long. The marginal magazines folded, one after another—and stayed folded. Yet the list of stories appearing in general periodicals grew steadily year by year.

Today American science fiction supports only seven titles, two of which are reprint magazines and two bi-monthlies—thus, only four new-material magazines a month. But there is hardly a publication in which fiction appears at any time in any form— newspapers, trade journals, house organs, men's magazines, women's magazines, literary reviews, everything—in which s-f does not sometimes appear. And the big market is still in books. The specialty magazines no longer dominate, or even represent, the genre.

All of this is much as Boucher, and Bretnor, foresaw it fifteen years ago. What they did not foresee was the back-water swirl of conservatism that would engulf the field in America in the first years of respectability, burying most of what was original or truly speculative in a flood of polished mediocrity and formularized paperback pap. They saw the specialty field remaining as a nucleus, and a breeding-ground for new writers (which it is), but not as the sad manifestation of a mystique-turned-cult; symptomatic are the interminable "series" stories, featuring the patterned exploits of a Beloved Character, and the long articles treating minor, and already unreadable, authors of twenty or thirty years ago as "master" writers of "classic" stories.

Nor could anyone have anticipated, fifteen years ago, the emergence of a British specialty field as a major force, not only in s-f, but increasingly in contemporary British writing and publishing. (The tiny market in the U. K. supports two magazines a month, plus a modest distribution of the American magazines, and a paperback market as flourishing as our own.)

Reginald Bretnor came closer than anyone else. His own essay in *Modern Science Fiction,* "The Future of Science Fiction," still ranks as the outstanding critical insight into the nature and direction of the genre. It falls short, even today, only in its failure to specify the influence of certain forces outside the field. Bretnor saw, and described, the *shape* of the influences; he simply failed to identify the names and faces.

- - -

As it happens, Bretnor and Boucher are fairly-near neighbors in Berkeley, California; professionally and personally, they are congenial, with much in common in tastes and attitudes. Their expressed views in 1952 varied little in surface applicability, but radically in underlying philosophy.

Boucher was discussing the place in literature of an area of fiction whose special province is science; Bretnor was thinking about a fiction form emerging from the interaction between science and literature, and possibly embodying some synthesis of the two. "The emergence of science fiction as a genre," he stated as his first premise, "is rooted in our failure to understand the scientific method and to define it adequately for the average individual and the average scientist." And, second, "Science fiction is not a genre. Its scope is universal. It holds the promise of an entire new literature."

Some of his predictions:

(1) To say that science fiction holds within itself the seed of an entire new literature does not mean that science fiction as we know it, *is* that literature. Nor does it mean that we can now foretell the exact forms that literature will take when it evolves from science fiction *and* non-science fiction. . . .
(2) . . . The impossibility of stretching the "old maps" to fit the new terrain, or of preserving them by trying to exclude it, will become constantly more obvious. The unperceptive reader will react to this as he is reacting now, but even more intensely; he will demand and get, on levels appropriate to his own complexity, stronger and stronger "emotional shock" values in his non-science fiction . . . .

(3) All fiction derives from the experience of reality. All fiction creates imaginary times, imaginary worlds, to be experienced only through acts of "the imagination." And the subjective reality of fiction depends, not on the spacio-temporal coordinates assigned to it, but on the author's direct or indirect experience of reality, on his frames of reference for the interpretation of reality, on his ability to abstract and synthesize fictional experiences, and on his selection of symbolic media capable of evoking these experiences completely for his readers.

(4) Therefore, the "serious" writer of non-science fiction . . . will find that the expansion of his frames of reference will neither force him to write about the future nor forbid him to write about "the present" and the past. If he determines to write science fiction as we know it now, he will learn that a hypothetical future is merely an interesting and plausible device particularly well suited to the presentation of those human problems and experiences promised by the nature of the scientific method and by its continued exercise. He will see that it is possible to write science fiction set in "the present" or the past—possible, and sometimes necessary, and usually just a bit more difficult.

(5) Eventually, we will again have an integrated literature. It will owe much, artistically, to non-science fiction. But its dominant attitudes and purposes . . . will have evolved from those of modern science fiction. . . .

It is the evolution of that literature that I am discussing here. It has not yet achieved a distinctive form; it is, possibly, just now experiencing the inception of its first "Movement"—but up till now it has had not even that much cohesiveness. Yet I presume to believe that I can see its directions, and recognize some of its early practitioners, and identify some of its immediate antecedents.

Only to the extent that I am able to do so, does this essay become more than an annotation of Bretnor's earlier one. His thinking influenced me so strongly that I frankly did not realize, until I went back to the book for the references here, how closely I had paralleled his structure and reasoning, considering the state of science and the state of fiction as prerequisites to an appraisal of the state of science fiction. Our conclusions are very much the same; the difference up to this point has been only in the perspective of fifteen years, which has allowed me to fill in detail, and verify predictions.

In what follows, I am dealing with events-in-process, events moreover in which I myself am involved. I have not attempted to analyze the literature of the Boucher period as I did that of the preceding decade; I do not have sufficient perspective as yet to do anything but describe the overall mood and direction—or alternatively, itemize memorable individual stories, of which there were a great many during the fifties. In approaching the events of the sixties, I cannot begin to be comprehensive, and shall not attempt it.

Since Walter Miller redefined the term in 1959 with *A Canticle for Leibowitz* (which may be thought of as the climax of the "Boucher Period") the number and diversity of *good s-f novels* is such as to require a complete essay in itself. There is no brief characterizing discussion possible of a collection of books which includes, for example, *The Child Buyer, Nova Express, Stranger in a Strange Land, Flowers for Algernon, The Crystal World, A Clockwork Orange, Dorsai!, Journey Beyond Tomorrow, Cat's Cradle, The Wanderer, The Genocides,* etc.

One becomes involved not only in questions of style, approach, and treatment, but subject matter. The line of definition between "science" and "non-science" is difficult to find when stories and newspapers both are full of talk of the chemical treatment of emotional disorders, and psychiatric cures for somatic malfunctions; "subjective time"; "computer art" (and music, and poetry); the Theory of Games (with its statistical predictions of human behavior); "brainwashing" (a precise technological/psychiatric operation, involving chemical, electronic, semantic, and physiological components); or even the existence of the "Think Tanks" as a growing facet of industry and government. ("R&D man" rolls off the tongue disturbingly like "R&A Director" or "R&B band.")

But in all this I believe I can see a direction—not of "science fiction," but of the "new literature" emergent from it. And again, because it is new, and still formative, it would take as much space to discuss, in any useful manner, the still very small body of work involved as to cover all the rest of the field since 1960. I am not going to attempt to define, explain, explicate, or justify any of the work I mention in this section. As with my first listing of the antecedents of "science fiction," I am only pointing to a location. In the first case, it was an area determined by much past discussion and definition-seeking. Here it is an area existing more in my own intuition, perhaps, than anywhere else.

Bretnor specified three "attitudes" of science fiction as significant in the role he predicted for it: "(1) it is not self-restrictive; nor is it restrictive of its readers; (2) it is not a literature of false dichotomies, conventionalized; (3) it is integrative." (The meaning of these attitudes is implicit in the following paragraphs.)

> In writing, as in the other arts, there have been a number of responses to the problem posed by the new complexity of knowledge and the breakdown of the older synthesis. Characteristic of almost all of these, especially in this century, is a peculiar process which can quite accurately be called the intellectual renunciation of 'the intellect.' Actually, this rebellion against 'reason' is a revolt against the scientific method, reason's cold instrument in the old scheme of things. It is a revolt prompted by the failure to understand, and by a fear of the un-understandable. It has varied in degree; it has been more or less conscious, more or less deliberate. It has included such seemingly diverse phenomena as the complete Dadaist denial, the Existentialist dramatization of fashionable despair, and a highly verbalized insistence on restrictive neo-Aristotelian frames of literary reference which themselves are a retreat from the Aristotelian balance of the Renaissance. The trend, in our most 'serious' fiction, has been increasingly toward a focus of all emphasis on 'the emotions,' on 'feeling' rather than on 'thought'—as though the two were mutually antagonistic and mutually exclusive.

And later:

> To science fiction, man is the proper study of the writer—man, and everything man does and thinks and dreams, and everything man builds, and everything of which he may become aware —his theories and his things, his quest into the universe, his search into himself, his music and his mathematics and his machines. All these have human value and validity, for they are of man.

Let me rephrase the opening of that last paragraph slightly: "Man is the *proper* study of any artist—man and" . . . etc. Call it the Bretnor-Merril Uncertainty Principle: you cannot define or describe a man except in terms of the universe of which he is aware; you cannot define or describe the universe except in terms of man's orientation within it.

This is what I meant when I said at the beginning, "Art at any time can achieve validity only if it is rooted in the accumulated human experience of its day, and touches somewhere on the nerve center of the culture from which it springs." It is still possible today to read Greek drama and Elizabethan poetry with delight; it is *not* possible for a modern writer to create Greek drama or Elizabethan poetry—only to imitate them. I refer not only to the mutability of language and form, but to a complete cultural complex. In our culture, within the last quarter century, purely technological accomplishments have radically altered (though not *quite* erased) the meaning of a phrase like "American literature." The young American writer today is likely to owe as much to Kafka or Kierkegaard as to Whitman and Emerson. In the same way, our culture today—not "American" or "Indonesian" or "Eskimo," but our increasingly global culture—is inescapably involved with the implications of modern scientific thought: if not with its philosophy, then at the very least, with its artifacts and their influence on human existence. In the arts, as in the sciences, the conflict between the response to the new challenges, and the reaction against them, is still raging; and within the growing ranks of those who have begun to accept the new concepts there is further inevitable experimental dissension.

An explosive experimental dissidence was in progress when Boucher and Bretnor were writing their respective essays in 1952. Between Berkeley and North Beach, the distance is short and the traffic is heavy; but between pre-*Sputnik* science fiction and the pre-Burroughs Beats, there were no bridges of any sort to span a distance no one on either side thought worth measuring.

I claim no prescience here; I didn't take the San Francisco scene seriously enough to do more than glance at a few pages. But I must add I had done little more with the big guns of the twentieth century literary revolution. The fact is, I did not know that Jack Kerouac or Henry Miller, *or* James Joyce represented anything more revolutionary than the Great Obscenity Rebellion—on which ground I distantly approved of them. (Remember, I was the Noble Savage at large in the world of Literature—nor am I sure how much I have changed since.) The only real difference I saw between (what I have since learned to call) the *avant garde* and the Establishment was what appeared to be a greater facility with language and more attention to form in the latter group; but my indifference to Faulkner and Eliot was almost as massive. I simply was not *disenchanted*. Dis-involvement, "alienation," the "search for identity"—the whole "cool" scene—were, and are, so foreign to my outlook (and my concern with writing, in particular) that I rejected all of it, even in its most elegant forms.

I do not mean to present my own benighted state as representative of science fiction. Bretnor, Boucher, Knight, Blish, and a good many other critical observers were able to make educated distinctions between the varieties of literary experimentalists (they certainly did not, like me, confuse the *New Yorker* with *New Directions*). Obviously, Bretnor neither ignored what was happening across the Bay, nor dismissed it as cursorily as I.

But dismiss it he did—we did—validly, I think, insofar as it related to "science fiction." Or any fiction.

- - -

The one thing I did know by then was fiction. I had been reading it for twenty-five years, and writing it for seven, and by that time I knew what made it work, and what worked *in* it—and even a little about writing (as distinct from selling) it. I think I speak for an overwhelming majority of the other writers I knew when I add that fiction was the only prose form that mattered; you might do other things for the exercise, or for the money. You might write an exquisite prose style, or create unforgettable characters; but if you couldn't tell a story, you were simply out of it.

And the stuff they were doing on the bongo beaches—or on the Left Bank—just wasn't in it for fiction—wasn't and *isn't*. No matter whose rules you're playing, projection, not involution, is what stories are made of. Fiction is not poetry slowed down; it is drama spread out. Some narrative poems are also fiction, and some great fiction is also, in large part, poetry. In the hands of a good writer, a drama too subtle or complex to make a good stage-play may be a great story; humor particularly (aside from slapstick) lends itself more readily to the flat-page technique than to the stage, where there is no technique equivalent to prose narrative for distortion of perspective. But stage or page, comic strip or Greek chorus, the only thing you cannot dispense with in story telling is externalized dramatic action. It can be realistic, symbolized, dreamlike, anticipatory, remembered; it may be witnessed, experienced, heard-of, imagined. It may illustrate any theme, convey any mood, dramatize any insight, act out any idea. It may have two characters or three or four or, rarely, more. (Almost always, when you get past three, they fall into alignments and groups, becoming for purposes of the *story*, two or three composite figures.) But it cannot have *one*.

There are stories with only one person on stage, and a few with only one person evident; but when that happens, some part of the environment acquires an animistic character. (Back in the wings a Manichean devil chuckles wickedly at the protagonist's efforts to overcome malicious—or malignantly indifferent—nature.)

There is no protagonist without an antagonist; in a story the confrontation between the two is acted out. Given these two basics, you may be as subtle or interior or stalemating as you please; you may not have a *popular* story, but you will still have a story. With less than those two essentials, it may be poetry, it may be essay, it may be monologue: it is not drama, and not fiction.

Psychiatric introspection makes fiction only when it involves remembered drama, symbolized drama, or delusional drama; a recital of symptoms, like a travelogue, may be frightening, fascinating, even beautiful, but it is not a *story*. Equally, the Battle between Good and Evil—or Life and Death—or Man and Woman—becomes drama instead of treatise only when the principles become principals, capable of *acting out* the conflict.

Obsessive introspection and agonizing reappraisals of morality seemed to be the whole range of subject matter for the serious non-science-fiction writers, and they did not seem to know how to turn this stuff into *story*.

The Beats of course were not trying to write fiction. I don't believe it ever occurred to me, in 1952, that they might be trying *not* to write fiction. (If the idea crossed my mind, it would have been as an example of absurd perversity.)

As for the "literary" types, the Quarterly and Review writers, the backbone of *Atlantic* and *Harper's* and *New Yorker,* they were trying, all right, and mostly doing a poor job of it. Their diction was graceful and their insights often profound, but they (literally) did not seem to know which way was up—by which I mean, they wrote in limbo, not on Earth, nor elsewhere in any real or sharply imagined universe. In this, it seemed to me, they could claim no distinction from the slick women's magazine writers or comic strip continuity writers.

The Beats seemed to me a crude, sometimes grotesque, malformed variety of the Establishment Litterateurs. I have no doubt at all that that is exactly how science fiction looked when viewed from North Beach. Oppositely oriented, there was not sufficient interest in either rebel camp to discover how similar our views of the middle really were. To the literary-artistic *avant garde,* science fiction's struggle for literary respectability, for acceptance by the very Establishment they had contemptuously abandoned, gave us a clownish aspect; their attempt at total rejection of modern technological society made our determined involvement with its dynamics look like a crude, sometimes grotesque, malformed variety of 19th century "materialism." They were too involved with the dynamics of meaning and expression, and the search for new modes of language and literature appropriate to the ambivalences and relativistic realities of modern life, to concern themselves with unorthodox experiments in interpretation of these realities, or with any philosophy more complex than existentialism. Our rockets and planets and alien creatures, unconnected with their immediate realities, appeared as absurd caricature-symbols of (not just "neurotic" but) childish "escapism." To us, their howls and bongo rhythms and cut-up-fold-ins were, just as obviously, the rococo entertainments of sterile decadence. We were much too intent on communicating our intellectual insights to have time or patience for experiments in unorthodox form.

Bretnor's view of "science" and "non-science" fiction suffered from the same limitation afflicting most "mainstream" critiques of s-f; it contrasted the *best* science fiction with the *bulk* of the rest. When he attacked the "anti-intellectualism" of "non-science" fiction, he was penetrating and accurate; but when he claimed an "integrative, non-restrictive" nature for s-f, he was talking about what he knew it could and should be—not what, for the most part, it was, or is.

There were people, in 1952, who understood emotionally/intellectually that both intellectual/emotional components of man were indivisibly meaningful: that new ideas required new forms, that new modes of experience demanded new techniques of expression: but most of them were mathematicians, cyberneticists, and air- or space-craft designers. A very few (like Bretnor) had begun to comprehend that the same principle applied to literature, and fewer yet (I know of three) had attempted the application.

Although I did not think of it that way at the time, retrospectively, I believe I would identify Cordwainer Smith's first science fiction story, "Scanners Live in Vain" (*Fantasy Book*, 1950), as the first effective—and possibly deliberate "integrative" effort I read. The impact of the story was tremendous, and baffling. Both Fred Pohl and I recommended it promptly to Robert Heinlein for the anthology (*Tomorrow the Stars*) he was then preparing for Doubleday. But I could not understand my own response. The piece was so "clumsily" written: the prose, the structure, the characterization—everything was subtly *wrong*. In the arguments that followed its publication, I was one of those who contended (wrongly) that "Cordwainer Smith" was not a pen-name, because the story was so "amateurish."

"Scanners" was neither the first such effort, nor the best early one: just the first *I* saw. It is a reasonable inference, since "Smith" is an accomplished linguist, and—according to his "momentary prologue" in *Space Lords* (Pyramid, 1965)—particularly fond of the French Symbolists, that when he turned to science fiction writing he was already familiar with the work of Alfred Jarry; it is almost as probable that he also knew some of Jorge Luis Borges's work.

(Boucher knew of Borges; he did the first English translation of Borges's fiction for *Ellery Queen's Mystery Magazine* in 1948; "The Circular Ruins" appeared in *New Directions,* and there were at least three others in the next five years. But Boucher used none of them, and—incredibly—overlooked, or decided against, translating "Tlön, Uqbar, Orbis Tertius" for *F&SF*.)

For most of us, however, Borges and Jarry might as well never have existed until after 1962, when Grove issued *Ficciones, New Directions* published *Labyrinths,* and *Evergreen Review* had its all-Jarry "Pataphysics" issue; at that, it took two or three years of word-of-mouth for more than the handful of two-camp people who then existed to become aware of what had been written in Paris in 1900 and in Argentina in 1940.

To all intents and purposes, it was 1962 before American readers heard of Anthony Burgess, either—or of J. G. Ballard.

Only one Ballard story appeared here before then, and I am happy to say it was his first published story, "Prima Belladonna" (from the British magazine, *Science Fantasy*), reprinted in my Second Annual SF in 1957.

1957 was also the year that David R. Bunch's strange grim short stories began to appear; he was the first writer, as far as I know, to grow up with a foot in both camps. From the beginning he was published simultaneously in the "little magazines" and in *Amazing* and *Fantastic*. Post-Beat rather than Symbolist, Bunch had none of the bright-fairy-tale appeal of "Smith" (who had done nothing after "Scanners" till 1955, when "The Game of Rat and Dragon" appeared in *Galaxy*; he got into full swing only in 1958-59). Bunch is still a highly controversial figure in American s-f—and I think almost unknown in England.

R. M. McKenna's "Casey Agonistes" came out in 1958. Again, the impact was explosive; but this time we were a little more ready, a little more knowledgeable—and McKenna was available for comment. He knew exactly what he was doing, and was able to convey a great deal of it to other writers.

A diffused cumulative influence began to be visible in 1958-59 with tentative approaches to the new direction like Carol Emshwiller's "Pelt," Knight's "The Handler," Leiber's "Mariana," Sturgeon's "The Man Who Lost the Sea." The next year, Vance Aeandahl emerged suddenly from nowhere (and apparently returned there, after three years of ill-received exciting new work). That same year Brian Aldiss' "Shards" and "Old Hundredth" appeared here. In 1961, it was R. A. Lafferty, with a bright humorous streak that made his approach more acceptable to the magazine audience.

And we are back at 1962, when Thomas Disch and Roger Zelazny began publishing strange provocative stories in *Amazing* and *Fantastic*.

There have been others since—Norman Kagan and Sonya Dorman, most recently—but most of what has happened has not been in the American science fiction magazines at all.

I do not know exactly when William Burroughs' influence began to make itself felt among the Post-Beat writers here—or whether there were other influences inside the group preceding him. But by 1962, the San Francisco little magazines were experi-

menting—wildly, sometimes satirically, not often successfully—
with their own "integrations," a good deal more consciously and
enthusiastically than "science fiction" as a whole. Out of that
group and/or affected by its widespread influence, began to come
a steady trickle of stories, appearing most frequently in the better
men's magazines (*Cavalier*, *Escapade*, sometimes *Playboy*, the late
lamented *Nugget*), and in *Mademoiselle*, and *The New Yorker*.

And of course, there have been others: a scattered handful of
names approaching the same area from the Establishment end, or
simply developing independently in the obviously appropriate
direction for our times: George P. Elliott, John Anthony West,
Donald Barthelme, John Updike, and most notably Kurt Vonnegut. But the main stream of the new integration has not been in
this country at all.

- - -

The shortest route across the Golden Gate turned out to be
by way of England. That it should have developed mainly in E. J.
Carnell's magazines is appropriately absurd for modern writing.
That I should have been a box-seat observer was pure happen-
stance.

At least six different s-f magazines were started in England
and Scotland between 1949 and 1955; the two that survived were
New Worlds and *Science Fantasy* (now *Impulse*), both founded
and edited (until 1964) by Carnell.

Carnell was a latter-day Gernsback—but it was not only
another time, but another country—and besides, Technocracy was
dead.   Carnell had the same energetic optimism about science
fiction, the same persistent evangelical streak, something of the
same sort of curiously innocent capacity for astonishment by the
world's wonders as Gernsback did—and the same head for business,
as well as a remarkably similar indifference to, or unawareness of,
literary technique.

Also he had a vanishingly small budget, and one of the things
he did about it was to turn agent on the side. From the time he
heard about my Annuals, Carnell was sending me stories—anything
he thought I might *possibly* like; shortly afterwards, he began sending me the magazines regularly.

Once again, I must avoid attempting an inadequate history or appraisal of the development of what is now a conscious, if somewhat elliptical infant "movement," centered around *New Worlds*, under the editorship of Michael Moorcock, *and* around a point in space in British poetry determined by the relative positions of Peter Redgrove, George MacBeth, D. M. Thomas, Bill Butler, *Ambit* magazine, a bookshop called Better Books, and I-don't-know-how-many other factors. (I hope to accomplish a more knowledgeable survey when I complete an anthology of the British "new wave" now in preparation for Doubleday.) But there is no doubt that the outstanding figure in this movement is J. G. Ballard, both in terms of his own work, and of the influence he wields.

I have discussed Ballard's work at considerable length in a review of his two most recent books (*The Crystal World*, 1966; *The Impossible Man and Other Stories*, 1966) in the August, 1966, issue of *Fantasy and Science Fiction*. Some of what I had to say there, while primarily applicable to Ballard, could be generalized to serve as a description of the nature of the "new literature" I see emerging:

> Because he has borrowed so much from the surrealists, and works for direct conveyance of concepts (however abstruse) through imagery, sensory clues, symbology, and associative language and structure, rather than overtly verbalized intellectualizations, it is easy to think of Ballard as the unconscious purveyor of potent magic-in-fantasy. To some small extent, this is probably true . . . But for the most part, he is an intensely conscious and purposeful speculative writer, and the modes he elects to use are those best suited to his vital interest in the philosophic basis of the contemporary revolutions in both scientific thinking and artistic expression. He is concerned with relationships rather than isolated definitions; with the synthesis of varieties of acquired knowledge, rather than the further dissection or analysis of the parts; with the opposites to be found in apparent equalities, and the identities to be derived from contrasts. The most recent stories are reaching toward a slightly different area of exploration and experimentation, but the main focus of the first ten-year phase was on Time—most specifically, man's orientation in Time, in the universal flow of event, the place of the hour, or flower, or single human consciousness, in the birth-to-death movement of cosmos, planet, species, culture . . . .

Ballard climaxes his first decade as a writer—and in another sense, the first phase of his career—at a point where the criteria of genre criticism are totally inadequate to judge his work; and while most of what he has done in the last two years comes off satisfactorily (and occasionally brilliantly) under examination by the established rules of 'serious' literary criticism, those rules are themselves far short of satisfactory for examination of most of his work. In the phase he now seems to be entering (to which "Terminal Beach" was a preliminary—as, five years earlier, was the far less complete "Voices of Time"), either set of standards will be about as useful as one axis on a sheet of linear graph paper for charting the course of a rocket: by using *both* axes, we can determine two dimensions of the trajectory; without some fairly sophisticated mathematics (the as-yet unformulated critical vocabulary) we have no way of indicating the third dimension.

And here, clearly I must stop. I can deliver no comprehensive summation or resounding conclusion, because there is no adequate critical vocabulary, as yet, with which to make wise statements about a literature so new-born that we hardly know how to distinguish hunger from temper from lung-exercise in its cries.

Fifteen years from now, someone else will have to point out my errors and omissions.

LIONEL STEVENSON

THE
ARTISTIC PROBLEM:
SCIENCE FICTION
AS
ROMANCE

I must begin by insisting in the most emphatic possible terms that I am not an authority in the field of science fiction. My reading in this area has been entirely desultory, and I stand in proper awe of the experts whom I have heard speak at previous sessions of this group. But I am keenly interested in observing how any particular sub-species of prose fiction relates itself to the total historical and aesthetic context of the English novel; and it is my impression that from this point of view science fiction has been unduly neglected.

The general histories of the novel barely mention it; even the encyclopedic Ernest A. Baker allows it only a few sentences in his chapter entitled "Satirists and Utopians, Revolutionaries and Evolutionaries," and this heading is revelatory of the directions from which it is usually approached. Even the specialized treatises on science fiction seem to deal with any other consideration rather than the artistic. It has been discussed in relation to utopian visions and dystopian warnings, to social protest and political satire, and of course it has been analysed in relation to the accuracy or plausibility of its scientific data. These are all highly significant topics, but their significance is not essentially relevant to the artistic merit of a work of literature. The total status of science fiction can be greatly enhanced if it can be shown to possess this

This paper derives from the discussion led by Professor Stevenson at the MLA Seminar on Science Fiction in December, 1962. It was first published in *Extrapolation*, 4 (May 1963), 17-22. Reprinted by permission of the author.

96

sort of merit in addition to its other, extraneous, qualities.

To begin with, it is plain that the real prominence of science fiction as a literary genre began about seventy years ago. This fact is likely to be passed over on the obvious ground that it coincided with an intensified public interest in the physical sciences, their inclusion in school and college curricula, and the acceleration of inventions that affected everyone's daily life. But these influences might more probably have eventuated in an increase in popular publications of a factual, informative nature, rather than in the development of a fresh type of creative literature.

In order to estimate the innovation in proper perspective, a glance must be directed toward its historical background. As with most (perhaps all) new genres, it was produced by several separate currents which eventually flowed together when external forces brought their channels to a point of conflict.

So far as literary eminence is concerned, the most distinguished precursors are those that belong to a genre not properly to be considered in the category of the novel at all. Plato's *Republic,* Bacon's *New Atlantis,* Campanella's *City of the Sun,* even *Gulliver's Travels* and *Erewhon,* use some of the superficial devices of fiction merely to render the author's social theories or his satirical grievances palatable to a wider public. A modicum of invented action, dialogue, and description of settings lent vividness to material that would otherwise be tediously abstract. It is doubtful whether anyone has enjoyed these books primarily for the suspense of the narrative or the sense of identification with the characters. One is not apt to feel painful tension as to whether Lemuel Gulliver will escape from Laputa, or to weep in sympathy for the dilemma of the visitor to Erewhon in his affection for Arowhena Nosnibor and his dislike for her sister Zulora.

Exactly opposite conditions apply to the second of the separate literary antecedents—the tale of terror. For addicts of Gothic romance, the agonies of suspense and the tears of pity were supremely important, and intellectual concepts were conspicuous by their absence. The effects of fear and sympathy were immensely heightened by the inclusion of supernatural elements, whether literal, as in *The Castle of Otranto,* or illusory, as in *The Mysteries of Udolpho.* But these responses depended directly upon the reader's innate superstition, and the rationalism of the nineteenth century steadily eroded the superstitions that lay in the substratum of intelligent minds.

Third among the literary types that preceded science fiction was the fantasy. In the Renaissance even the most highly cultivated minds could appreciate fiction that portrayed life in some delightful fairyland, in such a book as Sydney's *Arcadia*. But here again the growing dominance of utilitarian common sense scorned indulgence in dream worlds as a waste of time and a reprehensible avoidance of responsibility. By the nineteenth century, fantasy had been wholly relegated to juvenile literature, and even the satiric masterpieces of my first category, such as *Don Quixote* and *Gulliver's Travels*, were bowdlerized to serve as children's books. On the other hand, the expanding market for juvenile books led to an improvement in their quality, with the result that several authors of genius produced works in this category that are now recognized as masterpieces of fantasy meriting serious respect from adults—notably *The Water Babies, Alice in Wonderland,* and *Phantastes.* Thus the vital flame of fantasy was not merely kept alive but was enshrined in the very core of every literate mind, so that in mature life, though it might be ignored, it could not be extinguished.

Having thus listed the principal precursors of science fiction and noted that they were all reduced in prestige during the nineteenth century, it is necessary to consider the antagonist that had temporarily displaced them. All the dominant pressures upon the novel had combined to produce an earnest, somewhat monotonous type of domestic realism. Scientific thought was essentially in the fact-finding stage, laboriously observing phenomena and accumulating evidence as a basis for formulating strictly rational explanations of physical principles. The scientific mind of the era was inclined to regard imagination as a superficial but distracting adornment and emotion as a menace to the cool functioning of the human reason. Under this influence the novelists assumed that their duty was to record social and psychological details with scrupulous accuracy and austere detachment. Thackeray, Trollope, George Eliot, Henry James, all agreed in avoidance of exciting action or unfamiliar circumstances. The prevalent concept of realism reached its apogee in the confident assertions by W. D. Howells that all fiction was immoral unless it was confined to the everyday behavior and language of ordinary people. Writing in 1887, he thundered:

> We must ask ourselves before we ask anything else, Is it true?—true to the motives, the impulses, the principles that shape the life of actual men and women? This truth, which necessarily includes the highest morality and the highest artistry—this truth given, the book cannot be wicked and cannot be weak; and without it all grace of style and feats of invention and cunning of construction are so many superfluities of naughtiness. . . . I can hardly conceive of a literary self-respect in these days compatible with the old trade of make-believe, with the production of the kind of fiction which is too much honored by classification with card-playing and horse-racing. But let fiction cease to lie about life; let it portray men and women as they are, actuated by the motives and the passions in the measure we all know; let it leave off painting dolls and working them by springs and wires . . . and there can be no doubt of an unlimited future, not only of delightfulness but of usefulness, for it.

General adherence to this criterion imposed grave limitations upon prose fiction—limitations that isolated it from the main tradition of creative literature. One example must suffice. Mario Praz's challenging book on *The Hero in Eclipse in Victorian Fiction* has amply demonstrated how the domestic realism of the era obliterated the figure of the superior individual, the person whose virtues or vices raised him far enough above the average level to render him an object of envy or emulation or hatred or fear. This leveling of the characters of fiction to a commonplace mediocrity combined with the rejection of violent action and of exotic environment to make prose fiction once more ancillary to a non-artistic purpose. It was now providing specific details as equivalents for the documentary evidence of the social sciences. Carlyle's stigmatization of economics as "the dismal science" could well have been paralleled in the 1880's by terming fiction "the dismal art."

The whole realistic premise was profoundly contrary to the principle that the arts are not concerned with fact and logic but with imagination and feeling. Just as the neo-classical Age of Reason had locked poetry into a strait-jacket for more than a century, until the explosion of romanticism released the human spirit to its proper artistic freedom, so the new rationalism of the Age of Science was imprisoning fiction in solid walls of drab conformity, and a romantic revolt was once again required, if fiction were ever to reclaim its birthright of tragic dignity and comic absurdity and poetic beauty.

The new romantic novelists, who found their chief critical spokesman in Robert Louis Stevenson, were determined to employ themes and settings that could supply the excitement of danger, the glamour of unfamiliar surroundings, and the exaltation of heroic behavior. Many of them turned to the past as the most accessible source of these elements; but the historical novel had become so rigidly standardized in the mold set by Walter Scott that all the technical competence and scholarly research of Weyman, Quiller-Couch, and the others could not restore it to eminence. Even the historical novels of Conan Doyle, the best of the group, have not proved able to withstand the attrition of time.

Greater novelty, and therefore greater distinction, came to the writers whose experiences in remote regions of the world qualified them to write with authentic local color about primitive mores, lonely enterprises, and perilous physical conditions. In their various ways, Rider Haggard, Rudyard Kipling, and Joseph Conrad all brilliantly profited by this opportunity. Two of them, however, proved to have associated themselves with themes that the rapid tempo of social change has rendered not only obsolete but unpopular. The concept of imperialism, which sixty years ago connoted unselfish nobility and picturesque audacity, has now degenerated into a dirty word, and the stories of Kipling and Haggard are irremediably tarnished thereby.

More lasting success came to Conan Doyle when he turned away from historical romances to create his great detective. Here all the romantic essentials were present—suspense, danger, and a hero of supreme ability—but located in a modern urban environment and embellished with an aura of intellectual acumen. The author, as a physician, had been trained in a scientific discipline, and Sherlock Holmes employed the scientist's methods in solving his problems. Indeed, criminology itself was one of the newly emerging behavioral sciences. Hence the hero's essentially romantic exploits were rendered uniquely pleasurable to the ultra-rational new intelligentsia.

The quasi-scientific elements in the Sherlock Holmes cycle point the way by which the new romantic fiction achieved its most startling triumph. In an age when the mental attitudes of science had vitiated the traditional resources of romance, the alternative was to exploit the romantic potentialities of science itself. It was in 1894 that Kipling wrote his cogent poem, "The King":

"Romance!" the season-tickets mourn,
   "*He* never ran to catch his train,
But passed with coach and guard and horn—
   And left the local—late again!"
Confound romance! . . . And all unseen
Romance brought up the nine-fifteen.

His hand was on the lever laid,
   His oil-can soothed the worrying cranks,
His whistle waked the snowbound grade,
   His fog-horn cut the reeking Banks;
By dock and deep and mine and mill
The Boy-god reckless laboured still.

It was not only, however, that applied science was providing a dizzying succession of new inventions that changed the whole pattern of human life. At the same time the pure sciences were emerging from the plodding thoroughness of empirical research to the bold flights of speculative theory. Relativity and the quantum hypothesis and atomic energy were lurking just around the corner, ready to nullify the supposedly immutable laws of nature that had reigned unchallenged since Copernicus and Newton.

H. G. Wells chanced to be the person equipped with exactly the right qualities for recognizing the opportunity. With a respectable education in biology and physics he combined a journalist's agile intelligence and lively curiosity and an impudent disregard for established tradition. He seized upon the naive tale of adventure for boys, which had brought renown to Jules Verne, and transformed it into something new and astonishingly subtle. On the one hand, he retained a firm affiliation with the realistic fiction that was currently predominant. The compelling plausibility of *The Time Machine*, the weird intensity of *The Invisible Man*, the cataclysmal terror of *The War of the Worlds,* arise from their being liberally interspersed with scenes of everyday English life in the current year. Into this texture of domestic realism he interwove sturdy threads from all the earlier kinds of imaginative narrative that are now recognized as antecedents of science fiction; but he handled these potentially unconvincing ingredients so expertly that they merged into the pattern without incongruity.

The element of horror and dread was just as effectual as in a Gothic romance, but no skeptical reader could accuse the author of trading on the supernatural, since all the future developments that he described were consistent with the scientists' ever-accelerating control of the forces of nature. Similarly, even the earliest of Wells's novels contain perceptible implications of social criticism or utopianism, but the reader is seldom aware of any overt propagandizing. Rather, any suggestions of sneers at contemporary life or proposals for alternative forms of society seem to be latent in the narrative itself, and the story gives no impression of having been manipulated to serve as a vehicle for indoctrination. Hence each story belongs indubitably to the category of prose fiction, and not to that of allegory or satire.

Perhaps, however, it is the relationship of science fiction with pure fantasy that offers the most suggestive clues to its artistic status. Without drawing any serious inferences from the fact that Kingsley was an amateur biologist and Lewis Carroll a professional mathematician, one may nevertheless point out a significant relationship between science fiction and Victorian children's literature. *The Water Babies* and *Alice in Wonderland* are both imaginary voyages to realms where ordinary experience is distorted but not negated. One of them is on the same theme as *Twenty Thousand Leagues Under the Sea*; the other, on that of *A Journey to the Center of the Earth.* The immense enthusiasm for such books a century ago arose from their being the only current literature that gave untrammeled and indeed exuberant freedom to the imagination. All the work-a-day shackles of common sense and practical utility were joyously flouted, and staid mid-Victorian citizens reveled in the temporary liberation, while pretending that they were merely reading harmless fairy tales to their children. In the twentieth century, however, the literary respect for books of this type arises from their being essentially dream-narratives, and therefore richly susceptible to symbolic interpretation. When science fiction appeared upon the scene, it too partook of this dream (or often nightmare) quality of unearthly vividness and elusively distorted logic. At the time when Wells began to write, he could not have been aware that the psychoanalysts and the anthropologists were on the eve of launching a revolutionary thesis that within a generation totally overturned the concept of realism. The essential truth of human nature (and, consequently, of literary representation) ceased to depend upon external, material appearances, but was to be sought through dreams, wishes, irrational fears. And the most potent literary correlatives were primitive fairy tales and symbolic dreams—all the stuff that had been contemptuously lumped in the category of fantasy. Science fiction amply provided these fairy-tale elements, with the wizard disguised in the white jacket of a laboratory researcher and the ferocious giants and conniving dwarfs metamorphosed into Martians or into the Morlocks of the eight-thousandth century. Jack's beanstalk reappeared as the space-capsule bearing the first men to the moon; the spell put upon the sleeping beauty or upon Rip van Winkle was now supplied by the whirring gears of the Time Machine.

In this transformation the romantic hero, of course, regained his hereditary stature. No longer a brawny warrior or a captivating seducer of maidens, he was now an austere intellectual, but still irresistible through his mastery of secret physical processes. That he was sinister as often as beneficent, a Doctor Moreau as well as a Professor Redwood, was in itself a revival of the villain-hero role of Faust or Manfred or Milton's Satan himself. Stevenson, the arch-begetter of the new romanticism, had already symbolised the dichotomy in his nearest approach to science fiction, *Dr. Jekyll and Mr. Hyde.*

The kinship of the new science fiction with the other subtypes in the romantic revival was further demonstrated when several of the most skillful practitioners in those areas successfully invaded this one. Kipling's "With the Night Mail" and "As Easy as A. B. C." or Doyle's *Lost World* and *Poison Belt* challenge comparison with the best works of Wells.

As a solution, then, to the problem of evaluating science fiction on strictly aesthetic grounds, I suggest that the only criterion can be the extent to which any given specimen lives up to the fulfilment of these multiple roles. If the originality of its scientific hypothesis and the credibility of its data can be combined with realism in the scenes of contemporary life, a background of mature social consciousness in the utopian or satiric implications and rich symbolic potential in the fantasy, then it can honestly lay claim to a permanent niche in literature.

RUDOLF B. SCHMERL

FANTASY
AS
TECHNIQUE

E. M. Forster's essay on fantasy in his *Aspects of the Novel* is now perhaps most famous for its quite incidental characterization of "Ulysses" as "a dogged attempt to cover the universe with mud." If so, a ray of light has been obscured by a speck of dust, for Forster's essay, which does not quite define fantasy, illuminates almost all its relevant elements.

First, a disagreement. "Fantasy," says Forster, "asks us to pay something extra"; by which he means that we must be even more willing to suspend our disbelief when we read a fantasy than when we read ordinary fiction. The London of "Mrs. Dalloway" is not really London; the London of *Brave New World* or of *1984*, even less so. We can grant the point without admitting its pertinence. Virginia Woolf's London is a reality her readers share, coming into conflict with no London that exists. The Londons of Huxley and Orwell cannot be shared. They are satiric projections of sociological perspectives, not literary creations; and the reader is to agree to (not at all the same thing as sharing) the existence of implications making the projections plausible. To suspend disbelief when reading a fantasy may mean to fail to understand it. If fantasy asks us to pay something extra, it is extra attention.

Second, a quotation. ". . . Were that type of classification helpful," Forster writes, "we could make a list of the devices which writers of a fantastic turn have used—such as the introduction of a god, ghost, angel, monkey, monster, midget, witch into

Originally published in *The Virginia Quarterly Review*, 43 (Autumn 1967), 644-656.

ordinary life; or the introduction of ordinary men into no man's land, the future, the past, the interior of the earth, the fourth dimension; or divings into and the dividings of personality; or finally the device of parody or adaptation." How helpful such a classification might be can be seen by contrasting it with assertions about fantasy by Philip Van Doren Stern, who claims that "tales of fantasy all have in them at least one assumption which no sane person would be willing to grant," or by Ray Bradbury, who writes in his introduction to "The Circus of Dr. Lao," in an anthology, that "each fantasy assaults and breaks a particular law." Forster's specificity makes us focus on what the writer is doing, not on our sanity or on laws of literature—whatever either may be. Still, both Bradbury and Stern are talking about the essential characteristic of fantasy; it contradicts our experience, not the limited experience we can attain as individuals, but the totality of our knowledge of what our culture regards as real. Realistic fiction can corroborate, amplify, even exceed our individual experience; Yoknapatawpha, for example, abounds with perversion and violence most of us are not likely to encounter anywhere but in Faulkner's private world. Yet fantasy, as a generic term, is reserved to denote an entirely different kind of imaginative construction. Necrophilia may be as alien to us as a Martian, but it is not at all incredible, as all portraits of Martians have had to be. The Emily of "A Rose for Emily" is within the bounds of possibility; the *hrossa* of C. S. Lewis's Malacandra are not, at least, not yet. The "assumption" of *Out of the Silent Planet* no sane person would be willing to grant, or the "law" the novel breaks, is, however, not the existence of forms of life on Mars, but Dr. Ransom's trip to that planet. As far as we know, no human being had bodily left the earth when the novel was published. We would not claim, however, that necrophilia exists only in Faulkner's imagination.

The sophistication, then, not of the individual reader, but of the culture which a work of art simultaneously reflects and is received by, provides a criterion of fantasy. What one age regards as indisputable may seem superstition to the next, and what seems random speculation at one time may later turn out to be a feasible hypothesis; but we cannot regard "Hamlet" as a fantasy merely because a ghost is a character in the play, nor the *Nautilus* of

Jules Verne as the scientific forerunner of its namesake in the United States Navy. To be fantasy, a work of literature must be so regarded by its author and his contemporaries, and their judgment is final. Fantasy, in other words, is deliberate; it is intentionally fantasy. George Orwell, writing of abused farm animals rebelling against their drunken owner, is deliberately writing fantasy, just as Margaret Mitchell, writing of the fortunes and misfortunes of a Southern belle during the Civil War, is deliberately writing an historical novel. The accomplishments of later generations in their laboratories may turn matter into energy, but not fantasy into reality.

There is, of course, another possibility: fantasy may be misunderstood as realistic fiction or even as historical documents by a future society severed from its roots. Should we ever revert to a belief in witches, for example, Thorne Smith's *The Passionate Witch* might become an important piece of evidence to substantiate that belief. Or *Brave New World* and *1984* may be regarded as factual accounts of early European civilizations. John Atkins exploits this possibility in his fantasy about fantasies, *Tomorrow Revealed*, in which a twentieth century library full of science fiction and fantasies is the only link to the past that remains for a reader in the third millennium. A variation of this theme is the possibility that history may be intentionally distorted to suit the changing policies of a totalitarian state. In Orwell's *1984*, Winston Smith is employed in the Ministry of Truth for just this purpose.

The significance of the intention of the author may be made more apparent by considering religious literature. The vision of a mystic may seem fantastic to us, but its transcription, to the mystic, may be the record of an intimate experience with ultimate reality. It is irrelevant to declare that, whatever his mystical experience may have been, his interpretation of it is incorrect. The unicorn is no mythical beast to the man who sees one in his garden.

Or consider an obvious difference between fantasy and realistic fiction. The latter requires a willing suspension of disbelief; to try to suspend disbelief while one is reading fantasy can lead to absurd misconceptions. A bishop is said to have remarked, shortly after the publication of *Gulliver's Travels,* that he personally believed the book to be a pack of lies. The writer of realistic fiction may not want to be taken literally, but certainly he does not encourage skepticism about the underlying reality of his novel. A fantasist, however, if he is writing responsible fantasy —a qualification to be elucidated later—*must* be taken as meaning something other than what he is saying.

In the past, fantasists have been at some pains to make their tales at least superficially plausible. What pretended to be an account of a journey to the remote corners of the world was more likely to be read than a book blatantly "unreal" by readers who were dubious of the worth, even of the morality, of mere works of fiction. But today's prefaces or epilogues, such as those in *Out of the Silent Planet* and *Perelandra* by C. S. Lewis, pretending to attempt to persuade the reader of the veracity of the story, are rarely germane to the story itself, although they may provide an author with opportunities for sharper satire or more explicit didacticism than does the fantasy. Richard Gerber, in his *Utopian Fantasy,* considers protestations of the truth of the story an integral part of the fantasy; such protestations, he says, "are meant to ensure a superficial verisimilitude as well as a deeper ironical effect." One might point out that such superficial verisimilitude creates the deeper ironical effect, and thus is not an end but a means. More importantly, however, a fantasist's pretense of actuality, if well carried out, cannot be exposed as pretense. It is impossible to disprove the existence of goblins once upon a time, or that of Lilliput in uncharted seas, or the origins of Raphael Hythloday and the traveler from Altruria. But in modern fantasies, events of the future are often described in the past tense, and sometimes these events take place in another galaxy. Or, relying on the relative completeness of our knowledge of our own planet, a fantasist describes a place or an event, ostensibly in this world or within recorded time, that has no parallels in our experience. Koestler's Rubashov is clearly a figure from the Moscow trials; Robert Penn Warren's Willie Stark, even more clearly, or more specifically, a version of Huey Long; but Rex Warner's Governor, in *Men of Stones*, is a totalitarian who never existed. Two other Warner novels, *The Aerodrome* and *The Professor,* are fantasies for similar reasons: they describe events ostensibly important enough to be found in the files of any newspaper, but the events take place not in real but in representative countries.

Occasionally, it is true, one comes across a modern fantasy embedded in one of the old framework devices; the manuscript of Willy Johns' *The Fabulous Journey of Hieronymus Meeker* was found by the "editor," according to the epilogue, while he was traveling through some islands in the Pacific Ocean, some time after a mysterious object, hurtling down from the sky, had exploded in the vicinity. Hieronymus's journey, however, takes place after the Fourth World War, and the combination of this setting with the epilogue produces a curious mixture, quite appropriate to this unusual book, of an old device and modern indifference to it. Yet this is not new; Bellamy's *Looking Backward*, published in 1887, is another such mixture, pretending to attempt to convince readers in the twenty-first century of the author's birth in 1857. Generally, contemporary writers seem to scorn such efforts at plausibility as Johns' epilogue. Aldous Huxley's *Ape and Essence*, doubly framed as a movie script with a realistic introduction, is an extreme instance of the dropping of pretenses, employing the framework as an announcement of intentions. His earlier *Brave New World*, bluntly set in the year 632 After Ford, is more typical. The dream, a framework favored by medieval authors, has apparently been relegated to the psychoanalysts; at least most science-fiction writers seem to agree with Arthur C. Clarke, a scientist and author of science fiction, that the dream is "an annoying device which has been used all too often in fantastic literature."

A fantasy's theme cannot significantly depend on a pretense of actuality. "A great part of the pleasure derived from reading such books," writes Gerber, "consists in reading them at a double level, in continuously imagining . . . a naive reader who is taken in by these devices." That is, a reader who is not sufficiently sophisticated to recognize fantasy, to disregard pretenses of actuality, cannot understand it. Gerber maintains that such pretenses can be achieved not only through direct protestations of truth, but also through evasion, "which leads the reader away from the well-known into the regions of uncertainty." As an example of evasion, he quotes a passage from C. S. Lewis's *Out of the Silent Planet*, in which Weston, aboard his spaceship en route to Mars, answers his kidnaped prisoner's question about the working of the machine as follows:

> "As to how we do it—I suppose you mean how the spaceship works—there's no good your asking that. Unless you were one of the four or five real physicists now living you couldn't understand: and if there were any chance of your understanding you certainly wouldn't be told. If it makes you happy to repeat words that don't mean anything—which is, in fact, what unscientific people want when they ask for an explanation—you may say we work by exploiting the less observed properties of solar radiation."

Gerber does not find this sort of evasion as "satisfactory" as the technique of H. G. Wells, which, as Gerber describes it, consists of "a detailed explanation . . . presented with sufficient energy and with a considerable amount of pseudoscientific terms which will leave the reader in a state of resigned bewilderment." But if evasion is the goal, it seems that Lewis's swift and sure means of achieving it is at the very least as satisfactory as Wells's "detailed explanation." And the fact is that every fantasy is evasive, whether or not there is a passage which sidesteps explanation of the improbabilities the fantasy presents. Not to present any explanation at all (common in modern fantasies set in the future) is surely as evasive as to present an explanation of some kind. Thus evasion should not be regarded as an alternative to direct protestations of truth, either of which method achieves a pretense of actuality. Evasion, whether it can be pointed out as in the C. S. Lewis passage, or whether it is inherent in the whole of a book, as in Rex Warner's *The Wild Goose Chase*, is the method through which fantasy can present improbabilities; or rather, it is composed of one or more of certain of the methods suggested by Forster—the use of unverifiable time, place, characters, or devices.

The sacrifice of pretenses of actuality distinguishes modern fantasy much more sharply than the machines and monsters which clutter the imagination of our less talented science-fiction writers. The machines and monsters are simply the necessary magic, different in degree but not in kind from Aladdin's lamp or fire-breathing dragons. To dispense with attempts at credibility, no matter how thin they may be, allows a writer complete freedom. It is not merely that he can now play sociologist, anthropologist, psychologist, and, of course, astrophysicist—for who knows his creatures and their planet better than he?—but he does not *want* anyone to believe him. That would entail responsibility, and that, in turn, is a curb to freedom. Impatient with the difficulties of writing well about the real world, either realistically or as a responsible fantasist, he succumbs to the call of the wild blue yonder. His disease, a profitable one at the moment, is an undisciplined imagination.

John W. Campbell, Jr., a science-fiction writer and editor, claims that "we can safely practice anything in imagination—suicide, murder, anything whatever." To give this astonishing statement its most favorable interpretation, Campbell seems to be reassuring us about the relative safety of speculation compared to the absolute danger of actual experimentation, although his examples are unfortunate; suicide and murder are within our powers, and surely Campbell does not mean that there is no relationship between what we imagine and what we do. At best, Campbell's remark is a platitude, significant only for what it reveals of a leading science-fiction writer's attitude towards imagination. It is the attitude of a scientist in the laboratory, concerned about possible explosions, not that of a writer at his desk, struggling to unite his conception of reality with literary form.

The fantasist who wraps his tale in a mantle of plausibility usually has a purpose beyond his bank account. The wrapping, however, is not indispensable. Orwell's *1984* has none but the ominous potentialities of contemporaneity, a transparent mantle indeed. Yet this suffices to make *1984* responsible fantasy; its distortions are satiric, and only reality can be satirized. At the end of the novel, Winston Smith, crushed, drained, and all but physically obliterated, is left loving Big Brother, a fiercely satiric reply to the ostrich cult of muddling through; Arthur C. Clarke's *Childhood's End*, to choose one of the more literate science-fiction novels, closes with a metamorphosis of the last generation of humanity into Clarke himself knows not what. The difference between responsible and irresponsible fantasy, between the disciplined and the undisciplined imagination, is in their relation to reality.

Unfortunately, we are no longer sure that we know reality when we see it; we cannot kick it and thus refute Berkeley. It might be a flying saucer, a hoax, a secret weapon of uncertain origin, or, more simply and comfortingly, a manifestation of some psychosis. It is possible to dismiss *1984* as the nightmare of a sick and dying man, and it has, in fact, been so dismissed by a disturbingly large number of critics. And the adherents of science fiction have claimed as one of the cardinal virtues of their imagination precisely the valid relation to reality that has been denied to *1984*. We are told of prophecies that have come to pass, warned of the inscrutable mystery of the universe, reminded of the head-shakers and nay-sayers whom technology proved false Cassandras, and proudly informed that eminently sensible scientists both read and write science fiction. Further, the previously implied distinction between *1984* and science fiction would be vigorously rejected by the champions of science fiction, who have claimed it for their own, as they have *Gulliver's Travels* and Plato's *Republic*. The champions are inverted Don Quixotes, mistaking hostile giants for friendly windmills. They neglect still another characteristic of responsible fantasy: purpose. Even if we grant that reality is subjective, that Orwell's *Weltanschauung* is peculiarly his own, it remains obvious that *1984* satirizes reality as Orwell sees it. We can accuse him of pessimism, but not of irresponsibility. It is unthinkable, however, that *Childhood's End* satirizes the reality that Clarke sees, or that it is an allegory, or that it is, in fact, anything but an exercise of Clarke's undisciplined imagination. Writers of science fiction sometimes declare that they simply assume the truth of certain hypotheses and proceed to extrapolation. But this is in no way similar to assuming the truth of one's conception of reality (a necessary assumption under almost any circumstances), for the hypotheses, usually related to some branch of engineering or the natural sciences, rest on nothing but the writer's fancy. This clearly has nothing to do either with science, which rests on the reproducible experiment, or with literature, which is written about people. In fact, the problem posed by an admission of the subjectivity of reality becomes unnecessarily complex when we consider science fiction based, not on the probable, but merely on the mathematically possible. The reality to which responsible fantasy is related is one of whose existence the author and a sizable number of his contemporaries are convinced. It is for this reason that "science fiction" is a self-contradictory term; neither an author nor any of his contemporaries can be genuinely convinced that what is suggested as a scientific hypothesis can be elaborated verbally rather than empirically.

A different problem, at least to a non-Christian reader, is presented by, for instance, the C. S. Lewis trilogy, *Out of the Silent Planet, Perelandra,* and *That Hideous Strength.* The reality to which the three novels are related is Christian metaphysics. Like others of Lewis's books, the trilogy is belligerently affirmative; that is, his purpose is not to satirize but to proselytize. Orwell's deliberately distorted horror can be interpreted as necessary exaggeration, and the reader who has a rosier crystal ball can at least extend a certain esthetic tolerance to *1984.* He has not been told to save his soul, merely that the future will very probably not allow him to have any. But the Lewis trilogy, no matter how much of it is simply suspense and entertainment, is unflinchingly didactic, and it is of obvious significance that Lewis's Christ figure, Dr. Ransom, wins no final victory over the forces of darkness. The reader who is incapable of belief in Christianity can well inquire whether a religion whose truth is far from evident to him can provide a more legitimate framework for responsible fantasy than can pseudo-scientific speculation about the ultimate destiny of humanity.

But such a reader's skepticism is in itself an indication of his awareness of Christianity as a part of his world. Flying saucers, whatever they might be, seem at least to be something; not all the evidence for the phenomena has been exposed as fraudulent. But flying saucers have not as yet made an appreciable impact on man's mind. Perhaps they *are* the space craft of forms of life from outer planets, and perhaps every last item in the metaphysics of Christianity has no more relation to reality than do primitive superstitions; but as of this moment, Christianity is a living force in our world, and flying saucers have not yet penetrated its consciousness. Orwell and Huxley, with their telescreen and bottle babies, satirize contemporary uses of science and technology, and are in that respect writing responsible fantasy. Lewis is concerned with a reality just as tangible; although the reader, if he is not of his persuasion, has to translate that reality into terms meaningful to himself. That is not a difficult task, and is, in fact, the reader's obligation to perform. Should he refuse it, should he decide to read only those works which correspond to his personal view of reality, he will be left, ultimately, turning the knobs of his television set.

Fantasy, then, is the intentional and purposeful contradiction of our experience, the deliberate presentation of improbabilities. Its methods are to employ temporal or spatial distance, or characters or devices whose nature or qualities cannot be verified by the usual criteria of credibility one brings to a novel. And fantasy is addressed to a typical reader within a culture whose level of sophistication will enable that reader to recognize the improbabilities.

The emphasis of this view of fantasy as a technique is on objectively ascertainable elements. Apart from deciding whether the fantastic elements are integral to the novel, a reader will have no difficulty, using the criteria suggested here, in deciding whether a novel is a fantasy. It seems reasonable to ask why he should bother.

The answer is that fantasy, like anything else, cannot be understood if it is taken for something else. The novelist's task is not the same as the historian's, and we use different criteria in assessing their work. Similarly, the possibilities open to the fantasist are not identical with those the writer of realistic fiction can exploit, and the limitations within which they work differ correspondingly. Further, a general understanding of fantasy is needed to evaluate the ways in which fantasists present improbabilities. (I have tried to show elsewhere, for example, that Orwell's use of unverifiable time in *1984* is esthetically superior to that of Huxley's in *Brave New World*.) And such an understanding can also prevent misleading identifications of fantasy with Forster's "parody or adaptation."

Brave New World, for instance, is obviously a satire as well as a fantasy, and at first glance it may seem just as appropriate to evaluate the book on the basis of criteria derived from a definition of satire as on the basis of those derived from a concept of fantasy. Huxley's novel, like *Gulliver's Travels* and *Erewhon*, employs fantasy as a vehicle for satire. Swift's Lilliputians are not only unverifiable characters but also, and more importantly, satiric portraits of the smallness of man. Butler's Erewhon is an unverifiable country whose customs are satiric inversions of England's. The World State, as it exists in the unverifiable year 632 A.F., is a satiric projection of popular values and associated uses of science in the real world of 1932. Nevertheless, to treat *Brave New World* as primarily a satire would involve difficulties which it might be wiser to avoid than to confront. In the first place, satire is much easier to recognize than to define; unlike fantasy, it is not so much a technique as a manner. The underlying assumption of fantasy is that the reader can distinguish between what is verifiable and what is not. If he cannot, the distinction can be made for him. The underlying assumption of satire is that the reader's social and moral values are basically akin to the values implicit in the satire. If they are not, the satire's purpose—to sharpen the reader's perception of the applicability of these values, of implications inherent in them—is defeated, and nothing can be done about it. In other words, the fantastic technique lends itself to objective description in ways that the satiric manner does not.

Second, *Brave New World*, is wholly a fantasy (that is, unverifiable time and devices are integral to the novel) but not wholly satiric. John's suicide serves as a final symbol of universal death, or of the ultimate horror of the road civilization may be traveling, but it is not a satiric symbol. Much in the real world simply cannot be satirized. A satire of the concentration camps at Auschwitz is inconceivable. Yet the horror of the camps can be reflected in fantasy: in *1984*, Room 101 in the Ministry of Love is such a reflection. Most modern fantasies with a political theme combine satire with reflections of those aspects of reality which must be treated differently. Not even Orwell's *Animal Farm*, which is far more consistently satiric than *Brave New World*, maintains its satiric manner thorughout. Napoleon's purge of the animals is an allegorical, not a satiric, version of Stalin's purges of the Russian Communist party. Stalin's purges did not represent the kind of absurdity a satirist can seize on.

Fantasy, then, not only does not exclude satire and allegory, but sometimes merges with them. But not indistinguishably.

BRIAN ALDISS

THE
WOUNDED
LAND:
J. G. BALLARD

Terminal Beach is a much better collection than we have
any right to expect in this wicked world. Not only have the
stories virtue in their own right; they show Ballard developing in a
way that did not seem likely from his earlier writing.

Ballard's first (English) volume, *Four Dimensional Nightmare*, showed him limited as to subject. There were too many
stories about time, more particularly about the stoppage of time.
In the new volume, he remains limited as regards theme, but the
limitation represents an absorbed concentration and the theme
pours forth its rewards. And that in fact is his theme: that limits
whether voluntary or imposed bring ample compensation by
deflecting attention to occurrences and states of mind not available to the 'normal' world-possessed man.

Not the least damn bit incidentally, as H. L. Gold once put
it, this is also a parallel with Ballard's own position in the science
fiction field. By refusing to go joy-riding all over the universe, he
has brought his readers more rich strangeness than any hack ever
dredged out of far Andromeda.

Some of the best stories in the *Terminal Beach* collection
hover—as all good sf should—on the verge of being something
other than sf. "The Drowned Giant", for instance, is an apparently straightforward eyewitness account of the dismemberment of a

Originally published as part of the article, "British Science Fiction
Now," *SF Horizons*, no. 2 (Winter 1965), pp. 13-37. Reprinted in its present
form by permission of the author, who edited *SF Horizons* with Harry
Harrison. (Punctuation follows that used in original printing.)

gigantic, though otherwise human, body cast up on an unspecified shore. The manner of telling recalls such stories of Kafka's as "Metamorphosis" or "The Giant Mole". It begins with this sentence: 'On the morning after the storm the body of a drowned giant was washed ashore on the beach five miles to the north-west of the city.' The important thing, the narrator tells us, is to remember where the giant appeared, not the fact that he was a giant; to be amazed would be impolite. And by describing the dismemberment of the giant corpse, Ballard weans us of our desire to know where he came from. He concentrates on the important things, and by so doing makes the ends pursued by most sf seem trivial ones. In the hands of the first fifty sf writers you care to name, this story would end with other giants coming down from Akkapulko XIV to rescue him, and the shooting beginning. By eschewing sensationalism, Ballard makes us realise how much sf is given over to sensationalism.

The Unifying Wit

He replaces sensationalism with wit. The critics have not noticed how witty Ballard is, yet a unifying wit is his dominant characteristic. Fandom seems to have decided he is the prophet of despondence and let it go at that. Ballard is seldom discussed in fanzines (nor for that matter is anyone but Heinlein), but the occasional reference tends to be disparaging. Thus a correspondent in *Vector* calls Ballard a 'melancholy johnnie'. An instance of Ballard's wit is the dry way the pedantry of Pelham is drawn in "The Reptile Enclosure". (Chatting to his wife on the beach, Pelham remarks, "It's remarkable how popular sunbathing has become", and cannot resist adding, "It was a major social problem in Australia before the Second World War.") The situation in "Billenium", where seven people move one by one into a small room, is treated with an appreciation of its comic side, while irony is always present in Ballard's writing, often seeming to turn against the author himself, except on the rare occasions when it is dethroned by melodrama. "Track 12", an early story, skilfully combines melodrama and irony, where a man is drowned to the amplified noise of his own adulterous kiss.

"A Question of Re-entry", which deals with a Lieutenant in the Amazon, looking for a missing astronaut, has a humorous denouement, if the humour is wry. But Ballard's wit lies chiefly in imagery that, like the imagery of such metaphysical poets as Carew or Donne, can surprise and delight by its juxtaposition of hitherto separate ideas. In "The Drought", such imagery is, perhaps appropriately, more dessicated, more of the order of Ransome's remark to Catherine: "I've always thought of the whole of life as a kind of disaster area." Such juxtapositional imagery abounds in "The Terminal Beach". Here is a sample from the eponymous story: 'The series of weapons tests had fused the sand in layers, and the pseudo-geological strata condensed the brief epochs, micro-seconds in duration, of thermo-nuclear time.' Paradox is closely allied to this form of wit and in fact this passage continues, 'Typically the island inverted the geologist's maxim. The key to the past lies in the present. Here the key to the present lay in the future. This island was a fossil of time future, its bunkers and blockhouse illustrating the principle that the fossil record of life was one of armour and the exoskeleton'.

Traven's minute vision, exampled in the above-quoted passage, is sharpened by premonitions of death. He is metaphorically in the same position as Knight, in an early novel of Thomas Hardy's, *A Pair of Blue Eyes.* Knight clings desperately to the face of a tall cliff; like Traven, he is isolation personified, and the author makes his predicament stand for all mankind. A few inches from Knight's eyes, a fossil is embedded in the cliff, regarding him sightlessly. 'It was the single instance within reach of his vision of anything that had ever been alive and had had a body to save, as he himself had now . . . He was to be with the small in his death . . . Time closed up like a fan before him. He saw himself at one extremity of the years, face to face with the beginning and all the intermediate centuries simultaneously'.

Hardy's intentions here (and often elsewhere) are to achieve the sort of sf frisson that Ballard is after. Indeed, an echo of Hardy's fossil episode may be found in Ballard's "Deep End" (contained in *The Terminal Beach*) where the solitary fish that Holliday discovers in a pool is intended as a symbol of life—in "The Drought" this symbol is perhaps the dominant one. It is not my intention to draw strong parallels between Ballard and Hardy—parallels which I do not believe are there—but there are times when Ballard, in using symbols to convey massively passing time in a somewhat cumbrous prose, sounds remarkably like the great Victorian novelist: 'But the enigmatic presence of the terrace city, with its crumbling galleries and internal courts encrusted by the giant thistles and wire moss, seemed a huge man-made artefact [sic] which militated against the super-real naturalism of the delta. However, the terrace city, like the delta, was moving backwards in time, the baroque tracery of the serpent deities along the friezes dissolving and being replaced by the intertwined tendrils of the moss-plants, the pseudo-organic forms made by man in the image of nature reverting to their original.' (From "The Delta at Sunset").

In this extract, too, one sees at work the sort of wit of which I was speaking earlier—a unifying wit that seems to me entirely successful. Sometimes one detects the writer having a joke with himself. For instance, in *The Terminal Beach*, a young woman flier arrives on the blasted island. Traven sees her and 'as she turned, Traven rose involuntarily, recognising the child in the photograph he had pinned to the wall of the bunker'. What a twist in the plot that would be, how welcome in the slicks and the sticks, with its breath of conventional romance! But Ballard continues unfalteringly, 'Then he remembered the magazine could not have been more than four or five years old'.

The unifying wit seeks always to combine opposites and incongruities. In "The Subliminal Man" (published in *New Worlds* and not yet collected), the hideous giant subliminal signs are erected all over town but, as 'an appeal to petty snobbery, the lower sections had been encased in mock-Tudor panelling'—a typical wry Ballard joke. In "The Drought", Catherine strides along with her white lions, a contrast of weak and strong; Mrs. Quilter is buried in the back seat of a limousine. These are typical instances of college methods, the wit of a cataloguer who is discontented with everyone else's categories. They represent a sensible attempt to deal with the dislocations of our times, and are Ballard's most notable contribution to science fiction.

Dethronement of the Hero

Humour is not Ballard's forte, however much wit is. The most serious flaw in the best Ballard novel, *The Drowned World*, is the villainous Strangman who, with his alligators, his 'handsome saturnine face', his 'crisp white suit, the silk-like surface of which reflected the gilt plate of his high-backed Renaissance throne', and his henchman, 'a huge hunchbacked Negro in a pair of green cotton shorts . . . a giant grotesque parody of a human being' reminds one irresistably of the prewar villains in *Boy's Own Paper* or *Modern Boy*. *Modern Boy's* sf hero, Captain Justice, with his 'cigar in mouth, cap tilted jauntily over one eye', is characterised about as subtilely as Strangman. One laughs at the latter chiefly, I think, because the author does not; indeed, Strangman is designed as some sort of apocalyptic figure with great significance in the plot. He buckles under the weight of the author's intentions and is forgotten as soon as he disappears, leaving Kerans to his love-hate relationship with the smouldering submerged world about him.

As I say, one laughs; yet it is a mistake to underestimate Ballard. And it may even be that on a deeper level Strangman is intended as parody. There are frequent signs in Ballard's work that he is parodying or mocking or at least remembering all the bad things of the medium in which he has chosen to write (often it is difficult for the intelligent sf writer to do otherwise); we have already had one such example, where Traven thinks he recognises the girl aviator.

Ballard's attitude is such that we are often reminded of sf by the very things he is ostentatiously not doing. Ballard likes to regard himself as something of an outcast among the sf fraternity. He avoids most other authors, he believes—in sharp distinction to adulation expressed by other writers—that 'H. G. Wells has had a disastrous influence on the subsequent course of science fiction', he seems to regard William Burroughs as the greatest of sf writers, and of course he is the apostle of "Inner Space".

Making the most worthwhile contribution to the series of Guest Editorials in *New Worlds,* Ballard said that he believed sf should jettison such ideas as interstellar travel, aliens, and other staple ideas of the genre, turning more towards the biological sciences than the overworked physical ones. 'The only truly alien planet is Earth'. Not only should subject matter change; style should alter. He says: 'Science fiction must jettison its present narrative forms and plots. Most of these are far too explicit to express any subtle interplay of character and theme. . . . I think most of the hard work will fall not on the writer and editor but on the readers. The onus is on them to accept a more oblique narrative style, understated themes, private symbols and vocabularies.'

This is a conscious reaction against conservative sf. Nor does Ballard, unlike most prophets, fail to practise what he preaches. His central characters, sensitive, sinful, defeated, wounded, wry, are poles away from Heinlein's swaggering heroes, Asimov's world savers, Bester's anger-propelled demons, or Wright's sour conspirators, or of all the snarlingly brave guys with blasters and cloaks and big boots that have been with us since Verne's day. Against the doers, Ballard ranges his non-doers. He is as much against galactic heroes as Bill, The Galactic Hero.

In his early stories, his non-doers were also non-runners. His central characters struggle very little against their various worlds: too little, so that we find a faint sense of anti-climax lingering about early stories like "Prima Belladonna", "Waiting Grounds", "Sound Sweep", "Zone of Terror" and "Build-Up". But at this time, Ballard had still not found his tenor, and was writing stories like "Mobile", "Escapement", and "Now: Zero", all of which are too feeble and derivative to find equivalents in his later work. (Incidentally, all the stories mentioned in this paragraph, excepting "Escapement", can be found in one or other of Ballard's first two published volumes, *The Voices of Time* and *Billenium*, both put out courageously by Berkley of New York in the same year, 1962.)

Yet, just as he began with such masterly stories as "Manhole 99" and "Track 12", so his non-runners still appear in his latest stories. But this is where I think Ballard's development comes in. The non-doing was at first a disadvantage because Ballard had yet to forge the 'oblique narrative style, understated themes, and private symbols' he needed. In the volume called *The Terminal Beach,* he presents a series of stories in which the non-doing of the central character is essential to the structure; it has become the structure. His characters, like the characters of Jules Feiffer's cartoons, stand still and give themselves away. Apart from a certain amount of running through a forest in "The Illuminated Man", there is almost no action in the dozen stories. You could hear a finger stir.

Characteristic Lack of Hope

This is the effect Ballard needs. He has junked the old types of sf narrative and found space for nuance and for inner space. His settings too have moved from the cities and suburbias into desert places, almost as though this gives Ballard more room for his manoeuvres. Not only is the style more oblique than formerly; the proceedings are looked at from a more oblique angle. The examination now is less of failure than of the private glories often enshrined in failure. This is a major progression in which tales like "The Subliminal Man"—where Franklin, the chief character, is torn between doing and non-doing—perhaps mark a transitional stage. The curiously named James B- in "Illuminated Man", Pelham in "The Reptile Enclosure", Charles Gifford in "The Delta at Sunset", Traven in the title story, Holliday in "Deep End", Maitland in "The Gioconda of the Twilight Noon" can all be regarded as men who are failures from a worldly point of view; but the writer convinces us that there is more of interest to them than that; rejected by or rejecting the world, they are free to discover and suffer in unfrequented ways.

Many writers have freed themselves from the sort of tyrannies Ballard has rejected; but Ballard is probably the only one to do it in sf (at least without relapsing into the formless whimsy that mars the writing of Cordwainer Smith). So one is interested to see what the sf world makes of Ballard's writing. The people one might expect to cheer have cheered: Damon Knight in America, Michael Moorcock in Britain, John Baxter in Australia. Kingsley Amis devoted a long and appreciative review to "The Drowned World" in the *Observer*. Fan reaction has naturally been mixed; most of them do not understand and do not want to. But Peter White, a young man who shows promise as a critic, printed an interesting analysis of "Terminal Beach" in *Vector*. Even the fans and editors must be let off lightly; at the least they read and tolerate Ballard and provide a market for his pot-boilers like "The Wind from Nowhere". As Ballard himself has said, 'As with most specialised media (sf) needs a faithful and discriminating audience'. We must all be grateful that the audience is at least faithful.

Moorcock claimed in a fanzine, *Les Spinge,* that William

Burroughs is 'the only sf writer (with the exception of Ballard) worth reading'. Whether Burroughs is an sf writer is open to debate. Perhaps he seems important in a dislocated world because his theme is dislocation. Ballard's techniques are much more conservative than Burroughs's. Indeed, only in a conservative little corner of writing like sf could he ever be suspected of being revolutionary. He relies, as do the rest of us, on the logical effect of a cumulative progression of detail, so that his stories reach a climacteric point arrived at from the qualities inherent in the start of the account; and he attempts to 'write well' as, say, Sir Arthur Quiller-Couch would have defined the term. He enjoys encrusting his sentences with adjectives and rare words until, like the transformations in *The Illuminated Man,* they hand in 'huge pieces of opalescent candy, whose countless reflections glowed like giant chimeras in the cut-glass walls'. I'm not sure that Sir Arthur in his more Platonic moods would have approved of all that.

It may have been this encrustation process that led Amis to speak of Ballard's power as being 'reminiscent of Conrad'. More deeply, Amis sees that "Drowned World's" 'main action is in the deeper reaches of the mind, the main merit [is] the extraordinary imaginative power with which whatever inhabits these reaches is externalised in concrete form'. Conrad's men of action are not Ballard's; he traffics with the sedentary encapsuled men of our proto-space age. He seems to see in us a sickness that corresponds with something in nature. Nature, in Ballard's works, produces some considerable horrors—horrors which the older type of sf writer such as Williamson or Wyndham would have been glad to devise for the sake of a rattling adventure through ruined America or England—but the vital point Ballard seems to make is that man, being sick, conspires with these horrors, so that he does not feel their full effect. Ransome in *The Drought,* like the long line of suffering central figures before him, would never think of complaining of the decay of all earthly hopes—largely because (so one diagnoses from his prototypes in earlier stories) he has never had any earthly hopes.

Similarly, Kerans in "The Drowned World" is unmoved by the chaos about him, even when this takes the nastiest forms. 'He remembered again one ghastly cemetery over which they had moved, its Florentine tombs cracked and sprung, corpses floating out in their unravelling winding sheets in a grim rehearsal of the Day of Judgment.' The mood seems to be one of grim humour; Kerans gives no indication of discomfort.

In the same way, James B- wishes to return to the swamps of Florida in "The Illuminated Man". Here perhaps the identification of hero and author is over strong, for James B- is made to feel too clearly for conviction the pleasure that Ballard evidently gets from his prismatic effects.

This direct identification is given away in a sentence like 'For some reason I suddenly felt less concerned to find a so-called 'scientific' explanation for the strange phenomenon we had seen'. Which brings us to another point that must be considered when examining Ballard's work in relation to science fiction in general, his hostility to science and technology, which is linked with his indifference to providing us with a scientific explanation. In his contempt for 'a so-called 'scientific' explanation', he often neglects even a logical one. This shows up most badly, as one would expect, in the writings nearest to traditional sf in flavour—notably "The Wind from Nowhere": inauspiciously titled, for the wind indeed comes from nowhere and appears to go nowhere, and dies as it rises without reasons given.

Wrecking the Space Stations

It is at this point that Ballard most resembles Ray Bradbury, whose writings he admires, although the ambiguity of his feelings even towards science makes him the more interesting writer. His refuge from life in a scientific age is Bradbury's refuge, a seeking for the childhood world of feeling without thought.

Children are absent from Ballard's stories, sometimes obtrusively (two of the central characters in The Terminal Beach collection have lost wives and young children in car smashes), but many characters have the childlike trait that they will brave danger to return to the time/place where they feel most intensely. (Their boldness is generally rewarded, for few of them come to grief, even when surrounded with the most inauspicious circumstances). Kerans is a notable example of this, and Ransome, who is a pallid copy of Kerans, as "The Drought" is a pallid copy of "The

Drowned World". Kerans loses his identity; in the last lines of the novel, he is reduced to the anonymity of 'a second Adam'; Ransome merely loses his shadow. Maitland, in "The Gioconda of the Twilight Noon", tears out his eyes to attain the child's vision.

Perhaps here we have the reason why Ballard, like Bradbury, has become a figure of controversy. Whether his turning away from the striding he-man of sf is an intellectual or an instinctive act (and one must suppose that by its power in Ballard's work it is the latter, aided by intellectual window-dressing), it does not go down smoothly with the addict reader, who wants big tough figures he can identify with.

The shifting ambiguities of Vermilion Sands and all the other dune-ridden landscapes are too perplexing for them.

Ballard is a sensitive writer, and it is hard sometimes not to feel that his stories are written in a perverse spirit. This, of course, is one way to survive the criticism of the ignorant. After the first spate of ill-judged criticisms, Ballard's stories seemed to contain more wrecked space vehicles lying in the sand, more derelict ones orbiting overhead, more modern gadgets going wrong, more motels and hotels sinking in water or dust, more launching ramps and gantries rusting away. In some of the stories in *The Terminal Beach* you can almost hear him say "That's one for Arthur Clarke!"

One of his most notable bits of machine-wrecking occurs towards the end of "The Drought", where Ballard reveals himself as the literary luddite par excellence. He describes a small pavilion, 'its glass and metal cornices shining in the sunlight. It had been constructed from assorted pieces of chromium and enamelled metal—the radiator grills of cars, reflectors of electric heaters, radio cabinets and so on—fitted together with remarkable ingenuity'.

This is collage again, and another example of the unifying process at work. It is in part Ballard's way of commenting on the meaninglessness of the original gadgets; although they have been perverted from their intended usages, they now make something more worth while on a sane scale of values, 'a Faberge gem'. Analogously, this is what Ballard has done with the materialist values of the average sf tale. He finds most of the usual trappings not worthwhile. His editorial on Inner Space was impatient about 'the narrow imaginative limits imposed by the background of rocket ships and planet-hopping', and he is accustomed to refer to fictional space travels as old hat.

Personally, I disagree with much of this, I cannot see how his constant wrecking of the biosphere is to be reckoned as newer than space travel; nor do I think that symbols such as rockets and robots, which have been created as it were by agreement over several decades, should be lightly scrapped. But one welcomes the fact that Ballard has a point of view; it is the only way to create original work. Many writers are copying, Ballard is doing original work.

It is a pity, then, that in "The Drought" he seems momentarily to be copying himself. It may be that there is a fallacy in his inner space thesis. If, as I have suggested, his manifesto was conceived to justify his work (and we all need justification), it might be that in times of lower creative pressure, he would fall back on it consciously; on such occasions, the fallacy would be more likely to show through. Ballard's characters are forced to inhabit inner space by their failure to communicate, sometimes to communicate even on an elementary level. Several of his protagonists could be saved or could save themselves just by speaking out. A case in point is Maitland in "The Gioconda of the Twilight Noon". We can see no reason why he should not have spoken to the doctor concerning his blindness. Is it convention that keeps him silent, or the conventions of a Ballard story? The same question might be asked of Gifford in "The Delta at Sunset"; the last we see of him, he is refusing to answer his wife, his one contact with reality.

The Dislocated World

This dislocation with the outer world continues even when the outer world is itself dislocated. It reaches maximum severence in passages of "The Drought".

Ransome goes to some trouble to drive into Mount Royal to see Catherine Austen, who is working in a zoo. She pretends he is the vet at first, then says, "I'm glad to see you, doctor. Have you come to help?"

"In a sense," says Ransome. The answer seems to satisfy her, and she tells him how she will look after the animals.

"And then?" he asks.

"What are you trying to say, doctor?" is her reply. After more desultory talk, she asks him, "Why don't you join me, doctor? We'll teach the lions to hunt in packs."

Ransome's answer is to pick up his valise and walk away. The fashion today is for oblique and ambiguous conversation; Pinter has many imitators, and one or two of them might be more interesting in science fiction than the Hemingway imitators. Ballard is as fascinated by futility as Pinter or N. F. Simpson; but this sample of conversation, not untypical of many others, reveals him failing to make a point, perhaps because he is caught juggling different conventions—the situation on the surface is too like a scene from *Day of the Triffids,* with good old Bill driving into the ruined town to do a bit of shopping, for us willingly to accept anything like metaphysical ambiguity. Ballard is a surprising man; it may be that this is a new direction—it's needed!—towards which he alone is moving, and that *The Drought* represents a transitional point.

He probably regards all of literature as a transitional point, if we may paraphrase one of his own dicta. One direction in which he has moved is deeper into natural landscapes and away from man-made ones. The enveloping cities of "Billenium", "Chronopolis", "The Subliminal Man" (which contains the most brilliant obsolescence-speeding gadgets anyone has dreamed up) and a dozen more stories, are left behind.

One may regret this. At times, subtopia seemed almost like a patent Ballard invention. With his fondness for collages, Ballard should occupy a fallow period by mounting a metropolis novel from shuffled sections of his city stories. It might make his most striking novel yet.

Whichever way he is going, Ballard is still careful to maintain his books within a science fiction framework, even when this hardly seems necessary. The explanation of the drought in *The Drought,* which appears in Chapter 6, is a traditional one, served in the traditional way, isolated so that an uninterested reader can skip that bit, a shuffling of the customary phrases, 'world-wide attempts at cloud-seeding', 'off-shore waters of the world's oceans', 'thin but resiliant mono-molecular film from a complex of saturated long-chain polymers . . .' anyone who has composed any catastrophe story has dealt in this knowledgeable and inoffensive journalistic language. Ballard does the job as efficiently as anyone —better, indeed, than some, for the immediate follow-up of this last quote about the long-chain polymers is a mention of 'vast quantities of industrial wastes discharged into the ocean basins', which thus with a nudge of guilt (over-consumption and biosphere pollution) takes our attention away from any doubt about the science.

Despite his care to keep within the science fiction framework, Ballard is often careless with his facts. Or perhaps it is more accurate to say that he is rather lordly about his material, just as he is about his readers. At the beginning of "The Drowned World", the identity of the submerged city is left vague: 'Had it once been Berlin, Paris, or London? Kerans asked himself'. Ballard seems to put his own thought into Kerans' head when he says, a few pages later, 'despite the potent magic of the lagoon worlds and the drowned cities, he had never felt any interest in their contents, and never bothered to identify in which of the cities he was stationed'. But you'd think someone would know; the navigator, perhaps.

Later, the city turns out to be London, and Leicester Square is drained of water. Here it is the brute facts of hydrodynamics which are dealt with in a lordly way. It is hard to see how a dam of ships could keep the water out, even when we are told that the lagoon was sealed off by 'fungi growing in the swamp mud outside (which) consolidated the entire mass'.

These inaccuracies are not too troublesome in themselves; but Ballard's attitude to inconsistency is less comfortable. I find them easy to forgive when, to hark back to the last example, we are offered as a result of the draining of Leicester Square, such amusing novelties as the bats 'darting from one dripping eave to another', and the scow which 'ran aground on the sidewalk, pushed off again and then stuck finally on a traffic island'. This is how I like my science fiction, with the world topsy-turvy, and something unlikely on every page following from the original premise.

Jim Ballard, in private conversation, enjoys giving the impression that science fiction has little to offer him and that it is a form of cheating, of 'unearned experience'. I have argued that on the contrary it is often a record of psychic experience. Ballard's writing itself seems to support this proposition, even if Ballard won't. He uses sf to a fresh end, but it is hard to see what other field of writing would suit his gift for conjuring up vivid and alien landscapes and describing strange and disconnected states of mind.

His witty and nervous worlds, littered with twitching nerves and crashed space stations, carry their own conviction that will eventually win him popular support. For his characters, the worst blow is always over, they are past their nemesis and consequently free. One can only hope that for Ballard too the worst misunderstanding is over, so that he will be free to create in a more intelligent atmosphere. Despite some shortcomings, his stories represent one of the few stimulating forces in contemporary sf.

SAMUEL R. DELANY

ABOUT
FIVE THOUSAND
ONE HUNDRED
AND
SEVENTY FIVE WORDS

Most of the following ideas are not new. But since I lack the critical apparatus to cite *all* my sources, I will not cite any—beyond acknowledging the debt all such semantic analysis must pay to Ludwig Wittgenstein.

Every generation some critic states the frighteningly obvious in the *style/content* conflict. Most readers are bewildered by it. Most commercial writers (not to say, editors) first become uncomfortable, then blustery; finally, they put the whole business out of their heads and go back to what they were doing all along. And it remains for someone in another generation to repeat:

Put in opposition to "style," there is no such thing as "content."

Now, speculative-fiction is still basically a field of commercial writing. Isn't it obvious that what makes a given story sf *is* its speculative content? As well, for the last three years there has been much argument about Old Wave and New Wave sf. The argument has occasionally been fruitful, at times vicious, more often just silly. But the critical vocabulary at both ends of the beach includes ". . . old style . . . new style . . . old content . . . new content . . ." The questions raised are always: "Is the content meaningful?" and "Is the style compatible with it?"

This paper expands upon the discussion of "Speculative Fiction" given at the MLA Seminar on Science Fiction by Mr. Delany December 27, 1968. It has been reprinted in *Science Fiction Review*, 33 (October 1969), edited by Dick Geis, and in *The Disappearing Future* (London, Panther Books, 1970), edited by George Hay. Reprinted by permission of the author.

Again, I have to say, "content" does not exist. The two new questions that arise then are: One) How is this possible, and Two) What is gained by atomizing content into its stylistic elements?

The words *content, meaning,* and *information* are all metaphors for an abstract quality of a word or group of words. The one I would like to concentrate on is: *inform*ation.

Is content real?

Another way to ask this question is: Is there such a thing as verbal information apart from the words used to inform?

The entire semantics of criticism is set up to imply there is. Information is carried by/with/in words. People are carried by/with/in cars. It should be as easy to separate the information from the word as it is to open the door of a Ford Mustang: *Content* means something that *is contained.*

But let us go back to *information,* and by a rather devious route. Follow me:

red

As the above letters sit alone on the paper, the reader has no way to know what they mean. Do they indicate political tendencies or the sound made once you pass the *b* in *bread?* The word generates no significant information until it is put in *formal relation* with something else. This formal relation can be with a real object ("Red" written on the label of a sealed tin of paint) or with other words (The breeze through the car window was refreshing. Whoops, red! He hit the brake).[1]

The idea of *meaning, information* or *content* as something contained by words is a misleading visualization. Here is a more apt one:

Consider meaning to be a thread that connects a sound or configuration of letters called a "word" with a given object or group of objects. To know the meaning of a word is to be able to follow this thread from the sound to the proper set of objects, emotions, or situations—more accurately, to the images of these objects/emotions/situations in your mind. Put more pompously, meanings (*content* or *information*) are the *formal relations* between sounds and images of the objective world.[2]

Any clever geometry student, from this point, can construct

a proof for the etymological tautology, "All information is formal," as well as its corollary, "It is impossible to vary the form without varying the information." I will not try and reproduce it in detail. I would like to say in place of it, however, that "content" can be a useful word; but it becomes invalid when it is held up to oppose style. Content is the illusion myriad stylistic factors create when viewed at a certain distance.

When I say it is impossible to vary the form without varying the information, I do not mean any *formal change* (e.g. the shuffling of a few words in a novel) must completely obviate the entire informational experience of a given work. Some formal changes are minimal; their effect on a particular collection of words may be unimportant simply because it is undetectable. But I am trying to leave open the possibility that the change of a single word in a novel may be all important.

"Tell me, Martha, *did* you really kill him?"
"Yes."

But in the paperback edition, the second line of type was accidentally dropped. Why should this deletion of a single word hurt the reader's enjoyment of the remaining 44,999 words of the novel . . .

In a book of mine I recall the key sentence in the opening exposition described the lines of communication between two cities as ". . . now lost for good." A printer's error rendered the line ". . . not lost for good," and practically destroyed the rest of the story.

But the simplicity of my examples sabotages my point more than it supports it. Here is another more relevant:

I put some things on the desk.
I put some books on the desk.
I put three books on the desk.
I put Hacker's *The Terrible Children,* Ebbe Borregaard's *Collected Poems,* and Wakoski's *Inside the Blood Factory* on the desk.

The variations here are closer to the type people arguing for the chimera of content call meaningless. The information generated by each sentence is clearly different. But what we know about what was put on the desk is only the most obvious difference. Let's assume these are the opening sentences of four different stories. Four tones of voice are generated by the varying specificity. The tone will be heard—if not consciously noted—by whoever reads. And the different tones give different information about the personality of the speaker as well as his state of mind. That is to say, the *I* generated in each sentence is different.

As a writer utilizes this information about the individual speaker, his story seems more dense, more real. And he is a better artist than the writer who dismisses the variations in these sentences as minimal. This is what makes Heinlein a better writer than James Blish.

But we have not exhausted the differences in the information in these sentences when we have explored the differences in the "I . . ." As we know something about the personality of the various speakers, and something about what the speaker is placing down, ranges of possibility are opened up about the desk itself—four different ranges. This information is much harder to specify, because many other factors will influence it: does the desk belong to the speaker, or someone about whom the speaker feels strongly, or has he only seen the desk for the first time moments before laying the books on it? Indeed, there is no way to say that any subsequent description of the desk is wrong because it contradicts specific information generated by those opening sentences. But once those other factors have been cleared up, one description may certainly seem "righter" than another, because it is reinforced by that admittedly-vague information, different for each of the examples, that has been generated. And the ability to utilize effectively this refinement in generated information is what makes Sturgeon a better writer than Heinlein.

In each of those sentences the only apparent *formal* variation is the specificity of what *I* put on *the desk*. But by this change, the *I* and *the desk* change as well. The illusion of reality, the sense of veracity in all fiction, is controlled by the author's sensitivity to these distinctions. A story is not a replacement of one set of words by another—plot synopsis, detailed recounting, or analysis. The story is what happens in the reader's mind as his eyes move from the first word to the second, the second to the third, and so on to the end of the tale.

Let's look more closely at what happens on this visual journey. How, for example, does the work of reading a narrative differ from watching a film? In a film the illusion of reality comes from a series of pictures each slightly different. The difference represents a fixed chronological relation which the eye and the mind together render as motion.

Words in a narrative generate pictures. But rather than a fixed chronological relation, they sit in numerous semantic relations. The process as we move our eyes from word to word is corrective and revisionary rather than progressive. Each new word revises the complex picture we had a moment before.

Around the meaning of any word is a certain margin in which to correct the image of the object we arrive at (in grammatical terms, to modify).

I say:

dog

and an image jumps in your mind (as it did with "red"), but because I have not put it in a formal relation with anything else, you have no way to know whether the specific image in your mind has anything to do with what I want to communicate. Hence that leeway. I can correct it:

Collie dog, and you will agree. I can correct it into *a big dog* or *a shaggy dog,* and you will still concur. But a *Chevrolet dog?* An *oxymoronic dog?* A *turgidly cardiac dog?* For the purposes of ordinary speech, or naturalistic fiction, these corrections are outside acceptable boundaries: they distort some essential quality in all the various objects that we have attached to the sound "dog." On the other hand, there is something to be enjoyed in the distortions, a freshness that may be quite entertaining, even though they lack the inevitability of our big, shaggy collie.

A sixty thousand word novel is one picture corrected fifty-nine thousand, nine hundred and ninety-nine times. The total experience must have the same feeling of freshness as this turgidly cardiac creature as well as the inevitability of Big and Shaggy here.

Now let's atomize the correction process itself. A story begins:

The

What is the image thrown on your mind? Whatever it is, it is going to be changed many, many times before the tale is over. My own, un-modified *The* is a greyish ellipsoid about four feet high that balances on the floor perhaps a yard away. Yours is no doubt different. But it is there, has a specific size, shape, color, and bears a particular relation to you. My *a*, for example, differs from my *the* in that it is about the same shape and color—a bit paler, perhaps—but is either much farther away, or much smaller and nearer, In either case, I am going to be either much less, or much more, interested in it than I am in *the*. Now we come to the second word in the story and the first correction:

The red

My four-foot ellipsoid just changed color. It is still about the same distance away. It has become more interesting. In fact, even at this point I feel vaguely that the increased interest may be outside the leeway I allow for *The*. I feel a strain here that would be absent if the first two words had been *A red* . . . My eye goes on to the third word while my mind prepares for the second correction:

The red sun

My original *The* has now been replaced by a luminous disk. The color has lightened considerably. The disk is above me. An indistinct landscape has formed about me. And I am even more aware, now that the object has been placed at such a distance, of the tension between my own interest level in *red sun* and the ordinary attention I accord a *the*: for the intensity of interest is all that is left with me of the original image.

Less clearly, in terms of future corrections, is a feeling that in this landscape, it is either dawn, sunset, or if it is not another time, smog of some sort must be hazing the air (. . . *red* sun . . .); but I hold all for the next correction:

The red sun is

A sudden sense of intimacy. I am being asked to pay even greater attention (in a way that *was* would not demand, as it is the form of the traditional historical narrative). But *is* . . .? There is a speaker here! That focus in attention I felt between the first two words is not my attention, but the attention of the speaker. It resolves into a tone of voice: "The *red* sun is . . ." And I listen to this voice, in the midst of this still vague landscape, registering his concern for the red sun.   Between *the* and *red* information was generated that between *sun* and *is* resolved into a meaningful correction in my vision.   This is my first aesthetic pleasure from the tale—a small one, as we have only progressed four words into the story.   Nevertheless, it becomes one drop in the total enjoyment to come from the telling.   Watching and listening to my speaker, I proceed to the next corrections:

The red sun is high,

Noon and slightly overcast: this is merely a confirmation of something previously suspected, nowhere near as major a correction as the one before.   It adds a slight sense of warmth to the landscape, and the light has been fixed at a specific point. I attempt to visualize the landscape more clearly, but no object, including the speaker, has been cleared enough to resolve. The comma tells me that a thought group is complete. In the pause it occurs to me that the redness of the sun may not be a clue to smog at all, but merely the speaker falling into literary-ism; or, at best, the redness is a projection of his consciousness, which as yet I don't understand.   And for a moment I notice that from where I'm standing the sun indeed appears its customary, blind-white gold. Next correction:

The red sun is high, the

In this strange landscape (lit by its somewhat untrustworthily described sun) the speaker has turned his attention to another grey, four-foot ellipsoid, equidistant from himself and me. Again, it is too indistinct to take highlighting. But there have been two corrections with not much tension, and the reality of the speaker himself is beginning to slip. What will this become?

The red sun is high, the blue

The ellipsoid has changed hue. But the repetition in the semantic form of the description momentarily threatens to dissolve all reality, landscape, speaker, and sun, into a mannered listing of bucolica. The whole scene dims. And the final correction?

The red sun is high, the blue low.

Look! We are worlds and worlds away. The first sun is huge; and how accurate the description of its color turns out to have been. The repetition that predicted mannerism now fixes both big and little sun to the sky. The landscape crawls with long red shadows and stubby blue ones, joined by purple triangles. Look at the speaker himself! Can you see him? You have seen his doubled shadow . . .

Though it ordinarily takes only a quarter of a second and is largely unconscious, this is the process.

When the corrections as we move from word to word produce a muddy picture, when unclear bits of information do not resolve to even greater clarity as we progress, we call the writer a poor stylist. As the story goes on, and the pictures become more complicated as they develop through time, if even greater anomalies appear as we continue correcting, we say he can't plot. But it is the same quality error committed on a grosser level, even though a reader must be a third or three-quarters of the way through the book to spot one, while the first may glare out from the opening sentence.

In any commercial field of writing, like sf, the argument of writers and editors who feel *content* can be opposed to *style* runs, at its most articulate:

"Basically we are writing adventure fiction. We are writing it very fast. We do not have time to be concerned about any but the grosser errors. More important, you are talking about subtleties too refined for the vast majority of our readers who are basically neither literary nor sophisticated."

The internal contradictions here could make a book. Let me outline two.

The basis of any adventure novel, sf or otherwise, what gives it its entertainment value—escape value if you will—what sets it apart from the psychological novel, what names it an adventure, is the intensity with which the real actions of the story impinge on the protagonist's consciousness. The simplest way to generate that sense of adventure is to increase the intensity with which the real actions impinge on the reader's. And fictional intensity is almost entirely the province of those refinements of which I have been speaking.

The story of an infant's first toddle across the kitchen floor will be an adventure if the writer can generate the infantile wonder at new muscle, new efforts, obstacle, and detours. I would like to read such a story.

We have all read, many too many times, the heroic attempts of John Smith to save the lives of seven orphans in the face of fire, flood, and avalanche.

I am sure it was an adventure for Smith.

For the reader it was dull as dull could be.

The Doors of His Face, the Lamps of His Mouth by Roger Zelazny has been described as ". . . all speed and adventure . . ." by Theodore Sturgeon, and indeed it is one of the most exciting adventure tales sf has produced. Let me change one word in every grammatical unit of every sentence, replacing it with a word that ". . . means more or less the same thing . . . ," and I can diminish the excitement by half and expunge every trace of wit. Let me change one word and *add* one word, and I can make it so dull as to be practically unreadable. Yet a paragraph by paragraph synopsis of the "content" will be the same.

An experience I find painful (though it happens with increasing frequency) occurs when I must listen to a literate person who has just become enchanted by some hacked-out space-boiler begin to rhapsodise about the way the blunt, imprecise, leaden language reflects the hairy-chested hero's alienation from reality. He usually goes on to explain how the ". . . sf content . . ." itself reflects our whole society's divorce from the real. The experience is painful because he is right as far as he goes. Badly-written adventure fiction is our true anti-literature. Its protagonists are our real anti-heroes. They move through un-real worlds amidst all sorts of noise and manage to perceive nothing meaningful or meaningfully.

Author's intention or no, that is what badly written sf *is* about. But anyone who reads or writes sf seriously knows that its particular excellence is in another area altogether: in all the *brouhaha* clinging about these unreal worlds, chords are sounded in total sympathy with the real.

". . . You are talking about subtleties too refined for the vast majority of our readers who are basically neither literary nor sophisticated."

This part of the argument always throws me back to an incident from the summer I taught a remedial English class at my Neighborhood Community Center. The voluntary nature automatically restricted enrollment to people who wanted to learn; still, I had sixteen and seventeen-year-olds who had never had any formal education in either Spanish or English continually joining my lessons. Regardless, after a student had been in the class six months, I would throw him a full five hundred and fifty page novel to read: Demetry Merejakowsky's *The Romance of Leonardo da Vinci*. The book is full of Renaissance history, as well as sword play, magic, and dissertations on art and science. It is an extremely literary novel with several levels of interpretation. It was a favorite of Sigmund Freud and inspired him to write his own *Leonardo da Vinci: A Study in Psychosexuality*. My students loved it, and with it, lost a good deal of their fear of Literature and Long Books.

Shortly before I had to leave the class, *Leonardo* appeared in paperback, translated by Hubert Tench. Till then it had only been available in a Modern Library edition translated by Bernard Gilbert Gurney. To save my latest two students a trip to the Barnes and Noble basement, as well as a dollar fifty, I suggested they buy the paperback. Two days later one had struggled through forty pages and the other had given up after ten. Both thought the book dull, had no idea what it was about, and begged me for something shorter and more exciting.

Bewildered, I bought a copy of the Tench translation myself

that afternoon. I do not have either book at hand as I write, so I'm sure this will prove an exaggeration. But I do recall, however, one description of a little house in Florence:

Gurney: "Grey smoke rose and curled from the slate chimney."

Tench: "Billows of smoke, grey and gloomy, elevated and contorted up from the slates of the chimney."

By the same process that differentiated the four examples of putting books on a desk, these two sentences do not refer to the same smoke, chimney, house, time of day; nor do any of the other houses within sight remain the same; nor do any possible inhabitants. One sentence has nine words, the other fifteen. But atomize both as a series of corrected images and you will find the mental energy expended on the latter is greater by a factor of six or seven! And over seven-eighths of it leaves that uncomfortable feeling of loose-endedness, unutilized and unresolved. Sadly, it is the less skilled, less sophisticated reader who is most injured by bad writing. Bad prose requires more of your mental energy to correct your image from word to word, and the corrections themselves are less rewarding. That is what makes it bad. The sophisticated, literary reader may give the words the benefit of the doubt and question whether a seeming clumsiness is more fruitfully interpreted as an intentional ambiguity.

For what it is worth, when I write I often try to say several things at the same time—from a regard for economy that sits contiguous with any concern for skillful expression. I have certainly failed to say many of the things I intended. But ambiguity marks the failure, not the intent.

But how does all this relate to those particular series of corrected images we label *sf*? To answer that, we must first look at what distinguishes these particular word series from other word series that get labeled *naturalistic fiction, reportage, fantasy*.

A distinct level of subjunctivity informs all the words in an sf story at a level that is different from that which informs naturalistic fiction, fantasy, or reportage.

Subjunctivity is the tension on the thread of meaning that runs between word and object. Suppose a series of words is presented to us as a piece of reportage. A blanket indicative tension informs the whole series: *this happened.* That is the particular level of subjunctivity at which journalism takes place. Any word, even the metaphorical ones, must go straight back to a real object, or a real thought on the part of the reporter.

The subjunctivity level for a series of words labeled naturalistic fiction is defined by: *could have happened.* Note that the level of subjunctivity makes certain dictates and allows certain freedoms as to what word can follow another. Consider this word series: "For one second, as she stood alone on the desert, her world shattered and she watched the fragments bury themselves in the dunes." This is practically meaningless at the subjunctive level of reportage. But it might be a perfectly adequate, if not brilliant, word series for a piece of naturalistic fiction.

Fantasy takes the subjunctivity of naturalistic fiction and throws it in reverse. At the appearance of elves, witches, or magic in a non-metaphorical position, or at some correction of image too bizarre to be explained by other than the super-natural, the level of subjunctivity becomes: *could not have happened.* And immediately it informs *all* the words in the series. No matter how naturalistic the setting, once the witch has taken off on her broomstick, the most realistic of trees, cats, night clouds, or the moon behind them become infected with this reverse subjunctivity.

But when spaceships, ray guns, or more accurately any correction of images that indicates the future appears in a series of words and marks it as sf, the subjunctivity level is changed once more: These objects, these convocations of objects into situations and events, are blanketly defined by: *have not happened.*

Events that have not happened are very different from the fictional events that *could have happened,* or the fantastic events that *could not have happened.*

Events that have not happened include several sub-categories. These sub-categories define the sub-categories of sf. *Events that have not happened* include those events that *might happen:* these are your technological and sociological predictive tales. Another category includes *events that will not happen:* these are your science-fantasy stories. They include *events that have not happened yet* (Can you hear the implied tone of warning?): there are your cautionary dystopias, *Brave New World* and *1984.* Were

English a language with a more detailed tense system, it would be easier to see that *events that have not happened* include past events as well as future ones. *Events that have not happened* in the past compose that sf specialty, the parallel-world story, whose outstanding example is Phillip K. Dick's *Man in the High Castle.*

The particular subjunctive level of sf expands the freedom of the choice of words that can follow another group of words meaningfully; but it limits the way we employ the corrective process as we move between them.

At the subjunctive level of naturalistic fiction, "The red sun is high, the blue low," is meaningless. In naturalistic fiction our corrections in our images must be made in accordance with what we know of the personally observable—this includes our own observations and observations of others that have been reported to us at the subjunctive level of journalism.

Considered at the subjunctive level of fantasy, "The red sun was high, the blue low," fares a little better. But the corrective process in fantasy is limited, too: when we are given a correction that is not meaningful in terms of the personally observable world, we *must* accept any pseudo-explanation we are given. If there is no pseudo-explanation, it must remain mysterious. As fantasy, one suspects that the red sun is the 'realer' one, but what sorcerer, to what purpose, shunted up that second azure globe, we cannot know and must wait for the rest of the tale.

As we have seen, that sentence makes very good sf. The subjunctive level of sf says that we must make our correction process in accord with what we know of the physically explainable universe. And the physically explainable has a much wider range than the personally observable.[3] The particular verbal freedom of sf, coupled with the corrective process that allows the whole range of the physically explainable universe, can produce the most violent leaps of imagery. For not only does it throw us worlds away, it specifies how we get there.

Let us examine what happens between the following two words:

winged dog

As fiction it is meaningless. As fantasy it is merely a visual correction. At the subjunctive level of sf, however, one must momentarily consider, as one makes that visual correction, an entire track of evolution: whether the dog has forelegs or not. The visual correction must include modification of breast-bone and musculature if the wings are to be functional, as well as a whole slew of other factors from hollow bones to heart-rate; or if we subsequently learn as the series of words goes on that grafting was the cause, there are all the implications (to consider) of a technology capable of such operation. All of this information hovers tacitly about and between those two words in the same manner that the information and *I* and *the desk* hovered around the statements about placing down the books. The best sf writer will utilize this information just as he utilizes the information generated by any verbal juxtapositioning.

I quote Harlan Ellison describing his own reaction to this verbal process:

> . . . Heinlein has always managed to indicate the greater strangeness of a culture with the most casually dropped-in reference: the first time in a novel, I believe it was in *Beyond This Horizon,* that a character came through a door that . . . dilated. And no discussion. Just: 'The door dilated.' I read across it, and was two lines down before I realized what the image had been, what the words had called forth. A *dilating* door. It didn't open, it *irised!* Dear God, now I knew I was in a future world . . .

"The door dilated," is meaningless as fiction, and practically meaningless as fantasy. As sf—as an event that hasn't happened, yet still must be interpreted in terms of the physically explainable —it is quite as wondrous as Ellison feels it.

As well, the luminosity of Heinlein's particular vision was supported by all sorts of other information, stated and unstated, generated by his words.

Through this discussion, I have tried to keep away from what motivates the construction of these violent nets of wonder called speculative fiction. The more basic the discussion, the greater is our obligation to stay with the reader in *front* of the page. But at the mention of the author's 'vision' the subject is already broached. The vision (sense of wonder, if you will) that sf tries for seems to me very close to the vision of poetry, particularly poetry as it concerned the nineteenth century Symbolists. No matter how

disciplined its creation, to move into an 'unreal' world demands a
brush with mysticism.

Virtually all the classics of speculative fiction are mystical.
In Isaac Asimov's *Foundation* trilogy, one man, dead on page
thirty-seven, achieves nothing less than the redemption of mankind from twenty-nine thousand years of suffering simply by his
heightened consciousness of the human condition. (Read 'consciousness of the human condition' for 'science of psycho-history.')

In Robert Heinlein's *Stranger in a Strange Land* the appearance of God incarnate creates a world of love and cannibalism.

Clarke's *Childhood's End* and Sturgeon's *More Than Human*
detail vastly differing processes by which man becomes more than
man.

Alfred Bester's *The Stars My Destination* (or *Tiger, Tiger,* its
original title) is considered by many readers and writers, both in
and outside the field, to be the greatest single sf novel. I would
like to give it a moment's detailed attention. In this book, man,
both intensely human yet more than human, becomes, through
greater acceptance of his humanity, something even more. It
chronicles a social education, but within a society which, from our
point of view, has gone mad. In the climactic scene, the protagonist, burning in the ruins of a collapsing cathedral, has his senses
confused by synesthesia. Terrified, he begins to oscillate insanely
in time and space. Through this experience, with the help of his
worst enemy transformed by time into his savior, he saves himself
and attains a state of innocence and rebirth.

This is the stuff of mysticism.

It is also a very powerful dramatization of Rimbaud's theory
of the systematic derangement of the senses to achieve a higher
awareness. And the Rimbaud reference is as conscious as the
book's earlier references to Joyce, Blake, and Swift.

I would like to see the relation between the Symbolists and
modern American speculative fiction explored more thoroughly.
The French Symbolists' particular problems of vision were never
the focus American poetry. But they have been explored repeatedly not only by writers like Bester and Sturgeon, but also newer
writers like Roger Zelazny, who bring both erudition and word
magic to strange creations generated from the tension between
suicide and immortality.

But to recapitulate: whatever the inspiration or vision,

whether it arrives in a flash or has been meticulously worked out over years, the only way a writer can present it is by what he can make happen in the reader's mind between one word and another, by the way he can maneuver the existing tensions between words and objects.

I have read many descriptions of 'mystical experiences,' not a few in sf stories and novels. Very, very few have generated any *feel* of the mystical—which is to say that as the writers went about setting correction after correction, the images were too untrustworthy to call up any personal feelings about such experiences. The Symbolists have a lesson here: the only thing that we will trust enough to let it generate in us any real sense of the mystical is a resonant aesthetic form.

The sense of mystical horror, for example, in Thomas M. Disch's extraordinary novella, *The Asian Shore,* does not come from its study of a particularly insidious type of racism, incisive though the study is; nor does it come from the final incidents set frustratingly between the supernatural and the insane. It generates rather in the formal parallels between the protagonist's concepts of Byzantine architecture and the obvious architecture of his own personality.

Aesthetic form . . . I am going to leave this discussion at this undefined term. For many people it borders on the meaningless. I hope there is enough tension between the words to proliferate with what has gone before. To summarize, however: any serious discussion of speculative fiction must first get away from the distracting concept of sf content and examine precisely what sort of word-beast sits before us. We must explore both the level of subjunctivity at which speculative fiction takes place and the particular intensity and range of images this level affords. Readers must do this if they want to fully understand what has already been written. Writers must do this if the field is to mature to the potential so frequently cited for it.

NOTES

¹I am purposely not using the word 'symbol' in this discussion. The vocabulary that must accompany it generates too much confusion.

²Words also have 'phonic presence' as well as meaning. And certainly all writers must work with sound to vary the rhythm of a phrase or sentence, as well as to control the meaning. But this discussion is going to veer close enough to poetry. To consider the musical, as well as the ritual, value of language in sf would make poetry and prose indistinguishable. That is absolutely not my intention.

³I throw out this notion for its worth as intellectual play. It is not too difficult to see that as *events that have not happened* include the sub-group of *events that have not happened in the past,* they include the sub-sub group of *events that could have happened* with an implied *but didn't.* That is to say, the level of subjunctivity of sf includes the level of subjunctivity of naturalistic fiction.

As well, the personally observable world is a sub-category of the physically explainable universe. That is, the laws of the first can all be explained in terms of the laws of the second, while the situation is not necessarily reversible. So much for the two levels of subjunctivity and the limitations on the corrective processes that go with them.

What of the respective freedoms in the choice of word to follow word?

I can think of no series of words that could appear in a piece of naturalistic fiction that could not also appear in the same order in a piece of speculative fiction. I can, however, think of many series of words that, while fine for speculative fiction, would be meaningless as naturalism. Which then is the major and which the sub-category?

Consider: naturalistic fictions are parallel-world stories in which the divergence from the real is too slight for historical verification.

PATRICK J. CALLAHAN

THE
TWO GARDENS
IN
C. S. LEWIS'S
THAT HIDEOUS STRENGTH

Charles Moorman writes of C. S. Lewis's "space trilogy" that "science fiction provides him with a method and a plot, the theology of the Church with a theme." He goes on to write, "the main tenor of Lewis's myth is Christian orthodoxy; his vehicle is science-fiction."[1] Likewise, Claude Kilby refers to *That Hideous Strength* as "the longest of [Lewis's] religious books."[2] Finally, in an attack upon Lewis's writings, Roger Sale writes that Lewis is "the propagandist for Anglo-Oxford and for the Old things it defends—medieval and Renaissance literature, classical education, traditional Christianity. . . ."[3] Sale not only assumes that "the Old things" precious to Lewis are not worth defending, he shares Moorman's and Kilby's over-readiness to pigeonhole Lewis's fiction as "religious," devoted to "orthodox Christianity," or "theological." Such ready generalizations seem to reduce Lewis to the status of an outdated G. K. Chesterton. Worse, they are misleading and unjustified.

Quite how a novel such as *That Hideous Strength,* or the trilogy of which it forms a part, may be considered "theological," much less an apology for church orthodoxy, is difficult to understand. One may grant that Lewis's stress upon human frailty and his recasting of the Biblical Genesis in *Perelandra* derive from his deeply felt Christianity. Yet Lewis's concern in *Out of the Silent Planet* and *Perelandra* is neither religious nor theological, but moral. Lewis is interested in the human response to choices of good and evil. The novels are set in a theocentric cosmos because

147

Lewis was a believer, just as Olaf Stapledon's novels are set in a godless universe because he was not. Yet the focus of Lewis is upon the moral challenge posed to Ransom, upon the moral deterioration of Weston, and upon the monumental temptation offered to the Green Lady. The conflict in *Perelandra* would be little less forceful if divinity or demon had never been specifically mentioned. In the discussion that follows, and focusing on the concluding novel of the trilogy, I propose to explicate Lewis's moral emphasis, and to do so by attention to the symbolism of the two gardens, which, in my view, is central to the novel's investigation of the nature of good and evil.

The third novel of Lewis's trilogy differs markedly from the first two. Lewis himself writes in the preface to *That Hideous Strength* that "it concludes the trilogy . . . but can be read on its own."[4] The great difference between the first two novels and the last is in the shift of scene from the "moral laboratory" of the planets back to the world of everyday experience. Ransom tells Merlin, "the Hideous Strength holds all this Earth in its fist to squeeze as it wishes" (*THS,* 293). *This* earth. One leaves Mars and Venus for a small, sleepy English university town. Thus the trilogy follows an archetypal pattern well established in literature. Just as Shakespeare's characters in *As You Like It, Midsummer Night's Dream,* or *The Tempest,* having become wiser through a visit to a fantasy world, must eventually return to the mundane world from which they have come, Ransom has journeyed to the unfallen worlds of Mars and Venus to achieve a kind of enlightenment, but it is to Earth that he must return, and it is on Earth that his greatest battle must be fought. *That Hideous Strength* puts the moral insights of the first two novels to the test. They must be applicable to a recognizable world. *That Hideous Strength* becomes at once the "proof of the pudding" for Lewis's insights into good and evil, and a coda that unites and expands all the themes developed before.

The shift of setting with the third novel is accompanied by a shift of mode from the romantic, with its allegorical strain, to the ironic, with its satiric one. While in the first two novels, Lewis sought to involve the reader, now he tries to disengage him. As does Jonathan Swift in *Gulliver's Travels,* Lewis inserts a series of grim jokes to prevent our becoming too sympathetically engaged, to keep us at a certain critical distance. For example, the diabolic institute is "N.I.C.E.," the truncated head of a criminal is literally the "head" of that institute, and some of the symbolic names have a comic ring: "Fairy Hardcastle" for a lesbian, or "Mr. Fisher-King" for Elwin Ransom. Lewis wishes his reader to treat the surface of the story with a certain detachment, so that he may perceive overtones which make the fictional plot a means of attacking real social perils.

Although Lewis has as acute a Christian consciousness as had Swift, he, like Swift, refrains from preaching. He renders his morality into the image, symbol, and dramatic situation of art. Satire has often been rendered by its masters as a conflict between two societies, one real and one fictional: Candide's France versus Eldorado, Gulliver's England versus Brobdingnag. In *That Hideous Strength,* Lewis opposes two fictional societies, the remnant of Arthurian Logres, focus of traditional, spiritual Britain, versus the National Institute of Co-ordinated Experiments, focus of scientistic, materialistic Britain. Two gardens represent these two societies, and form the symbolic center of the novel. On the one hand, the fertile garden of St. Anne's, where reside the company of Logres, draws its name from the patroness of mothers and motherhood. On the other, Belbury, the location of N.I.C.E. headquarters, has the unmistakable resonance of funeral bells and burial to it. Its name may have been suggested by Belbury, site of Arthur's great battle against the invading Saxons.[5]

St. Anne's is a garden *par excellence.* Lewis's rich description of it gives a sense of size, and of variety subjugated to order. As Jane Studdock arrives at St. Anne's for the first time, she describes the garden as she sees it:

> The woman led her along a brick path beside a wall on which fruit trees were growing, and then to the left along a mossy path with gooseberry bushes on each side. Then came a little lawn with a see-saw in the middle of it, and beyond that a greenhouse. Here they found themselves in the sort of hamlet that sometimes occurs in the purlieus of a large garden—walking in fact down a little street which had a barn and a stable on one side and, on the other, a second greenhouse, and a potting shed and a pigstye— inhabited, as the grunts and not wholly agreeable smell informed her. After that were narrow paths across a vegetable garden that

seemed to be on a fairly steep hillside, and then, rose bushes, all
stiff and prickly in their winter garb (*THS*, 61).

The garden contains fauna as well as flora, plants of beauty as well
as plants of utility, and its expansive layout with "little streets"
suggests a sort of floral city.

The garden at St. Anne's is in the tradition of the symbolic garden, emblem of harmony between man and nature, emblem of order within variety, subject to the principle of individual
development within a harmonious whole. It was thus that Spenser
used the Garden of Adonis in the *Faerie Queene,* or Shakespeare
used the garden in *Richard II,* or Milton used Eden in *Paradise
Lost.* Jane's further reflections on St. Anne's make Lewis's symbolic intentions unmistakable:

> This [St. Anne's] reminded Jane of something. It was a very
> large garden. It was like—like—yes, now she had it: it
> was like the garden in *Peter Rabbit.* Or was it like the garden in
> *Romance of the Rose?* No, not in the least like really. Or like
> Klingsor's garden? Or the garden in *Alice?* Or like the garden on
> top of some Mesopotamian Ziggurat which had probably given
> rise to the whole legend of Paradise? Or simply like all walled
> gardens? Freud said we liked gardens because they were symbols
> of the female body (*THS,* 61-62).

In this passage, St. Anne, patroness of mothers, and the garden,
symbolic of the female body, are brought together. In the traditional garden as in woman, the pattern of nature and the pattern
of the ordering mind become one.

The company of the Fisher-King reside in a large house located at the very heart of the garden. As Jane first discovers the
house, "they suddenly emerged from between plantations of
rhododendron and laurel, and found themselves at a small side
door, flanked by a water butt, in the long wall of a large house"
(*THS*, 62). Within, the company of Logres, a group dedicated to
the goal of revivifying England, are themselves a garden. The
group contains characters such as Camilla Denniston, Ivy Maggs,
and the strong-willed Miss Ironwood. Mrs. Dimble and her husband are passionate gardeners, especially fond of roses, and even
Ransom has taken the name Fisher-King, after the fertility king of

the old vegetation-cycle religions. Those characters outside of the immediate company but acting in sympathy with it also take on the garden imagery. Professor Hingest, for instance, the one scientist with enough courage to repudiate N.I.C.E., is a gardener who has "judged flower shows" (*THS*, 70).

Fisher-King, who presides over St. Anne's, is as different from the Ransom of the trilogy's first two novels as, say, Henry V from Prince Hal. He is what Ransom has become, and his description evokes the sun. When Jane Studdock first meets him, she remarks his golden hair, and the way it seems to attract the light in the room: "The light of the fire with its weak reflection, and the light of the sun with its stronger reflections, contended on the ceiling. But all the light in the room seemed to run towards the gold hair and the gold beard of the wounded man" (*THS*, 142). The Fisher-King is seated against a backdrop of blue: "she had an impression of massed hangings of blue . . . behind the man, so the effect was that of a throne room" (*THS*, 142), or, one might add, of a golden sun against a blue sky. The Fisher-King is the sun to the human garden of his company, perhaps because he has consecrated himself to life and its fulfillment just as completely as his enemies have devoted themselves to life's annihilation.

Acting in antagonism to St. Anne's is Belbury, N.I.C.E. head-quarters. It is many things, including a scientific institute, a "blood transfusion center," and a ruining estate, but it is also, very clearly, a garden. It is described by Mark Studdock:

> After lunch he explored the grounds. But they were not the sort of grounds that anyone could walk in for pleasure. The Edwardian millionaire who had built Belbury had enclosed about twenty acres with a low brick wall surmounted by an iron railing, and laid it all out in what his contractor called Ornamental Pleasure Grounds. There were trees dotted about and winding paths covered so thickly with round white pebbles you could hardly walk on them. There were immense flower beds, some oblong, some lozenge-shaped, and some crescents. There were plantations —slabs would almost be a better word—of that kind of laurel which looks as if it were made of cleverly painted and varnished metal. Massive summer seats of bright green stood at regular intervals along the paths. The whole effect was that of a municipal cemetery (*THS*, 101).

The Belbury garden contains growing flora, but Lewis's choice of diction strangles any brightening effect the flora might have by emphasizing non-vegetative elements: "low brick wall . . . iron railing . . . round white pebbles . . . slabs . . . varnished metal . . . massive summer seats." Belbury is, as its name connotes, a cemetery.6

Like St. Anne's, this garden has a building at its heart, but it contrasts sharply with the rustic manor of Fisher-King. Belbury was originally a gauche Edwardian manor built in imitation of Versailles, but "at the sides, it seemed to have sprouted into a widespread outgrowth of newer cement buildings, housing the Blood Transfusion Office" (THS, 51). The words "sprouted" and "outgrowth" may suggest a cancerous growth. Belbury is, at its best, grotesque.

If the characters at St. Anne's bear the names of flowers, the characters of Belbury bear names which suggest forces deadly to gardens. Mr. Wither is deputy director of Belbury, and Dr. Frost is his right-hand man. Department heads include Mr. Steele and Mr. Stone. The sinister Divine of Out of the Silent Planet returns under the alias of Lord Feverstone, a name which suggests disease. The religious director of Belbury, whose doctrine of hatred well suits his name, is Rev. Straik (strike). Fairy Hardcastle, leader of the secret police at Belbury, suggests her sadism and lesbianism by her name. If St. Anne's symbolizes the life-giving female body, Fairy Hardcastle, as the only woman at Belbury, suggests the perversion and sterility of N.I.C.E.

Animal life at Belbury is tormented in the name of scientific experiment. Mark Studdock, walking about the grounds, hears "a loud melancholy howl . . . , all manner of trumpetings, bayings, screams, laughter even, which shuddered and protested for a moment and then died away into mutterings and whines" (THS, 102). The beasts protest against Belbury's "immense program of vivisection" which evokes the Nazi "medical experiments," senseless orgies of cruelty. Strong contrast indeed with St. Anne's beloved pet bear, its well-fed pigs, and contented horses!

Belbury's antagonism to all life soon becomes apparent. Its "rubberoid floors and distempered walls," its mixture of chemical smells, all suggest a cross between a hospital and a mortuary. Belbury's leaders advocate the extermination of all living things, and announce that as an important objective. As Feverstone explains, "the . . . problem is our rivals on this planet. I don't only mean insects and bacteria. There's far too much life of every kind about, animal and vegetable. We haven't really cleared the place yet" (*THS*, 42). Professor Filostrato, head of the scientific staff at Belbury and an obese eunuch, advocates the extermination of all life, floral and faunal, and the replacement of all forests with "civilized trees . . . light, made of aluminum" (*THS*, 72).

Belbury's antagonism toward living things tends to expand the antagonism of the two gardens into a battle between gardeners of life and gardeners of death. Evil, as Lewis's presentation of the "un-man" Weston made clear in *Perelandra*, is a kind of destructive cancer within the living universe which turns it to self-destruction and death. The evil of Belbury tends toward death, and indeed, Filostrato makes clear that "the conquest of organic life," as he calls it, is the reign of death, and is the true goal of Belbury. As Filostrato explains it, "we do not want the world any longer furred over with organic life, like what you call the blue mold—all sprouting and budding and breeding and decaying." The moon represents Filostrato's ideal of a world: "Thousands of miles of polished rock with not one blade of grass, not one fibre of lichen, not one grain of dust. Not even air. Have you thought what it could be like, my friend, if you could walk on that land?" (*THS*, 173).

Should there be any question as to the effect of a philosophy such as Feverstone's or Filostrato's when actually applied to a society, Lewis proceeds to remove all doubt. Belbury delights in the destruction or derangement of living processes for the sheer sake of it. The Dimbles discover "a lorry on the drive . . . unloading a small army of what looked like criminals, with picks and spades" (*THS*, 74). They proceed to dig up and destroy the Dimbles' rose garden, and to saw down their trees. No reason for such destruction is ever given, but a clue may be found in Filostrato's buoyant delight at commanding the destruction of a grove of birch trees. Mark Studdock is bewildered by the order, and comments, "I shouldn't have thought they did much harm at that distance from the house" (*THS*, 172). Filostrato's reply makes clear that the destruction was for its own sake, irrational except in terms of Belbury's hatred of life. Like a cancer, Belbury feeds its own processes through purposeless destruction.

An ironic reversal in the novel tends to reveal the essence of the N.I.C.E. institute. As the novel begins, N.I.C.E. seems flawlessly organized, and its move to force Bracton College to sell its little wood is so smoothly put over that the reader envisions the institute as a well-oiled machine, sinister in its purposes, but brilliantly efficient in their achievement. As the narrative proceeds, that impression is progressively undermined, and then destroyed. It is no coincidence that the novel's title derives from a description of the Tower of Babel.[7] The organization is a chaos, and contains within itself the contradictions that destroy it—a garden inimical to growth, a disorganized organization. Mark Studdock's initial respect for N.I.C.E. deteriorates as soon as he learns that no one at Belbury has any idea what is going on, excepting possibly Wither, the Deputy Director, and, as Fairy Hardcastle tells Mark, "making things clear is the one thing the D.D. can't stand" (THS, 97). Consequently, department heads such as Steele simply do not know what their departments are supposed to be doing.

The use of language at Belbury seems chaos, an attack upon meaning itself. The institute is a bureaucracy, but supposedly dedicated to a "crusade against red tape." Murders are "sanitary cases." "Remedial treatment" is torture. It is appropriate that Merlin should inflict a "curse of tongues" at the Director's dinner to precipitate the destruction of N.I.C.E., since he has only unleashed a chaos already implicit in the organization. As Marjorie Wright points out, the inner circle of N.I.C.E. meet their end chanting nonsense syllables to Alcasan's head, symbolically indicating that the impetus of N.I.C.E. derives not from "scientific reasoning," but from an irrational, libidal primitivism.[8]

The core of Lewis's insight into evil is contained in images of organization versus images of discord. Philosophically, Lewis does not accept a positive existence to evil. Evil is a negation, a distortion or perversion of the good. If the garden at St. Anne's represents the fecund and harmonious pattern of life, Belbury can only be its grotesque parody, and thus it must contain the seeds of its destruction: order is chaos, the "conquest of organic life" is death, liberation is slavery. The eldils of the planets who help destroy N.I.C.E. make for an entertaining display of cosmic fireworks, but they destroy N.I.C.E. only in the sense that they amplify its internal contradictions.

If the abeyance of reason is madness, N.I.C.E. is wholly and thoroughly mad. Surely in many ways N.I.C.E. suggests Nazi Germany; the novel was written in 1943, and Mrs. Dimble, getting her first taste of N.I.C.E. procedures, says "it's almost as if we'd lost the war" (*THS*, 76). Lewis himself tells that he intended to attack bureaucratic totalitarianism more so than science itself: "what we are up against throughout the story is not scientists but *officials*. If anyone ought to feel himself libelled by this book it is not the scientist but the civil servant; and, next to the civil servant, certain philosophers."[9] Lewis goes on to say, "Miss Hardcastle, the chief of the secret police . . . is the common factor in all revolutions," and certainly she and her hired rowdies are intended to evoke Hitler's Brownshirts.

In sum, Lewis accedes to no moral relativism. The garden of St. Anne's, the garden paralleled to a woman's body, suggests a harmonious order of nature, an order in terms of which man must live if he is to be human. Lewis believes, in contradiction to Feverstone and Filostrato, that man does not "make himself," but that his reason is capable of apprehending a rational universe, and thus, that there is a natural moral order. Such a stance places him in opposition to all principles of infinite human progress, to all philosophies of the superman.[10] Lewis would accept Blake's maxim that "in trying to be more than man, we become less."

In such views, Lewis is traditional rather than "modern." Yet more often than not great satirists have been conservative traditionalists, lashing out at excesses of "modern" thought. Lewis shares this role with both Jonathan Swift, who attacks the Enlightenment in *Gulliver's Travels*, and with Samuel Johnson, who attacks it in *Rasselas*. Swift attacks the Enlightenment goal of a "heavenly city on earth" with the same insistence upon man's frailty and need for rational governance that characterizes Lewis; Johnson offers *Rasselas* as an anodyne to "modern" ideas of perfect societies and infinite human progress. No critic to my knowledge has narrowly characterized either Swift or Johnson as "theological," or as advocates of "Christian orthodoxy." As with them, so with Lewis. All three men are concerned with issues far more social and moral than theological.

Lewis owns as his literary antecedents not such theologically-oriented writers as Langland, Bunyan, or the Pearl Poet, but rather, men such as Swift, Johnson, or Voltaire.[11]

NOTES

[1]Charles Moorman, *Arthurian Triptysch* (Los Angeles, 1960), pp. 107, 109.

[2]Clyde S. Kilby, *The Christian World of C. S. Lewis* (Grand Rapids, Mich., 1964), p. 107.

[3]Roger Sale, "England's Parnassus: C. S. Lewis, Charles Williams, and J. R. R. Tolkien," *Hudson Review,* XVII (Summer, 1964), 205.

[4]C. S. Lewis, *That Hideous Strength* (New York, 1960), pp. 7-8. Further references to this, the Macmillan paperback edition, will be found within the text.

[5]Charles Williams and C. S. Lewis, *Arthurian Torso* (New York, 1948), pp. 9-10.

[6]Leaves like "cleverly painted and varnished metal" evoke Spenser's deadly Bower of Bliss in Book II of the *Faerie Queene.* Spenser's Bower has metal leaves disguised to seem real.

[7]The anagram which explains the novel's title is from *Ane Dialog* by Sir David Lyndsay, and describes the Tower of Babel: "The shadow of that hyddeous strength Sax myle and more it is of length."

[8]Marjorie E. Wright, "The Cosmic Kingdom of Myth: A Study in the Myth Philosophy of Charles Williams, C. S. Lewis, and J. R. R. Tolkien," unpublished doctoral dissertation, University of Illinois, 1960, p. 109.

[9]"A Reply to Professor Haldane," in C. S. Lewis, *Of Other Worlds* (London, 1966), pp. 78, 82.

[10]Lewis attacks repeatedly in his critical writings such "scientific" estheticians as J. B. S. Haldane, C. H. Waddington, and George Bernard Shaw. For a sample, see his *The Abolition of Man* (Oxford, 1943), or essays in *Of Other Worlds.*

[11]For a discussion of Lewis's trilogy as a satire, but from a perspective different from mine, see Mark R. Hillegas, *The Future as Nightmare* (Oxford, 1967), pp. 133-144.

MICHEL BUTOR

SCIENCE FICTION:
THE CRISIS
OF
ITS GROWTH

I

If the genre Science Fiction is rather difficult to define—
disputes among the experts afford superabundant proof of that—
it is, at least, one of the easiest to designate. It is enough to say:
"You know, those stories that are always mentioning interplanetary rockets," for the least-prepared interlocutor to understand
immediately what you mean. This does not imply that any such
apparatus occurs in every SF story; it may be replaced by other
accessories which will perform a comparable role. But it is the
most usual, the typical example, like the magic wand in fairy tales.
Two remarks are immediately relevant:
1. There exists for the moment no interplanetary rocket. If
there ever has been one, or there is one now, the ordinary reader
knows nothing about it. A narrative in which a device of this kind
occurs is therefore a narrative of fantasy.
2. But we all believe quite firmly that such devices will soon
exist, that the question is no more than one of time—a few years
of development. The apparatus is possible. This notion is fundamental, and requires some explanation.
It might be claimed that for the Arab storytellers, who
believed in the power of magicians, flying carpets were also "possible." But for most of us, the possibility of rockets is of an

Originally published in *The Partisan Review*, 34 (Autumn 1967),
595-602. Copyright 1967, 1968 by Simon and Schuster, for *Inventories*.
Reprinted by permission of Simon and Schuster.

altogether different order. It is guaranteed by what we might call, by and large, *modern science,* a sum of doctrines whose validity no serious Occidental dares to question.

If the author of a narrative has taken the trouble to introduce such a device, it is because he chooses to depart from reality only to a certain degree, he wants to prolong, to extend reality, but not to be separated from it. He wants to give us an impression of realism, he wants to insert the imaginary into the real, anticipating results already achieved. Such a narrative naturally situates its action in the future.

We can imagine, taking modern science in its broadest acceptation, not only other devices, but technologies of all kinds— psychological, pedagogical, social, etc.   .   .   .   This scientific guarantee may become increasingly loose, but it nonetheless constitutes the definable specificity of SF: a literature which explores the range of the possible, as science permits us to envision it.

It is, then, a fantasy framed by a realism.

The work of Jules Verne is the best example of SF to the first degree, which is justified by the results achieved and which uniquely anticipates certain applications. Wells inaugurates a SF to the second degree, much more audacious but much less convincing, which anticipates the results themselves. He lets us assume behind Cavor's machine, which will take the first men to the moon, an explanation of a scientific type, one that conforms to a *possible* science which will develop from the science of his time.

II

The SF tourist agencies offer their customers three main types of spectacles which we can group under the following rubrics: life in the future, unknown worlds, unexpected visitors.

1) Life in the Future

We start from the world as we know it, from the society which surrounds us. We introduce a certain number of changes whose consequences we attempt to foresee. By a projection into the future, we open up the complexity of the present, we develop certain still larval aspects. SF of this type is a remarkable instrument of investigation in the tradition of Swift. It readily assumes a satiric aspect. We shall find excellent examples in the works of Huxley (*Brave New World*), Orwell (*1984*), Werfel (*Star of the Unborn*), Hesse (*Magister Ludi*), Bradbury, etc.

2) Unknown Worlds

It suffices to mention the name Ray Bradbury, whose best-known work is called *The Martian Chronicles*, to see that an altogether different element occurs here, almost of necessity.

Technological progress has for its goal not only the transformation of our daily life, but also the satisfaction of our curiosity. The new instruments, the new sciences must allow us to discover domains of reality which are hidden from us today. Within the scientific representation of the world, there are enormous districts which our imagination is free to populate with strange beings and landscapes according to its whim, subject to several very broad restrictions. Here we can project our dreams.

This aspect of SF links up with a very respectable tradition. Dante, when he locates his inferno inside the globe, his purgatory at the antipodes and his paradise in the stars, is merely projecting his theology, and a good deal more, into the empty spaces which medieval cosmology reserved.

Thus Verne scrupulously inventoried the lacunae of the geography of his age and filled them with myths inscribed within the extension of the known facts, achieving a synthesis which strikes us as naive but which by its breadth and harmony outstrips anything his successors have attempted.

When an author of the eighteenth century wanted to give his story some appearance of reality, he had a ready-made site in which to locate it: the islands of the Pacific. (*Cf.* Diderot: *Supplement to Bougainville's Voyage.*) Today, when the exploration of the earth's surface is quite advanced, we prefer to locate our islands in the sky. But if we once knew nothing, of course, of the archipelagos which had not yet been discovered, we were at least quite sure that apart from certain remarkable peculiarities they could not be very different from those we knew already. We were still on the same Earth, with the same general conditions.

On the contrary, the little we know today about the islands in the sky proves to us that everything must be very different there. We know that gravity is more powerful on Venus, less powerful on Mars, than on Earth, etc. These several elements oblige the writer who respects them to make an enormous effort of imagination, force him to invent something truly new. Unfortunately, the creation of another "nature," even when based on elementary information, is a task so arduous that no author, so far, has undertaken it methodically.

In order not to acknowledge ourselves vanquished, we raise our sights: instead of describing what might happen on Mars and Venus, we leap at once to the third planet of the *Epsilon* system of the Swan, or else, since in fact there is nothing to stop us once we have started on this path, planet *n* of star *n* in galaxy *n*. At first the reader is impressed by these cascades of light years; the solar system was certainly a wretched little village, here we are launched into the universe *at large*. But he soon realizes that these ultra-remote planets resemble the earth much more than they do its neighbors.   Out of the immense number of stars which populate space, it is always permissible to imagine one on which the conditions of life are very close to those we know. The authors have rediscovered the islands of the eighteenth century.   They employ a vaguely scientific jargon and decorate the sky with charming fantasies; the trick is turned.

This infinite freedom is a false freedom. If we flee infinitely far into space or time, we shall find ourselves in a region where everything is possible, where the imagination will no longer even need to make an effort of coordination. The result will be an impoverished duplication of everyday reality. We are told of an enormous war between galactic civilizations, but we see at once that the league of the democratic planets strangely resembles the UN, the empire of the nebula Andromeda stands for the Soviet Union as a subscriber to *Reader's Digest* might conceive that nation, and so on.   The author has merely translated into SF language a newspaper article he read the night before.   Had he remained on Mars, he would have been obliged to invent something.

At its best moments, the SF that describes unknown worlds becomes an instrument of an extreme flexibility, thanks to which all kinds of political and moral fables, of fairy tales, of myths, can be transposed and adapted to modern readers. Anticipation has created a language by whose aid we can in principle examine everything.

3) Unexpected Visitors

The description of unknown worlds, in SF, necessarily becomes part of our anticipation, however rudimentary it may be; it is natural that it should affect that anticipation. It is not so much by the improvement of commercial relations that the invention of the compass transformed the Old World, but by the discovery of America. The description of unknown worlds and beings involves the description of their intervention in the future history of humanity.

We can easily imagine that the inhabitants of other planets have a civilization in advance of our own, hence that they have a realm of action superior to our own, that they are ahead of us in discovery.

All of space becomes threatening; strange beings may intervene even before we know of their existence. Most of the pre-Columbians had no expectation that a deadly invasion would come out of the East.

It is in Wells's *War of the Worlds* that we encounter this theme for the first time, and his countless imitators have not added much to it. It is a profoundly modern theme (it never occurred to anyone in the sixteenth century that Europe might be discovered in its turn) and an extremely powerful one (as several memorable radio broadcasts have demonstrated).

Thanks to this notion of intervention, SF can assimilate those aspects of the fantastic which at first seem most opposed to it: all that we might classify under the heading: "Superstitions."

In the *Divine Comedy*, Beatrice transports Dante from planet to planet; in Father Kircher's *Iter Extaticum,* an angel does the job; we are not yet in SF, which implies that the journey is made as a result of techniques developed by man. But these techniques will allow us to enter into contact with beings to whom we can attribute knowledge we do not possess, techniques we do not understand. It might, of course, occur to one of them to come to

Earth, to carry off one of *us* and transport him elsewhere by means which there is no longer any need to explain. The difference between such a being and Kircher's angel becomes infinitesimal; only the language has changed. As a matter of fact, it is necessary today, in order to gain a sufficient suspension of disbelief, that the being be described in the same way as a being that man might have discovered on another planet. Thus we could unite within SF all the narratives of phantoms and demons, all the old myths dealing with superior beings which intervene in the life of men. Certain tales by H. P. Lovecraft illustrate this possibility.

C. S. Lewis begins his curious antimodern trilogy with a novel which has all of SF's characteristics: *Out of the Silent Planet*. Two wicked scientists transport a young philologist to Mars by means of a spaceship furnished with every modern convenience. In the second volume, *Perelandra*, the author drops his mask: it is an angel who transports the philologist to Venus; as for the scientists, they are Satan's henchmen.

III

We see that all kinds of merchandise can be sold under the label SF; and that all kinds of merchandise seek to be packaged under this label. Hence it seems that SF represents the normal form of mythology in our time: a form which is not only capable of revealing profoundly new themes, but capable of integrating all the themes of the old literature.

Despite several splendid successes, we cannot help thinking that SF is keeping very few of its promises.

This is because SF, by extending itself, is denaturing itself; it is gradually losing its specificity. It furnishes a very particular element of credibility; this element is increasingly weakened when it is utilized without discernment. SF is fragile, and the enormous circulation it has achieved in recent years merely renders it more so.

We have already noted that the flight to ultra-distant planets and epochs, which seems at first glance a conquest, actually masks the authors' incapacity to imagine in a coherent fashion, in conformity with the requirements of "science," the planets or the epochs which are closer at hand. Similarly the divination of a

future science affords, surely, a great freedom, but we soon discover that it is above all a revenge of the authors against their
incapacity to master the entire range of contemporary science.

The day is long past when an Aristotle could be the first
researcher of his age in every domain, and the day when a Pico
could claim to defend a thesis *De Omni Re Scibili*; but the day is
almost past when a Verne could easily handle the notions implied
in all the technological applications achieved in his age, and anticipate other applications while remaining perfectly clear to the high
school students who formed his public.

Today the notions implied in devices as common as a radio
set or an atomic bomb exceed by a good deal the average reader's
level of scientific culture. He uses without understanding; he
accepts without asking explanations; and the author takes advantage of this situation, which frequently causes him to multiply his
blunders, for he too generally lacks a sufficient knowledge of the
notions he is obliged to use or else seem backward, a grave
possibility when one is claiming to reveal the mysteries of two
hundred thousand years hence.

As a result SF, which should derive the greatest part of its
prestige from its precision, remains vague. The story does not
truly manage to *take shape*. And when the scientists themselves
begin writing, they quite often prove their ignorance of the disciplines unfamiliar to them and their difficulty in vulgarizing their
specialty.

SF is distinguished from the other genres of the fantastic by
the special kind of plausibility it introduces. This plausibility is in
direct proportion to the solid scientific elements the author introduces. If they fail, SF becomes a dead form, a stereotype.

IV

Hence we understand why few authors risk specifying the
details of their image of a transformed world. It is an undertaking,
indeed, which supposes not only a scientific culture far above the
average, but also a knowledge of present reality comparable to that
supposed by a novel of the realistic type, and finally an enormous
effort of coordination. The author is generally content to evoke a
future world "in general," one which might just as well be located

in 1975 as in 19750, a world characterized by the widespread use of plastic substances, of television and of atomic-powered rockets. It is within this setting that he will briefly develop what is often a highly ingenious idea. In another tale, he will use this same background in order to develop another idea, without taking the trouble to coordinate them. The result is an infinity of variously sketched futures, all independent of one another and generally contradictory. We shall have, in the same way, an infinity of Venuses, each of which diminishes the plausibility of the rest.

This dispersion has monotony as its direct consequence, for the authors, since they renounce constructing systematically, can describe only in a rudimentary fashion and depart only slightly from banality.

It appears that SF has begun with the cake. It had things too much its own way: it was once enough to mention Martians to enthrall the reader. But the time has come when the reader will notice that most of these monsters, despite their crests, their tentacles, their scales, are much less different from the average American than an ordinary Mexican. SF has cut the grass under its own feet, has spoiled thousands of ideas. The doors have been thrown open to start on a great quest, and we discover we are still walking round and round the house. If the authors scamp their texts, it is because they realize that an effort to improve them would lead to an impasse.

The SF narratives derive their power from a great collective dream we are having, but for the moment they are incapable of giving it a unified form. It is a mythology in tatters, impotent, unable to orient our action in any precise way.

V

But the last word has not been said, and it is certainly possible that SF will surmount this crisis in its growth.

It has the power to solicit our belief in an entirely new way, and it is capable of affording, in its description of the possible, a marvelous precision. But to realize its full power, it must undergo a revolution, it must succeed in unifying itself. It must become a collective work, like the science which is its indispensable basis.

We all dream of clean, well-lighted cities, so that when an

author situates a narrative in such a place, he is certain of striking a sympathetic note. But we find ourselves, in the present state of SF, facing an enormous choice of barely sketched future cities among which the imagination hesitates, unsatisfied.

Everyone knows Heraclitus' famous fragment: "Those who are awakened are in the same world, but those who sleep are each in a separate world." Our dreamers' worlds are simultaneously without communication and very much like one another. The classical mythologies united the common elements of these dreams into unique and public myths.

Now let us imagine that a certain number of authors, instead of describing at random and quite rapidly certain more or less interchangeable cities, were to take as the setting of their stories a single city, named and situated with some precision in space and in future time; that each author were to take into account the descriptions given by the others in order to introduce his own new ideas. This city would become a common possession to the same degree as an ancient city that has vanished; gradually, all readers would give its name to the city of their dreams and would model that city in its image.

SF, if it could limit and unify itself, would be capable of acquiring over the individual imagination a constraining power comparable to that of any classical mythology. Soon *all* authors would be obliged to take this predicted city into account, readers would organize their actions in relation to its imminent existence, ultimately they would find themselves obliged to build it. Then SF would be veracious, to the very degree that it realized itself.

It is easy to see what a prodigious instrument of liberation or oppression it could become.

(Translated from the French by Richard Howard)

ON
SCIENCE FICTION
CRITICISM

Michel Butor's "Science Fiction: The Crisis of its Growth" (*Partisan Review*, Fall 1967) has two serious deficiencies: it gives a completely misleading impression of the present state of the genre, and it proposes a future course for it which would destroy everyone's interest in either writing or reading it.

I

For some reason, most critics who undertake to discuss science fiction for a literary but non-specialised audience do so from a limited and largely antiquarian knowledge of the field, heavily weighted toward Jules Verne (d. 1905). That this is true of M. Butor may be seen in the fact that he mentions no living science-fiction author but Ray Bradbury.

This might be of little importance in older genres, but science fiction is uniquely dominated by living authors, since it is based upon modern technology. There are, to be sure, a few dead giants —Verne, Wells, C. S. Lewis, Orwell—but the field as a modern phenomenon dates back only to 1926 (when it diverged from the mainstream of fiction into specialised magazines of its own); and as M. Butor's title admits, it is still growing vigorously. Hence a critic who fails even to mention such figures as Isaac Asimov, Arthur C. Clarke, Robert A. Heinlein or Theodore Sturgeon may reasonably be suspected of having lost track somewhere around 1940; so that if there is a "crisis" in modern science fiction, his

Originally published in *Riverside Quarterly*, 3 (August 1968), 214-217. Reprinted by permission of the author and Leland Sapiro, editor of *Riverside Quarterly*.

chances of identifying it cannot be of the best.

Had M. Butor been keeping up with his reading, he would have known that much of what he says about modern science fiction is in fact untrue. He says, for example: "We know that gravity is more powerful on Venus, less powerful on Mars, than on Earth, etc. These several elements oblige the writer who respects them to make an enormous effort of imagination, force him to invent something truly new. Unfortunately, the creation of another 'nature,' even when based on elementary information, is a task so arduous that no author, so far, has undertaken it methodically." No critic who has read the works of Heinlein, Clarke, Hal Clement, Lester del Rey or Don A. Stuart—all well-known authors active for more than twenty-five years, all still alive, and all in print in France—could have permitted himself so categorical an error.

A closely related point is M. Butor's abdication of any attempt at a definition of the field he is talking about. The best he manages is, "You know, those stories that are always mentioning interplanetary rockets." (And two paragraphs later he is saying that "There exist for the moment no interplanetary rockets," a statement which denies existence to a long and well-reported series of such probes.)

Within the field itself, there is wide agreement on the following rule by Theodore Sturgeon: "A good science fiction story is a story with a human problem, and a human solution, which would not have happened at all without its science content." (N.B. the second word.)

By this rule, it can be seen that such examples of M. Butor's as H. P. Lovecraft and Ray Bradbury are not science fiction writers at all, since their works contain no trace of any science whatsoever. (Both in fact were terrified of science; they belong to that part of the Faustian tradition which may be summarised in a line common to all horror movies, "There are things that Man was not meant to know.") They are writers of pure fantasy. M. Butor seems to think Bradbury to be one of those authors who tries to stick to the few known facts about such a place as Mars; but the "Mars" of Bradbury bears not the faintest resemblance to the real planet of that name—it is, instead, a sentimentalised, displaced rural Illinois county.

Clothing quite ordinary Earth settings (and, it might be added, plots) in a few futuristic trappings is a common failing of routine commercial science fiction. M. Butor stresses this point, but omits the two key words: "routine commercial." As specialists in the field are bitterly aware, no other genre in literary history has been so consistently judged by its worst examples. This observation, too, was made some years ago by Sturgeon, who went on to note that non-specialist critics seem to take a positive delight in pointing out that ninety per cent of all science fiction is worthless —without pausing to reflect that there is *no* field of human endeavor which is immune to exactly the same stricture.

If a field is to be considered worthy of critical examination for an audience of non-specialists, the critic owes it to that audience to weigh the field's achievements as well as its failures. If its failures are vastly more numerous, why should we be surprised—or, worse, gratified? Good work in any field is always scarce; why otherwise do we prize it at all?

After many years of reading critiques like M. Butor's, I am driven to the conclusion that schoolboy questions like these simply never get asked when the subject is science fiction. Hence I am emboldened to offer an elementary prescription to the next such man who wants to interpret science fiction to non-experts. The prescription does not require him to read every awful story in every routine issue of every commercial science fiction magazine; indeed, it is designed to save him that trouble, by sending him instead to what might be called the semi-permanent exhibits of modern science fiction, as follows:

(1)   Three different collections of "best" science fiction stories are published annually, edited respectively (in order of decreasing age) by Judith Merril, by Terry Carr and Donald Wollheim, and by Harry Harrison. They all have their biases, but together they offer a reliable sampling of the non-routine work that is going on in the genre.

(2)   Each year, too, two sets of awards are offered in the field: the "Hugo" awards (from the readers) and the "Nebula" awards (from the writers). The shorter award-winning stories appear in annual collections; the award-winning novels are so identified on their jackets by their publishers.

There is nothing infallible about these choices, of course; but a critic who has failed to pay any attention to them is incompetent to talk about the past of science fiction, let alone its future. It might also be useful for him to have read the specialist critics in the genre.

II

From his gallery of dead authors M. Butor proceeds to derive a prescription of his own for science fiction: "It must become a collective work, like the science which is its indispensable basis." He offers a specific example of how this might be done:

> We all dream of clean, well-lighted cities, so that when an author situates a narrative in such a place, he is certain of striking a sympathetic note. But we find ourselves, in the present state of SF, facing an enormous choice of barely sketched future cities among which the imagination hesitates, unsatisfied.
>
> Now let us imagine that a certain number of authors, instead of describing at random and quite rapidly certain more or less interchangeable cities, were to take as the setting of their stories a single city, named and situated with some precision in space and in future time; that each author were to take into account the descriptions given by the others in order to introduce his new ideas. This city would become a common possession to the same degree as an ancient city that has vanished; gradually, all readers would give its name to the city of their dreams and would model that city in its image.
>
> SF, if it could limit and unify itself, would be capable of acquiring over the individual imagination a constraining power comparable to that of any classical mythology. Soon all authors would be obliged to take this predicted city into account, readers would organize their actions in relation to its imminent existence, ultimately they would find themselves obliged to build it. Then SF would be veracious, to the very degree that it realized itself. (pp. 601-2)

Can anyone imagine a more totalitarian view of the function of creative writing? *Quis custodiet ipsos custodes?* Who would hand down the "descriptions" in this *Zukuftskulturkammer?*

The prescription would freeze the very worst elements of routine commercial science fiction—its paucity of imagination and its tendency to conventionalise the future—into a set of dogmas much like thirteenth century canon law. At best it would limit the scientific or technological substrate of all science fiction to whatever some appointed tenth-rate engineer deemed "possible" at the time of writing (as all of Verne's stories were limited, though apparently M. Butor doesn't know this); no room would be left in which to extrapolate from the known to the unrealised possibilities, in the sciences alone, although science itself is today in a ferment of speculation utterly unlike the body of dogma M. Butor imagines it to be. (In fact M. Butor knows nothing about science either, as his remarks on gravity, his vagueness over what is meant by a "galaxy," and his failure to differentiate between science and technology make painfully evident.)

Secondly, such an agreed-upon or dictated city (or universe) would preclude the individual human speculation upon the future which is the life blood of the *fiction* part of science fiction. Let us not forget that it is above all else a branch of fiction that we are talking about here, not a body of myth, or an attempt at a self-fulfilling prophecy like *Das Kapital.*

As it happens, there does exist a collection of eleven science-fiction stories each one of which is set in a completely different vision of a future city (Damon Knight, ed. *Cities of Wonder* (New York, 1967)), each one utterly personal to the writer. M. Butor's recipe would rule out all of these visions, and all others like them, without giving us anything better in their place but another of those "interchangeable" cities of which he simultaneously complains. What he wants us to do, in fact, is to become less imaginative and more interchangeable than ever, by limiting ourselves to *his* version of a "clean, well-lighted" city of the future, as laid down in every important particular by some combination of the French Academy and Robert Moses. It seems never to have occurred to him that the city of the future may be even less clean and well-lighted than our own—or that a rational future may choose to abolish the folk-custom of the huddling-place entirely.

It is, I submit, a curious sort of critic who wants not only the future, but fiction about the future to be put in a strait-jacket.

MILTON A. MAYS

FRANKENSTEIN,
MARY SHELLEY'S
BLACK
THEODICY

Mary Shelley's *Frankenstein* is a very bookish book, permeated with literary allusions, quotations, references, and parallels. From what might have been a literary *olla podrida* of Romantic themes and types, however, the firm mind of the author has finally drawn a coherent thematic pattern worthy of serious regard. Two great literary sources stand behind this pattern, it seems to me, the Faust-myth and Milton's *Paradise Lost*. These principal *Einflüsse* intermingle to the extent that the various actions of the romance—those involving Frankenstein and Walton, on the one hand, and that of the Monster on the other—can all be said to raise questions of the relationship of man to God, or nature, or, more narrowly, of universal law or justice.

One of the more interesting of contemporary reviews, that in the *Edinburgh Magazine* for March of 1818[1] while admiring *Frankenstein*, expressed a certain uneasiness as to its import: "It might, indeed, have been the author's view to show that the powers of man have been wisely limited, and that misery can follow their extension." Yet there is something disturbing to the reviewer in the use of the expression "Creator" "applied to a mere human being," and in general something "bordering too closely on impiety" about the work. This writer is very close: there can be said to be *two* themes to *Frankenstein*, an "outer," or more obvious, and an "inner," the latter of which the following comments will suggest is indeed impious.

Originally published in *Southern Humanities Review*, 3 (Spring 1969), 146-153. Reprinted by permission of the editors.

These two themes take their source from the Faust-myth and *Paradise Lost*, respectively. Frankenstein is more of a chastened Faust, in my opinion, than a Prometheus; the "moral" of his story to Walton, whom he sees as infected with his own obsession, is "Learn from me . . . how dangerous is the acquirement of knowledge." Frankenstein is Faustian in his meddling in a bastardized mixture of alchemy and empirical science, out of pride and intellect and desire for glory; but, unlike Goethe's more ambiguous Faust, he is not saved by striving. He admits on his deathbed, after a life of horror, that his studies have been "unlawful, that is to say, not befitting the human mind." Frankenstein has offended against "law" (whether of nature or God—Mary Shelley does not put Frankenstein in a theological frame of reference); and thus his story implies a just universe, against which he has offended.

Far different, and darker, is the story of the Monster; he is, rather, the victim of universal injustice—from man, and from his "God," Frankenstein, a god who, after casting him botched into a world in which he inspires horror, abandons him. If behind Frankenstein stands the Faust-type, the Monster's story gains its peculiar resonance from *Paradise Lost*. The epigraph chosen by Mary Shelley indicates the relation of the romance to Milton's epic:

> Did I request thee, Maker, from my clay
> To mold me man? Did I solicit thee
> From darkness to promote me?
> (*Paradise Lost* X, 743-745)

It should also indicate the priority of the Monster in this work—for the point of view of the rebellious Adam in no way pertains to Frankenstein.

The inner story of Mary Shelley's *Frankenstein* is a kind of "black theodicy"; its secret hero, the Monster, a great Romantic rebel who reflects many Romantic archetypes, but finally stands in most interesting relationship to Adam and Lucifer. The sore Adam who speaks the lines of the epigraph goes on to say, "inexplicable / Thy justice seems . . ." (X, 754-755). Yet Milton's Adam has had a contract with God, as he admits; has "enjoyed the good" provided by this God; is indeed made in God's image, beautiful, happy, and companioned. Such is Milton's "justification of God's ways to man"; Adam's outburst is a temporary one, which must give way to a broader view of the fortune even of his fall.

But the Monster's condition is far worse than, if parallel to Adam's. That amazing autodidact has read *Paradise Lost* "as a true history," and seen his situation vicariously in Adam's (Mrs. Shelley places her literary sources squarely before us). Adam's state, says the Monster, "was far different from mine . . ." in that "he had come forth from the hands of God a perfect creature, happy and prosperous, guarded by the especial care of his Creator; he was allowed to converse with, and acquire knowledge from, beings of a superior nature: but I was wretched, helpless, and alone . . ." This above all: "No Eve soothed my sorrows, nor shared my thought; I was alone." (The poignance of this aspect of the Monster's fate reveals the personal emotion of his author, who records "spasms of anguish" at a solitude "no other human being ever before, I believe, endured—except Robinson Crusoe."[2] —and not only after PBS's death, it would seem.)

The Monster's description of his dawning consciousness might almost parody Adam's in Book VIII of *Paradise Lost.* "For man to tell how human life began / Is hard . . ." says Adam (11. 250-251); "It is with considerable difficulty that I remember the original era of my being . . ." begins the Monster in Chapter XI. Adam and the Monster share early sensations of light and dark, sleep and waking, appetency and satisfaction, the awareness of other creatures, such as the birds. But whereas for Adam "all things smiled; / With fragrance and with joy my heart o'erflowed" (11. 265-266) the hapless Monster, born not to Paradise but at Ingolstadt in November feels "pain invade me on all sides" and weeps. The rationality of one creation is further illustrated by Adam's facility: "To speak I tried, and forthwith spake; / My tongue obeyed, and readily could name / Whate'er I saw" (11. 271-273). The Monster (whose innate aesthetic response to Nature is one of the details which make him such a touching if ludicrous creature) tries to "imitate the pleasant songs of the birds, but was unable." And "sometimes I wished to express my sensations in my own mode, but the uncouth and inarticulate sounds which broke from me frightened me into silence again." Adam's satisfaction in "perusing" himself as creature contrasts with the Monster's "terror" in seeing himself in a pool: "I became fully convinced that I was in reality the monster that I am" and "was filled with the bitterest sensations of despondence and mortification." Both creatures ask the immemorial questions: "Who I was, or where, or from what cause, / Knew not" says Adam (11. 270-271), but the Monster's "What was I?" can be "answered only with groans." Little wonder that Adam's "how came I thus, how here" he answers "by some great Maker then, / In goodness and in power pre-eminent," a Maker he desires only to "adore" (11. 278-279, 280). The Monster has access to Frankenstein's journal of his creation, and so knowledge of his creator's purpose and attitudes granted to no other creature, but its effect is to sicken him, and he curses his creator. The Monster's is knowledge with a vengeance: his "god" has been revulsed by him, and has abandoned him. Finally, his condition is rendered absolutely unendurable by his loneliness: "I remembered Adam's supplication to his Creator [for a mate]. But where was mine? He had abandoned me: and, in the bitterness of my heart, I cursed him."

But this true prototype, the Monster sees, is not Adam, but Satan; and if he has less reason than Adam to adore, he is even justified as the devil. "I am thy creature," he says to Frankenstein in that first dramatic confrontation on the glacier above Chamonix. "I ought to be thy Adam; but I am rather the fallen angel, whom thou drivest from joy for no misdeed." Satan, then, is "the fitter emblem of my condition"—the Satan of Romanticism, proud sufferer of Divine injustice, and rebel against God's power. And, at a level of abstraction beyond this, Mary Shelley's Monster is a type of the Romantic hero-villain, the ambivalent man of "archangelic grandeur" (as Melville describes Ahab) who may be poet, or genius, but is always of different stature from other men, and an "isolato." The Monster suffers "for no misdeed"; his "evil" is the fruit of his suffering, rather than the reverse.

Even if the Monster did not know Milton so well, even if he did not make the analogies of his fate and Adam's, or Satan's, so explicitly, so habitually salt his narrative with literary allusion (e.g., the shepherd's hut appears to the suffering Monster "as exquisite and divine a retreat as Pandemonium appeared to the demons of hell"), Mary Shelley's debt to Milton would be evident in the Monster's character, action, and situation. The "heroic villain" stance of the Monster derives in varying degrees from Lucifer's envy, pride, disdain, and from his central motive of revenge.

Envy is less developed in *Frankenstein* than in *Paradise Lost*, which differs from *Frankenstein* in that the central action is the onslaught of the evil principle on innocence; whereas for the Monster hatred of the "Creator" is kept central. But Frankenstein's Monster does at one point feel "the bitter gall of envy" rise at the happiness of mankind around him; and when his overtures to them are repulsed in horror he recoils from thwarted love into a possession of "rage and revenge" in which he could "with pleasure have destroyed the cottage and its inhabitants," the idyllic family he has come to love in secret. But, as it happens, the Monster does violence to no one not intimately connected with Frankenstein, and, as we shall see, is even in so doing tortured with a self-hatred completely foreign to Milton's Satan. Envy, the base passion, is not so characteristic of the Monster as of Satan. The Monster's revenge is essentially motivated by his sense of injustice, rather than springing from wounded pride; and is directed at the source, rather than diverted in impotent meanness at the Creator's new favorite:

> Revenge, at first though sweet
> Bitter ere long back on itself recoils;
> Let it; I reck not, so it light well aimed,
> Since higher I fall short, on him who next
> Provokes my envy, this new favorite
> Of heaven, this man of clay . . .
> (PL IX, 171-176)

But Lucifer-derived is the Monster's "mine shall not be the submission of abject slavery," comparable to Satan's "Who can think submission? War then, war / Open or understood must be resolved" (I, 661-662). The Monster's "proud villain" attributes, his "disdain and malignity" are the more remarkable considering that he shares none of Satan's awful grandeur of person, even thunder-scarred and darkened in Hell; the Monster is created of an "unearthly ugliness . . . almost too horrible for human eyes." Yet if the Monster is not an operatic evil hero, he has a doubleness that is very characteristic of the Romantic protagonist. The Monster's "difference" from most men is to the last degree ambivalent—to himself, as well as to others. Is he grander, or more despicable?

The basest of all, or a superman? Frankenstein's Monster literally walks two feet taller than most, and if he is horrified at himself, he is far from abject: "I was . . . endowed with a figure hideously deformed and loathsome; I was not even of the same nature as man. I was more agile than they, and could subsist upon coarser diet; I bore the extremes of heat and cold with less injury to my frame; my stature far exceeded theirs. When I looked around, I saw and heard of none like me." I think the Monster indisputably more complex than Frankenstein. By the end of his story we may feel him to have achieved an ambiguous grandeur all his own.

A bitter sense of exclusion from all pleasure, and in particular the sensuous beauties of nature characterizes both the Monster and Milton's Satan. As Satan walks among Eden's woods and rivers he thinks "With what delight could I have walked thee round, / If I could joy in aught . . ." (IX, 114-115); now "the more I see / Pleasures about me, so much more I feel / Torment within me . . ." (119-121). The Monster has an inborn sense of beauty; yet it is mocked by the pain he has felt from his first miserable moments, alone, cold, and hungry in the woods; just as his innate benevolence is mocked by man's cruelty at their every encounter. After the Monster has received a painful gunshot wound from a "rustic" whose child he has rescued from drowning, the "bright sun or gentle breezes" no longer alleviate his condition: "All joy was but a mockery . . . I was not made for the enjoyment of pleasure." (Here, as so often, Herman Melville has given supreme statement in modern prose romance to this interesting Romantic theme of the "enjoying power": as Ahab watches the sunset over the Pacific he says "Oh! time was, when as the sunrise nobly spurred me, so the sunset soothed. No more. This lovely light, it lights not me; all loveliness is anguish to me, since I can ne'er enjoy.") Perhaps we can say that this "loss of pleasure," the sense of being excluded from the healthy range of sensuous response is the counterpart of some "cosmic" disorder, perceived by both Ahab and Frankenstein's Monster.

But the more poignant exclusion occurs where the sensuous shades into the human experience: here the Monster's plight far surpasses Satan's: "the fallen angel becomes a malignant devil. Yet even that enemy of God and man had friends and associates in his desolation; I am alone." Satan is capable of envying the embraces of Adam and Eve (". . . half her swelling breast / Naked met his under the flowing gold / Of her loose tresses hid . . .") but his attraction remains at the sexual, rather than the social level; Milton's, like Goethe's, is a lubricious devil.

> Sight hateful, sight tormenting! thus these two
> Imparadised in one another's arms,
> The happier Eden, shall enjoy their fill
> Of bliss on bliss, while I to Hell am thrust,
> Where neither joy nor love, but fierce desire,
> Among our other torments not the least,
> Still unfulfilled with pain of longing pines . . .
> (IV, 505-511)

The Monster's loneliness, on the other hand, is absolute, and his desire for a mate is couched in social rather than animal terms (the popular notion of the Monster as a sexual fiend has no foundation in Mary Shelley's creature). The being for which he petitions his "god," Frankenstein, is one "with whom I can live in the interchange of those sympathies necessary for my being." Paradoxically, the Monster's very departure on a career of crime—his murder of Frankenstein's small brother—springs from agonized loneliness. Seeing the child in the forest, following his experiences of rejection everywhere, the Monster thinks "that this little creature was unprejudiced, and had lived too short a time to have imbibed a horror of deformity. If, therefore, I could seize him, and educate him as my companion and friend, I should not be so desolate in this peopled earth." But, after struggling and reviling the Monster, the child is killed when he reveals that he is a Frankenstein. Where Satan's approach to Adam and Eve is with malice aforethought, as creatures weaker and more exposed than God, their creator, and in whose torment he can "interrupt [God's] joy," the rather similar exultation of the Monster on killing William Frankenstein is after the fact: feeling "exultation and hellish triumph" he cries "I too can create desolation; my enemy is not invulnerable; this death will carry despair to him . . ."

The significant feature of contrast between Milton's Satan, who, orthodoxly understood, does his part in justifying God's ways to man, and Mary Shelley's Monster, is that Satan's misery springs from his crime, the Monster's crime from his misery. At point after point the monster offers benevolence and love, is rejected, and recoils into violence: at the house of the blind man, on rescuing the child from drowning, or in his dealings with his creator, whom he acknowledges (with what we may think an excess of fairmindedness) as "worthy of love and admiration." At any point up to the crime with which, the Monster claims, he crossed irretrievably into "insatiable" evil—the murder of Frankenstein's bride—he could have been reclaimed by one act of love, one experience of mere justice. Yet even this crime, according to the Monster, occurred only because of the cruel disparity between "haves" and one absolute "have not."   After the murder of Frankenstein's friend Clerval in his rage at the destruction of his mate, the Monster abhors himself, and pities Frankenstein. But when Frankenstein marries, the Monster is again overcome with rage: "When I discovered that he, the author at once of my existence and of its unspeakable torments, dared to hope for happiness; that while he accumulated wretchedness and despair upon me he sought his own enjoyment in feelings and passions from the indulgence of which I was forever barred, then impotent envy and bitter indignation filled me with an insatiable thirst for vengeance."   Frankenstein's marriage seems a taunt to his loneliness, the insult added to the injury of the destruction of his mate-to-be. This is the superficial parallel of Satan's destructive envy of Adam and Eve's felicity, but with how great a difference in significance! With the death of Frankenstein's bride the Monster seems to cross a watershed, abandoning conflict with his better self to embrace evil as a principle: "Evil thenceforth became my good." The Monster speaks here with the very voice of his great literary ancestor. But the verbal echo of Satan's "Evil be thou my good" serves to underline the difference between Mary Shelley's Monster, outcast from life's feast, and Milton's Satan, who rejects repentance out of pride and ambition.

The concluding episodes of *Frankenstein* are among the most impressive. We have a pursuit and a revenge, as in *Moby Dick*, and it is a revenge effected by pursued on pursuer. Paradoxically, the hatred of the Monster, born of thwarted love and abused affection, in the end forms a kind of relationship in itself with Frankenstein, the sole being to whom he can claim a tie. Only a remarkable intelligence in the service of an immense force of poisoned emotion could be capable of the exquisite refinements of torture the Monster exacts from his pursuer. As they move across the face of the globe toward the polar fastnesses of the north, the Monster leaves clues by which he can be followed, taunting messages, even food, and advice as to equipment. Like Hawthorne's Chillingworth, resolved to preserve his enemy Dimmesdale so as to wring from him every ounce of suffering, the Monster draws out his revenge until Frankenstein dies of exhaustion on the polar icecap. Only Frankenstein's obsessive force could keep him following, only the Monster's malignant ingenuity motivate his pursuer: "Come on, my enemy . . ."

It is indeed a relationship to the death, of a kind Hawthorne has acutely characterized in *The Scarlet Letter*: "It is a curious subject of observation and inquiry, whether hatred and love be not the same thing at bottom. Each, in its utmost development, supposes a high degree of intimacy and heart-knowledge; each renders one individual dependent for the food of his affections and spiritual life upon another; each leaves the passionate lover, or the no less passionate hater, forlorn and desolate by the withdrawal of his subject . . ." So in Frankenstein's death the Monster finds him "worthy of love," and saying "my crimes are consummated" he mounts his funeral pyre triumphantly, to achieve the death wherein "must I find my happiness."

But even in his last moments the Monster does not let us forget that the issue is justice—a word Godwin's daughter has run through every portion of this work. With scathing irony the Monster defends himself to Walton. All his antagonists, "all human kind" are "virtuous and immaculate beings! I, the miserable and the abandoned, am an abortion, to be spurned at, and kicked, and trampled on. Even now my blood boils at the recollection of this injustice." If, as God pronounces in *Paradise Lost*, III, Satan's fate, and man's fall, but ultimate achievement of grace, all proclaim his "mercy and justice" throughout heaven and earth, Mary Shelley's world in *Frankenstein* is a dark one in which fundamental injustice prevails among men, and, in the allegory of the Monster and his Creator, between man and God.

NOTES

[1]As quoted in R. Glynn Grylls, *Mary Shelley* (London, 1938), Appendix E, p. 317.
[2]Muriel Spark, *Child of Light* (Hadleigh, Essex, 1951), p. 5.

NORMAN SPINRAD

STAND ON ZANZIBAR:
THE
NOVEL
AS
FILM

At the core of every science fiction novel, from the most sublime to the sheerest pandering drivel, is an attempt to resolve a paradox which in the final analysis may in fact be unresolvable. Unlike the "mainstream" novelist, the sf novelist *really* starts out with blank paper: he must not only create characters, theme, forces of destiny and plot but (unlike the mainstream novelist) must create from scratch a universe entire in which character, plot and destiny interact with each other and with the postulated environment.

This is why that rare creation the genuine sf novel (a work of art that is both genuinely sf and genuinely a novel) is, all other things being equal, a higher form of art than the "mainstream" novel. (Of course you knew that already on some visceral level, else why would you be reading this publication?)

However, the infuriating thing about writing sf novels is that the novelistic imperatives of plot, destiny and character are in conflict with the sf imperative of universe-creation. While one is in the process of creating in detail the sf context, the characters and plot hang in limbo; while one is advancing plot and characterization, one's grip on one's created universe tends to loosen. This explains, among other things: why New Wave advocates dislike

Originally published in *Science Fiction Review*, no. 29 (January 1969), pp. 12-14. Richard Geis edits *SFR*; both in 1969 and 1970, the annual Worldcon has voted *SFR* the best amateur magazine (fanzine). Reprinted by permission of Richard Geis and Norman Spinrad.

181

"Old Thing" novels in which the sf imperatives over-ride the novelistic imperatives; why "Old Thing" fans dislike hard-core "New Wave" in which traditional novelistic imperatives over-ride the sf imperative; why so few sf novels satisfy both camps; and why God felt constrained to rest on the seventh day—creating a universe *and* real people is no mean task, even if one has the advantage of omnipotence.

Basically, sf novelists have attempted to solve this fundamental problem in one of two ways. The first alternative is to hold up plot and characterization here and there and throw in chunks of background either with overt author-exposition or long quotes from non-existent books or worse still by having one's characters describe the scientific and historical background of the universe they inhabit.

The second alternative is to stay strictly within the viewpoints of the characters and let the reader pick up the background by a kind of osmosis, by letting him live the lives of real people as they move through their environment. It would seem that these two techniques or an unsatisfactory combination of the two are the *only* ways of writing a genuine science fiction novel.

Now, however, John Brunner has come along with *Stand* On *Zanzibar* and invented a third alternative.

One needs no crystal ball to predict that much will be made of this book for the wrong reasons. It is probably the longest sf novel ever written and there is some mysterious force operating in the sf field that tends to create a worship of giganticism. But after all, a long dreadful novel has no real advantage over a short dreadful novel except in the eyes of a confirmed masochist. Perhaps the worship of huge sf novels is merely the extension of the traditional American equation of quantity equals quality. So, in a way, it's a shame that *Stand On Zanzibar* is so long because it is not its length which makes it an important book but its form.

In the book itself, Brunner calls *Stand On Zanzibar* a "nonnovel." He has a point. *Stand On Zanzibar* is a literary construct consisting of one novel, several short stories, a series of essays and a lot of what can only be called schticks intercut and put together like a film. *Stand On Zanzibar* is not a novel; it is a film in book form.

This is stated quite candidly in the table of contents (one of the longest tables of content extant).

Brunner lists the sections of the book that constitute the novel about the two main viewpoint characters, Donald Hogan and Norman House, under the heading "Continuity." The essays are listed under "Context." The independent short stories about minor characters who inhabit the world of 2010 (and which have only tangential relationships in most cases to the "Continuity" novel) are listed under "Tracking with closeups." The schticks, the bits and pieces of such things as headlines, tv shows, commercials, quotes from books, etc., are listed under "The Happening World."

What we have here is the cinematic technique of the split-screen applied to the "novel."

Perhaps the only way to discuss such a book is to borrow some of Brunner's own technique.

Context

The world of 2010 is overpopulated. An interminable semi-war is being waged by the U.S. and China for control of the Pacific Basin through a series of proxies. (Sound familiar?) Eugenic legislation is prevalent throughout the Developed World. A Developing Country which fits the description of Indonesia but which Brunner calls "Yatakang" is developing a program for producing genetically-engineered supermen, the news of which program is producing political turmoil in the developed countries where the masses chafe under the eugenic legislation which forbids people with proscribed genes from having children. In the tiny impoverished African country of Beninia, the Shinkas, despite their squalid condition, have somehow achieved a tranquil "noble savage" culture.

Continuity

Norman House and Donald Hogan are roommates in super-crowded New York. House, an "Afram" (Brunner's 2010 slang for Negro, a mistake only a non-American would make), works for a large corporation which closes a deal with the dying President of Beninia to develop that country, a kind of benevolent neo-colonialism. House is appointed to head the corporation's effort in Beninia; in Beninia it is discovered by Chad Mulligan (sociologist whose works are quoted extensively in "Context" and "The Happening World") that the Shinkas' non-violent nature is a genetic mutation.

Meanwhile, Hogan is activated as a kind of CIA agent, "eptified" into a human killing machine and sent to Yatakang to kill Dr. Sugaiguntung, the key scientist in the Yatakang superman breeding program.

After many twists and turns in plot and motivation, Hogan achieves his end, which, in light of the discovery of the "peace" gene in Beninia, has ironic but not totally tragic overtones.

The Happening World

Legalized pot. Bizarre parties. Chad Mulligan's *Hipcrime Vocab*. Various sinister psychedelics. Yonderboys. Shalmaneser, the conscious (?) computor. Shiggies. Bleeders. Muckers. The shiggy circuit. *Scanalyzer*. TV shows.

Tracking with closeups

Chad Mulligan, sociologist playing at misanthropy and not making it. Various old colonial types dying to get in on the Beninia project. Eric Ellerman blackmailed, then murdered by yonderboys. Poppy Shelton, pregnant flower-child taking drugs so that her unborn child will never have to see the dreary straight world. Bennie Noakes, psychedelic vegetable. Guinevere Steel, Bitch-priestess of fashion.

Brunner has dealt with the paradox of sf imperatives versus novelistic imperatives by the simple process of dissociation. He gives the reader background in the "Context" and "The Happening World" sections. He writes a rather conventional unexceptional and unexceptionable sf novel in the "Continuity" sections. He gives his world depth and extension in the "Tracking with closeups" sections.

"Continuity" with a minor rewrite could've been published as an ordinary sf novel. "Tracking with closeups" could be re-edited (in the filmic sense) into a series of conventional sf stories.

If *Stand On Zanzibar* proves anything, it proves that the whole can be greater than the sum of its parts. None of the sections (the unedited film) are particularly brilliant by themselves. The total book is. It's all in the editing.

William Burroughs produces slices of his novels by randomly

cutting up pieces of coherent prose. The result is gibberish which adds nothing to the coherent sections of his novels.

Brunner takes a lot of ordinary sf and speculative non-fiction and edits it non-randomly into a brilliant non-novel.

John Brunner would make one hell of a film editor.

Stand On Zanzibar is a brilliant and dangerous book. Brilliant because with it Brunner has invented a whole new way of writing book-length sf.

Dangerous because what he has done looks so damned easy. I predict (while hoping I am wrong) that a lot of other sf writers are going to try their hands at books like this. It looks like the easy way out: write a conventional sf novel, a few short stories with the same background and a bunch of essays, and put together a most successful novel from them. Then go collect your Hugo.

But unfortunately, most sf writers (and especially those who would stoop to copying another man's success, the trend-riders) are most deficient in that area in which Brunner proves himself the master in *Zanzibar*: sense of structure.

Brunner is not a great master of prose, nor a great master of characterization, nor a great master of plotting. Yet he has written a great book. So there is the temptation to conclude that he has simply invented a gimmick which lesser writers can copy.

But what he has really done is applied a film technique to prose fiction and it works because Brunner has a great talent for film editing, whether he ever thought of it in those terms or not.

Those writers who believe it was all done with mirrors proceed at their own peril. Not to mention at the peril of their readers.

JANE HIPOLITO

THE LAST
AND FIRST
STARSHIP
FROM
EARTH

The Sphinx has many imitators. To duplicate her ancient feat—to capture the meaning of all human experience in a single nagging riddle—has formed the perennial ambition of philosophers and artists. Her enigma has challenged the talents of some of the world's best writers. Dostoevsky, Kafka, Joyce, Eliot, and Borges all have sought to play the Sphinx's role for mankind. To this distinguished company must now be added another, for in his first novel, *The Last Starship from Earth*, John Boyd has laid claim to be the latest and perhaps the most diverting of the Sphinx's successors.

Boyd insinuates his version of the age-old enigma in his title. *The Last Starship from Earth* may seem by its name to promise only the mindless thrills of the ordinary space opera; the book's bewildered reader, however, quickly discovers that in fact Boyd's title propounds the same philosophical conundrum that forms the heart of Boyd's novel. For him to determine which of the book's three starships is the last to leave earth, he must consider complex metaphysical problems of the nature of time and space, as well as their relation to human experience. He must realize how true are the paradoxes that last is first, then is now, and there is here.

Time and space become crucial mysteries in the novel's opening paragraph: "Rarely is it given man to know the day or the hour when fate intervenes in his destiny, but, because he had

This will be published in a forthcoming issue of *Speculation*, edited by Peter Weston in Great Britain.

checked his watch just before he saw the girl with the hips, Haldane IV knew the day, the hour, and the minute. At Point Sur, California, on September 5, at two minutes past two, he took the wrong turn and drove down a lane to hell." One is immediately tantalized by the incompleteness of Haldane's information; what, one wonders, is the year of this momentous encounter, and where is Haldane's hell located, in space or in metaphor? These are the questions that vex Boyd's reader throughout the novel.

Boyd first indicates that Haldane IV inhabits our earth at some indefinite future time. In this space age the pope is a computer, religion has been converted into theological cybernetics, and hell is a distant and peculiarly dismal planet which serves earthmen as a penal colony. Like the future anti-utopia of Aldous Huxley's *Brave New World*, Haldane's is a rigidly stratified culture, divided into professional and proletarian castes; and Haldane's world is also brave and new in its reverence for science and its contempt for poetry and passion. Still another sign that Boyd envisions a future earth is the patriotic, puritanical Citizens' Creed: here, as in George Orwell's *1984*, sex must be held "sacred to the purposes of the state," and "it is folly for a professional to endanger the social welfare for a tremor in the loins" (p. 33).

In other respects, however, Haldane IV seems very much our contemporary. In his world, as in ours, many assume that "every problem can be solved by the pope or a prostitute" (p. 10); Haldane researches a project which engages our own scientists, inventing a machine to analyze literature; and the novel's discussions of integration and miscegenation unmistakably refer not to any future or fictional society, but to race relations in twentieth-century America. In fact, *The Last Starship from Earth* clearly has as one of its primary purposes to satirize contemporary culture. Thus Haldane IV becomes an instrument of satire as Boyd attacks the modern reverence for the great God Justice, Whose three instruments are Sociology, Psychology, and Church; this novel devastatingly lampoons "those who would come to us with persuasive smiles and irreproachable logic in the name of religion, mental hygiene, social duty, come with their flags, their Bibles, their money credits" (p. 132). Finally, the impression that Haldane's world is essentially ours ornamented with some futuristic frippery seems decisively confirmed by the specific references to "Haldane IV of the twentieth century" (p. 25) and to "September 5, 1969, the very date of his accidental meeting with the then-virgin and extracategorical student, Helix" (p. 120).

Yet this certainty falters before the baffling impossibility of other specific chronological and geographical references in the book. Haldane IV describes Henry VIII as a famous sociologist influenced by Dewey; Haldane's Lincoln "brought about the political hegemony of the United Nations" (p. 59) and delivered a Johannesburg Address on the abuses of laser science; and Haldane's Christ lived to the age of seventy, died doing battle against Roman archers, and left as His sign not the Cross, but the Cross-bow. Moreover, Fairweather I, the post-Einsteinian mathematician who designed the pope, directed the first explorations of outer space, and masterminded the starflights to hell by his Fairweathian Mechanics—Fairweather I turns out to be a nineteenth-century figure: Haldane's studies disclose that "the man who had assembled the last representative of Saint Peter on earth" (p. 41) was also a nineteenth-century poet, whose only son was born in 1822 and who was censured by the last human pope in 1850.

Confronted with these and other historical absurdities, the reader of The Last Starship from Earth may well wonder with Haldane IV whether history is "a state secret" (p. 41) in this world, as it is in Orwell's 1984.   Indeed, Boyd's satire, like Orwell's, pictures an authoritarian, repressive regime which controls its citizens' deeds, words, and thoughts; and until the epilogue Boyd's reader must continually ask if Haldane, like Winston Smith, is the dupe of governmental "double-think," the official distortion of reality for propaganda purposes.   Perhaps Haldane's rulers have retold history in order to enforce the puritanism and patriotism which their Orwellian Citizens' Creed expresses.

Certainly one of the most powerful elements of Boyd's novel is its deft evocation of Orwell's anti-utopia.   Yet Boyd's power extends beyond satire and into areas unvisited even by Orwell's earlier anti-utopian vision.   For Boyd conceives reality to be much more conjectural than the objectively-minded Orwell permits. Hence Haldane's society is much more complicated than a revisited 1984, and Haldane's plight is even more complex than Winston Smith's.   As Haldane explains in the epilogue, his predicament is not as straightforward as Smith's: "[No] deliberate lies had been told; it was rather that the truth behaved strangely in the presence of Fairweathers" (p. 180).

In fact, the true explanation of Haldane's world totally transcends common sense: " 'My understanding isn't intelligence,' Haldane modestly admitted. 'You understand Fairweather by a trick of the mind. You have to think in non-human concepts' " (p. 91).

The particular non-human concepts which are required to understand Boyd's book may be subsumed under Fairweather's Simultaneity Theory. According to this theory, one solid can occupy two places at the same time and parallel lines do meet in space, for "time and light are . . . the same phenomena expressed in different media," and jumping the time warp means jumping the space warp as well (p. 121). At first glance such a theory may appear merely a fanciful philosophical exercise, "non-human" indeed in its removal from real life. But John Boyd not only makes this apparently fantastic theory the real basis of Haldane's whole career: he also suggests that our lives, like Haldane's, are fundamentally "simultaneous."

Haldane's experiences begin to make sense to us when he leaves earth for hell aboard the starship *Styx*: "Silent, bodiless, immune from the hurtling detritus of space, they moved inside the ship, vanished as sound vanishes to ears above Mach 1. They were light, riding a wave of simultaneity that would have sent them hurtling through the core of the sun unscathed. For three earth months, Haldane slept, and every minute on the ship's clocks reversed a day on earth" (p. 138).

In other words, Haldane flies backward both in space and in time; and the hell to which the *Styx* transports him is actually a primitive earth, 355 years younger than the one he left. In its flora, fauna, and climate this seventeenth-century world is naturally much like Haldane's native twentieth-century America. In its social aspects, however, hell differs drastically from Haldane's original environment. As a matter of fact, the two societies are absolutely antithetical. Ruled not by the earthly god Justice but by the opposite god Love, hell has none of the sterile amusements and repressive regulations of that law-and-order civilization; instead, hell's citizens display a rambunctious frontier individualism as they pursue their only common aim, "to fertilize and be fertilized" (p. 161).

What Haldane learns in exile, then, is that hell is not at all the horror he had imagined. He learns that Fairweather I deliberately fostered the illusion of hell's ugliness, by scheduling all starflights to arrive during hell's winter and by making the hell ships as hideous as possible, "horrible gray slugs" manned by toad-like pilots and moaning Gray Brothers (p. 56). And Haldane also learns that the men and women sent to hell for their criminal atavism and deviationism are far from being the monsters and corpses described by Fairweather's devotees, the sociologists, psychologists, and theologians. In Haldane's new view of things, the true "living dead" are the law-abiding earthmen, while hell's residents possess the tremendous vitality, charm, and heroism we associate with Elizabethan explorers and American pioneers.[1]

Holding such a favorable opinion of hell, Haldane responds to hell's sovereign, Fairweather II, who proposes that he "help us overthrow the Department of Sociology and set free the human spirit on earth" (p. 173). By re-entering earthly history at a particularly critical moment and thus altering the pattern of events, Haldane hopes to accomplish his wildest dream, "that someday earth and Hell will reunite in the final synthesis of the thesis and antithesis," Justice and Love (p. 152). His heroic deed is to commit deicide: Haldane IV, re-incarnated as Judas Iscariot, is to keep Christ from establishing His church, for, as Fairweather II points out, "There are few periods in history, and those come early, when one man could alter the course of nations. To eliminate the power of the sociologists, we must destroy the seeds of that power, which were planted before the sociologists came into being" (p. 173).

So everything that happens to Haldane after he leaves earth contributes to the reader's understanding of John Boyd's puzzling spatial and temporal schemes. Haldane's adventures in hell indicate that the strangely futuristic twentieth-century California in which he first appears is neither a future nor a contemporary earth, but rather a never-never land which occupies no time and no place. This is a world that never was, is not now, and never will be, because Haldane had meddled with history. *Non omnia secula seculorum.*

By contrast, the world of the novel's epilogue is our own twentieth-century earth, rich in "television publicity, student sit-ins, boycotts" (p. 178) and the omnipresent whine of "that gosh-derned country and western music" (p. 182). Conspicuous in this real twentieth century are social inequities, turbulence, and disharmony. Yet this is the world Haldane made, and according to his careful plan it should be perfectly just and perfectly loving.

The reason Boyd gives for the continuing imperfection of human existence is that Haldane himself bungled. Instead of assassinating Christ and returning immediately to hell, Haldane "side-tracked history or derailed it when he laid the hissop-drugged body of Jesus into the one-seater right after the Crucifixion" (p. 180). By thus yielding to the pleas of Mary Magdalene, he has doomed mankind in general and himself in particular to a long, tedious wait: "at the present rate of scientific progress it would be another two thousand years before he could catch a starship off this cruddy planet. There was another possibility he dreaded. He might have to tarry until He returned, and that would mean Purgatory if he were doomed to walk the earth, somewhere between the sophomore and junior class, for the next ten thousand years" (pp. 181-82). Haldane IV, alias Judas Iscariot, has become the Wandering Jew.

After reading the epilogue, then, Boyd's reader finally understands that the "first" starship from earth is the one that never flew, the *Styx* which ferried Haldane IV from a purely hypothetical 1969 to an equally fantastic 1614 (fantastic because Haldane's actions in the real 33 A.D. made both this 1614 and his original 1969 impossible). The novel's "second" starship from earth took Christ to hell in 33 A.D. And the third and "last" starflight, like the "first," cannot be dated, for it too has only potential existence: it may or may not happen.

Further, Boyd's reader comes to understand that in still another sense there have been no starships from earth. First, last, and always Boyd's astronauts fly to, not from, earth, arriving at their own hellish beginnings.

The most important of the epilogue's revelations, however, is that any attempt to define human experience in such terms as first and last, then and now, there and here, must inevitably fail. The profoundest truth about Boyd's starships is that they are continuously in operation, eternally and essentially simultaneous. For man perpetually shuttles from present to past and back to present again; as Freud, Jung, and other modern psychologists have shown, the human mind must forever return to its primitive beginnings for inspiration. And man's history, like man's mind, is patterned. As Haldane puts it, speaking with the ultimate wisdom of the Wandering Jew, "Patterns never changed. The tides of history were [forever] sweeping back" (p. 179).

Archetypal as Boyd makes this sound, the eternal return of *The Last Starship from Earth* is not simply Jungian. The novel also has the circularity of *Finnegans Wake*, and the very name of the heroine, Helix, evokes Yeats' gyre as well as the Irish poet's Sphinxian vision of "The Second Coming." Thus the company John Boyd keeps is good as he incarnates his illusion of the reality of the human condition. Whether the cross or the cross-bow challenges mankind represented by Haldane, and whether the time-space continuum of the novel is September 5, 1969, in whatever parallel universe, Boyd restates emphatically the enigmantic question of the Sphinx: what is man? And he answers the question with a Joycean affirmative.

WILLIS E. McNELLY

SCIENCE FICTION
THE
MODERN MYTHOLOGY
[VONNEGUT'S
SLAUGHTERHOUSE-FIVE]

On February 13, 1945, the United States Air Force dropped several thousand tons of incendiary bombs on Dresden, Germany. In the ensuing firestorm, over 135,000 people died, surpassing the number who perished in the later atomic bombing of Hiroshima and Nagasaki. Historians now agree that the destruction of Dresden, virtually an open city, amounted to an act of wanton cruelty to a nation only a month from death. The flames served no military purpose.

One of the survivors of the fire bombing was a fourth generation German-American, a U. S. Infantry prisoner of war named Kurt Vonnegut Jr. He escaped death only because the fallen cement blocks and insulation of an abattoir gave him a womb from which he eventually emerged into isolation.

Now, after 25 years of remembering, this horror has provided Vonnegut with the subject matter of a major novel, *Slaughterhouse-Five or the Children's Crusade* (Delacorte Press Bk. 1969). It is a work of transparent simplicity, a modern allegory whose hero, Billy Pilgrim, shuttles between earth and its timeless surrogate, Tralfamadore. In these journeys, Billy, who is both Vonnegut and a modern Everyman, seeks an answer to the inevitable questions about suffering. In addition, he ponders the incredible violence of war, its insanity and blind cruelty, and probes the proud flesh of an American society that—an even

Originally published as "Science Fiction—The Modern Mythology," *America*, 5 Sept., 1970, pp. 125-127. Reprinted with permission from America Press, Inc., 106 West 56 St., N. Y., N. Y. 10019. All rights reserved.

greater horror to Vonnegut—has managed to ignore the moral responsibility for Dresden as well as the ethical implications of the senseless attack. Vonnegut and Billy Pilgrim see both worlds—and which is real and which is fictional?—in innocent terms, but in the same shades as Picasso's "Guernica"—"deathing" color.

Reviewers of Vonnegut's novel have raised one basic question about its execution while they almost uniformly praise its conception, its empathy and its power. Why, they ask, did Vonnegut choose science fiction as his medium? Has he not outgrown the vagaries of *Player Piano, Cat's Cradle* or *God Bless You, Mr. Rosewater*—all of them ostensibly out-and-out science-fiction novels? These juvenilia, some critics maintain, are interesting oddities where Vonnegut learned his trade; but now, faced with problems of tragic intensity if not tragic import, he has flawed his vision by reverting to science fiction. His message, they imply, has been lost in his medium. Someday, they add, Vonnegut might write a great novel, but he will do so only when he abandons such standard science-fiction devices as probability worlds, alternate universes, cyclic time and time travel.

How valid are these objections? An unprejudiced analysis of *Slaughterhouse-Five* might reveal that none are true; that in fact Vonnegut's novel achieves stature precisely because it *is* a science-fiction novel. For it is only through science fiction that Vonnegut can bring himself and his readers to face or understand both the terrifying and the incomprehensible fact of the Dresden holocaust.

The best science fiction treats of the interface between man and the machine, the human problems issuing from the common boundary of differing disciplines. It considers the human problems affected by an extrapolation of some scientific hypothesis or device. In the hands of skilled verbal technicians like Vonnegut, Ray Bradbury, Arthur C. Clarke and John Boyd, science fiction becomes what a recent Modern Language Association conference called "the modern mythology." And like any mythology, science fiction works best on two levels, the objective as well as the subjective. It permits its readers to understand the implications of a hypothesized action, possible invention or transcendent machine. Because we live in an increasingly technological age, science fiction has become a contemporary form of Eliot's objective correlative, enabling us to face problems we cannot otherwise face directly;

permitting us to comprehend the tragic consequences of our mis-
use of science, science that should be a tool rather than a master, a
servant rather than a *dybbuk*.

So it is the soulless, violent spirit of man that Vonnegut is
attempting to exorcize in *Slaughterhouse-Five*. Man had, after all,
created the guns that Vonnegut fired before his capture and
imprisonment in Dresden. The mind of man had conceived the
plan for fire-bombing, manufactured the bombs, ridden the planes,
engaged the autopilots and aimed the intricate bombsights. In the
end, 135,000 men, women and children died in the fatal interface
of the machine. Their bodies were buried in the corpse-mine of
Dresden.

How does science fiction become the objective correlative in
Vonnegut's hands? Eliot originally used the term to explain how
the reader moves from the known to the unknown. In Eliot's
words, it is "a set of objects, a situation, a chain of events which
shall be the formula of that particular emotion; such that when
the external facts, which must terminate in sensory experience, are
given, the emotion is immediately evoked." The objective correlative can also transmute ideas into sensations or an observation
into a state of mind. As a consequence of this literary theory,
allusions of all kinds crowd Eliot's lines; the reader is led to associate Prufrock with Hamlet, Polonius and Osric, or the Fisher King
with Ariel. The conclusion is not mere comparison, but an
empathic symbiosis where the disparate esthetic emotions in the
mind of the artist are recreated by the reader.

So also with Vonnegut. Faced with the horror of Dresden,
its omnipresence of cruel disaster and accidental slaughter, he wills
that the reader share his incomprehension. He calmly states: "I
was in Dresden when it was bombed. I was a prisoner of war. I
just want you to know. I was there." Vonnegut can no longer
cope with the casual massacre of innocents. To enable himself,
and, by extension, his readers to cope with these matters, even if
only stoically, Vonnegut invents the planet Tralfamadore, whose
inhabitants (shaped like a green "plumber's friend") see time as
discontinuous, with all moments eternally present. Billy Pilgrim,
kidnapped by Tralfamadorians on a flying saucer, writes of his
experience:

The most important thing I learned on Tralfamadore was that when a person dies he only appears to die. He is still very much alive in the past, so it is very silly for people to cry at his funeral. All moments, past, present and future, always have existed, always will exist. The Tralfamadorians can look at all the different moments just the way we can look at a stretch of the Rocky Mountains, for instance. They can see how permanent all the moments are, and they can look at any moment that interests them. It is just an illusion we have here on Earth that one moment follows another one, like beads on a string, and that once a moment is gone it is gone forever.

When a Tralfamadorian sees a corpse, all he thinks is that the dead person is in bad condition in that particular moment, but that the same person is just fine in plenty of other moments. Now, when I myself hear that somebody is dead, I simply shrug and say what the Tralfamadorians say about dead people, which is 'So it goes.'

And *so it goes*. The phrase becomes incantatory; these are the magic words that exorcise, enchant, stoicize. They are repeated by Vonnegut and echoed by Pilgrim to convince Earthlings of Tralfamadorian fourth-dimensional reality. The words become a fatalistic chant, a dogmatic utterance, to permit Vonnegut himself to endure. In creating Tralfamadore, Vonnegut is suggesting that cyclic time or the eternal present will enable himself and mankind to accept the unacceptable. The sin of Dresden is so great that it will require an eternity to expiate. But eternity is not available to all men—only to the Tralfamadorians and the Pilgrim soul of man, and Vonnegut has, out of his science-fiction heritage, created both.

Billy Pilgrim is captured by the Tralfamadorians, caged by them, but always treated kindly. If Pilgrim attempts escape, however, he will die, for the Tralfamadorians are symbols of both death and life. They breathe cyanide and will eventually destroy the universe when a Tralfamadorian flying saucer pilot initiates a chain reaction in testing a new fuel. So it goes, says Pilgrim-Vonnegut, unconcerned by this cataclysmic tragedy, because he and the Tralfamadorians will spend eternity contemplating only the happy, pleasurable moments when the universe is not destroyed, when no one dies, when Dresden does not burn, when peace endures, and Pilgrim-mankind has eternal hope. In short, heaven—the eternal present.

Peculiarly enough, Vonnegut denies that he is writing science fiction. The bookjacket, in fact, maintains: "Once mistakenly typed as a science fiction writer, he is now recognized as a mainstream storyteller often fascinated by the tragic and comic possibilities of machines." He further indicates his antipathy to the form by introducing a hypothetical science-fiction writer named Kilgore Trout, whose one claim to fame was that in 1932 he "predicted the widespread use of burning jellied gasoline on human beings." Kilgore Trout's prose, however, is frightful, his books do not sell and his publishers fail. So with all science fiction, Vonnegut implies.

If Vonnegut has such an apparent antipathy to science fiction, why has he deliberately used its devices to tell his story?

Vonnegut himself provides the answer:

> Billy had seen the greatest massacre in European history which was the fire-bombing of Dresden. So it goes.
> So they were trying to re-invent themselves and their universe. Science fiction was a big help.
> Rosewater [the Eliot Rosewater of Vonnegut's earlier novel, *God Bless You, Mr. Rosewater*] said an interesting thing to Billy one time about a book that wasn't science fiction. He said that everything there was to know about life was in *The Brothers Karamazov* by Feodor Dostoevsky. 'But that isn't enough any more,' said Rosewater.

Humanity, then, is no longer enough to explain inhumanity. Man's inhumanity can be understood only tangentially, through the science fiction devices of flying saucers, alternate universes, probability worlds or time travel. As a consequence of Vonnegut's invention of the plunger-shaped, cyanide-breathing, non-human, science-fictional Tralfamadorians, the novel itself becomes its own statement of hope. Only the Tralfamadorian notion of time, where life becomes death becomes life, permits Vonnegut to say: "So it goes." In the end the apparently stoic, almost hopelessly pessimistic texture of the novel is transformed by the objective correlative of science fiction into affirmation: the song of a bird can conquer death.

In addition, science fiction devices employed in *Slaughter-*

house-Five function much as the devices of the pastoral do in elegaic poetry. The complex is expressed through the simple; intolerable pain shades into reconciliation. For the final statement of *Slaughterhouse-Five* is not one of death and its concomitant "So it goes." Rather it is a statement of rebirth, the cyclic return of springtime and singing birds that tell Billy Pilgrim "Poo-tee-weet." If, as Vonnegut suggests, mankind has come unstuck in time through the dissociation engendered by slaughter, Earthlings can find stoical, hopeful acceptance in the pattern presented by Tralfamadore. On the final page of the novel, mythic cycles incarnate into trees that are leafing out. Time and eternity, fiction and science fiction fuse to become Vonnegut's parable. Ultimately, through science fiction, despair becomes hope.

BRUCE FRANKLIN

FOREWORD
TO
J. G. BALLARD'S
"THE SUBLIMINAL MAN"

The increase in the quantity of objects is accompanied by an extension of the realm of the alien powers to which man is subjected, and every new product represents a new possibility of mutual swindling and mutual plundering. Man becomes ever poorer as man, his need for money becomes ever greater if he wants to overpower hostile being. The power of his money declines in inverse proportion to the increase in the volume of production: that is, his neediness grows as the power of money increases.

> —Karl Marx,
> *The Economic and Philosophical Manuscripts of 1844*

We talk a lot about science fiction as extrapolation, but in fact most science fiction does not extrapolate seriously. Instead it takes a willful, often whimsical, leap into a world spun out of the fantasy of the author, who then casually throws in some improbable hints about how that world developed out of (or into) our own. Certainly science fiction has enriched our common imagination by projecting worlds millions of years and light-years away, but such projections become increasingly less scientific and more fantastic the farther they are from us. Meanwhile, we have a desperate need for scientific, fictional extrapolation into the immediate future. This job, which rightfully belongs to science fiction, is being usurped, and performed dangerously, by paid ideologues of the political-economic status quo, as in *Markets of the Seventies,* by the editors of *Fortune,* and *Here Comes Tomorrow: Liv-*

Originally published in *The Mirror of Infinity*, Robert Silverberg, ed. (New York: Harper & Row, 1970), pp. 239-242.

ing and Working in the Year 2000, written by the *Wall Street Journal* staff and published by Dow-Jones. "The Subliminal Man" is a superb example of one of those too rare science-fiction stories that seriously extrapolate into the next few decades and do so with some sense of the ideological content of such an extrapolation.

In this respect, "The Subliminal Man" is an unusual story for Ballard himself. Ballard is a poet of death whose most typical fictions are apocalyptic imaginings, beautiful and ghastly visions of decay, death, despair. His early novels show the conscious origins of this desperate imagination (whereas "The Subliminal Man," as I shall try to demonstrate, analyzes these sources with more precision). *The Wind from Nowhere* (1961) and *The Drowned World* (1962) are science fictions of the wasteland. In one, London looks like "a city of hell"; in the other, it appears "like some imaginary city of hell." On the literal level, both books ascribe the destruction of the human world to a cosmological freak of nature. In the first, a global wind tears down all human buildings and tears apart almost all human relationships, converting the opening scenes of normal sexual alienation and sterility into a dry and dusty inferno. In the other, solar storms have caused the loss of part of the ionosphere, and the sun, burning through the thinner envelope, has converted the world into a steaming swamp, where human buildings lie drowned and human relationships melt back into a primeval and preconscious world dominated by reptiles. Ballard, however, clearly sees his own imaginings as only ostensibly caused by an unnatural quirk of nature. The world of his fiction already exists in the imaginations of a decadent society:

> Over the mantelpiece was a huge painting by the early 20th century surrealist Delvaux, in which ashen-faced women danced naked to the waist with dandified skeletons in tuxedos against a spectral bone-like landscape. On another wall one of Max Ernst's self-devouring phantasmagoric jungles screamed silently to itself, like the sump of some insane unconscious [p. 27].

Later the nightmare paintings, the actual jungle world, and the shared nightmares of the characters merge into each other: the painting by Ernst and the jungle "more and more . . . were coming to resemble each other, and in turn the third nightscape each of them carried within his mind. They never discussed their dreams, the common zone of twilight where they moved at night like the phantoms in the Delvaux painting" (pp. 73-74). As this world develops—that is, reveals its true "nature"—"the once translucent threshold of the womb had vanished, its place taken by the gateway to a sewer," and the hero, an impotent Fisher-King, leaves Beatrice behind and finally loses himself in the festering jungle bubbling out of his author's fantasy. Over and over, Ballard calls that jungle "subliminal," which gives us a clue to understanding the significance of "The Subliminal Man."

In "The Subliminal Man," Ballard goes to the actual sources of his own decadent imaginings of transfiguring death—his own society. It is not nature conquering man but man's own creations, his own productivity, attaining the dumb, senseless, uncontrolled power of primeval nature over him. Here Ballard explores the basic contradiction of decadent capitalism. The economic system, with its fantastic productivity and preposterous inability to satisfy real human needs, has become so completely irrational that it can survive only by enslaving the unconscious to its own most grotesque needs. Man himself must be reduced to a consuming animal below the threshold of conscious thought; he must become subliminal, literally "under the threshold," less than man.

If the products of overdeveloped capitalist society satisfied real human needs, they could be sold through rational explanations of their value. But such is clearly not the case. So in the present stage advertising uses a variety of means to get around rational thinking, which would reject its message, in order to jam that message into our unconscious processes. Behind the simplest singing commercial and the most intricate manipulation of our desires for success, power, fame, riches, and sex lies a vast industry of research on how advertising can exploit us unconsciously. Even the product's container is designed to make us irrational robots, as Gerald Stahl, Executive Vice-President of the Package Designers Council, so eloquently put it: "You have to have a carton that attracts and hypnotizes this woman, like waving a flashlight in front of her eyes." In 1956 some advertising companies took the logical next step and briefly (so far as we know) tried out the mechanism of Ballard's giant signs. Ballard merely extrapolates one stage.

The value of a story like "The Subliminal Man"—that is, how "good" it is—must be measured partly by the accuracy of its extrapolation. This means that we have to do some measuring.

A fashionable idea these days is that advanced industry reduces the amount of human work available, so that one of the main problems of the future will be finding things to do. "The Subliminal Man" displays the opposite: more and more laboring time is required to subsist (that is to satisfy the basic necessities as defined by society), and hence individual laboring time lengthens as the quality of life diminishes. Which is true? The average weekly hours worked by manufacturing production workers in the United States has been consistently rising for over 35 years; the 1962-67 average of 40.8 hours represents a 12% increase over the 1932-35 average and a 2% increase over the 1955-61 average. By 1966, one out of five nonfarm workers—that is, 9.4 million workers—worked 49 hours or more per week. In the average working family, the wife must also work in order to keep up with the credit payments (women now constitute 40% of the civilian work force). Meanwhile, automobile installment credit has gone from $455 million in 1945 to $6 billion in 1950, $18 billion in 1960, and $29 billion in 1965; total installment credit (not counting mortgages) has gone from $2.5 billion in 1945 to $14.7 billion in 1950 and $68.6 billion in 1965; private debt has gone from $250.9 billion in 1950 to $1 trillion 8.5 billion in 1967; and by 1965 the per-capita individual and noncorporate debt—that is, the average amount personally owed by each man, woman, and child—had reached $2,250. And none of this includes the public debt, national, state, and local. Government statistics on take-home pay are misleading, for out of this come all those new sales, property, and state and municipal income taxes needed to pay the interest on the public debt, as well as the payments on that huge private debt. In 1949, the average family was paying 11 cents of every take-home dollar in interest on household debt. By 1967, this figure had doubled: 22 cents out of every take-home dollar was paid to banks and finance companies as interest.

But even more impressive than its description of how the economics of capitalism is developing is the story's portrayal of some of the psychological consequences of this development. Ballard perceives that this superproductivity not only fails to meet actual human needs, but that it must constantly make people needier, more dissatisfied, more voracious, until they themselves become objects of no value to each other or to themselves. Mechanical men and women only make the nightmare more grotesque when they call each other "angel" and "darling" with the same unconsciousness they use in buying, consuming, or hiding the piles of cigarette butts and chocolate wrappings. This wasteland—dry, barren, sterile—can finally be compressed into that magnificent closing image of mechanical death.

My only substantive disagreement with the message of "The Subliminal Man" (and this is nothing if not a story with a message) is that it fails to recognize that more than a lone Hathaway will see "the signs" and revolt. Although Ballard accurately foresees the present widening police terror, he does not project the forces that now oppose that terror—and its source. Here, as the newspaper tells us each day, Ballard's imagination was certainly too conservative. But then, of course, the opening question is addressed to all of us.

BERNARD BERGONZI

THE
PUBLICATION
OF
THE TIME MACHINE,
1894-1895

It is generally agreed that H. G. Wells's first novel, *The Time Machine*, is a finer artistic and imaginative achievement than any of his later fiction. In March 1895, when it was appearing as a magazine serial, W. T. Stead wrote, 'Mr. H. G. Wells, who is writing the serial in the *New Review*, is a man of genius',[1] and in recent years Mr. V. S. Pritchett has remarked, 'Without question *The Time Machine* is the best piece of writing. It will take its place among the great stories of our language'.[2]

Yet *The Time Machine* is remarkable not only for its literary merits, but for its complex bibliographical history, which must be unparalleled among works of modern fiction. The basic facts have already been made known by Wells himself and other writers.[3] The earliest draft of the story was called *The Chronic Argonauts* and was serialized in the *Science Schools Journal*, the students' magazine of the Royal College of Science, in 1888. It had only the bare idea of 'time travelling' and a few lines of dialogue in common with the later versions. Wells subsequently made two further drafts, which are lost, and early in 1894, in response to a request by W. E. Henley, he returned to the story and rewrote it as a series of loosely connected articles for the *National Observer*. The first of them appeared in March, and six more were published between March and June, but the series was discontinued after Henley gave up the editorship. These articles have a fairly close resemblance to the story as we now know it, particularly the first

---

Originally published in *Review of English Studies*, 11, N.S. (1960), 42-51. Reprinted by permission of the author and the Clarendon Press, Oxford.

of them, but contain only a fraction of the material. Wells, with Henley's encouragement, continued to work on the story, though without any specific plans for its publication. In a newspaper interview given in 1906, Wells stated that *The Time Machine* was written in a fortnight of sustained effort.[4] If this was so, Wells could only have been referring to a draft of the story, and probably an early one, since letters written to him by Henley in September and November 1894 suggest that the story was still being worked on at that time. At the end of the year Henley took over the editorship of the *New Review* and arranged for the novel to be serialized there: it appeared in five instalments from January to May 1895. At the end of May *The Time Machine* was published as a book by William Heinemann, and this version is still in print. It is largely, though not entirely, the same as that serialized in the *New Review.* Some years later Wells made a few minor changes in the text, which mainly consisted of removing the chapter headings and running various chapters together; and this revised text was included in the Atlantic Edition of his works; it has since been reprinted in *The Short Stories of H. G. Wells* and the Everyman's Library edition of *The Wheels of Chance and The Time Machine.*

Allowing for minor revisions, this makes seven versions of *The Time Machine*, of which five have survived. But neither Wells nor his commentators have remarked that the first American edition, published in 1895 by Henry Holt and Co. of New York, contains a number of significant variations from both the *New Review* and Heinemann versions. Geoffrey H. Wells, in his bibliography, merely refers to the curious fact that the author's name appears on the title page as 'H. S. Wells'.[5] This American edition was published some time before the British one (copies were received by the Library of Congress on 7 May 1895, and the *Publishers' Weekly* for 18 May lists the book in its 'Weekly Record of New Publications'; the Heinemann edition was not published until 29 May), though it is not listed in I. R. Brussel's bibliography of nineteenth-century works by British authors which were first published in the United States.[6] It is, in fact, the true first edition.

The differences in the text, however, add considerably to the importance of the American edition. But before discussing them it will be necessary to summarize the differences between the *New Review* and Heinemann texts.[7] There are two places in which NR differs substantially from H. The first chapter, 'The Inventor', is much longer, since it corresponds to the first two chapters, 'Introduction' and 'The Machine', of H. And the first part of 'The Inventor' is quite different from 'Introduction' as printed in H. The former contains a lengthy account of the 'Time Traveller' and his friends, and shows them engaging in a somewhat leisurely discussion of the scientific and metaphysical aspects of time-travelling. Wells appears to have inserted into this discussion what may have been part of his early paper, 'The Universe Rigid', which had been accepted by Frank Harris for the *Fortnightly Review* in 1891 and then rejected as 'incomprehensible'.[8] The first chapter of H opens much more directly and omits this material: the first few pages are in fact a revision of the first of the *National Observer* articles, which had appeared on 17 March 1894. This suggests that the changes made in NR were somewhat provisional and were removed before publication in permanent form. There are some unpublished letters from Henley to Wells which suggest precisely this.[9] On 6 December 1894 Henley wrote:

> I am very strongly urged that it would be most unwise to reprint from the *N.O.* What is more, I see the force of the objection. Can you help me to a new first chapter? I send you the existing one. It is hard to beat, I know; but I shall be properly grateful if you'll try.

And the following day he wrote again:

> 'Tis in your hands, and you must use it as seems best to you. The great thing is not to keep too closely to the old *N.O.*

A postcard dated 12 December, bearing the terse inscription 'Excellent! W. E. H.' can be taken as evidence of the receipt of the new opening chapter from Wells. But it is reasonable to assume that Wells also thought that the original opening had been 'hard to beat', and so took the opportunity to restore it when the novel was published as a book.

The other principal difference between NR and H also concerns certain passages which appear in the former but not in the latter. In Chapter XIII of NR (which becomes Chapter XIV in H), published in the May issue, the 'Time Traveller', after leaving the world of the Eloi and the Morlocks, travels into the remoter future and finds that the remnants of humanity have dwindled into puny creatures like 'some small breed of kangaroo' who are preyed upon by huge monsters resembling centipedes. This episode of about 1,000 words is not reproduced in H, where the Traveller does not stop the machine until he reaches the desolate period when the earth has ceased to rotate and the only visible life consists of giant crabs. The episode is vividly written, but it fits rather uneasily into its context, and it is not surprising that Wells chose to remove it. Curiously enough, however, it was singled out for special praise by W. T. Stead, not only in another laudatory reference made while the serial was appearing, but also in a retrospective article on Wells's work published three years later: Stead had evidently only read *The Time Machine* in the serialized version and had not noticed the disappearance of the 'kangaroo' episode from the book.[10] In point of fact, this episode also seems to have been added as a result of the exigencies of serial publication. In a letter of 1 April 1895 Henley wrote:

> Our printers led me a dance last month which ended in the clapping on, against my will, of an extra chapter. Consequently, this last instalment is a little short: it runs in fact to less than nine pages.
>   Have you any more ideas? I should be glad to have a little more for my last; and it may be that you would not be sorry either. Of course, it would be tommyrot to write in for the sake of lengthening out; but I confess that, as it seems to me, at this point—with all time before you—you might very well give your fancy play, &, at the same time, oblige your editor. The Traveller's stoppings might, for instance, begin some period earlier than they do, & he might even tell us about the last man & his female & the ultimate degeneracy of which they are the proof and the sign. Or—but you are a better hand at it than I! I will add (1) that I honestly believe that to amplify in some sense will be to magnify the effect of the story; & (2) that I can give you a clear week for the work.

Henley's habit of editorial interference was notorious,[11] but in this case Wells seems to have gracefully agreed to what was suggested. Many years later, however, he remarked in an introduction to *The Time Machine:*

There was a slight struggle between the writer and W. E. Henley
who wanted, he said, to put a little 'writing' into the tale. But
the writer was in reaction from that sort of thing, the Henley
interpolations were cut out again, and he had his own way with
the text.[12]

Apart from the passages just discussed, the only other differences
between NR and H consist of the occasional alteration, addition,
or removal of single words or short phrases, and a certain modification of the chapter divisions.

NY, however, contains several major differences from both
NR and H, and a considerable number of minor ones. The opening
of the novel, in particular, differs from both the other two
versions. Like NR it contains a long first chapter called 'The
Inventor', equivalent to Chapters I and II of H. The first 800
words are identical with NR, but thereafter it corresponds with H.
The Traveller's account of the Rigid Universe which comes in
Chapter I of NR is not included. This first chapter of NY in fact
follows the first *National Observer* article rather more closely than
does H. Thus, though the 'Time Traveller' is referred to as such in
the first 800 words (as in NR), in the next few pages (corresponding to Chapter I of H) he is called the 'Philosophical Inventor' or
the 'Philosophical Person' as in the *National Observer.* In H, on
the other hand, he is consistently the 'Time Traveller'. This suggests very strongly that Chapter I of NY was not all written at the
same time and that the part of it which corresponds to Chapter I
of H was written first. At the same time, there are certain places
where Chapter I of NY follows NR rather than the *National
Observer* article or H. The character, for instance, who is called
the 'Provincial Mayor' in the *National Observer*, becomes the
'Rector' in NR; in NY he is the 'Provincial Mayor' at the beginning
of the chapter and the 'Rector' at the end; in H he is once more
the 'Provincial Mayor' throughout. There are other cases where
Wells has made several successive alterations of the same phrase.
Thus, in the second *National Observer* article, published on 24
March 1894, the Traveller, describing the sensations of time-
travelling, remarks, 'the night is like the flapping of a black wing';
in NR and NY this is replaced by the inept phrase, 'day followed
night like the flap, flap, flap of some rotating body' (Chapter III);

but in H we find once more, 'night followed day like the flapping of a black wing' (Chapter IV).

In Chapter IV of NR and NY there is a curious fossil-like survival of an earlier stage of the story: the Traveller refers there to 'the people of the year Thirty-two thousand odd', whereas in NR, NY, and H the age of the Eloi and Morlocks is A.D. 802701, and in the *National Observer* articles it had been merely A.D. 12203. Evidently Wells had provisionally adopted another date before deciding on one sufficiently far in the future, and it is remarkable that the allusion should have been allowed to pass, at least in NR, which bears every sign of being a carefully corrected text. In H, however, it has been corrected to 'the people of the year Eight Hundred and two thousand odd' (Chapter V).

There is another major difference between NY and the other texts in the chapter containing the 'kangaroo' episode in NR (XIII of NY and NR, XIV of H). Though the episode is not included in NY, the chapter is somewhat different from the corresponding one of H. The arrangement of several paragraphs at the opening corresponds with NR rather than H, and though it also incorporates what in NR is Chapter XIV and in H Chapter XV (the penultimate chapter of each), the part actually corresponding to Chapter XIV of H is shorter and less elaborately written: the following collation will show the kind of expansion introduced in NR-H.

NY	NR-H
But as my motion became slower there was, I found, no blinking change of day and night. A steady twilight brooded over the earth. And the band of light that had indicated the sun had, I now noticed, become fainter, had faded indeed to invisibility in the east, and in the west was increasingly broader and redder. The circling of the stars growing slower and slower had given place to creeping points of light. At last, some time before I	As I drove on, a peculiar change crept over the appearance of things. The palpitating greyness grew darker; then—though I was still travelling with prodigious velocity—the blinking succession of day and night, which was usually indicative of a slower pace, returned, and grew more and more marked. This puzzled me very much at first. The alternations of night and day grew slower and slower, and so did the passage of the sun across the

stopped, the sun, red and very large, halted motionless upon the horizon, a vast dome glowing with a dull heat. The work of the tidal drag was accomplished. The earth had come to rest with one face to the sun even as in our own time the moon faces the earth.

sky, until they seemed to stretch through centuries. At last a steady twilight brooded over the earth, a twilight only broken now and then when a comet glared across the darkling sky. The band of light that had indicated the sun had long since disappeared; for the sun had ceased to set—it simply rose and fell in the west, and grew ever broader and more red. All trace of the moon had vanished. The circling of the stars, growing slower and slower, had given place to creeping points of light. At last, some time before I stopped, the sun, red and very large, halted motionless upon the horizon, a vast dome glowing with a dull heat, and now and then suffering a momentary extinction. At one time it had for a little while glowed more brilliantly again, but it speedily reverted to its sullen red-heat. I perceived by this slowing down of its rising and setting that the work of the tidal drag was done. The earth had come to rest with one face to the sun, even as in our own time the moon faces the earth.

The third major difference between NY on the one hand, and NR and H on the other, comes at the very end of the book. In NR-H there is an eloquent 'Epilogue' of about 250 words which begins:

> One cannot choose but wonder. Will he ever return? It may be that he swept back into the past, and fell among the blood-drinking, hairy savages of the Age of Unpolished Stone; into the abysses of the Cretaceous Sea; or among the grotesque saurians, the huge reptilian brutes of the Jurassic times.

It concludes:

And I have by me, for my comfort, two strange white flowers—
shrivelled now, and brown and flat and brittle—to witness that
even when mind and strength had gone, gratitude and a mutual
tenderness still lived on in the heart of man.

In contrast to this highly coloured but dramatically effective conclusion, the final sentences of NY merely offer a flat and abrupt
return to the Kiplingesque manner of the opening pages:[13]

> Up to the present he has not returned, and when he does return
> he will find his home in the hands of strangers and his little
> gathering of auditors broken up for ever. Filby has exchanged
> poetry for playwriting, and is a rich man—as literary men go—
> and extremely unpopular. The Medical Man is dead, the Journal-
> ist is in India, and the Psychologist has succumbed to paralysis.
> Some of the other men I used to meet there have dropped com-
> pletely out of existence as if they, too, had travelled off upon
> some similar anachronisms. And so, ending in a kind of dead
> wall, the story of the Time Machine must remain for the present
> at least.

Apart from these substantial additions to or omissions from
the text, NY has a great many stylistic differences from NR and H,
particularly in the latter two-thirds of the book. The possibility of
editorial changes made by the New York publisher must be
allowed for: there is evidence of such changes where spelling is
concerned, since American spellings ('Traveler', 'clew', 'somber',
'color', &c.) have been consistently introduced and 'damned' has
been expurgated throughout to 'd———d'. In fact, the innumer-
able differences of punctuation, capitalization, and paragraphing
may be mostly ascribed to Holt and Co. or their printer. NY has,
in particular, many more paragraph divisions than H. But it seems
less likely that the purely verbal alterations were made by the
publisher, since in most cases their effect is to make NR-H seem
less clumsy or more vivid and precise than NY. The following
collation of selected passages will make apparent the kind of
stylistic differences in question.

NY	H
This again was a question I delib-erately put to myself, and upon	This, again, was a question I de-liberately put to myself, and my

which my curiòsity was at first entirely defeated. Neither were there any old or infirm among them.

(VII)

curiosity was at first entirely defeated upon the point. The thing puzzled me, and I was led to make a further remark, which puzzled me still more: that aged and infirm among this people there were none.

(VIII)

And finally the evident confusion in the sunlight, the hasty flight towards dark shadow, and the carriage of the head while in the light, re-enforced the idea of an extremely sensitive retina.

(VII)

And last of all, that evident confusion in the sunshine, that hasty yet fumbling and awkward flight towards dark shadow, and that peculiar carriage of the head while in the light—all reinforced the theory of an extreme sensitiveness of the retina.

(VIII)

[The next passage, substituting 'suddenly' for 'evidently', first appeared in the National Observer, 19 May 1894.]
You can scarcely imagine how nauseatingly inhuman those pale chinless faces and great lidless, pinkish-gray eyes seemed, as they stared stupidly, evidently blinded by the light. So I gained time and retreated again, and when my second match had ended struck my third.

(VIII)

You can scarce imagine how nauseatingly inhuman they looked—those pale, chinless faces, and great, lidless, pinkish-grey eyes! —as they stared in their blindness and bewilderment. But I did not stay to look, I promise you: I retreated again, and when my second match had ended, I struck my third.

(IX)

I held it flaring, and immediately the white backs of the Morlocks became visible as they fled amid the trees.

(XI)

I held it flaring, and saw the white backs of the Morlocks in flight amid the trees.

(XII)

Somehow this gave me strength for another effort.

(XI)

It gave me strength.

(XII)

I walked about the hill among them and avoiding them, looking for some trace of Weena, but I found nothing. (XI)	I walked about the hill among them and avoided them, looking for some trace of Weena. But Weena was gone. (XII)

A number of conclusions may be drawn from the evidence so far presented. As I have implied, there is a very strong probability that NY is an early and unrevised version of NR-H. Apart from the stylistic differences this assumption is supported by the fact that Chapter XIII of NY somewhat resembles the corresponding chapter of NR but lacks the 'kangaroo' episode, which Wells presumably inserted at Henley's request in early April 1895. (And since NY was published early in May the manuscript would certainly have been with Holt before Wells made the addition.) The differences in the concluding paragraphs of the novel also support this opinion: in fact, it seems likely that the 'Epilogue', as published in NR-H, was also added by Wells, in response to Henley's letter of 1 April, at the same time as the 'kangaroo' episode, and that, unlike the latter, he decided to keep it when the novel was published as a book.

The evidence of the opening chapter is less conclusive, admittedly. But the probable sequence of events would appear to be as follows. Wells had originally intended to open the story with the introduction as printed in the *National Observer*, 17 March 1894, but being asked early in December 1894 for a new opening chapter he supplied one, and this was published in the *New Review* in January 1895. Wells kept the first 800 words of this new chapter for NY, but removed the rest, and added on instead the original *National Observer* article: hence the inconsistencies in the description of the 'Time Traveller'/'Philosophical Person' and the 'Provincial Mayor'/'Rector'. Before the publication of H, however, Wells removed all trace of the new first chapter he had written for NR, and merely kept the original *National Observer* opening, somewhat revised, with the inconsistencies that had appeared in NY removed. Chapter I of NY, therefore, appears to be an intermediate version between NR and H, though the rest of the text would appear to be earlier than NR. Unfortunately there is no surviving external evidence relating to NY: Wells does not refer to it in his autobiography, the records of Henry Holt and Co. do not go so far back, and there is apparently nothing bearing on the edition in the Wells papers at the University of Illinois. So any account of the history of NY must be conjecture based on internal evidence.

I think it probable that the text of NY is in fact the version that Wells developed from the *National Observer* articles in the summer and autumn of 1894, and that in December 1894 (or January 1895 at the latest) he was negotiating with Holt or an agent of theirs for an American edition of the book. There is a curious piece of evidence in Chapter XIV of NY, where we find the sentence, 'I heard the door of the laboratory slam, seated myself in a chair, and took up the *New Review*.' In NR-H 'a daily paper' is substituted for the name of the magazine. It is very likely that Wells inserted this little advertisement for Henley's new venture at about the time when Henley took over the editorship— i.e. in November or December 1894—but afterwards removed it as rather pointless. Before the manuscript was dispatched to America Wells rewrote the first chapter, adding part of the new opening he had written for NR. Thereafter it was out of his hands. It may also be significant that NY does not contain the dedication to Henley which appeared in H, and about which Wells and Henley were corresponding at the end of January 1895.

However, as the monthly parts appeared in the *New Review* Wells continued to revise the text, and the March, April, and May instalments were extensively rewritten, with the 'kangaroo' episode and the 'Epilogue' added to the May instalment. Finally, before the story was published as a book by Heinemann at the end of May, he made a few more verbal revisions, restored the opening chapter to something like his original intention of December 1894, and removed the 'kangaroo' episode but kept the 'Epilogue'. Wells may have virtually disowned the New York edition, since it represented an unrevised text, and this may account for his subsequent silence about it.

Wells was never again to bestow such care on revising his work, though he did make a number of changes to the text of *When the Sleeper Wakes,* first published in 1899, before it was reissued in 1910 as *The Sleeper Awakes.* In later years his writing became increasingly hurried and undistinguished, and in 1915 he wrote to Henry James, 'I had rather be called a journalist than an artist, that is the essence of it. . . .'[14] But a study of the successive versions that he made of *The Time Machine* between the summer of 1894 and the spring of 1895 suggests that the young Wells had an artistic scrupulosity almost rivalling that of James himself.

NOTES

[1]*Review of Reviews*, xi (1895), 263.

[2]*The Living Novel* (London, 1946), pp. 119-20.

[3]See H. G. Wells, *Experiment in Autobiography* (London, 1934), i. 309, ii. 515-519, 530; Geoffrey West [Geoffrey H. Wells], *H. G. Wells* (London, 1930), pp. 287-94; Georges Connes, 'La première forme de la Machine à explorer le temps', *Revue Anglo-Americaine*, i (1924), 339-44.

[4]*New York Herald,* 15 April 1906.

[5]*H. G. Wells: A Bibliography* (London, 1926), p. 4.

[6]*Anglo-American First Editions 1826-1900: East to West* (London, 1935).

[7]Henceforth the *New Review* version will be referred to by the symbol NR, the Holt edition by NY, and the Heinemann edition by H; NR-H will be used for passages where NR and H are identical.

[8]Wells, *Experiment in Autobiography* (London, 1934), i. 356-9.

[9]I am indebted to Professor Gordon N. Ray for permission to quote from this correspondence. The originals are in the Library of the University of Illinois.

[10]'How the World Will Die', *Review of Reviews,* xi (1895), 416. 'The Latest Apocalypse of the End of the World', *Review of Reviews,* xvii (1898), 389-96.

[11]See Kennedy Williamson, *W. E. Henley* (London, 1930), p. 240.

[12]Wells, *Works* (Atlantic Edition, London, 1924), I. xxi-xxii.

[13]The influence of Kipling on some of Wells's short stories was remarked on in a review of *The Stolen Bacillus* in the *Saturday Review,* 21 December 1895.

[14]James, *Letters* (London, 1920), ii. 505.

I. F. CLARKE

THE
SHAPE
OF
WARS
TO COME

The first battles in the Great War, long foretold by Bismarck and Moltke, had already been reported and described at the beginning of the twentieth century. According to one German writer, Karl Eisenhart, the Great War began on the grey morning of a nameless day in an unknown month when swift German cruisers steamed out from North Sea ports. Their task, as Eisenhart explained in *Die Abrechnung mit England* in 1900, was to destroy British commerce on the high seas—the indispensable preliminary to the final defeat of the United Kingdom.

But that was only one version of the future, for in the years of 1900 and 1901 British, French, and German writers between them produced at least a dozen different accounts of the Great War. In 1900, for example, Colonel Maude described the initial success of a French invasion in *The New Battle of Dorking*. He planned his imaginary war on the fact that "there are three months in every year—July, August, September—during which the French Army is ready for immediate warfare. And every year during these months there is a constantly recurrent probability of a surprise raid on London by the 100,000 men whom they could without difficulty put on board ship, land in England, and march to within a dozen miles of London in less than three days from the receipt of the order to move."

The stratagems of the enemy varied according to the know-

Originally published in *History Today*, 15 (February 1965), 108-116. Reprinted by permission of the author and publisher.

ledge and intentions of the authors of these tales of imaginary warfare. One device much used by popular writers of the period was to describe a treacherous attack by a Fifth Column of alien workers. In *The Invaders*, written by the journalist Louis Tracy in 1901, disguised French and German troops pour from their hiding places to seize Liverpool, Birmingham and Derby. The hero looks out of his window one morning to see mysterious figures assembling in the street. "The light of the street lamps revealed to him British horses and arms, British cannon and ammunition carts, portions of a howitzer battery, British commissariat carts, Army Hospital waggons—all the paraphernalia of war, and all unmistakeably belonging to his own service. But the officers and men! They were clothed in khaki, but not of British cut. They were quite unmistakeably foreigners."

Even more remarkable was Max Pemberton's very popular account of the French attempt to construct a secret tunnel under the Channel for the purpose of invading England. In this story of 1901, *Pro Patria*, a courageous officer stumbles on the French plans, and in a way that anticipates Erskine Childers in the *Riddle of the Sands* he tracks down the danger to its source. "The vigilance of one man," so ran the post-script to *Pro Patria*, "defeated this great scheme; he shut the gate, as he says, in the face of France. But the tube of steel still lies below the sea. No living man, outside the purlieus of the secret, can say how far that tunnel is carried, or where the last tube of it is riveted. It may even come to Dover's cliffs."

The French versions of the coming conflict were equally fantastic and equally popular. In March 1900 the highly respectable French weekly, *Le Monde Illustré*, devoted an entire number to an illustrated account of a future war against Great Britain, *La Guerre Anglo-Franco-Russe*. Similarly, in *L'Agonie d'Albion* Eugène Demolder related the defeat and fall of the British Empire; and in *La Guerre Fatale: France-Angleterre* the French military writer, Capitaine Danrit, described a swift invasion and conquest of the United Kingdom. With a band playing *Sidi Brahim* and to the cry of *En avant! la garde du drapeau*, the men of a crack Chasseur regiment storm ashore at Deal. The rest of the tale goes off with the enviable celerity of a staff exercise. The British defence crumbles before the ferocity of the French attacks and London falls within weeks of the first landings. The point of all this appears in the author's conclusion at the end of *La Guerre Fatale*. His intention had been to show that, "although the ancient enemy of France pursues an admirably conducted policy and is unusually daring, nevertheless Britain is really a colossus with feet of clay. Up to now she has imposed on the world by her arrogance, by her capacity to foresee the trend of events, and by her lack of scruples. But she has a miserable army, and in my story I have actually given it too big a rôle; for even though British officers died bravely in South Africa, there is only one word with which to describe their men and that is—cowards."

These tales of the war-to-come were one of the more extraordinary literary activities that engaged the attention of readers in the principal European countries between 1871 and 1914. During the half-century before the First World War there was a constant succession of short stories and book-length anticipations of what reviewers liked to call "the next great war." At first they appeared occasionally in sudden bursts of publication in response to some commotion of the moment like the alarm at the proposals for a Channel Tunnel in 1882, or the indignation of the French at British activities in Egypt during the eighteen-eighties, or the anxiety caused by the isolation of Britain in the eighteen-nineties. By the beginning of the twentieth century, however, the publication of these stories had reached flood proportions; and from 1900 onwards, when German accounts of the *Zukunftskrieg* began to appear in growing numbers, tales of future warfare came out by the dozen every year right up to the outbreak of the war that most of the writers had so signally failed to anticipate.

One of the more curious facts about these imaginary wars of the future is that they were among the first-fruits of the new technologies and the new primary schools. They began after the Franco-German War as an attempt to inform the middle classes of the changes brought about by the breech-loader, the iron-clad warship, and the new warfare of great numbers and rapid movement made possible by the use of railways. And then in the eighteen-nineties, with the coming of universal literacy and the beginnings of the mass newspapers, the scope of the war-to-come widened to include the whole nation. Thus, the tale of imaginary warfare began to develop after the publication of *The Battle of Dorking* by Lieutenant-Colonel George Chesney in the May issue of *Blackwood's Magazine* in 1871. Later on it entered on a new and wider phase of activity after the appearance of book-length stories like *The Great War in England in 1897.* This first appeared as a serial in *Answers* during the war scare of 1893. In the following year it came out as a book, ran through twenty-six editions, and was translated into most European languages.

After the continental success enjoyed by Chesney's *The Battle of Dorking* it became common practice for British, French, and German writers to describe imaginary defeats—or victories—in some future period in order to demonstrate the need for the appropriate reforms in the armed forces, or to advertise the advantages of the measures and policies they recommended. In the course of this literature from 1871 to 1914 there was always a close correlation between the politics of the day and the projections of the future. Until the early years of the twentieth century, British writers generally selected France as the principal enemy; and most of the writers agreed with the author of *The Sack of London in the Great French War of 1901* that French hostility was a matter of pure envy: "envy of England's great Empire, envy at her freedom, envy at the stability of her Government, of her settled monarchy, and of her beloved Queen." Propaganda of this kind continued until 1904 in such stories as *The Coming Waterloo, A New Trafalgar, Pro Patria, The Invaders, Seaward for the Foe, Starved into Surrender, Black Fortnight, Trafalgar Refought.* All were variations on the theme that, as one author wrote, "Great Britain stood face to face with allied France and Russia for the death-grip."

The French, however, were divided between the duty of describing the great war of *la revanche* against Germany and a sense of fierce indignation at British policies that issued into satisfying visions of a conquered and humiliated Albion. And then, quite suddenly, with the beginning of the Entente the British were no longer the enemies of France in imaginary wars of the future. From 1904 to 1914 French writers confined themselves to the business of relating the defeat of Germany in stories like *Une Guerre Franco-allemande, La Bataille de 1915, Les Ailes de la Victoire, Le partage de l'Allemagne, La fin de la Prusse.* The first World War, it seems, had been desired and described before it began.

With the Germans it was quite different at first. While British and French writers were turning out vivid accounts of future battles between 1871 and 1900, the German interest was all for prosaic staff appreciations of the next war, or for translations of foreign accounts like Admiral Colomb's *Great War of 1892*. Only after Germany started to build a fleet did writers begin to produce forecasts of great wars in which heroic German soldiers conquered Europe in the name of the Kaiser. And then, after the appearance of the *Riddle of the Sands* in 1903 and the translation of August Niemann's *Der Weltkrieg* as *The coming conquest of England* in 1904, the great war between the British and the Germans commenced in earnest. For the first time since *The Battle of Dorking* the Germans began the large-scale production of tales like *Der Deutsch-englische Krieg, Die "Offensiv-Invasion" gegen England, Mit Deutschen Waffen über Paris nach London*. Their common theme was victory, the expansion of the Reich, and the pleasing episode at the end of Niemann's *Der Weltkrieg*: "His Majesty the Emperor will enter London at the head of the allied armies. Peace is assured. God grant that it may be the last war which we shall have to wage for the future happiness of the German nation."

On the British side, the war against Germany opened with two publications of 1903. The first was *Modern warfare; or how our soldiers fight* by Captain Guggisberg. It attracted little attention, although the writer described a German invasion of Belgium and a British warning that any attack on Belgium would be considered a hostile act. In consequence, when the German armies cross the Belgian frontier on July 1st, 1905, "the telegraph lines from London flash the order to 'mobilize' to the Army and Navy in all parts of the United Kingdom. Before midday every corner of the Empire knows that Britain and Germany are at war."

The other story of 1903, although less spectacular than this account, was far more successful. In the *Riddle of the Sands* that brave and chivalrous yachtsman, Erskine Childers, devised the ideal myth in which to convey the anxieties of a nation beginning to be alarmed at a menace from overseas. The exciting detective work in the stage-by-stage account of the discovery of the German invasion plans was admirably calculated to express contemporary fears for the future. The rapid narrative, the constant mystery and adventure, the excellent sailing episodes, and the appearance of the All Highest himself combined the advantages of realism and romance. The story seemed as if it ought to be true; and for this reason it caused a sensation when it came out. Several hundred thousand copies of the cheap edition were sold, and in Germany the book was ordered to be confiscated.

Erskine Childers had presented the first stage of a legend that was taken up and enlarged by later writers. In William Le Queux's notorious *Invasion of 1910* and in Guy du Maurier's very successful play, *An Englishman's Home*, the invaders were shown in the act of conquering the British Isles; and in Saki's *When William Came* the end-stage of the operation could be observed in the detailed account of life under enemy rule in Hohenzollern Britain. All this had begun in the last chapters of the *Riddle of the Sands* after the hero had hidden himself on the German tug and so had discovered the purpose of the secret manoeuvers off the Friesland coast:

> The course he had set was about west, with Norderney light a couple of points off the port bow. The course for Memmert? Possibly; but I cared not, for my mind was far from Memmert tonight. *It was the course for England too.* Yes, I understood at last. I was assisting at an experimental rehearsal of a great scene to be enacted, perhaps, in the near future—a scene when multitudes of sea-going lighters, carrying full loads of soldiers, not half loads of coal, should issue simultaneously, in seven ordered fleets, from seven shallow outlets and under escort of the Imperial Navy traverse the North Sea and throw themselves upon English shores.

After this warning of intended invasion in 1903 and Niemann's forecast of war in 1904, stories of the coming conflict came out every year in Britain and Germany until a real war put an end to this literature. The first major increase in production took place in 1906, a bumper year which saw the appearance of several widely read books: *Volker Europas, Hamburg und Bremen in Gefahr, 1906: der Zusammenbruch der alten Welt, The Shock of Battle, The Enemy in Our Midst, The North Sea Bubble, The Writing on the Wall, The Invasion of 1910*. They were all written at a time when international affairs had deteriorated after Bulow had staged the Tangier incident in 1905.

In March 1906, the *Daily Mail* declared war on Germany in a serial that proved to be the most sensational of all the imaginary wars before 1914. It was written by Queen Alexandra's favourite novelist, William Le Queux; and his account of a German descent upon the British Isles aroused such interest that it was translated into twenty-seven languages—including Arabic, Japanese, and Chinese. The story sold a million copies throughout the world when it appeared in book form. At the special request of the Spanish government, so the *Daily Mail* announced, it was translated for the instruction of their army and navy officers. And in Germany an enterprising publisher gave it a different ending by removing all reference to the final defeat of the Germans. It was sold under the title of *Der Einfall der Deutschen in England* in a special edition for boys.

The story began in 1905 as another of Harmsworth's ideas for the *Daily Mail*. He commissioned Le Queux to do the writing; and, after four months spent in touring the likely invasion areas, Le Queux set to work on his story. In this he had help from the naval writer, H. W. Wilson, and from that untiring champion of Army expansion, Lord Roberts. Le Queux and the Field-Marshal worked out the most likely plan for a German invasion according to the best military principles. But, when the scheme was put before Harmsworth, they were told that, although the strategy might be faultless, it would not be in the best interests of the *Daily Mail* if major battles were to take place in areas where there was no chance of large sales. So, the Field-Marshal was defeated, and the plan of campaign was altered to allow the Uhlans to gallop into every town from Hull and York to Southen-on-Sea. One wonders what the Spanish officers made of it all.

Still with an eye to the sale of the *Daily Mail*, Harmsworth placed full-page advertisements in London dailies and in the larger provincial newspapers. These showed a map of the district the Germans were to be invading the next day in the *Mail*. Another stunt was to send sandwich-men through London, dressed in Prussian-blue uniforms and spiked helmets, carrying notices of the Le Queux serial. And later on, in 1906, when it came out in book form, it carried a specially reproduced letter in the hand of Lord Roberts. He commended the story to all readers: "The catastrophe that may happen if we still remain in our present state of unpreparedness is vividly and forcibly illustrated in Mr. Le

Queux's new book which I recommend to the perusal of every one who has the welfare of the British Empire at heart."

Other writers joined in the imaginary war against Germany; and most of them accepted the convention of an invasion as the framework and basis of their arguments in favour of naval, or military, or political measures. The Royal Navy, for example, in *When the Eagle Flies Seaward* put the case against the politicians with the customary terseness of the Senior Service: "Why the hell didn't you electors scrap this Government for cutting down naval construction?" The navy placed the blame for disaster squarely on the shoulders of the feckless electorate: "You sat ashore here rolling your eyes in thankfulness at 'economy, economy'; you didn't care a damn about the Navy so long as you had a penny off your beer and twopence off your tobacco."

Although stories of this type may strike the modern reader as the work of alarmists, there can be no doubt that they expressed the fears of many Edwardians. The growth of a bellicose German imperialism, the international disputes with France and later with Germany, and the decision to abandon our traditional isolation were all factors that helped to encourage an expectation of war. As Sir Henry Newbolt said of his generation, "we spent all our lives among warring nations, and in grave anticipation of the supreme danger which broke upon us at last." This fact and the inevitable failure to foresee the scale and slaughter of the first great technological war were major influences in encouraging writers to imagine the shape of the conflict-to-come. War still seemed both natural and inevitable to most people; and in their projections of imaginary wars writers carried over into a mythical future a vision of war that was a simple affair of charging cavalry, quick infantry actions, and a campaign that ended after a decisive battle or two.

Although the language of these stories recalled the heroic moments of Trafalgar and Waterloo, the fears behind them were real enough. During the naval manoeuvers of 1908, for instance, the news that the Royal Navy was engaged on anti-invasion exercises caused much anxiety. It was this fear of a possible invasion, ably encouraged by papers like the *Daily Mail*, that created the hot-house atmosphere in which so many tales of future wars were able to flourish. Indeed, there can be no doubt that by 1906, certainly by 1908, these forecasts of German intentions had become a recognizable and potentially dangerous element in the European situation. The propaganda of one country attracted attention in another. Thus, the *Daily Mail* had an editorial in April 1906 that took Germany to task for such publications as *Der Deutsch-englische Krieg* and *Der Kommende Krieg.* In like manner the important German naval journal, *Marine Rundschau,* brought out a special article in November 1908, which examined British anxieties at the possibility of invasion. The writer noted the influence of Le Queux, and observed that the British were "once more troubled by the idea of invasion—naturally by German armies only. German espionage is almost a standard feature of one section of the press."

Some German periodicals found the matter amusing. The comic weekly, *Kladderadatsch,* printed cartoons from time to time that poked fun at British fears of invasion. On occasions there were ironical poems about the perils facing Britain. One of these opened with the following verse:

Das bedrohte England

Lord Roberts sprach im Oberhaus
Und kramt' sein Oberstubchen aus,
In dem es leider offenbar
Nicht mehr vollstandig richtig war.
Er rief in furchtbar ernstem Ton:
Uns drogt von Deutschland Invasion.
Wir mussen darauf gefasst sein!

This was a direct reference to Lord Roberts's campaign for a bigger army, especially to his speech in the Lords on November 23rd, 1908, when he put forward the argument for conscription. Two months later, the Field-Marshal had dramatic support in the sensational success of the play, *An Englishman's Home,* which opened at Wyndham's Theatre. The play was by Guy du Maurier, then second-in-command of The Royal Fusiliers. The plot dealt with invasion by the forces of "the Emperor of the North"; and it so caught the public mood that it played to packed houses for eighteen months. The illustrated weeklies carried pages of photographs from the principle scenes; a gramophone company made a

record of the more memorable speeches; and a recruiting office
was set up in the theatre to deal with the rush of volunteers to join
the newly formed Territorial Force.

While London audiences were cheering episodes in *An
Englishman's Home*, a very different forecast of the next war by
Rudolf Martin, *Der Weltkrieg in den Luften*, was appearing in the
German bookshops. Like so many of the German authors of
imaginary wars, Martin had composed a magnificent wish-fulfil-
ment fantasy in which Germany and Austro-Hungary triumph over
the combined forces of Britain, France and Russia. War breaks out
on November 11th, 1915, after German ultimatum to France. By
the following December, Paris has fallen, an Austro-German army
occupies Moscow, and the Low Countries have been overrun. In
1915 Wilhelm II appoints Graf Zeppelin to command air opera-
tions against Britain; and, while 500,000 air-landing troops descend
upon key points throughout southern England, a great seaborne
invasion begins. London falls, the enemy G.H.Q. is established at
10 Downing Street and King Edward is brought prisoner to
Germany. The point of this prospective epic was entirely political.
As the Crown Prince explained to a son of the Prince of Wales:

> You British entered into increasingly closer relations with France
> and Russia whilst my father all the time wanted to separate you
> from those countries for the sake of our common interests. And
> now Uncle Edward himself seems to realize that father acted
> quite rightly and has looked after British interests better than
> Uncle Edward. This unhappy war, conducted so unwillingly by
> my father and disliked by all of us, would never have begun if our
> two countries had entered into an alliance. Today Germany and
> the United Kingdom would be immensely rich and would be
> advancing to the highest level of civilization, if you British had
> agreed to divide the Turkish Empire with us, and if you had not
> prevented the division of Morocco between France and ourselves.

On the British side, the production of less happy stories of
German invasions went on unchecked throughout 1909 and into
1910: *The Swoop of the Vulture, When England Slept, The Invasion That Did Not Come Off, The German Invasion of England,
The Horrors of War in Great Britain*. One story was the work of a
promising young writer who saw a very different opportunity in

the invasion legend. He seized on the stock device of a German descent on the United Kingdom and turned it upside down for his own tale of the great invasion, *The Swoop! or, how Clarence saved England.* The young writer was P. G. Wodehouse.

Wodehouse made fun of the invasion myth by a process of inversion and comic inflation. In his first chapter he converted the plot of Guy du Maurier's play into the comedy of "An English Boy's Home." The patriot who warns an indifferent and bored family of their country's peril is the hateful boy, Clarence Mac-Andrew Chugwater, "one of General Baden Powell's Boy Scouts." The news of a German landing reaches a complacent nation in the Stop Press column of the newspapers: "Fry not out, 194. Surrey 147 for 8. A German Army landed in Essex this afternoon. Lancashire Handicap: Spring Chicken, 1; Salome, 2; Yip-i-addy, 3. Seven ran." But the invasion was not a simple matter of a single German army. Eight more invasion forces arrive. Russians, Swiss, Chinese, Young Turks, and Moroccan brigands advance in parallel with the forces of the Mad Mullah and the Prince of Monaco. The British ignore them; golfers play on through the charging infantry; Londoners complain of the crowds; and a theatrical agent persuades the enemy commanders to relate their part in the invasion to the music halls. Then liberation comes when trouble breaks out between the enemy forces, after Russian troops had hissed the German commander off the stage with cries of "Get Offski! Rotten Turnovitch!"

The book was not a success. After years of tales about the coming German invasion and the rumours of spies active throughout the country, it had become accepted doctrine with many citizens that one day there would be a war with Germany. And yet, in spite of all the efforts devoted to predicting the shape of the next great war, it is remarkable how almost all these prophets failed entirely to describe the type of warfare that burst upon the nations at Verdun and the Somme. In all the forecasts and predictions there were only two writers, H. G. Wells and Conan Doyle, who can be said to have come close to guessing what happened later on. Wells is still celebrated for his forecast of armoured fighting vehicles in the short story of *The Land Ironclads*; and in *The World set free* he had the dubious distinction of describing the first war with atomic weapons. Twenty-six years before Einstein wrote the letter warning President Roosevelt that the discoveries of the nuclear physicists had made possible the development of "extremely powerful bombs of a new type," Wells had already given the term "atomic bomb" to the English language. His forecast of 1914 makes melancholy reading today:

> For the whole world was flaring then into a monstrous phase of destruction. Power after power about the armed globe sought to anticipate attack by aggression. They went to war in a delirium of panic, in order to use their bombs first. . . . By the spring of 1959 from nearly two hundred centres, and every week added to their number, roared the unquenchable crimson conflagrations of the atomic bombs.

But this forecast of unheard-of weapons seemed too far-fetched to the general reader in 1914. The book was a failure. A prophecy much more to the point in those days was Conan Doyle's short story about unrestricted submarine warfare, *Danger*, which won the interest of all Europe and excited the scorn of many naval experts. The story appeared in the July number of the *Strand Magazine* in 1914, although it had been written eighteen months earlier as propaganda in aid of the Channel Tunnel project. The story followed the familiar pattern of showing what ought to be done by demonstrating the consequences of failure. In a few thousand words Conan Doyle described the defeat of Great Britain by a small—and imaginary—European country after enemy submarines had established an effective blockade outside all approaches to our ports.

Doyle's forecast appeared two months before Kapitänleutnant Otto Weddigen showed what the U-Boats could do when he sent three British cruisers to the bottom; and, five months after that, the Chief of the German Naval Staff proved the accuracy of *Danger* by proclaiming a submarine blockade of the British Isles. Before this happened, however, several admirals had dismissed Conan Doyle's story as fantastic. Admiral Sir Compton Domvile thought it was "most improbable and more like one of Jules Verne's stories." Admiral William Hannam Henderson declared that there was no reason for thinking that "territorial waters will be violated, or neutral vessels sunk. Such will be absolutely prohibited, and will only recoil on the heads of the perpetrators. No nation would permit it, and the officer who did it would be shot."

Within a few months of that remark authors of imaginary wars, like Saki and Capitaine Danrit, were committed to a conflict very different from anything they had described. Saki dies with a sniper's bullet in his head, and Colonel Driant—to give Danrit his real name—fell at Verdun in the heroic defence of the Bois des Caures. The best that can be said for them, and for all who wrote about the next great war, is that they often stood for high patriotic ideals at a time when few understood how technological innovations would transform the nature of modern warfare. They represent the last stage in the brief honeymoon between science and humanity, before the military technologies of poison gas, barbed wire, machine-guns and tanks showed what could be done with war, given the science to do it.

Three weeks after the appearance of *Danger*, the fateful ultimatum had been sent to Serbia. And then the armies began to move, discharged at each other like so many ballistic missiles according to the calculations of the Schlieffen Plan and Plan XVII. By late August the British Expeditionary Force was fully engaged with the enemy in the area of Mons. And out of that episode came the last of the old-world tales of imaginary warfare. In Authur Machen's story of *The Bowmen*, which grew into the legend of the Angels of Mons, the hard-pressed troops heard a great cry of *Adsit Anglis Sanctus Georgius!* Beyond their positions stood a long line of gleaming shapes. "They were like men who drew the bow and with another shout, their cloud of arrows flew singing and tingling through the air towards the German hosts."

RICHARD D. MULLEN

THE
UNDISCIPLINED
IMAGINATION:
EDGAR RICE BURROUGHS
AND
LOWELLIAN MARS

The most widely read science-fiction stories of all were those wonderful tales of John Carter of Mars by Edgar Rice Burroughs—which might more properly have been labeled "by Edgar Rice Burroughs and Percival Lowell," for Burroughs laid his wild adventures of swords and semi-science on a Mars designed according to the beliefs of Percival Lowell.

—John W. Campbell[1]

Those who have gained a stereotyped concept of Burroughs as a writer who conveys his plot line on a nonstop jetstream of action, moving his characters along so swiftly that readers cannot react to his flaws, are in great error.

The fascination of Burroughs rests in his careful delineation of the *setting* in which he has placed his characters.

—Sam Moskowitz[2]

Edgar Rice Burroughs began writing his Martian series in the latter half of 1911; the first four volumes were produced at the rate of one a year in 1911-1914 and the remaining seven, with intervals of several years, between 1921 and 1941.[3] If he had been interested in setting his stories on "a Mars designed according to the beliefs of Percival Lowell," he could have found the information he needed in any number of places,[4] but most conveniently, perhaps, in either of two books by Lowell himself—

I. *Mars and Its Canals* (New York, 1906)
II. *Mars as the Abode of Life* (New York, 1908)

229

—or in a science-fiction novel written with Lowell's blessing by
Mark Wicks, *To Mars via the Moon* (London, 1910).[5] The novel
would have been the most convenient of the three, for it contains
not only a very full summary of Lowellian fact and theory but
also a discussion of something that Lowell ignores: the Martian
satellites.

My purpose here is to demonstrate that Lowell's vision of
Mars was far different from Burroughs's, that Burroughs probably
knew no more about Lowellian Mars than could have been learned
from the casual reading of newspapers and popular magazines, and
that Barsoom, the Burroughsian Mars, was almost entirely the product of an undisciplined imagination—that is, that Burroughs made
it up as he went along and felt free to change it whenever anything
he had previously written proved inconvenient for present purposes, or even when it was just hard to remember.

1

The year of Lowellian Mars "consists of 687 of our days, 669 of
its own [I, 161]. On Barsoom there is an infamous prison known
as the Temple of the Sun:

> consisting in six hundred eighty-seven circular chambers, one
> below another. . . . As the entire Temple of the Sun revolves
> once with each revolution of Barsoom about the sun, but once
> each year does the entrance to each separate chamber come
> opposite the mouth of the corridor which forms its only link to
> the world without. [M2:20]

Since the length of a Barsoomian day is "a trifle over 24 hours, 37
minutes" [M2:16], a Barsoomian year must be somewhat longer
than a Lowellian year.

On Lowellian Mars there is no permanent glaciation:

> Once formed, an ice sheet cools everything about it and chills
> the climate of its hemisphere. It is a perpetual storehouse of cold.
> Mars has no such glaciation in either hemisphere, and the absence
> of it, which is due to lesser precipitation, together with the clear-
> ness of its skies, accounts for the warmth which the surface
> exhibits and which has been so hard hitherto to interpret. [I, 53]

At the Barsoomian south pole is a warm sunken valley; surrounding this valley and shutting it off from the rest of the world is an "area of eternal ice" [M2:10], an area which extends, when viewed from an airship, "as far as eye could reach in any direction" [M2: 8]. The arctic region is also shut off from the rest of Barsoom, being surrounded by a "towering wall of white . . . a mighty ice-barrier, from which outcropped great patches of granite hills which hold it from encroaching further toward the south" [M3:8], and within this barrier there is naught but snow, ice, and hot-house cities [M3:9]. Here the temperatures are so low that a wicked ruler can keep a million soldiers in the suspended animation of permanent deep-freeze by storing them outside the walls of his city [M10:12]. To be sure, it is also true that in the far-famed Carrion Caves, one of the passages through the northern ice-barrier, the temperatures are evidently above freezing—"Can man breathe this polluted atmosphere and live?" [M3:8]—but this could perhaps be explained away by positing an underground river such as those that flow beneath Manator [M5:12] and Tjanath [M7:7].

The axial tilt of Lowellian Mars is virtually the same as Earth's, and the Martian seasons are therefore comparable to ours except in being longer [II, 77-78]: "the arctic polar night . . . is 305 of our days long; the antarctic, 382" [I, 48]. Barsoom evidently has no axial tilt, for night and day recur at the poles with the same frequency as at the equator, as witness first a speech made not more than fifty or sixty miles from the south pole—

"It was midnight when you released me from my chains. Two hours later we reached the storeroom. There you slept for fourteen hours. It must be nearly sundown again. Come, we will go to some nearby window in the cliff and make sure." [M2:5]

—and then this account of adventures very near the north pole:

In accordance with Talu's suggestion, we deferred attempting to enter the city until the following morning. . . . As he had said, we found numerous caves in the hillsides about us, and into one of these we crept for the night. Our warm Orluk skins kept us perfectly comfortable, and it was only after a most refreshing sleep that we awoke shortly after daylight on the following morning. [M3:9]

In the "depths of winter" on Lowellian Mars, the polar caps "stretch out over much more than the polar zones, coming down to 60° or even 50° of latitude north or south as the case may be, thence melting till by mid-summer they span only five or six degrees across" [I, 138]. But in the eleven volumes of the Barsoomian series, our heroes and heroines, when outside the polar zones, never encounter anything that could be called winter weather: "During the daylight hours it is always extremely hot; at night it is intensely cold" [M2:5]. There are no seasons on Barsoom.[6]

On Lowellian Mars there occasionally appears "a vast dust-cloud travelling slowly over the desert and settling slowly to the ground" [I, 106], and a "sort of steaming" regularly appears in the spring over the northern polar cap; on the other hand, for the southern polar cap, "no such regularly recurring spring haze has yet been noted" [I, 64-66]. For Barsoom we are told that a certain morning "dawned hot and clear, as do all Martian mornings except for the six weeks when the snow melts at the poles" [M1:14]. As for clouds of dust: "there is no dust on Mars except in the cultivated districts during the winter months, and even then the absence of high winds renders it almost unnoticeable" [M1:15]. But on Barsoom every rule has its exceptions, as Tara of Helium discovers one evening when she braves "ominous clouds" in her little airship. The gale that follows the ominous clouds is so strong that it topples the great tower of Lesser Helium and carries her airship halfway round the planet [M5:2-3].

For Lowellian Mars "the evidence is conclusive that great irregularities of surface do not exist. . . . Elevation there of over two or three thousand feet in altitude are absent" [I, 62]. On Barsoom the cliffs of the Valley Dor tower "a good five thousand feet" [M2:2], the Valley of the First Born is "perhaps two miles deep" [M10:1], and the mountain upon which Sola finds herself is "the highest peak of a lofty range" with "a vast panorama of sea bottom and distant hills lying far below" [M2:18]. While we will grant that elsewhere the hills of Barsoom seem always to be low, as in "a landscape of rolling hills that once had been lofty mountains upon a Martian continent" [M5:3], even here we have a difference from Lowellian Mars, for in its surface the absence of great irregularities comes not from weathering but from the laws of planetary formation [II, 27-28].

2

On both planets the "canals" are vegetated strips stretching from pole to pole (or, to be more accurate of Barsoom, from ice-barrier to ice-barrier), each strip being irrigated by water pumped through a covered conduit from the polar areas toward the equator [II, 202-09; M1:21]. The Lowellian canals range in width from two to twenty miles, with ten miles as a probable average [I, 182; II, 49]. The Barsoomian canals would seem to be somewhat wider, if the two crossed by the Tharkian caravan are typical, for "it required five hours to make one of these crossings without a single halt, and the other consumed the entire night" [M1:16].

There are 437 canals on Lowellian Mars:

> This great number of lines forms an articulate whole. . . . It resembles lace-tracery of an elaborate and elegant pattern, woven as a whole over the disk, veiling the planet's face. . . . None of the large ochre areas escapes some filament of the mesh. No single secluded spot upon them could be found, were one inclined to desert isolation, distant more than three hundred miles from some great thoroughfare. [II, 151-52]

The presentation of the canals in M1, especially the map drawn by Dejah Thoris, is apparently consistent with this:

> It was crisscrossed in every direction with long straight lines, sometimes running parallel and sometimes converging toward some great circle. The lines, she said, were waterways; the circles, cities. [M1:16]

But it is still true that the Tharkian caravan crosses only two canals in its twenty-day journey from Korad to Thark. In M2, M3, and M4, the canals are mentioned, but only mentioned. In the other seven volumes they are completely ignored except for one sentence in the Foreword of M7 and one more in the first chapter of M10a. And this last appearance of the Barsoomian canals helps make my point, for we are told that John Carter crossed only two of them in his 5000-mile flight from Helium to Horz. In sum, the canals of Barsoom, except in the comparatively small region mapped by Dejah Thoris, are few, far between, and of very little importance.

For Percival Lowell, "next in interest to the canals, come the oases," which number 186 [II, 156-57]:

> We are certainly justified in regarding them as the apple of the eye of Martian life—what corresponds with us to centres of population. . . . That the largest are some 75 miles across, seems to give sufficient space for living and the means to live. [II, 213-14]

The word *oasis* is not used of any Barsoomian feature, and the cities of Barsoom are not described in any way that would make them equivalent to the oases of Lowellian Mars.

From the standpoint of physiography, Barsoom differs from Lowellian Mars most completely, most drastically, most needlessly, and most foolishly in not having an overriding distinction between sea bottom and barren plateau. Only about two-fifths of the surface of Lowellian Mars consists of those dark areas which change with the seasons from "blue-green" to "brown," which he believed to be "not seas, but areas of vegetation" [I, 127], but which "suggest old sea bottoms" [I, 164]. Contrasting with the dark areas are the "ochre tracts," which

> occupy nine-tenths of the northern hemisphere and a third of the southern. Three-fifths, therefore, of the whole surface of the planet is a desert. . . . The picture that the planet offers us is thus arid beyond present analogue on earth. Pitiless as our deserts are, they are but faint forecasts of the state of things existent on Mars at the present time. Only those who as travelers have had experience of our own Saharas can adequately picture what Mars is like and what so waterless a condition means. Only such can understand what is applied in having the local and avoidable thus extended into the unescapable and the world-wide; and what a terrible significance for everything Martian lies in that single word: *desert.* [I, 156-59]

Since the nomadic green men of Barsoom are always depicted as roaming the sea bottoms, one would expect to find the Lowellian distinction reflected in a three-way division of Barsoomian territory: (1) the plateau, except for the canals and oases, as uninhabited desert, (2) the sea bottoms, except again for the canals and oases, as steppe over which the green men roam with their herds, and (3) the canals and oases as the cultivated districts inhabited by the red men. But the "yellow moss" on which the green men graze their herds covers "practically the entire surface of Mars with the exception of the frozen areas at the poles and the scattered cultivated districts" [M1:3], the sea bottoms are not blue-green changing to brown and back to blue-green but are instead "ochre" [M2:14; M4:3; M5:7; M7:2; M9:2; M10a:1], and in the eleven volumes only two small areas are depicted as deserts [M5:9; M7:9]. Hence we have to say that on Barsoom there are no great areas of barren plateau and therefore no apparent reason why the green men should confine themselves to the sea bottoms— unless, indeed, as sometimes seems to be the case, the sea bottoms cover virtually the whole surface of the planet.

3

The figures given for the Martian satellites in M1 are correct as far as they go, but in one respect the interpretation of these figures is wildly wrong:

> The nearer moon of Mars makes a complete revolution around the planet in a little over seven and one-half hours, so that she may be seen hurtling through the sky like some huge meteor two or three times each night. . . . [M1:5]

Although apparently restricted to the nearer moon in M1, the participle *hurtling* is applied to both moons in M2 and M3:

> Then the moons come; the mysterious, magic moons of Mars hurtling like monster meteors low across the face of the dying planet. [M2:5]

> Beneath the hurtling moons of Mars, speeding their meteoric way across the bosom of the dying planet. [M3:1]

By 1921 Burroughs had learned that the two moons differ greatly in their apparent motion: "Thuria, swift racer of the night"; "far Cluros, stately, majestic, almost stationary" [M5:4].

On the basis of this difference we get a little myth about Mad Thuria and her aloof spouse, Cold Cluros:

I had watched Cluros, the further moon, take his slow deliberate way. He had already set. Behind him, Thuria, his mistress, fled through the heavens. [M6:5]

Mad, passionate Thuria raced across the cloudless sky; Cluros, her cold spouse, swung his aloof circle in splendid isolation. [M7:9]

Cluros . . . moved in stately dignity, while Thuria . . . hurtled through the night from horizon to horizon in less than four hours. [M10c: 1]

Even so, the original idea continues to crop up:

Gently they drifted [in their airship] beneath the hurtling moons above the mad shadows of a Martian night. [M5:9]

All that night we sped beneath the hurtling moons of Mars. [M6:13]

Thuria and Cluros were speeding across a . . . star-lit sky. [M9:2]

Deimos and Phobos, the two fast-moving moons of Mars, sped through the heavens. [M11a:12]

It was evidently not until about 1933 that Burroughs learned a certain fact about Phobos-Thuria that would have been available to him in Wicks or in any number of other places:

Thuria . . . apparently moved through the heavens from west to east, due to the fact that her orbit is so near the planet that she performs a revolution in less than one-third of that of the diurnal rotation of Mars. [M8:1]

Having learned it in 1933, he forgot it in 1940:

Both moons were now in the sky, Cluros just above the horizon, Thuria a little higher; by the time Cluros approached zenith, Thuria would have completed her orbit around Barsoom and passed him, so swift her flight through the heavens. [M10c:5]

It seems unlikely that Burroughs ever fully grasped the distinction between actual motion and apparent motion, for he continues to derive the length of the period Phobos-Thuria is above or below the horizon simply by halving the "little over seven and one-half hours" which he gave for its "complete revolution" in M1: "more than three and one-half hours" [M5:3], "three and three-quarters Earth hours" [M6:5], "less than four hours" [M10c:1]. That he ever worked out a table like the following seems doubtful:

	ACTUAL	APPARENT
Period of Luna around Earth	656 hours	25 hours
Period of Phobos-Thuria around Mars	8 hours	11 hours
Period of Deimos-Cluros around Mars	30 hours	133 hours

For then it would have been obvious that unless the observer looked steadily for several minutes, even Phobos-Thuria would seem to be stationary.

The ultimate origin of the hurtling moons of Mars is probably in newspaper accounts that compared their sidereal periods with that of Luna around Earth without making clear the difference between actual and apparent. Although Garrett P. Serviss had been a science writer for fifteen years in 1898, he was still capable of the following:

> Throwing myself on my back on the deck of the electrical ship, for a long time I watched the race between the two satellites, until Phobos, rapidly gaining on the other, had left its rival far behind.[7]

More important, even Mark Wicks, in a generally correct account of how the two satellites would look from the surface of Mars,[8] was capable of comparing the apparent motion of Phobos with the actual motion of Luna:

> Consequently it will be evident that Phobos must travel very rapidly across the sky. It really moves over a space of 32½ degrees in a single hour—a great contrast to the slow and stately movement of our moon, which only passes over half a degree in an hour. [p. 244]

From the similarity of the language used, it seems possible that
Burroughs had read Wicks by 1938:

> Thuria and Cluros were speeding across a brilliant starlit sky . . .
> quite different, John Carter told me, from a similar aspect above
> Earth, whose single satellite moves at a stately, decorous pace
> across the vault of the heavens. [M9:2]

When Burroughs first began writing about Mars the two satellites were generally believed to be considerably larger than is allowed by present opinion.[9] This being so, his depiction of their
brightness may be said to be exaggerated only to a reasonable degree. He says nothing about their apparent size in the first eight
volumes or in the last two. The one place in which he does speak
of it suggests again that he might have read Wicks by 1938:

> How pale and bleak must be the nights on Earth, with a single
> satellite moving at a snail's pace through the sky at such a great
> distance from the planet that it must appear no larger than a plat-
> ter. [M9:19]

For in Wicks he would have found a basis for the speaker's comparison: "Phobos appears rather larger than our moon, because it
is so near to the planet" [p. 243]. But even here there is a gross
inconsistency in Burroughs. Whereas Wicks's statement, made in
1910, was based on the belief that Phobos has a diameter of 36
miles [p. 243], Burroughs had already made use of later and presumably better opinion, having in 1933 given Phobos-Thuria a diameter of only seven miles [M8:12]. If Burroughs did indeed follow Wicks in these two places, it is ironic that he should have been
misled by what may well have been the only two errors in Wicks—
one an error that Wicks made himself, the other an error of his
time.

4

All in all, the greatest difference between Barsoom and Lowellian
Mars is in the social effects of the fact that Mars is a "dying
world." On Lowellian Mars those effects have been all to the
good:

Girdling their globe and stretching from pole to pole, the Martian
canal system not only embraces their whole world but is an organized entity. . . .

The first thing that is forced on us in conclusion is the necessarily intelligent and non-bellicose nature of the community that
could thus act as a unit throughout its globe. War is a survival
among us from savage times and affects now chiefly the boyish
and unthinking element of the nation. The wisest realize that
there are better ways for practicing heroism and other and more
certain means of insuring the survival of the fittest. It is something people outgrow. [I, 376-77]

On Barsoom one day, while prisoners in a dead city, John Carter
and Dejah Thoris take note of murals depicting a white race:

She told me that these people had presumably flourished over a
hundred thousand years before. They were the early progenitors
of her race, but had mixed with the other great race of early
Martians, who were dark, almost black, and also with the reddish
yellow race which had flourished at the same time.

These three great divisions of the higher Martians had been
forced into a mighty alliance as the drying up of the Martian seas
had compelled them to seek the comparatively few and always
diminishing fertile areas, and to defend themselves, under new
conditions, against the wild hordes of green men. [M1:11]

But that was a hundred thousand years ago. The nations of the
red race that resulted from the amalgamation of the three old
races now fight incessant wars not only against the green men but
also among themselves. The boyish element has long since regained the upper hand:

There are other and natural causes tending toward a diminution of
the population, but nothing contributes so greatly to this end as
the fact that no male or female Martian is ever voluntarily without a weapon of destruction. [M1:4]

To the objection that constructing a globe-encircling system
of canals would be an impossible task, Lowell responded in 1908
with arguments that "minified the task and magnified the worker":

Beings on a small planet could be both bigger and more effective than on a larger one, because of the lesser gravity on the smaller body. An elephant on Mars could jump like a gazelle. . . . The task itself would be seven times as light. For gravity on the surface of Mars is only about 38 per cent of what it is on the surface of the earth; and the work that can be done against a force like gravity with the same expenditure of energy is inversely as the square of that force. [II, 210]

Garrett P. Serviss offered the same argument in the same year:

Animal forms might obtain a far greater size upon Mars than upon the earth, with coincidentally greater muscular strength, without being oppressed by their own weight. In the second place, since all bodies are relatively light on Mars, mechanical powers could be more efficiently applied there than here. Thus a race of powerful giants might be able to achieve public works hopelessly beyond the range of man's capacity upon the earth.[10]

And so did H. G. Wells, who wrote that Martians might well have a mass 2-2/3 times as great as that of human beings, with a height half again as great.[11]

All three were drawing on a concept well established by 1908. How far back it goes I cannot say, but it was probably not new in 1896, judging from a novel of that year in which Martians are "nine to ten feet tall and proportionately large in every way":

You ought not to have been surprised to find us so large here. You knew before you came that Mars is much smaller than the earth and, therefore, the attraction of gravitation being less, that everything can grow more easily.[12]

Less sober traditions were also well established by 1908. The voyagers that Mark Wicks sent to Mars via the Moon arrived with three machine-guns "in readiness for any emergency, if some of the ideas of which we had read about the probable ferocity of the Martians should prove to be correct" [p. 55], only to discover that the Martians were not "the big, ugly giants, nor the strange animals, that some of our folks had imagined" but instead friendly people only "seven feet nine inches in height" and "splendidly proportioned" [pp. 165-66].

In 1898, in one of his less sober moments, Garrett P. Serviss had contributed "dark olive" giants to these traditions:

> His head was of enormous size and his huge projecting eyes gleamed with a strange fire of intelligence. His face was like a caricature, but not one to make the beholder laugh. Drawing himself up, he towered to a height of at least fifteen feet.[13]

The fifteen feet was presumably derived by applying the 2-2/3 factor to height rather than mass. Serviss says nothing about the mass of his Martians, perhaps because he dared not use such a large figure, but their proportions would seem to be similar to a man's.

The green men of Barsoom, sometimes described as "olive" or "olive-green" [M1:3,4], also with projecting eyes and also towering fifteen feet, "on Earth would have weighed some four hundred pounds" [M1:3], which would make them as grotesquely thin as the sorns of Malacandra. Since they are not so described, we can put the four hundred pounds down to the simple error of imagining that if they are 2-2/3 times as tall they must weigh 2-2/3 times as much, and then go on to something more important:

> While the Martians are immense, their bones are very large and they are muscled only in proportion to the gravitation which they must overcome. The result is that they are infinitely less agile and less powerful, in proportion to their weight, than an Earth man. [M1:3]

Whereas the traditional Martians were not only larger but more powerful in every way than their visitors from Earth, Burroughs has created a race of gigantic Martians that an Earth man like John Carter can kill with a right to the jaw [M1:4], as well as men of human size that any Earth man could defeat in any physical contest, being much more powerful—seven times as powerful, indeed, although Burroughs does not use this or any exact figure. Barsoom is thus a perfect world for puerile dreams: if you could go there you could lick every man in sight.

5

In 1912, when *A Princess of Mars* was serialized in *All-Story Magazine*, a reader might well have said that although the story is sentimental melodrama of the cheapest kind, its speculative content is both interesting and promising. Let us see what we can make of the Barsoomians as oviparous humanoids, pausing first to note that when unmodified the word *year* always indicates an earthly year.

Ranging in height from ten to fifteen feet, the green Barsoomians have four arms, protruding eyes, long, curving tusks, and a generally ferocious appearance [M1:4]. The red race, on the other hand, is said to be a "beautiful race whose outward appearance is identical with the more god-like races of Earth men" [M2:4], and similar terms are used of the remnants of the black, yellow, and white races from whose amalgamation long ago the red race originated [M1:11]. Barsoomians have a natural life span of a thousand years and show no signs of old age until near or past that mark, but since nearly all of them die violent deaths, few live to be more than three or four hundred [M1:4].

The egg laid by a green female is about the size of an ordinary goose egg [M1:14]. If stored in a shaded place, it will neither deteriorate nor develop but will instead remain unchanged for at least five years [M1:7]. If placed in the sun, it will grow until, at the end of five years, it is large enough to yield an infant as tall as four feet [M1:14], an infant fully developed except in size and immediately ready to begin learning how to talk and fight [M1:7]. At this point one may be permitted to wonder why there would be any need for agriculture in a world in which so much food can be absorbed from the rays of the sun.

With their strange dependence on the mundane calendar, or perhaps from a universal humanoid rhythm, "each adult Martian female brings forth about thirteen eggs each year" [M1:7]. Practicing eugenics and population control, the chieftains of a green community put a carefully selected gathering of eggs into the communal incubator once each five years and at the same time take into the community the newly hatched infants of the previous quinquennium [M1:7]. At one such moment, the community in which John Carter was a prisoner consisted of 250 females, 250 youths, 450 to 460 warriors, and 500 newly hatched infants [M1:7, 15]. It would seem to follow that during each quinquennium about half the infants die from one cause or another ("the greatest death loss comes during the age of childhood, when vast numbers of little Martians fall victims to the great white apes of

Mars" [M1:4]), the other half graduating into the female or youth class, and also that at the end of each period, the surviving youths graduate into the class of warriors, of whom a large number would in the meantime have died in battle. Of the newly hatched infants, presumably only six or eight would be females, no more being needed to keep their number at 250. The age range in the several classes, then, would be as follows: infants, up to five years; youths, five to ten; females, five to a thousand; warriors, ten to a thousand.

The green Barsoomians, except for an occasional atavism, are "absolutely virtuous, both men and women" [M1:7], the "brute passion" having been "almost stilled in the Martian breast" by the "waning demands for procreation upon their dying planet" [M1: 12]. Since there are twice as many warriors as females, since each high-ranking warrior has several females in his retinue, and since "mating is a matter of community interest only, and is directed without reference to natural selection" [M1:7], it seems likely that most of the warriors lead completely celibate lives, the task of fertilizing the females being assigned to those warriors who meet certain genetic specifications.

We are not told anything directly about the eggs of the red race, but from what we are told indirectly they would seem to be similar to those of the green race even in size, for the incubation period is the same five years [M1:27], and the red infant emerges from his shell "almost adult" [M4:2], "just short of physical maturity" [M9:2], and so evidently even larger than the green infant. For the males of the red race, moreover, the period of childhood and youth would seem to be even briefer than for the green men, for Carthoris, when only ten years out of the egg [M2:16, 20], has already been a warrior for almost a full Barsoomian year, if not longer [M2:10]. Over against this early entrance into the warrior class we have a statement that "the age of maturity" is "about forty" [M1:4] and also a statement that Sola, who is about thirty-five [M1:15], has been laying for less than a year [M1:7].

In a later volume we learn that among the red nations there is a wicked emperor who aspires to the conquest of all Barsoom:

For at least two hundred years. . .Tul Axtar has made man-

power his fetish; no eggs might be destroyed, each woman being
compelled to preserve all she laid. An army of officials and
inspectors took a record of the production of each female. Those
that had the greatest number of males were rewarded; the unpro-
ductive were destroyed. When it was discovered that marriage
tended to reduce the productivity of the females of Jehar, marriage among any classes beneath the nobility was proscribed by
imperial edict.

Since a well-serviced female would presumably produce thirteen
fertile eggs each year, we can hardly be surprised at what resulted,
and can only wonder that it took two hundred years:

> The result has been an appalling increase in population, until
> many of the provinces of Jehar cannot support the incalculable
> numbers that swarm like ants in a hill. The richest agricultural
> land upon Barsoom could not support such numbers; every
> natural resource has been exhausted; millions are starving, and in
> large districts cannibalism is prevalent. [M7:5]

Whether red nations with honorable rulers, such as Helium or
Gathol, practice eugenics or population control we are never told,
but it is obvious that, unlike the green nations, they have a family
system similar to that of "the more god-like races of Earth men."
And while we are not told that the red men are "absolutely virtuous," we do learn of "the Martian custom which allows female
slaves to Martian men, whose high and chivalrous honor is always
ample protection for every woman in his household" [M2:14].
Moreover, Barsoom is "a world that aspired to grace and beauty
and chastity in woman, and strength and dignity and loyalty in
man" [M5:1]. With all this I am inclined to imagine a ceremony
occurring each twenty-eight days in which unmarried women
bring their new-laid eggs to a stern paterfamilias for candling, but
Burroughs, alas, does not enter into such problems as might arise
from attempts to ensure the chastity of oviparous females.

We also have the rather astonishing fact that our oviparous
heroines are identical in outward appearance with Earth women
and thus have a navel, even though hatched from an egg, and nip-
pled and protruding breasts, even though they can produce no
milk. We are of course free to imagine, if we will, that the Barsoomians were once mammalian, having made themselves ovi-

parous for the purposes of population control upon their dying planet, and at the same time having bred to retain navels and mammary glands for esthetic reasons. But if we imagine this, we will then have to wonder why they did not also perfect a method of fertilizing the egg after it has been laid, thus eliminating any necessity for "that brute passion which the waning demands for procreation upon their dying planet has almost stilled in the Martian breast" [M1:12]. We are free to imagine such things, but there is nothing in the eleven volumes to warrant our doing so.

In simple fact, there is no warrant in the eleven volumes for much of anything, for in the ten sequels we find, not a filling in of the picture outlined in *Princess*, but instead a mere accumulation of disparate detail. In one place we learn that "there is practically no such thing as foreign commerce on warlike Barsoom, where each nation is sufficient to itself" [M3:5], but in others we hear of "great merchantmen such as ply the upper air between the cities of the outer world" [M2:8] and of "landing-stages that tower high into the heavens for the great international passenger liners" [M4:2]. In the first four volumes we have a nudist society with a weak sexual urge; in the last seven we have a clothed society in which attempted rape is as common as in the other worlds created by Burroughs.[14] In M3:8 we are told that except for the arctic region all Barsoom has recently been explored, but in each of the later volumes our heroine gets captured by the rulers of some community that has been utterly isolated from the rest of Barsoom for millennia. New societies are introduced in every volume, but none is ever really described, and in the end they are all alike.

Sam Moskowitz has included Chapters 3-13 of *Princess* in his recent anthology, *Under the Moons of Mars*.[15] If these chapters were typical of, rather than unique in, the work of Burroughs, we might see some justification for his claim that in that work the settings are carefully delineated. But they are unique rather than typical: in the other sixty-five books by Burroughs there is nothing comparable to them. More typical are the adventures of M2 and M3, which were presumably set in the Barsoomian polar regions because of the great contemporary interest in earthbound polar exploration. Given this interest, it is difficult to believe that Burroughs would not have known what every schoolboy knew in 1911, that day and night at the poles are six months long.

Whether we put this business down to his ignorance or to his contempt for his readers, it is still typical of the carelessness and vagueness with which he describes his various settings. If anyone wishes to praise Burroughs as a writer of action-packed thrillers in which superhuman heroes save beautiful heroines from being subjected by horrible villains to the fate worse than death, I will not complain. But to praise him for much of anything else is surely to talk nonsense of the most arrant kind.

NOTES

[1]John W. Campbell, "Good-Bye Barsoom," *Analog*, March 1970, p. 4.

[2]Sam Moskowitz, *Under the Moons of Mars* (New York, 1970), pp. 297-98.

[3]Since these books have been published in numerous editions, reference in this article is to chapter rather than page. The dates given in the following table are for publication in book form, which was often considerably later than the serialization.

M1. A Princess of Mars, 1917	M7. A Fighting Man of Mars, 1931
M2. The Gods of Mars, 1918	M8. Swords of Mars, 1936
M3. The Warlord of Mars, 1919	M9. Synthetic Men of Mars, 1940
M4. Thuvia, Maid of Mars, 1920	M10. Llana of Gathol, 1948
M5. The Chessmen of Mars, 1922	M11. John Carter of Mars, 1964
M6. The Master Mind of Mars, 1928	

The dates used here and in the article for Burroughs are from Robert W. Fenton, *The Big Swingers* (Englewood Cliffs, 1967), who had access to the notebook that Burroughs kept as a record of his literary production.

[4]William B. Johnson and Thomas D. Clareson, "The Interplay of Science and Fiction: the Canals of Mars," *Extrapolation*, V (1963-64), 37-48, which lists a large number of articles on Mars published prior to 1911.

[5]There was also a New York edition, dated 1911 but published, according to *The American Catalogue*, in December 1910. The paging in this edition may or may not be the same as in the London edition used here.

[6]The occurrence of the word *winter* in a passage quoted in the next paragraph is, I believe, unique in the Barsoomian series, and I have been able to find only one other occurrence of a seasonal name: in M2:13 it is both summer and nighttime at the south pole.

[7]Garrett P. Serviss, *Edison's Conquest of Mars* (Los Angeles, 1947), p. 132, which was reprinted from the New York *Evening Journal*, January 12 to February 10, 1898. According to the *National Encyclopedia of American Biography*, this story was "published simultaneously in many leading newspapers in 1898."

[8]My judgment as to Wicks's correctness is based on a comparison of his Chapter 22 with Isaac Asimov, "Kaleidoscope in the Sky," *The Magazine of*

Fantasy and Science Fiction, August 1967, pp. 115-24.

[9]Robert S. Richardson and Chesley Bonestell, *Mars* (New York, 1964), p. 91: "Phobos started out about 1900 at 30 miles in diameter but by 1960 had gotten down to only 5 miles; Deimos has undergone a similar decline, from 20 to 3 miles." Cf. Wicks, pp. 124-25, where the discussion concludes with the statement that "experiments have fixed the sizes as 36 miles for Phobos and 10 miles [for] Deimos."

[10]Garrett P. Serviss, *Astronomy with the Naked Eye* (New York, 1908), pp. 214-15.

[11]H. G. Wells, "The Things that Live on Mars," *Cosmopolitan Magazine*, XLIV (1908), 335-42,

[12]James Cowan, *Daybreak: a Romance of an Old World* (New York, 1896), pp. 51, 53.

[13]Serviss, *Edison's Conquest*, pp. 67-68, 172.

[14]Cf. Richard D. Mullen (the Elder), "Edgar Rice Burroughs and the Fate Worse than Death," *Riverside Quarterly*, IV (1969-70), 186-91; also my own forthcoming article in *RQ*, "Sex and Prudery in Haggard and Burroughs."

[15]See Note 2. The anthology bears the name under which *Princess* was serialized.

RICHARD HODGENS

A SHORT TRAGICAL HISTORY OF THE SCIENCE FICTION FILM

Cut is the branch that might have grown full straight,
And burned is Apollo's laurel-bough,
That sometime grew within this learned man.
Faustus is gone: regard his hellish fall,
Whose fiendful fortune may exhort the wise,
Only to wonder at unlawful things,
Whose deepness doth entice such forward wits
To practise more than heavenly power permits.
—Doctor Faustus, *Epilogue*

Some of the most original and thoughtful contemporary fiction has been science fiction, and this field may well prove to be of much greater literary importance than is generally admitted. In motion pictures, however, "science fiction" has so far been unoriginal and limited; and both the tone and the implications of these films suggest a strange throwback of taste to something moldier and more "Gothic" than the Gothic novel. But the genre is an interesting and potentially very fruitful one.

Science fiction publishing expanded spectacularly in the late '40's, and dwindled again in the early '50's. Science fiction filming as we know it today began in 1950 with *Destination Moon*, and has continued to the present, hideously transformed, as a minor category of production. Earlier examples, like Fritz Lang's *Metropolis* and *Frau im Mond*, H. G. Wells' powerful essay on future history, *Things to Come*, and such nonsupernatural horror films as *The Invisible Ray*, have not been considered "science fiction," although they were. One of the many painful aspects of most of the recent films involving space travel, alien visitors, or earthly monsters which have followed *Destination Moon* is that they *are* considered "science fiction," although most of them are something peculiarly different from the literature of the same label.

Motion picture adaptations have ruined any number of good works of literature without casting a pall, in the public mind, over literature in general. The science fiction films, however, seem to have come close to ruining the reputation of the category of fiction from which they have malignantly sprouted. To the film audience, "science fiction" means "horror," distinguished from ordinary horror only by a relative lack of plausibility.

Science fiction involves extrapolated or fictitious science, or fictitious use of scientific possibilities, or it may be simply fiction that takes place in the future or introduces some radical assumption about the present or the past. For those who insist upon nothing but direct treatment of contemporary life, science fiction has little or nothing to offer, of course. But there are issues that cannot be dealt with realistically in terms of the present, or even the past; and to confront such issues in fiction it is better to invent a future-tense society than to distort the present or the past. And in a broader sense there are few subjects that cannot be considered in science fiction, few styles in which it cannot be written, and few moods that it cannot convey. It is, to my mind, the only kind of writing today that offers much surprise—not merely the surprise of shock effects, but the surprise of new or unusual material handled rationally. And conscientious science fiction, more than any other type, offers the reader that shift of focus essential to the appeal of any literature. Often too it presents a puzzle analogous to that of the detective story, but with its central assumptions considerably less restricted.

Science fiction, as most science fiction readers define it and as most science fiction writers attempt to practice it, calls for a plausible or at least possible premise, logically developed. The most damning criticism one can make of a work of science fiction is that it is flatly impossible in the first place, and inconsistent in the second. To say the least, many things are possible; and readers may accept a premise that they believe impossible anyway, so long as they do not consider it "supernatural." Often, the distinction between science fiction and fantasy is simply one of attitude; but an impossible premise must at least not contradict itself, and it should be developed consistently in the story.

Science fiction films, with few exceptions, follow different conventions. The premise is always flatly impossible. Any explanations offered are either false analogy or entirely meaningless. The character who protests "But that's *incredible*, Doctor!" is always right. The impossible, and often self-contradictory, premise is irrationally developed, if it is developed at all. There is less narrative logic than in the average Western.

Although antiscientific printed science fiction exists, most science fiction reflects at least an awareness and appreciation of science. Some science fiction, it is true, displays an uncomprehending faith in science, and implies that it will solve all problems magically. But in the sf films there is rarely any sane middle ground. Now and then, science is white magic. But far more often, it is black, and if these films have any general implications about science, they are that science and scientists are dangerous, raising problems and provoking widespread disaster for the innocent, ignorant good folks, and that curiosity is a deadly sin.

The few exceptions to this bleak picture are the first three sf films produced by George Pal: *Destination Moon, When Worlds Collide,* and *War of the Worlds.* Perhaps there are one or two others. *Destination Moon* may be considered a good semi-documentary, educational film, although today its optimism is rather depressing. Despite its accuracy and consistency, and the extent to which the stereotyped characters were forced to go to explain it, most criticism indicated that the critics did not understand it. The special effects were the film's main attraction, and except for a few shots of the apparent size of the ship in space, and the appearance of the stars, were exact and superb. In a fascinating article about the technical problems of this film, Robert Heinlein credits its director, Irving Pichel, with saving it from an arbitrary addition of musical comedy and "pseudoscientific gimmicks which would have puzzled even Flash Gordon."[1]

Those who hoped that the financial success of *Destination Moon* would lead to equally convincing but more sophisticated science-fiction films were bitterly disappointed, for nearly everything since has been unconvincing and naive. There was a flood of "science fiction" on the screen, but it followed in the footsteps of *The Thing*, and it was unbelievably and progressively inane.

Pal's next two productions were satisfactory, however, and although they are not very impressive when compared with a film like *Things to Come*, in comparison with their contemporary science fiction competition they seemed masterpieces. In the '30's Paramount had considered *When Worlds Collide*, a novel by Edwin Balmer and Philip Wylie, for De Mille, and *War of the Worlds*, by H. G. Wells, for Eisenstein. Pal's films modernized the sources, but respected them. Unlike *Destination Moon*, however, both have themes of menace and catastrophe—the end of the world and interplanetary invasion. It appeared that even Pal had decided that sf films must be, somehow, *horrible*.

In *When Worlds Collide*, models were used extensively, and while many of them were not completely convincing, the only major disappointment to most people was the last shot of the lush, green new world, after the single escaping space ship had landed in impressively rugged territory. H. G. Wells' *War of the Worlds* is a good novel, and difficult to ruin. If *War of the Worlds* had been filmed as a period-piece, as Disney later treated Jules Verne's *20,000 Leagues Under the Sea*, it would still have been effective. The story was carefully modernized, however, as Howard Koch had modernized it in 1938 for Orson Welles' Mercury Theater of the Air. One unnecessary modern addition, though, was an irrelevant boy-and-girl theme because, Pal apologized, "Audiences want it."[2]

The theme of Wells' memorable "assault on human self-satisfaction" is still valid, if less startling. No one today expects to be visited by intelligent Martians, but granting this premise the film was quite convincing. The Martians' fantastic weapons were acceptable as products of a superior technology; the Martians themselves, though more terrestrial in appearance than Wells' original conception, were probably the most convincing Things to come from Hollywood, and they were used with surprising restraint and effectiveness—one brief glimpse and, at the end, a lingering shot of the hand of the dying creature. About half the film was painstaking special effect, and the models were nearly perfect.

These three films were spectacular productions, and if the

scripts contained moments rather similar to more traditional spectacles, they still contained powerful images that had never been
seen before: after take-off, virtually every shot in *Destination
Moon*; the red dwarf star nearing the doomed Earth; and the deadly Martian machines, like copper mantas and hooded cobras, glid-
ing down empty streets.

I do not mean to imply that everyone was pleased by these
films. Those who like plots with villains were bored by *Destination Moon*, and people who knew nothing about space travel, and
did not care, were baffled. *When Worlds Collide* drew harsh words
for its concluding shot and its models, and some people seem to
have been irritated by the undemocratic survival of the interplanetary Ark. And of *War of the Worlds* I heard someone say,
"That Orson Welles always was crazy, anyway."

George Pal's last science fiction production, *The Conquest of
Space*, was disappointing. Again there were some visually impressive shots, but unfortunately that was all. The script attempted to
"enliven" a subject that called for serious treatment; the result
was an inaccurate, misleading film ending with a miracle which,
unlike the "miraculous" end of *War*, was impossible and pointless. It was an expensive production which could have contributed
to the salvation of science fiction in motion pictures. But the
monsters had taken the field, and the facile *Conquest of Space*
merely seemed to prove that monsters are always necessary.

What the movies were likely to do with science fiction was
already evident when *Rocketship X-M* was released in 1950 to
compete with *Destination Moon*. An expedition sets out for the
moon. The ship's course is altered by the close passage of some
noisy meteors, however, and the explorers land on Mars, where
they learn that atomic warfare has destroyed Martian civilization.
The Martians appear to be entirely human—at least, if memory
serves, one savage female was beautifully human—but radiation has
bestialized them. The girl scientist and the boy scientist escape
from Mars, but, lacking fuel to land on the frantically spinning
Earth, they endure a stoic martyrdom. Though *Rocketship X-M*
seemed ludicrous, it was level-headed and superb compared with
what followed.

The great villain was *The Thing From Another World*, which
appeared in 1951. *The Thing* was based on a short novel by John

W. Campbell, Jr., the editor of *Astounding Science Fiction*, where it appeared in 1938 with the title "Who Goes There?" The story is regarded as one of the most original and effective science fiction stories, *sub-species* "horror." Its premise is convincing, its development logical, its characterization intelligent, and its suspense considerable. Of these qualities the film retained one or two minutes of suspense. The story and the film are poles apart. Probably for timely interest, the Thing crashed in a Flying Saucer and was quick-frozen in the Arctic. In Campbell's story "it had lain in the ice for twenty million years" in the Antarctic. In film as in source, when the creature thaws out it is alive and dangerous. In "Who Goes There?," when it gets up and walks away, and later when it is torn to pieces by the dogs and still lives, the nature of the beast makes its invulnerability acceptable. But there is little plausibility about the Hollywood Thing's nine lives. Since this film, presumably dead creatures have been coming back to life with more and more alacrity and with less and less excuse. Instead of the nearly insoluble problem created in Campbell's story, this Thing is another monster entirely. He is a vegetable. He looks like Frankenstein's monster. He roars. He is radioactive. And he drinks blood.[3]

Probably Campbell's protean menace was reduced to this strange combination of familiar elements in the belief that the original idea—the idea which made the story make sense—was too complex. This was probably incorrect, because monsters since that *Thing* have imitated the special ability of Campbell's Alien, although with far less credibility (*It Came From Outer Space*, *Invasion of the Body Snatchers*), and there is no indication that anyone found them difficult to understand.

Incidentally, the most stupid character in the film is the most important scientist. The script did its best to imply that his tolerant attitude toward the Thing was his worst idea. And the film ended with a warning to all mankind: "Watch the skies" for these abominably dangerous Flying Saucers.

The Thing is a most radical betrayal of its source, but since the source was generally unfamiliar, and since the idea of a monster from outer space seemed so original (though the monster itself had blood-brothers in Transylvania), the film earned both critical approval and a great deal of money.[4] In addition, it fixed the pattern for the majority of science fiction films that followed, for it proved that some money could be made by "science fiction" that preyed on current fears symbolized crudely by any preposterous monster, and the only special expense involved would be for one monster suit.

Not all sf films since *The Thing* have been about monsters, but the majority have. *The Day the World Stood Still,* also released in 1951, was almost, but not quite, a monster film. It was not a story of catastrophe as the title suggests, but of alien visitors. The screen-play deprived another popular science fiction story from *Astounding,* Harry Bates' "Farewell to the Master," of its good ideas, its conviction, and its point. *The Day* substituted a message: Earthlings, behave yourselves. Again, probably because like *The Thing* the story was novel but could be understood without much effort, *The Day* earned good reviews and good money. Whatever reservations one may have about the film, in comparison with *The Thing* and its spawn, *The Day* has a comparatively civilized air, at least.

It Came From Outer Space was another rare exception that appeared rather early in the cycle. One of the virtues of *It Came From Outer Space* is that It is here by accident, and wants to go home.

Following the precedent that *The Thing* set, *The Beast From 20,000 Fathoms* and *Them!* established major variations of the monster theme. *The Beast* was an amphibious dinosaur. I cannot remember whether nuclear physics was responsible for its resuscitation or its final destruction, but probably it was both. *The Beast,* like *The Thing,* thaws to life, but it was a menace of terrestrial origin. This simplifies the film-makers' problems. *The Beast* has been followed by several monsters revived, we are told, from the distant past, and all of them instinctively attack populous cities. (*King Kong,* unlike these "atom beasts," had some sort of motivation.) *Them!* were giant ants, also dangerous, in the sewers of Los Angeles. Impossibly large insects with a taste for human flesh have appeared in *The Deadly Mantis, The Spider,* and others. The milder *Creature from the Black Lagoon* proved so popular that he himself returned for *Revenge,* but of all the earthly monsters, only *The Magnetic Monster,* with a script by Curt Siodmak, displayed much originality and consistency.

The Incredible Shrinking Man created its bloated-insect horror by shrinking the hero until an ordinary spider became typically perilous. The unfortunate young man of the title passes through a strange cloud while sunbathing on his cabin cruiser and begins to shrink—evenly, all over. The screen play, by Richard Matheson from his own novel, is a protracted and occasionally amusing agony. Soon the incredible shrinking man is too small to live an ordinary life. He finds brief happiness with a beautiful midget, but he breaks off their relationship when he discovers that he has become too short for her. He is plagued by reporters. When his wife walks downstairs, the doll house in which he lives shakes with unbearable violence. The cat chases him. He gets lost in the cellar. Then the spider chases him. Although the premise of the story is impossible, the end improves upon it, for the incredible shrinking man does not die because "in the mind of God there is no zero." Even God, in the science fiction films, is a poor mathematician. *The Shrinking Man* began its own minor series of increasingly poor films about people who are too small or too big.

In a persuasive review of Matheson's novel and Frank M. Robinson's *The Power*, Damon Knight[5] argues that these works are popular successes precisely because they are irrational and antiscientific—considering, for instance, the inconsistent diminution of Matheson's hero, one of the novel's faults that is not repeated in the film, where one wouldn't notice it much. Knight goes too far, however, when he remarks that "Spiders don't scream, as even Matheson might know; but gutted scientists do." *The Shrinking Man* is certainly unscientific, but this sinister implication Knight suggests in the impalement of the screaming, "symbolic" spider does not follow. In many of the sf films, though, such sinister implications are conventional.

Invasions from space did not cease. *The Blob* came in color, and Martian Blood Rust sprouted in black and white in *Spacemaster X-7*. When Japan is invaded by *The Mysterians* the aggressors' one insupportable demand is intermarriage with human females "because there is so much strontium-99 in our bones." If one can safely judge by title and advertising, *I Married a Monster from Outer Space* involves a similar unlikely prospect, and takes the same attitude toward it. This is like expecting the Thing to pollinate Godzilla, but monstrous union is in line with this sort of film, and, considering the attitude they display toward almost every Thing in them, an intolerant view of mixed marriage is to be expected.   The Mysterians, incidentally, look very much like human beings, except that they melt.   Space travel is rare in sf films now, but we have discovered human beings native to Mars, Venus, and various nonexistent planets.   Sometimes space travel and monsters are ingeniously combined, as when *The First Man into Space* returns a monster.   *The Forbidden Planet* and *This Island Earth* were expensive color productions which involved space travel and managed to have their monsters too.   In *Forbidden Planet* it had something to do with the Id, but it might as well have been Grendel.   *This Island Earth*, an unbelievable adaptation of a somewhat less unbelievable novel by Raymond F. Jones, included a horrendous Thing called, of all things, a "Mutant."

The most recent big sf film is *The Fly*, in CinemaScope and Horror-color, and popular enough to call for a *Return* . . . . *The Fly* is not from the short story of that title by Arthur Porges, originally in *The Magazine of Fantasy and Science Fiction*, but from another story of the same title by George Langelaan, originally in *Playboy*.   Porges' story presents an interesting situation which could not be filmed without expansion and, inevitably, ruination; and it would be called *Invasion of the Atom-Fly from Another World*.   Since Langelaan's story is impossible to begin with, is inconsistent anyway, and is a horror story as horrifying as the most horrible sf films, one might expect that it could endure motion picture adaptation.   The film, however, managed to be more impossible and less consistent, to add clichés and bright blood, and to contrive a happier ending with some morally repugnant implications.

Even if one accepts, for the sake of entertainment, the initial premise that Andre Delambre has built, in his basement, a working matter-transmitter, nothing else follows. The machine behaves differently each time it makes a mistake. The molecular structure of a dish is reversed. A cat, with a pitiable wail, disappears entirely. Finally, Andre himself is somehow mixed up with a fly. The result is a handsome young scientist with ". . . the head of a fly" (and an arm, too) and "the fly with the head of a man!"[6] Of course, there is a certain ingenuity about the accident: it creates two "monsters" instead of one. But why is Andre with the head of the fly still Andre, and why does his fly-leg have (evidently) a fly's volition? Why was the part of the fly grafted to Andre enlarged to fit him so well? How does he eat? Breathe? Why does he gradually begin to think a bit like a fly, and why is he then tempted to maul his poor wife, Helene? Why destroy the lab? The series of physical impossibilities in the script is not helped by the psychology. After squashing the man with the head of the fly in a hydraulic press, Helene neither commits suicide nor is she confined, as in the story. Helene is saved from grief and inconvenience by Commissaire Charas who, at the last minute, notes the fly with the head of a man, and squashes it with a rock. What else, indeed, could be done with it? Although it is clear that Andre's death (i.e., Andre, in the press) was suicide in which Helene cooperated, the script chooses to ignore the moral problem presented by the suicide, or the mercy-killing, or whatever it was. Instead, the issue is that Helene killed a mere Thing. After all, it is not improper to kill a Thing, and one may safely kill a man if he is no longer entirely human. This follows repetitious dialogue about the Sacredness of Life, but apparently they meant natural, original life-forms only, and the cat is more sacred than Andre in either combination. In the last scene of the film, Andre's surviving brother delivers a little proscience speech to Andre's son while Helene listens, smiling sweetly. Father, the boy's uncle tells him, was like Columbus. What will be remembered, of course, is that Father was like a fly.

The Fly, like most sf films, has a rather strange, very old moral. A search for knowledge or any worldly improvements may go too far; it may be blasphemous; and one may be punished with an unnatural end.[7]

The premises of sf films are all antique, and carelessly handled. Twenty years ago, the matter-transmitter in the present-day cellar might have been almost convincing; but now one would expect it in a more credible context, and expect it to function with some consistency. Most sf films, however, do not take place in the future, where such an invention might be acceptable. 1984 is a rare, recent exception; but if Orwell's novel had not forced the date, it would have been 1960.

It is true that magazine science fiction developed and exploited the stereotyped mad scientist and the evil bug-eyed monster. But that, again, was about twenty years ago. Giant insects, shrinking men, and dinosaurs can be found in science fiction of the same period. It is true that some science fiction stories are as unoriginal, illogical, and monstrous as sf films; but you have to know where to look in order to find many of them.

Apart from such incidental lessons as the immorality of attempting to prolong life and the advisability of forgetting anything new that one happens to learn, there are two vague ideas that appear in sf films with some regularity. Sometimes, the menace or the Thing does not merely kill its victims, but deprives them of their identity, their free-will, or their individual rights and obligations as members of a free society. In *Attack of the Puppet People*, for instance, the combination doll-maker and mad super-scientist who shrinks the people he likes is a sort of pathetic, benevolent dictator. Many sf films derive whatever emotional effect they have from their half-hearted allegorization of the conflict between individuality and conformity. Usually, the conflict remains undeveloped, and although the characters tend to resist such menaces, their reasons may often be that the menace is a slimy, repulsive Thing, or that they would resist any change, even one for the better. *1984* is the only sf film that took this conflict as its subject, although it is common in science fiction novels.

The other vague idea is that atomic power is dangerous. The point has been made again and again, ever since the Geiger counter reacted to the presence of the first Thing. The point is indisputable, but these films rarely show any awareness of the ways in which the atom is dangerous. The danger of atomic war is explicit in Arch Oboler's *Five*, the recent *The World, the Flesh, and the Devil*, and the forthcoming *On the Beach*. These films are not only exceptional, they are not generally considered to be science fiction. In the ordinary science fiction film, atomic bombs raise dragons and shrink people. Even *The Fly*, which had nothing to do with the effects of radiation, real or imagined, was advertised as if its poor monsters were the realistic, possible outcome of fall-out on flesh. It may be argued that all the atomic monsters of sf films are symbols, and I suppose that they are, but they are inapt, inept, or both.

If the creators of monster films had intended any comment

on the problems raised by the atomic bomb, or even on feelings about it, as some kindly critics have assumed, they would not have made their monster films at all. The most obvious advantage of science fiction, and the three films mentioned above, is that one can deal with such problems and feelings by extending the situation into the future and showing a possible effect or resolution. There is no need for indirect discussion or for a plot with a "symbol" as its mainspring. A twelve-ton, woman-eating cockroach does not say anything about the bomb simply because it, too, is radioactive, or crawls out of a test-site, and the film-makers have simply attempted to make their monster more frightening by associating it with something serious.

One should realize that, like them or not, the invaders in Wells' *War of the Worlds*, the stranded Alien in Campbell's "Who Goes There?," or the parasites in Heinlein's *Puppet Masters* (clumsily parodied by *The Brain Eaters*, who are complex parasitic animals that evolved when there were no hosts for them) are a different sort of monster from those of most sf films. They may be symbols too, but first they are beings. Campbell may invent a creature that evokes a complex of ancient fears—fear of the ancient itself, the fear that death may not be final, that evil is indestructible, and fear rising from the imitation motif, fear of possession, of loss of identity, all the fears that gave rise to tales of demons, ghosts, witches, vampires, shape-shifters. But in "Who Goes There?" it is a realistically conceived being that evokes these fears and creates the suspense, not an impossible symbol; and the story is not hysterical, but a study of man under stress.

The sf films abuse their borrowed props and offer nothing but hysteria. The films resemble unpleasant dreams, but rarely resemble them well. One cannot condemn an attempt to make a film suggesting nightmare illogic, of course, but surrealism is not what the makers of these films have in mind.

Fantasy and science fiction are not convincing if they are not consistent. Convincing the audience to accept the initial premise of the story may be difficult enough, without violating that premise in each scene. Expensive and careful treatment of a careless script cannot overcome the script's bad logic in science fiction or anything else. And while careful sf scripts are rare, careful treatment is even more rare. Most of the special effects in sf films, for instance, would not deceive a myopic child in the back of the theater—not even all the third-degree burns and running sores that have become so popular. The films convey the impression that everyone involved is aware that he is working on something which is not only beneath his talent but beneath the audience as well. It seems that even the make-up department, called upon by the pointless turns of a morbid plot to disintegrate a bored actor, has neither the time nor the heart to waste any effort, and produces something that looks like the unraveling of an old vacuum-cleaner bag. Perhaps this is a good thing. But it is strange that if you hire a group of talented people and ask for another science fiction-horror, you will get a film that is not merely abominable in conception and perverse in implication but half-hearted in execution.

Reginald Bretnor's symposium, *Modern Science Fiction* (New York, Coward-McCann), contains an interesting article by Don Fabun, "Science Fiction in Motion Pictures, Radio, and Television," a detailed examination that concludes with this hope: "In time we may see the modern literary form called science fiction legitimately married to novel and exciting techniques of presentation, a combination which should bring us fresh and exciting entertainment superior to what we see and hear today." That was in 1953. Today, there seems little cause for hope from the present level where "science fiction" is indistinguishable from "horror," and "horror" from sadism. An audience for good science fiction films probably exists, but it is unlikely that producers will take that chance now. During the period when it seemed reasonable to expect some good sf films, the only chances that producers were willing to take with unfamiliar material were with material from contemporary life—"unfamiliar material" only in their previous films. With science fiction, every one has followed the easy examples of a few successful horror films, in cheaper and cheaper productions that plagiarized their poverty of ideas and their antiscientific tone. Perhaps the problem of producing good *sf* films is more difficult than that of producing simply good films. Complex, individual, and intelligent films are rare, and films of this quality with unfamiliar, fantastic subjects are few indeed. *Things to Come, Caligari, Orpheus,* or *The Seventh Seal* are uncommon individual achievements; probably, good science fiction films will appear only in the form of such unusual achievements.[8] For the rest, if sf films continue to be produced, they will take the easy way of the scream instead of the statement, and continue to tell their increasingly irrational and vicious stories of impossible monsters, evil professors, and helpless victims. ("See a strip-teaser completely stripped—of flesh!" invites the latest poster.)

A possible explanation for the impossible, self-contradictory creatures and plots of these films is that their creators do not think it could matter to anyone: the monsters are unnatural—or unnaturalness—anyway, and the calculated response is "Quick! Kill it, before it reproduces!" (Poor Andre, poor Thing.) The assumption may be partially correct; and if many people like this sort of entertainment, the clear impossibility of creatures and plots may help ease the conscience. If the monsters are anything, they are evil conveniently objectified. But the "evils" that they represent, while sometimes pain and death, are just as often man's power, knowledge, and intelligence. Their part used to be played by the Devil or his demons. The destruction of the Things and of the mad scientists, and the senseless martyrdoms of the more rare "good" (if not "sane") scientists, resemble nothing so much as exorcism and the burning of witches and heretics.

Unfortunately, science fiction films have associated science, the future, the different, and the unknown with nothing but irrational fear. There are enough dangers; in these films the dangers are not natural, but impossible and monstrous—of the same character as those that one was believed to risk when, in another time, one forsook the True Faith for the Black Arts. What the equivalent of the Black Arts is imagined to be is often all too clear in each film. But the True Faith is never plainly shown, perhaps because if it is anything at all it is simply an absence of any thinking.

NOTES

[1]"Shooting *Destination Moon*," *Astounding Science Fiction*, July 1950.
[2]"Filming *War of the Worlds*," *Astounding Science Fiction*, October 1953.
[3]It may be pointed out that Wells' Martians shared this improbable habit; but they were not vegetable bipeds, and that was about fifty years before.
[4]Vague approval of this film is found even today, when its "novelty" is

no excuse.   For instance, Frank Hauser, although aware of the fiction of Bradbury and Heinlein, makes this wild understatement: "The film, unfortunately, was not entirely successful." (In his "Science Fiction Films," in William Whitebait's *International Film Annual, No. 2*, New York: Doubleday, 1958.)

[5]*In Search of Wonder: essays on modern science fiction*, Chicago: Advent, 1956.

[6]In the story, Andre attempts to rectify this error and merely mixes himself with the vanished cat as well as the housefly; this explains why the author did away with the cat, if not how.   No doubt the makers of the film considered this too complicated, but retained the cat's disappearance for the unique poignancy of the scene.

[7]In *The Return of the Fly*, the same thing happens, and the moral is the same.

[8]Despite his success with *Beauty and the Beast*, Cocteau had trouble in obtaining backing for *Orpheus*.

MORRIS BEJA
ROBERT PLANK
ALEX EISENSTEIN

THREE
PERSPECTIVES
OF
A
FILM

I. *2001*: Odyssey to Byzantium
Morris Beja

Most of the commentary on Stanley Kubrick and Arthur C. Clarke's film, *2001: A Space Odyssey*, has concentrated on the second half of the title, and consequently on the way in which astronaut Dave Bowman's journey takes him to the infinite—from here to there. But the film presents us, as its full title indicates, with a journey which is temporal as well as spatial. The first half of the title—and the part given most stress by the graphics associated with the film— emphasizes the temporal nature of Bowman's odyssey, and consequently the way it takes him to the eternal—from now to then.

Indeed, the choice of the date strikes me as one of the most intriguing things about the movie. With its connotations of a new start (. . . 0001) built on past millennia (2000 . . .), it recalls many theories of the cyclical nature of universal history. For me, it has been illuminating in particular to consider this element of the film against the background of William Butler Yeats's stress on 2,000 year cycles, at the end of each of which we have a birth and take-over by a new god. Any student of Yeats, certainly, is not going to pass lightly over the crucial significance of the year 2001, of all possible dates. It seems especially enlightening to compare what Kubrick and Clarke are attempting in *2001* with what Yeats is attempting in such a poem as "Sailing to Byzantium."

Originally published in *Extrapolation*, 10 (December 1968), 67-68. Reprinted with the permission of the author.

I need hardly mention that my point is not that Kubrick, say, necessarily knows Yeats's poem, or that Yeats composed it after a vision-preview of the movie in 1926. Rather, the approach and goals of the two visionary and metaphysical works seem to me strikingly similar and mutually illuminating.

In "Sailing to Byzantium," of course, Yeats is concerned with what faces each individual soul as it tries to turn from our sensual and physical world—"that country," as Yeats calls it—to the next world, the world of the spirit and eternity, symbolized by the holy city of Byzantium. In his quest, he beseeches the aid of the "sages" in "God's holy fire," asking them to "come from the holy fire, perne in a gyre"—that is, to leave their condition of eternity for the mid-realm of the gyre, so that they may teach *him* how to be gathered "into the artifice of eternity."

The key to apprehending *2001* is the initial realization that—in this film about what is past, or passing, or to come—when Dave Bowman goes on his odyssey to outer (and inner) space, he is on precisely the same sort of journey that Yeats is making when he sails to Byzantium; only in Bowman's case it cannot be called a conscious quest as such, since initially he is not aware of the full significance of his "mission." But we are: we have been clued in by the appearance of the artifice of eternity—the monolith of the opening sections of the film. By the time we see Dave on his unwitting quest for it, we realize that it has awaited him, patiently, three or four million years, a monument of unaging intellect.

Unfortunately, Dave encounters obstacles on his pilgrimage: the most formidable is that monument of its own magnificence, Hal, the computer. But our pilgrim triumphs over that obstacle and finally goes through to, as the words on the screen inform us, "Jupiter—and Beyond—the Infinite." Clearly, when you go to the Infinite, what you are doing is, in Yeats's terms, going out of nature. And once out of nature, Dave goes through a prolonged and intense psychedelic experience, in order to be taken out of our world into the other. In Clarke's novel based on the film, we are told that Dave is here going through "some kind of cosmic switching device, routing the traffic of the stars through unimaginable dimensions of space and time."[1] The movie itself exposes us to varied and extreme visual and aural phenomena, designed to make it perfectly clear to any observer that what Dave is doing is perning in a gyre—and finally coming through God's holy fire.

By the time the extraterrestrial sages get him through, he is an aged man, and we are presented with the most perplexing sequence in this challenging film. We encounter Dave, in a French Provincial room, considerably aged since we last saw him. Moreover, he is not getting any younger, so pretty soon we see him as a tattered coat upon a stick, a mere paltry thing, a dying animal. But we must realize that that does not matter—that, indeed, his soul should clap its hand and sing, and louder sing for every tatter in his mortal dress. For Dave is to have his bodily form changed-and he is no more likely than Yeats to have it transformed into any natural thing.

He has been gathered into eternity, and that is no country for old men. So his bodily form is changed into that of a child. But a god-child: the new god coming in the *magnus annus*, the Great Year 2001—the beginning of the new 2,000 year cycle. Or, at least, he is a supernatural, anti-natural child: what the sequel to Yeats's poem "Byzantium," will hail as "the superhuman."

NOTES

[1]Arthur C. Clarke, *2001: A Space Odyssey* (NY: New American Library, 1968), p. 199.

II. 1001 Interpretations of *2001**
Robert Plank

The glory that was Greece reached its pinnacle in marble, so when you want to see it at its most glorious, you go to the Louvre, for the Venus di Milo and the Victory of Samothrace. And what do you see? Venus has no arms, Victory has no head.

The viewer has to complete the figure, and if your imagination is what it should be, you may produce something finer in your mind than any sculptor could have chiseled into stone. Absolute perfection is not within human reach; being imperfect, these statues are perfect.

*Originally published in *Extrapolation*, 11 (December 1969), 23-24. Reprinted by permission of the author.

They were not, of course, so designed: their fate perfected them. Few artists are as lucky as to have head or hands knocked off their works in just the right way. They have to leave room for imaginative completion intentionally. They have to build ambiguity into their design.

Yeats's poem "Sailing to Byzantium" and the Clarke/Kubrick film *2001: A Space Odyssey* are such works. Professor Beja has shown us their kinship in a lithe and lean paper in the last issue of this journal. His reasoning is as enchanting as it is convincing on internal evidence. That he sought to underpin it with something like a numerological proof was gratuitous.

Similar lines of thought could undoubtedly be spun from any date that Kubrick and Clarke might have chosen. To interpret the date 2001 differently is equally easy. It being but one step from the sublime to the ridiculous, let me demonstrate how simple a step it is:

Factorize the date. You get this equation: $2001 = 3 \times 23 \times 29$. If you don't believe this to be a true equation, recompute it; if you can't, ask your friendly neighborhood computer. Now the significance of the three prime factors:

Three has been a sacred number for so long that nobody remembers or cares any more, how it got that way. $23 = 12 + 11$, the number of the apostles plus the number of the apostles who remained faithful. 29 is a number of such awesome sacred secret power that even the numerologists don't know.

If you like the search for the meaning of God better than the search for the meaning of numbers, here is another tack: in *Citadelle,* Antoine de Saint-Exupéry relates a (perhaps fictitious) dream:

> . . . Obstiné, je montais vers Dieu pour lui demander la raison des choses . . . Mais au sommet de la montagne je ne découvris qu'un bloc pesant de granit noir—lequel était Dieu . . . Seigneur, lui dis-je, instruisez-moi . . . Mais le bloc de granit ruisselant d'une pluie luisante me démeurait impénétrable . . .

> (Undaunted, I climbed toward God, to ask him the reason of things . . . But on the summit of the mountain all I found was a heavy block of black granite—which was God . . . Lord, I said, teach me . . . but the block of granite, dripping with a luminous rain, remained, for me, impenetrable . . .)

Citadelle was published (in French) in 1948, four years after its author was lost in action. Clarke's short story *The Sentinel*—the gem of *2001*—was copyrighted in 1951. It is not impossible that Clarke could have known *Citadelle*, but—as Beja has shown—it does not matter. The kinship is strikingly there. Does it follow that the slab in *2001* is God, and that this is the explanation of the film?

Where a work of art has the requisite ambiguity, it is almost easier to interpret it than not to interpret it. These interpretations proliferate. If one of them is as good as the other, shouldn't we wonder whether any of them is any good?

The problem how to validate our interpretations is so vast and difficult that it would be presumptuous of me even to suggest any solutions; but I do think it is time that we seriously address ourselves to it.

III. The Academic Overkill of *2001*
Alex Eisenstein

While Morris Beja's general interpretation and conclusions are hardly arguable, his methods of arriving at them, and the actual relevance of the Yeats poem are highly questionable. "Any student of Yeats," says Beja, ". . . is not going to pass lightly over the crucial significance of the year 2001, of all possible dates." The "crucial significance" of 2001 is that it has long been one of several traditional dates (1999 and 2000 are others) favored by sf writers dealing with the semi-distant future. And more important than "Yeats's stress on 2000 year cycles" is the significance attached to the termination of *any* millenium by the multifarious prophets preceding the temporal juncture. Yeats is hardly the first mystic to predict the arrival of a god (or the end of the finite world) at the onset of a new (or the culmination of an old) millenium.

Beja disclaims all intentions of demonstrating some clear-cut literary influence of this esoteric poet on either Kubrick or Clarke, yet he insists that the "key to . . . 2001 is . . . that . . . Bowman goes on . . . precisely the same sort of journey" as that described by Yeats in "Sailing to Byzantium." It is an odd key indeed that manifests a perfect fit through coincidence only.

Yet   .   .   .

Beja fails to establish that the two "metaphysical works" in question are "strikingly similar and mutually illuminating"; they are no more so than most randomly-matched pairs of millennial forebodings (mystic or otherwise). (Plank politely hints as much in the last lines of his own brief rejoinder in the following issue.) That Dave's hypercosmic journey equals "perning in a gyre—and finally coming through God's holy fire," *apropos* of Yeats, is far from being "perfectly clear to any observor," if only because the poet's terminology, via Beja, does not correspond at all with the imagery, either metaphysical or literal, in this final portion of the film.

In his two encounters with specifics of the film itself (aside from the title), Beja errs twice. The first error is relatively minor and the result of an excusable ignorance of art history: the furnishings of the green bedroom are *not* French Provincial, but mostly Louis Seize, the outstanding exception to the period style being the modern, unadorned king-size bed upon which Bowman gasps his last.

Beja's second error of observation is more fundamental, but he compounds it with a very convenient misapprehension—and, thereby, spuriously rectifies his ultimate conclusion. In his analysis, the last sub-title reads, "Jupiter—and Beyond—the Infinite"; in other words, what lies beyond Jupiter, for Dave, is the Infinite. Sound reasonable? Yes, but it isn't really, for the sub-title actually reads, "Jupiter and *Beyond the Infinite*." (My italics.) There are great, glowing magnitudes of difference between these two captions! Nevertheless, Beja surmises that Bowman travels "out of our world [and] into the other"—i.e., outside the normal confines of our Universe and its Space/Time Continuum; beyond the usual matrix of matter and energy, into another plane of existence. His basic assumption is that "Clearly, when you go to the Infinite, what you are doing is, in Yeats's terms, going out of nature." Well, I cannot speak for Yeats, but in terms of present cosmological theory, one needn't necessarily search for Infinity outside the Universe; Infinity may be right at home, so to speak, as a function of the space/time we ordinarily experience. (Another theory describes the possibility of a finite Continuum, but most sf stories equate the dimensions of Time and Space with

Infinity.) Obviously, however, to go "*beyond* the Infinite" would definitely require transcendence of the normal physical framework; thus Beja derives the correct conclusion from faulty observation and assumption.

Some of Robert Plank's interpretive suggestions would be intolerable, were they not offered in an effort to ridicule all such extraneous interpretation. His introductory remarks involving aesthetics must displease the sincere artist. If the viewer of Venus di Milo may truly imagine more beautiful limbs than those it originally possessed, a probable explanation is that ideals of feminine loveliness have changed somewhat since 150 B.C. (Or perhaps that the Venus is not a particularly enchanting example of Hellenistic sculpture.) Although the greatest present appeal of the Nike lies in her enveloping drapery, which describes in stone the exciting, turbulent flow of wind about her figure, no historian or critic of art, nor any real artist, would suggest the foul notion that this statue was less a work of art before being damaged. To contend that accidents of deletion perfected the Victory denies the competence (and evident genius) of the artist who designed and created her; such a thought is the expression of an absolute philistine—the iconoclasm of Dada and Surrealism notwithstanding. I categorically reject Plank's assertion that any viewer with an adequate power of imagination "may produce something finer" in his mind "than any sculptor could have chiseled in stone." Being a graphic artist myself, I know something of the problems and process involved in such creation; rest assured that even a well-developed imagination is more slippery and insubstantial than Plank would have it. The question of the relative merits of the actual head of Nike and that imagined by Plank is, of course, absurdly moot: the original cannot be recovered, and Plank, I presume, cannot show us his version.

The permissible extent of intentional ambiguity—the whole point of Plank's facetiousness regarding Classical statuary—is a highly subjective area of debate, as witness Joanna Russ's seemingly opposite view.[1] Where must specific and literal exposition and description necessarily end? This self-query applies especially in the realm of sf writing: in a short story there is often not room to explain in detail all aspects of the author's marvelous inventions. Occasionally, apt naming must suffice. Nevertheless, I am not positive that Plank's acceptable ambiguity is consonant with mine.

The similarities between de Saint-Exupéry's *Citadelle* and Clarke's "The Sentinel" are interesting, but the correspondence is too slight for *Citadelle* to be relevant to the later story. *The Sentinel*, after all, is a translucent pyramid, and even the titles are closer in sound than in meaning. The black monoliths of the film are not so much symbols of specific content as *agents* of specific *involvement*, and they suggest many more entities of myth than they represent. As Richard Hodgens, for one, has observed, "This is art, not allegory."[2]

After demonstrating that Clarke could have read *Citadelle* before writing "The Sentinel," Plank offers the contingent, rhetorical question, "Does it follow that the slab in *2001* is God?" Because he never establishes any *probability* that Clarke knew *Citadelle*, and even dismisses the importance of such prior knowledge, the obvious answer is, "No, of course it does not follow—not from the story *Citadelle*." Nor does it necessarily follow, from any source, that only *one* slab exists—a pet notion of the literati. Whether or not the first monolith (or its later manifestations/cousins) is God depends almost entirely on how the Deity is defined. In a certain functional sense, the monolith acts as "God": it seems to strike the first spark of higher intelligence that separates Man from Beast; thus the Monolith may be said to "create" Man. And a literally vital idea is triggered (or imparted) by the monolith; the latter, therefore, is also saviour.

Of course, the monoliths are really minions of a collective High Power, one that apparently embodies both the omnipotence and omniscience ascribed to God in the modern Judeo-Christian conception. Yet neither the slabs nor the Master Intelligence are implicated in the Origin of the Universe when the Supreme Power displays the process to Bowman, during the so-called "psychedelic trip." The Creation is presented in two brief, successive shots: the first is often mistaken for a globular star-cluster hurtling at the viewer; the other is commonly interpreted, less understandably, as a spiral galaxy. Actually, these shots comprise a concise visualization of the "Big Bang" theory: the first illustrates the explosive disruption of the primal "cosmic egg" into myriad, glowing spherules; the other depicts the random whorls of proto-galaxies coalescing within a vast, amoeboid nebula (a later stage, presumably, of one of the incandescent ejecta in the first scene).

So God-the-Primogenitor is not a part of the fictional scheme of 2001—though all devout Christians would surely belabor the significance of the Cross over Jupiter and the many trinities scattered throughout the film. They would discount, of course, the possibility that those signs are included expressly to elicit such reflexive inferences (and to curry the favor of the Church—not the only group Kubrick attempts to placate with the multiplex freight carried by the film's imagery and story-line. But that's another story in itself.)

NOTES

[1]Joanna Russ, "Dream Literature and Science Fiction," *Extrapolation*, 11 (December 1969), 6-14.

[2]Richard Hodgens, "Notes on *2001: A Space Odyssey*," *Trumpet*, no. 9 (1969), p. 37.

MARK R. HILLEGAS

SCIENCE FICTION
AS
A
CULTURAL PHENOMENON:
A RE-EVALUATION

For more than a decade now science fiction has offered an almost irresistible attraction to those who enjoy using the method of content analysis to determine what are the values and attitudes for which popular literature is a vehicle.[1] But unfortunately for the analysts, science fiction is a very large domain (Harvard's Clarkson Collection contains more than 2000 paperback books plus every issue of some one hundred magazines), and so far no one has had the energy to do more than sample here and there. Even so, the analysts have been fairly successful in delineating the contours of science fiction as a cultural manifestation, and this has been possible because science fiction apparently is written and read by people who share a somewhat similar background of education and interests.[2] In general the analysts have come to the sensible conclusion that science fiction is an expression of two common elements in Western culture.

The first element is the Baconian faith that by the systematic investigation of nature man can master the secrets of this mysterious universe and in so doing improve the human condition. Such faith in the power of science has clearly been implicit in a great deal of science fiction, especially in the thirties, and sometimes it is directly stated, as recently, for example, as in Arthur

Professor Hillegas's paper was presented as one of a trio of papers under the topic, "The Cowboy, The Detective, and the Spaceman," at the ASA general meeting at MLA, Washington, D.C., in December, 1962. It was first published in *Extrapolation*, 4 (May 1963), 26-33.

Clarke's *Childhood's End* (1953). In this novel, the Overlords, a manifest symbol of science, invade our earth just in time to prevent men from turning their world into a radioactive wasteland and, by introducing reason and the scientific method into human activities, transform earth into a technological utopia where each individual can develop his potentialities to the fullest. As a carrier for the Baconian faith, science fiction is almost the exercise of a new religion, in which the scientist is priest and the scientific method creed.

The second element common to science fiction as a cultural manifestation is the belief that the universe is a machine, indifferent to man and lacking a divine plan or purpose. This belief darkens the following passage from Algis Budrys' *Rogue Moon* (1960):

> Death is in the nature of the universe, Barker. Death is only the operation of a mechanism. All the universe has been running down from the moment of its creation. Did you expect a *machine* to care what it acted upon?

And yet, as Robert West points out in a recent article in *The Georgia Review*, there is, in most science fiction, no failure of nerve in facing the cold infinities lying between the stars.[3] Science fiction holds that man, with the aid of science, is the measure of the universe—at least while he is alive. And so the analysts can also tell us that science fiction is the expression of what is a new myth, the embodiment of a uniquely modern vision of man and the cosmos.

But there is nothing surprising in the above analyses; for the analysts have done little more than point out that science fiction, as a kind of popular literature, is a vehicle for ideas about science and man's relationship to the universe which are generally widespread in the culture, something one might possibly surmise without having read any science fiction. If there is anything really unexpected in these analyses, it is the evidence as to the great vitality of these ideas, a vitality which the commentators have not so much directly described as indirectly suggested by the attention they have thought it worthwhile to give to science fiction. Yet even after this qualification is made, one has only said that science fiction presents a remarkably accurate index to certain elements in our culture, elements which are not altogether hard to detect in numerous other manifestations. All of this serves to suggest that we cannot expect to learn much more about science fiction by looking at it from the outside; and therefore it seems reasonable to turn to more humanistic methods in our attempt to understand this phenomenon. Here, I think, the fact that science fiction is a kind of popular literature (and hence may help to shape the attitudes and values of a great number of people) determines the scope and direction of our investigation. Specifically, we are forced to find answers to two questions. First, is science fiction a significant instrument for social criticism and comment on human life? Second, if it is such an instrument, how does it function?

The answer to the first question is that since World War II many science-fiction writers have turned to examining the whole relationship of human life to scientific and technological progress, have begun to deal with problems of human employment and activity, of freedom and social justice in a world dominated by machines, problems of ethics in an age of a new science of man, problems of the very survival of a species which seems to have outrun its intelligence. And so there has appeared a great flood of science-fiction novels and stories, critical not only of the impact of science and technology on human life but critical of man and society, works whose criticism would never pass, as Oscar Shaftel has pointed out, "the official or unofficial censorship that has fallen upon most mass media of communication."[4] And in case we doubt our own interpretation, there is the supporting opinion of "mainstream" literary critics like Kingsley Amis and C. S. Lewis, who testify to the actuality of this revolution in science fiction.[5]

As for the second question—how science fiction functions as social criticism—a partial answer has already been given, most notably in Amis's New Maps of Hell (1960), a work largely devoted to showing how satiric and inverted utopias written by professional science-fiction writers have been used for what Amis terms "diagnosis and warning."[6] But much more remains to be discovered as to how science fiction provides an instrument for criticism of human life. An effective way, I think, to conduct an investigation of this problem would be to apply the concept that science fiction is not one single type or form of fiction but instead a collection of many genres. Looked at this way, science fiction would be found, I think, to contain certain genres which have a potentiality for criticism which is uniquely a function of the particular genre. Three genres stand out in this respect: the dystopia, the post-catastrophe novel or story, and space fiction. Before going on to discuss these three genres, it is important to make the qualification here that each may have elements from the other two. Space travel is frequently a part of the dystopia and sometimes of the post-catastrophe novel or story; dystopian elements are common in novels and stories concerned with other worlds; and the threat of world holocaust can hang over other worlds as well as this earth.

The first genre, the dystopia, extrapolates "existing tendencies" in our world today to warn us what the future may be like. A dystopia can be anywhere on a spectrum whose two ends are the nightmare and the satire, and, of course, it is a manifestation in popular literature of a tradition which stretches at least as far back as the eighteenth century and *Gulliver's Travels*. As a genre in science fiction, it lends itself especially to the kind of criticism which requires the preface, "If this goes on . . ." Among recent dystopias which have made significant comment and attained the rank at least of minor literature are Kurt Vonnegut, Jr.'s *Player Piano* (1952), which brilliantly imagines an America of the near future in which automated production has replaced the average worker and the only people who have work worth doing are managers and engineers; Frederik Pohl and C. M. Kornbluth's *The Space Merchants* (1953), which extrapolates a plundered and polluted world run tyrannically by ad men and business executives and which warns against the possibility of using the discoveries of the behavioral sciences to manipulate people without their knowledge or consent; and Ray Bradbury's *Fahrenheit 451* (1954), which warns of a book-burning society in which wall television and hearing-aid radios enslave men's minds.

The second genre, which is like the first in being concerned with the future, is the post-catastrophe novel or story—that is, fiction which describes the collapse of civilization after a world disaster, usually a nuclear war. Relying heavily on the effect of shock, this genre is able to say things about human nature and human civilization which cannot be effectively said in any other way. The genre has achieved significance at the hands of science-fiction writers in two very good recent novels, John Wyndham's *Re-Birth* (1953) and Walter M. Miller, Jr.'s *A Canticle for Leibowitz* (1959), both of which find men, after the great atomic disaster, stumbling back to their previous level of civilization and another catastrophe.

The third genre is space fiction,[7] the novel or story set on another world. Let us turn to this genre now and study it in some detail, for space fiction, I believe, illustrates in its purest form the way a science-fiction genre can function as an instrument of criticism.

The first important point to establish is that the plausible other world of twentieth-century space fiction is a quite different instrument of social criticism from the imagined world of the utopia. Primarily the capacity of modern space fiction to criticize rests on what an English sociologist, in characterizing all forms of science fiction, has called "a new basis of credibility": that is, a suspension of disbelief eased by the popular faith that almost everything is ultimately possible to modern science and technology.[8] Such credibility seldom exists in the utopia, which is marked by a quality which Richard Gerber has termed "ironical realism."[9] "In utopian writing," Gerber explains, "there is always a double level, the implication being: 'Here in this really existing utopia things are like this; they could also be like this in our known reality, but of course they are not, and perhaps, after all, they could not really be so, for we know, don't we, that this utopia does not really exist.' " In space fiction, on the other hand, such a double level does not exist, and the author imagines a distant world which is intended to be taken much more seriously as real than the imagined world in any utopia. It is a world eminently plausible in terms of modern scientific knowledge, particularly biology and the theory of evolution, a world which is inhabited by alien forms of life, with other customs and ways of living. This plausible other world is, naturally enough, the chief instrument for social criticism in space fiction and may function as such through several distinct techniques.

One technique is to send a traveler to live for awhile on the plausible other world; and, in what the traveler sees and experiences—the differences can be at heart distortions, inversions, and exaggerations of characteristics of our world—the reader gains new understanding of life on our world. By means of the comparisons and contrasts offered by the new world, the reader, through the eyes of the traveler, is able to look at earthly life from a distance, and what the reader learns is rendered especially accessible because of the dissociation with which the reader views the phenomenon of the new world. On a grander scale, such a voyage is like an account of travel to other lands on this earth, except that the author has almost limitless possibilities for rearranging the order of time and space.

The two greatest examples in the twentieth century of the use in this fashion of plausible other worlds are H. G. Wells's *The First Men in the Moon* (1901) and C. S. Lewis's *Out of the Silent Planet* (1938). Wells brilliantly creates the gigantic anthill of the moon's interior to present a paradox still unresolved in the twentieth century: how, in an age of science and technology, can the world achieve economic, social, political stability and efficiency and, at the same time, not dehumanize the individual by completely controlling him? Lewis transcends the familiar conventions of the Martian romance to look at human life through the eyes of the Oyarsa and the three unfallen species of Malacandra, as Mars is called in Old Solar. But these two works, as excellent as they are, are really outside of our present discussion, which is restricted to space fiction written since the war by professional science-fiction writers. The same technique, however, is used by professional science-fiction writers, a good example being the first part of James Blish's *A Case of Conscience* (1958).

A Case of Conscience represents the blending of genres of which we spoke earlier. The first part of the novel takes place on a distant world, Lithia (made real by carefully worked out ecological details) and so is space fiction. The second part is set on earth and is a nightmare utopia; but the novel is first of all a representative of space fiction since the action in the second part is a direct consequence of what exists and takes place on Lithia. The Lithians, a twelve-foot-tall reptilian people, know no God yet live and think righteously because to do so is reasonable, efficient, and natural. Without constraint or guidance, without laws of any kind, they follow an ethical code equivalent to the highest ideals evolved on earth. The question is whether Lithia is an unfallen world (like Lewis's Malacandra), or whether it is, as the central character, the Jesuit biologist, Father Ruiz-Sanchez, reluctantly concludes, a "planet and a people propped up by the Ultimate Enemy" to demonstrate once and for all that God need not exist. In either case, the chief vehicle for criticism is the contrast between men, with their built-in imperfections—original sin, if you wish—and the seemingly unfallen Lithians. This criticism of human nature by presenting its antithesis becomes almost unbearable in the second part, the inverted utopia, when we see men, riotous and neurotic, still living in underground shelters some time after a threat of atomic war has been averted.

Much more commonly, though, the plausible other world of space fiction is used in another way for social criticism—that is, the focus is not so much on what a traveler sees on another world as on the contact between two species, the Earthlings and the aliens. Very often men exploit or corrupt the species or civilization with which they come in contact. Malcolm Jameson's "Lilies of Life" (*Astounding Science Fiction*, 1945), for example, speaks cogently about the relationship between religion and colonialism when it shows men of earth converting to Christianity the natives of Venus so that they will be useful, cooperative workers in the planet's uranium mines. Poul Anderson's "The Helping Hand" (*Astounding Science Fiction,* 1950) shows a world accepting technological aid from earth and thereby destroying its own unique potentiality for growth, for with the technological aid come the worst features of earthly civilization. But probably the best example of this kind of space fiction is Bradbury's *The Martian Chronicles* (1950). This collection of stories—incidents in a great migration from earth to Mars, where an old, dying race is killed off by a terrestrial disease—presents the hauntingly pathetic contrast between the civilization of the departed Martians—"a graceful, beautiful, philosophical people" who blended art into their living and never let science get out of hand—with the immature, materialistic, unstable civilization which is being transferred to Mars. Because it is set on another world, we are able to achieve sufficient detachment to see with understanding what happens as the men of earth energetically set about defacing the ancient and beautiful world, littering the proud canals with tin cans, the gray sea bottoms with dirty newspapers, the deserted cities with banana peels and picnic papers; and building prefabricated hot-dog stands at the crossroads of fifty-centuries-old high-ways—in short, demonstrating their total insensitivity to any values beyond the crudely materialistic. The book is also an instance of the merging of genres, of which we have spoken. In this case the apocalyptic element is joined to space fiction, for after awhile nuclear war breaks out on earth and the colonists return to their homelands in time for the final catastrophe.

Besides the two ways already discussed of using plausible other worlds to criticize human life, there are other possibilities in space fiction. One of these is the theme of the invasion of earth by superior creatures from another world. Most often, of course, this theme has been turned merely to the uses of terror, bringing forth an unending series of alien menaces in twentieth-century space fiction. But occasionally the theme has been used for criticism of human life, just as it was in the first important examples of the theme, Kurd Lasswitz's *Auf Zwei Planeten* (1897) and Wells's *The War of the Worlds* (1898). In this relatively small category there are several recent novels and stories about aliens who come to bring order out of earthly chaos—for example, the Overlords in *Childhood's End.* Finally one ought to add that space fiction can criticize without using a plausible inhabited world at all. Vonnegut's *The Sirens of Titan* (1961) turns space adventure to farce in order to smother in Gargantuan laughter the absurdities of American civilization and the human follies which support these absurdities. And Algis Budrys' *Rogue Moon* sends men to map a mysterious and hostile natural formation on the moon—a kind of "Alice in Wonderland with teeth"—in order to question the meaning of the human adventure in a universe without mind or purpose. But *The Sirens of Titan* and *Rogue Moon* are very much the exception in their methods of criticism.

The preceding discussion is sufficient, I think, to suggest the rich potentiality of space fiction for social criticism and comment. The same richness of potentiality also characterizes the other two genres which I have briefly discussed, and, to a lesser extent, still other genres which I have not discussed, such as novels and stories concerned with adventures in time, marvelous inventions, journeys into the hollow earth, and so forth. Science fiction demands further study, but one needs to resist the temptation to approach it in the wrong way—particularly one needs to resist the temptation to study it as myth.

In a broad sense, of course, science fiction is myth embodying the familiar ideas we mentioned at the beginning of our discussion—that is, the faith that man, using science and the scientific method, is the master of the mindless universe in which he finds himself. But this information is ultimately unenlightening, while further generalization about science fiction as myth is prevented by the very diversity of the novels and stories in the different genres of science fiction. Besides, the mythic constitutent is not what is important about science fiction.

What is really important about science fiction is that in its various genres it provides an extraordinarily flexible instrument for social criticism, that it is particularly able to deal with problems of life in a new age of science and technology, and that at the same time it is able to reach, because it is a kind of popular literature, a much larger audience than does most mainstream literature. In other words, science fiction has a significance in itself which far transcends its importance as an index to our culture. It is an interesting, vital phenomenon whose characteristics ought to dictate the nature of any investigation of it. There is a need to continue where Amis's *New Maps of Hell* has left off and to undertake a truly comprehensive survey of science fiction as social criticism.

NOTES

[1]Among numerous articles which analyze sf in this way, these are perhaps the most important: S. E. Finer, "A Profile of Science Fiction," *Sociological Review,* N.S. 2 (Dec. 1954), 239-255; S. Mendel and P. Fingesten, "The Myth of Science Fiction," *SR,* 27 August 1955, pp. 7-8; W. Hirsch, "Image of the Scientist in Science Fiction: A Content Analysis," *AJS,* 63 (March 1958), 506-512; R. H. West, "Science Fiction and Its Ideas," *Georgia Review,* 15 (Fall 1961), 276-286.

[2]See Finer, "A Profile of Science Fiction."

[3]See West, "Science Fiction and Its Ideas."

[4]Shaftel, "The Social Content of Science Fiction," *Science and Society,* 17 (Spring 1953), 97-118.

[5]Amis, *New Maps of Hell* (New York, 1960), 87-133; Lewis, *An Experiment in Criticism* (Cambridge, 1961), 108-109. Also, see Chad Walsh, *From Utopia to Nightmare* (New York, 1962).

[6]In addition to Amis's book (cited in preceding note), the function of post-war science fiction as social criticism is also pointed out in several articles, such as Finer, "A Profile of Science Fiction"; Shaftel, "The Social

Content of Science Fiction;" and M. R. Hillegas, "Dystopian Science Fiction: New Index to the Human Situation," *New Mexico Quarterly*, XXXI (Autumn 1961), 238-249.

[7]I make a distinction between cosmic voyage and space fiction. The cosmic voyage (a term used first by Professor Marjorie Nicolson) is a form of space fiction which describes an imaginary journey to another world; that is to say, the voyage itself is given considerable emphasis, sometimes as much as is the description of the strange new world. The cosmic voyage was the dominant form of space fiction from the seventeenth century and works like Kepler's *Somnium,* Godwin's *Man in the Moone,* and Cyrano de Bergerac's *Voyages to the Sun and Moon* to the nineteen thirties and Lewis's *Out of the Silent Planet,* Lewis's work being the last major example of this form. In the thirties, however, the pulp magazines created a new kind of space fiction in which very little emphasis is given to the voyage, a kind of space fiction which usually, unless concerned with some aspect of the journey—for example, human reaction to the several generations of time required to reach the stars—has been able to presuppose the voyage and all its conventions. This kind of space fiction, with us ever since the thirties, starts its adventures in space or on another world, sometimes as simply and matter-of-factly as in this opening sentence from Robert Heinlein's "The Black Pits of Luna": "The morning after we got to the Moon, we went over to Rutherford."

[8]Finer, "A Profile of Science Fiction," p. 244.

[9]Gerber, *Utopian Fantasy* (London, 1955), 89-104.

BEN FUSON

A
POETIC PRECURSOR
TO
BELLAMY'S
LOOKING BACKWARD

Eight years before the Julian West of Edward Bellamy's now-famed Utopian science-fiction classic awoke from his sleep, a Missouri lawyer allegedly did the same; like West, he recorded "a century hence" his observations of the 1980's, but he did it, mercifully, in just twenty-one 8-line stanzas of pleasantly rocking-horse anapaestic meter. This poem occupied pages 7-13 in Paxton's now rare volume, *A Century Hence and Other Poems* (Kansas City, Mo.: Ramsey, Millett & Hudson, 1880, 138 pp.); the remaining 25 poems are lackluster "remains" of a midwest Genteel-Tradition versifier, but the title poem intriguingly anticipates some of Bellamy's forecasts and observations, and is worth preserving. Incidentally, the book's dark green cover has a title stamped in gold featuring a "flying-saucer" wingless air machine aloft in the clouds, with three propellers, and the numeral "1991" (sic) proudly displayed on its hull! Here's the poem by our Platte City, Mo., lawyer:

A CENTURY HENCE

I. PROPHETIC VISIONS

If we could look down the long vista of ages,
    And witness the changes of time—
Or draw from Isaiah's mysterious pages,

Printed in The Kansas City *Star*, 27 June 1964, p. 8, c. 3; and in *Extrapolation*, 5 (May 1964), 31-36. Reprinted by permission of the author.

A key to his visions sublime,
We'd gaze on the picture with pride and delight,
    And all its magnificence trace—
Give honor to man for his genius and might,
    And glory to God for his grace.

II. PROGRESS

Behold, what astonishing progress appears,
    In literature, science and wealth,
Within the past era, of one hundred years,
    Of energy, virtue and health.
And now let us view the bright glories this land
    In the next hundred years shall possess—
When genius and science, with industry's hand,
    This country and people shall bless.

III. THE SEVEN SLEEPERS

We've all read the mythical story of old,
    How seven young sleepers withdrew,
And hid in a cavern, where, weary and cold,
    They slept a whole century through—
Then rose to return to their whole habitation,
    But found it dismantled and hoary;
Their kindred were dead, and the new generation
    Refused to give heed to their story.

IV. MY TRANCE

And I, too, have slept a whole century through,
    And rising, go forth through my land;
I seek for my home, and at length find the place,
    But all is so strange and so grand;
My cottage, that stood on the hill, is no more;
    A mansion now covers the ground;
I pass up the yard, and approach to the door,
    But none to receive me is found.

V. THE GARDEN

I go to the garden—in wonder I'm lost:
    The fruits of all countries are there:
The fig and the date are not hurt by the frost—

The orange is luscious and fair.
Each month brings renewal of all kinds of fruits;
    The tropical flowers grow wild;
The birds of the south and the African brutes
    Find the climate congenial and mild.

VI. THE FLYING FEMALE

In deep meditation I wandered alone,
    And lifted my gaze to the sky;
And lo! in the heavens a bright object shone,
    Approaching from regions on high:
As an angel it hovered, then drop't by my side:
    "Who are you?" I asked and retreated:
She folded her pinions and sweetly replied:
    "Your hostess; come in and be seated."

VII. RELATIVES

No words can express my surprise when I learned
    This lady possessed my own name;
She told me I'd hear, when her husband returned,
    He, too, would relationship claim.
By different lines, they their pedigree traced,
    Through four generations to me;
And my portrait the walls of the gallery graced,
    Where all of my race I could see.

VIII. THE DAGUERREAN ART

We turned to the hall, and my likeness selected,
    Mid pictures enchantingly bright;
She told me photography now was perfected,
    And colors were painted by light.
These pictures surpassed, in their scope and design,
    The paintings of masters of art;
Their colors were such as no art could combine,
    And nature alone could impart.

IX. RAIN PRODUCED

She saw that my mind was bewildered and dazed,
    And guided me forth to the green;
"And now," she observed, as to heaven she gazed,
    "Not a cloud in the sky can be seen;

And yet I will bring, in the course of an hour,
    A thunder-cloud, lightning and rain;
And languishing nature, refreshed by the shower,
    Will smile in soft beauty again."

X. SUNSHINE

She stepped to a rod, that extended on high,
    And touched it with magical craft—
The gathering vapors grew thick in the sky,
    And poured out a copious draught.
She again touched the rod, and the sun, from his path,
    Looked down with exhilarant ray;
All nature rejoiced in the life-giving bath,
    And mountain and meadow were gay.

XI. ACCLIMATURE

We walked through the nutmeg and cinnamon bowers,
    By statues and beautiful fountains,
Mid shrubbery, fruit trees and tropical flowers,
    By streamlets and miniature mountains—
Saw birds, of rich plumage, from Borneo's isle,
    And humming birds brought from Brazil;
While songsters from Europe, the Ganges, and Nile,
    Glad nature's rich orchestra fill.

XII. SCIENTIFIC ACHIEVEMENTS

The lady explained that, as science progressed,
    Man ruled upon sea and in air,—
That storms were forbidden—the sea kept at rest,
    And seasons made fruitful and fair;
That flowers and animals, far away reared,
    Were acclimated here and grew wild;
And a motor, much stronger than steam, had appeared,
    Yet cheap, economic and mild.

XIII. ATMOSPHERIC SHIP

"And look," she exclaimed, as she lifted her face,
    "There, now in the sky is a ship;
As swift as an eagle it moves to its place;
    'Tis my husband returned from his trip,"
He stepped from the vessel, as near us it came,

And dropped upon wings from above:
He knew, from my portrait, my kinship and name,
And hailed me in tenderest love.

XIV. AERIAL VOYAGE

He told of his visit to Paris and Rome—
    Of his flight over England and Spain;
He found in his travels, no land like his home,
    No place where he wished to remain.
He spoke of his trip to the banks of the Nile,
    To cities now crumbling to dust—
Of China, Japan and Australia's isle,
    Where all are in ruin and rust.

XV. DESOLATION IN THE EAST

He noted and wept, for the rapid decay,
    Of lands of the date and the lime,
Where ignorance, vice and oppression held sway,
    And men sought a happier clime.
But when he had passed o'er the isles of the ocean,
    And reached California's strand,
His spirit was filled with a thrilling emotion,
    Of pride for his own happy land.

XVI. VIEW FROM THE ROCKY MOUNTAINS

He rested on top of the high Rocky Mountains,
    And turned for a view of the West;
The land was a garden, with forests and fountains—
    A home for the free and the blest.
He turned to the East, and a picture more bright,
    Never rose in the poet's sweet dream;
The land was an Eden of love and delight,
    With mountain and valley and stream.

XVII. THE WHOLE CONTINENT OURS

In the midst, at St. Louis, the Capitol loomed,
    With lofty and glittering steeple—
The seat of a Nation, where freedom first bloomed,
    Containing a billion of people.
"And now," he exclaimed, "the whole Continent's ours,
    From Panama, North to the pole!

For naught but the ocean can fetter our powers,
Or give to us less than the whole!"

XVIII. INVENTIONS

As we walked to the house, my companions reported,
That roads through the land were not found,
That men, on light wings, in the atmosphere sported,
Or walked, as they pleased, on the ground.
With the new motive power, one man could do more
Than fifty, without it, could do;
So people were able to add to their store,
And be generous, noble and true.

XIX. TELEPHONE

An order for supper, by telephone, now,
Had scarcely been made, by my host,
When in sprang a servant, I cannot tell how,
With coffee, ham, biscuit and toast.
He'd come from St. Louis, three hundred miles out,
With dishes delicious and rare;
There were venison, and turkey, and salmon, and trout,
With pine-apple, orange and pear.

XX. ARTIFICIAL LIGHT

When supper was ended, I found it still light;
I looked for a lamp, and found none;
I stepped to the door, and looked forth on the night,
And lo! every house had a sun.
Above me in splendor, surpassing the moon,
A disk, in the heavens gave light;
And neighboring orbs gave the brightness of noon,
And scattered the darkness of night.

XXI. CONCLUSION

By reflectors, the light of these beacons was cast,
On parlor, and chamber, and hall;
And candles and lamps were consigned to the past,
And light, like the air, was for all.
Now worn by the scenes of the day, I need rest,
And find it in slumber elysian;
But rise in the morning, perplexed and distressed;
T'was all but a beautiful vision.

Color photography, artificially induced rain, controlled weather to support exhibits of tropical plants and animals, new power sources, individual human flight ability (with "pinions"), menus by telephone, diffused city-illumination devices (not yet rivalled by our stadium tower lights?)—our Platte City attorney's forecasting tempers science-fiction fantasy with extrapolative logic.   His political vision of St. Louis as the capital city of a United States covering "from Panama, north to the Pole" with a population of one billion may now seem jingoistic and macabrely Malthusian, but he set his sights high!   Paxton's poem deserves its niche, however tiny, in the bibliographies of Science-Fiction and Utopias.

FRANZ ROTTENSTEINER

KURD LASSWITZ:
A
GERMAN PIONEER
OF
SCIENCE FICTION

1–On Two Planets

On Two Planets (*Auf zwei Planeten*) was one of the best liked German science-fiction novels, selling seventy thousand copies between 1897, when it was first published, and 1930, the year of its last pre-war printing. Shortly after publication it was translated into Danish, Norwegian, Dutch, Swedish, and Czech; at the turn of the century it was probably the best known European novel of space fiction. (Curiously enough, it was never translated into English, and so had almost no *direct* impact on modern science fiction.)

Scientists applauded the novel, which, in Anthony Boucher's words, "probably had more influence upon factual science than any other work of science fiction" (*F&SF*, July 1955, 102). And Willy Ley reports in his *Rockets and Space Travel* that in 1927 he met an elderly gentleman in Berlin who had learned German just so he could read Lasswitz's book.

Ironically, the best article on Lasswitz—despite some minor factual errors and a few misinterpretations—was written by an American and published in a British journal. It is Edwin Kretzman's "German Technological Utopias of the Pre-War Period" in *Annals of Science* (Oct. 1938). In two recent scholarly works, Herbert Schwonke's "From the Political Novel to Science Fiction"

Originally published in *Riverside Quarterly*, 4 (August 1969), 4-18. Reprinted by permission of the editor, Leland Sapiro.

289

and Hans-Jurgen Krysmanski's *The Utopian Method*,[1] both writers profess a liking for Lasswitz, mention that he is the German author closest to modern American science fiction, and then proceed to ignore him. Perhaps this is because German doctoral theses are concerned more with philosophical foundations than with evaluations of individual works.

Lasswitz's thousand page novel begins with three explorers, Josef Saltner, Hugo Torm, and Grunthe (who seems to lack a first name) reaching the North Pole in a balloon. But the Martians have arrived first, and the balloon is destroyed by an "abaric field," generated by the Martian polar station. Torm escapes across the ice, but his companions are captured and brought to Mars.

Later the Martians return to Earth, where their spaceship is fired on by a British man-of-war and two of their crew taken prisoner. This pair is eventually rescued, but the incident has produced factions on Mars. The Philo-Baten ("Ba" meaning "Earth") wish to treat humans as equals, but the anti-Baten consider them as mere animals, whose planet should be exploited for its raw materials.

The Martians again come to Earth, this time with an entire fleet, which destroys the British navy. The Turks, no longer fearing British sea power, massacre all foreigners in their country; this results in a European fleet appearing in the Dardanelles and shelling the Turkish capital. The Martians, shocked at all this violence, decide that humans are indeed savages and turn Western Europe into a protectorate.

Meanwhile, on Mars, the anti-Baten party expands, as does the Terrestrial League of Humankind, in which Saltner and Grunthe play a leading role. While acknowledging Martian cultural superiority, the League disagrees with the Martian education by force and thinks that mankind must develop without outside help.

However, the anti-Batens win, and the Martians now extend their protectorate over Russia and the United States. Then the humans revolt and in a fleet of airships, copied from the Martian craft, attack the polar stations and the Martian artificial satellites hovering above them. The Martians, of course, could destroy the Earth by bombarding it from space, but genocide is repugnant to them. Eventually a peace treaty is signed and Earth becomes a world-state, with Martians and Terrestrials working closely to-gether.

Thus reason wins on both planets.

The writing is plausible, with the role of individual people not being ridiculously exaggerated as in many later works of science fiction. Grunthe, Torm, and Saltner play important roles, but they are not the prime movers of state (whom we never see directly). But there are structural weaknesses. After a carefully detailed and convincing picture of Mars, Grunthe and Saltner leave the planet permanently. The last part of the novel then turns into a satire on contemporary social and political conditions on Earth, but while skilfully done it is a disappointment after our glimpse of the alien world. And the scenes of flight and destruction are hardly convincing: Lasswitz did not excel in description of physical actions.

The greatest weakness of the book is its characterisation: not only the morally superior Martians, but also the main human characters are so idealised that it is difficult to tell them apart. Also, Earth's final sudden change in attitude is not convincing: after witnessing the petty quarrels and selfishness of humans, we find it hard to believe that Terrestrial countries would so suddenly accept a world league of nations.

Nevertheless, this story of colonialism in reverse, during the age of imperialism and Manifest Destiny, represents an important advance.

Lasswitz wrote very little "technological" science fiction, his main concern being personal conduct rather than practical scien-tific applications. Nevertheless his scientific prophecies were astonishingly accurate.

Most striking is Lasswitz's anticipation of the space station, his satellite having the form of a wheel and serving, in the author's phrase, as a "railway station to Mars." Instead of rotating around Earth like our modern satellites, it is held immobile 6,356 kilo-metres above the pole, by big electromagnets powered by solar energy. Between the satellite and ground station vehicles are propelled by a field of artificial gravity (an "abaric" field).

Sam Moskowitz[2] has taken great pains to show that an American writer, Edward Everett Hale (1822-1909) has priority with his story, "The Brick Moon," in *Atlantic Monthly* (Oct.-

Dec. 1869). Hale describes a satellite made of bricks, which is planned as a navigational aid to ships; the satellite is accidentally launched while the labourers are still inside—and the story then shows how the workers survive in free space. But while this author does forecast the navigation satellite, there is no indication that he was thinking about space travel. Hence we can say that Lasswitz was the first to embody in fictional form the idea of a satellite as a stopping platform *en route* to the planets.[3]

In his story Lasswitz accepts the conventional Martian canals, which are used to transport water from the poles. Mars is connected by rolling roadways, each of which consists of strips traveling at different velocities, with the greatest velocity at the middle. In addition, there is food synthesised from inorganic matter, photoelectric cells to open doors, and pills that remove the necessity of sleeping.

Lasswitz's Martians are thoroughgoing Kantians, who differentiate between personal inclination and duty, and never allow the first to interfere with the second. The most convincing character in the novel is Ell, son of a human mother and a Martian who had been stranded on Earth years before the invasion. Despite his love for Isma, Torm's wife, Ell does everything possible to rescue her husband (who has fled across the ice), thus showing the moral discipline of which Martians are capable.

The leading terrestrial characters are also Kantians. Grunthe, for example, would like to stay and see the wonders of Mars; but he considers it his duty to return to Earth—although he knows his story of the Martian invasion will not be believed.

Because of his Kantian outlook Lasswitz does not care about the organisation of society: he is interested only in the individual. Once the individual improves morally, believed Lasswitz, social improvement will be automatic. Mars is a pluralistic society; on this planet there are monarchies and republics, capitalism and socialism, with each citizen having the right to live under the system he likes best.

Naturally, the Martians find that conditions on Earth are quite different from this Kantian ideal, with terrestrials being ". . .engaged in a furious fight for living and enjoyment, with ethic and aesthetic ideals not clearly differentiated from theoretical statements. . . ."

As explained by a German character, Grunthe, the Martians can train their superior weapons on human beings only because of human moral inferiority:

> . . . no Martian is able to press the button of the nihilite apparatus if a human stands against him with a firm, moral will, a will that knows nothing but the desire to do what is good. But these Englishmen—and we are not any better—considered only their own interests, their specifically national advantages, not the dignity of humanity as a whole. . . .[4]

On Two Planets, then, is a fine though sometimes slow-moving adventure novel that tries to embody a philosophical notion in the action. We can only speculate whether H. G. Wells had read this story. Wells's cavorite is similar to our author's satellite; but his bacilli (and of course his Martians) are just the opposite of Lasswitz's, which merely spread a rather harmless Martian infection on Earth.

2—Pictures From the Future

Lasswitz's first collection of shorter stories, *Pictures From the Future* (*Bilder aus der Zukunft*) was published in 1878. The two novelettes in this volume differ from anything he wrote later— each having a melodramatic plot, a prevalence of technology, and frequent variations in tone from jest to sobriety. The first (a reprint of a story published seven years earlier, when the author was twenty-three) was "To the Zero-Point of Being: A Story of the Year 2371."

Aromasia Duftemann Ozodes is a performer on the ododion, or smell piano, an instrument that gives off exquisite odours to the sound of music. Her fiance is Oxygen Warm-Blasius, one of a party of rationalists (*Muchterne*) who think little of her art. Oxygen quarrels with the poet Magnet Reimert—Oberton (and with Aromasia) over the future status of art; Aromasia is so hurt by her lover's conduct that she and Magnet make fun of him in a written parody. For revenge, Oxygen changes some cylinders in Aromasia's ododion, so that when she begins to play, it gives off a horrid stench. The audience flees in panic, fire breaks out, and Aromasia burns to death. The repentant Oxygen flees in his space ship; on his departure Magnet writes a poem in which the lovers finally collide with a cosmic gas and thus assist in the formation of a new sun.

That Lasswitz did not take the story too seriously is suggested by its proper names and by various speeches, as when Magnet cries: "O great Aromasia, the most exalted woman ododist of the 24th century! The cells of my brain are vibrating for you; every fibre of my spine quivers for you! Just as the meadows long for the morning air . . . so the delicate membranes of my nose vibrate in harmony with the odours of your ododion!"

But for all his jesting Lasswitz had a more serious purpose: to show the conflict between reason and emotion or, more precisely, between reason alone and a blending of reason and emotion. Oxygen is a pure rationalist: his party claims "that only by the furthering of reason is progress . . . possible, that intellectual development . . . can free mankind from its passions and perfect its moral responses." He also believes that science will make art obsolete, with psychologists taking over the role of artists. "We will show how to stimulate the brain directly, so that it will experience the same emotions that you now . . . achieve so labouriously . . . by your art."

Magnet, on the other hand, believes that ". . . all this theoretical cognition is powerless against the elemental forces of the will to survive . . ."[5] Despite his love for science, he believes that emotional values should determine human actions.

The second story in this volume is "Against the Law of the World: A Story of the Year 3877." Its beginning is that of Huxley's *Brave New World* minus the test-tube babies. The director of a school is explaining to a visitor that the children enter at the age of five and leave at the age of nine, with their brains being stimulated by electric currents to make certain thought processes easier for them. Lasswitz does not think that this method will enable the children to acquire knowledge without studying:

"It would be a wrong picture if you thought the brain would accumulate knowledge as a glass is filled with wine; rather, a kind of schema is developed which accords with certain processes of our consciousness, just as the dancer, the swimmer do preliminary exercises, after which the muscular movements become easier."

The whole idea is based upon Gustav Fechner's theory of psycho-physics: that for every psychological process there is a physiological process in the brain corresponding to it; therefore by stimulating certain parts of the brain, one can create the desired thoughts and emotions.

Lasswitz also anticipated Huxley's alpha, beta, and gamma types. Man is so complex that a division of work is necessary—and the scientist, Atom, speculates that this differentiation may become more pronounced in the future. In the words of two other characters in the story:

> "If I have understood Atom correctly, he is thinking that the next step in the evolution of man is one in which the various activities, the various tasks and the various organs which are now united in a single individual, will be distributed among various individuals . . ."
>
> "Very good," Proprion laughed, "you think there also will be special people for thinking, special people for feeling, special people for working, and so on?"

The application of this science of the brain also leads to development of the "brain-organ" *(Gehirnorgel)* that can convey the desired moods and feelings directly.[6] (Odiodonics, however, has become obsolete by 3877, since most people have lost their sense of smell.)

Sinister applications of such a brain-organ (by thought-police for example) didn't occur to Lasswitz, whose primary interest was new art forms, such as a taste art in *On Two Planets* or a brain mirror, in the story of the same title, used to create a new art in which "the very soul of the artist paints."[7]

"Against the Law of the World" contains many other inventions: a substance called "diaphot" which confers on living things the refraction index of air, thus making them invisible, a computing machine for the mechanical solution of equations,[8] and underground tunnels connecting America and Europe. (These tunnels do not follow the Earth's curvature, but are perfectly straight, so that their mid-points are nearer the earth's centre than their ends. In these tunnels, cars are propelled by gravity through a vacuum.)

Lyrika, an artist on the brain organ, is in love with the botanist Clotyledo. Atom, the villain (who naturally wishes Lyrika for himself) persuades the mathematician Functionata to subject the proposed marriage to a mathematical analysis; she finds that if Clotyledo marries Lyrika he will die in exactly 6237 days from dissolution of his brain tissue. The analysis consists in tracing back the lovers' ancestors until a mutual progenitor can be found. In this case it is a man named Schulze, who lived in the nineteenth century and disappeared without a trace, with his disappearance being the ultimate reason why Clotyledo's marriage to Lyrika will cause his death.

Kretzman (*op. cit.*, 423) says that this is a parody of the theory of evolution. Actually, it is a lampoon on the genealogical-historical method employed by the German nobility of that time. In his story "Autobiographical Studies" (in another collection) Lasswitz also makes fun of this method:

> You begin before your birth . . . by considering yourself the product of a biological development. You will be able to deduce your own personal attributes from those of your ancestors, and this the better the less you know about them. That is the secret of the genealogical-historical method . . . This point of view is of high ethical value: what we once received from our ancestors we return to them—thankfully. They have created us and we create them again. But we are their betters: they created us according to their nature; we create them as we please.

(One character in this story traces his ancestors back to the lowest sea-organism of the Laurentian period, our author showing at this point more humour than God usually bestows on any single German.)

To prevent her lover's death, Lyrika disappears from his life by stealing Atom's diaphot and becoming invisible. Atom suspects Lyrika of the theft and hides the rest of diaphot in a grotto far beneath the earth's surface. For diaphot wears off, and when Lyrika comes to get more, he intends to take her prisoner. But she eludes him, and there ensues a pursuit through an earth tunnel and across two continents.

At last Lyrika falls into the sea, from which she is saved by Clotyledo, who had come to inspect a coffin found there. The occupant of this coffin is none other than his ancestor Mr. Schulze, who is then awakened from the suspended animation that had preserved him through the centuries. The obstacle to their marriage being removed, Clotyledo and Lyrika carry out their original nuptial plans; while Atom uses a tunnel that points toward Earth's centre as a space cannon, a la Jules Verne, to shoot himself into the sun.

Except for radar (which Hugo Gernsback in 1911 was in a much better position to predict than Lasswitz in 1878) most of the ideas from *Ralph 124C41+* are already here in Lasswitz: the same tunnels, flying machines, and pleasure resorts; and the same abduction (or attempted abduction) of a beautiful maiden. Each villain also used an invisibility device, although the basic principles are different. (Lasswitz also anticipates the "sleep school" of *Brave New World* by fifty years and Gernsback's hypnobioscope by thirty years.) There is no interplanetary background in Lasswitz's story, but this Gernsback might have derived from *On Two Planets*.[9] It seems likely, then, that Gernsback, who spent his youth in Luxembourg and could read German, derived most of his early ideas from Lasswitz.

Aside from Gernsback, however, there seems to have been no English-speaking author who was inspired by *Pictures from the Future*. The influence of this volume on German authors has also been small—a result, perhaps, of German science-fiction publishing being restricted to books and of the author's failure to have his works reprinted, except for a small second edition in 1879. Since his other books were reprinted in many editions, we conclude that Lasswitz didn't think very highly of these humourous early efforts.

3—The Short Stories

Lasswitz's shorter fiction[10] falls into three categories: fairy tales, technological stories, and philosophical stories. The first group can be dismissed as insignificant: his elves and fairies merely talk about Kant, Schiller, and the promotion of the German educational ideal. Sometimes there is a redeeming touch of satire, as in "Little Waterdrop," where two Germans profess a liking for nature because they can see the features of Bismark and Moltke in the landscape—but generally the stories are just sentimental. More interesting are the technological stories; but these form only a minority and again are mere expositions of ideas that are not embodied in action. What little plot these stories possess is that of a conventional romance, without basic connection to the problem. In "The Dream Maker" *(Der Traumfabrikant)*, e.g., the owner of a dream factory loves the daughter of a politician who is conducting a campaign for the socialisation of such factories. A special dream induced in the father averts this danger and the dream manufacturer wins the girl in the process.

"The Home School" *(Die Fernschule)* depicts pupils of the future sitting at home before their television sets, with their heads connected to a psychograph which turns off the television when the majority become too sleepy to follow the lesson. Again, there is no story.

More important are the philosophical tales, which are witty, satirical, and full of ideas—being true speculative fiction in Judith Merril's sense. As indicated by the title, *Soap Bubbles*, of the first such collection, the stories are free plays of fancy, not subject to the law of gravity or any other law, created joyfully by the artist and destroyed again at will.

The title story (*Auf der Seifenblase*) describes Uncle Wendel's apparatus that transports people to soap bubbles, where life is like that on Earth, but speeded up ten billion times. The reader may recall that FitzJames O'Brien's *The Diamond Lens* mixed this same theme with myths of Eden and Hermaphroditus, with his love story given a scientific tinge by detailed references to microscopes. And Ray Cummings' *Girl in the Golden Atom* is essentially an adventure fantasy of subjugation and revolt, whose locale could just as easily have been another country or planet. Lasswitz's story, however, is a light-hearted parallel to the trial of Galileo. Glagli of the microscopic world dares to question the teachings of an ancient Saponian philosopher (the equivalent of Aristotle) and pronounces the revolutionary thesis that the world is hollow and filled with air. He has to defend himself before the "Academy of Thinking Men," who will decide "whether his ideas are to be permitted in the interests of the state and public order"; and our travellers barely escape being cooked in hot glycerine after they confirm Glagli's opinion.

"Princess Yesyes" is a philosophical fairy tale that asks the question, how do we know we exist? Princess Yesyes, in the kingdom of Higgledy-Piggledy, has a fairy godmother named Krakeleia, who is fabricator of all unnecessary questions and mistress of all "inventors of puzzles, revenue collectors, policemen, and metaphysicians." One day our princess asks the fairy who her mother was; but the fairy has no mother (like Pallas Athena she has sprung directly from Zeus) and for punishment sentences the princess to remain unmarried until she has found and answered the most useless question of all. The question is whether or not she exists and the answer, that she simply has to believe in her own existence. This is one of Lasswitz's most amusing stories, with many references to German philosophical pomposity.

Lasswitz is at his best when least serious; when earnest, he shows a deplorable tendency towards sentimentality. "The Diary of an Ant" might have been amusing had not the ants chosen to report the romance of a human couple. The two are forbidden to marry (probably because she is his social inferior), but he writes love poems to her (which are included in the text) and there is a happy, happy ending.

The utopian tale "Apoikis" presents the converse side of *On Two Planets*. Apoikis is a secluded island in the Atlantic inhabited by descendants of Socrates' friends. Not being obliged to gain mastery over nature, they have concentrated upon spiritual development. "We are not the slaves of our customs as are the savages, nor masters of the material world as are the educated nations of Europe; but are masters of our own wills, masters of all consciousness, and therefore we are free."

Perhaps Lasswitz distrusted the masses, as Kretzmann suggests; but I think that he knew that for us there is no other alternative except technological development. In this story he shows awareness that science and technology are necessary and *possible* only for a mass society. Hence the different developments on Apoikis and Mars, despite the adoption of Kantian principles by both societies.

In "Aladdin's Lamp" (reprinted in *F&SF*, May 1953) Lasswitz anticipates Charles L. Harness's "The New Reality" (*TWS*, Dec. 1950), a story based on the Kantian notion that we know nothing about the *Ding an sich*, but are acquainted only with the appearances presented to our senses. Further, the supposed laws of nature are just categories already present in our minds. Harness takes Kant literally: that our consciousness creates reality. In his story the world changes with our conception of it: the earth really was flat as long as we conceived it so; it was spherical ever since we began to regard it as a sphere, and so on.

In Lasswitz's story a company sit together and discuss magic implements, at last agreeing that Aladdin's Lamp would be the most desirable. A lamp is at hand, and one of the company deduces that it is indeed the lamp of Aladdin. The spirit appears, but is unable to do anything he is told to do because he would be violating some natural law. Finally, he cannot even lift up a pencil. But why was the spirit able to comply with Aladdin's wishes?

> ". . . at that time the laws of conservation of matter and energy were still unknown."
> "What! Surely you wouldn't maintain that the laws of nature were not working then?"
> "The natural laws," answered the spirit, "are nothing but the expression of scientific perception in a given period. In my transcendental consciousness, I am independent of these laws; but when working in time, in your time, I cannot do anything contrary to the laws that are the pillars of your culture."

Two other stories are lampoons on German metaphysicians. In "Psychotomy" (translated in *F&SF*, July 1955) a private teacher, Dr. Schulze, is given the personified categories, some Kantian pure reason and other philosophical paraphernalia. These are handed to him accompanied by needling remarks: "Here in this red vase is freedom. I have only this small sample, for I could find no more . . . in the whole of Europe"; "Here is humanity; it is cheap—but is demanded only by Societies for the Prevention of Cruelty to Animals."

Two fine mathematical fantasies have been translated into English by Willy Ley: "When the Devil took the Professor" (*F&SF*, Jan. 1957) and "In the Universal Library" (Clifton Fadiman, ed., *Fantasia Mathematica*). The first of these is the familiar bargain with the devil, who takes a professor on a tour of the universe in a vessel that exceeds the speed of light. The professor is a mathematician and suspects that the universe is curved, as it actually proves to be. So the voyagers circumnavigate the universe after a flight of several billion light-years.[11]

"In the Universal Library"[12] is based on the idea that the total number of permutations of finitely many symbols is limited, so that a finite number of volumes could contain everything expressible in a given language—including the amusing nonsense of Lasswitz's story. And the universe wouldn't be big enough to contain all the volumes in this library.

Between his two volumes of short stories, Lasswitz published a biography of Gustav Theodor Fechner, who next to Kant was the single greatest influence on him. Fechner wrote humourous "articles" that might be called precursors of modern science fiction: "Proof that the Moon Consists of Iodine" (1821), "Panegryricus on Contemporary Medicine and Science" (1822), and "Four Paradoxes" (1846). In the last of these, for example, he "proves" that shadows are living things (whose projections are solid objects), that space has four dimensions, and that witchcraft actually exists.

Lasswitz stressed that Fechner's essays are not "scientific fairy tales" (this author's term for science fiction), since they lack the form of stories and have no living persons (an unfortunate deficiency in Lasswitz's own fiction).

A quotation from "Mirax," which is pure Fechner in method, will show Lasswitz's indebtedness. Mirax's "experimental metaphysics" is based on sentences collected from proverbs.

> . . . he applied these sentences to any . . . field. For instance, he proved that the sun was inhabited by beings who eat meteors. For, you must strike while the iron is hot, and since spectral analysis shows there is iron vapour in the sun, there must be entities in the sun who strike the iron. And since a magic table is a fine thing, we may assume that the solar inhabitants have food falling from the sky. Now, meteors fall from the sky and consist mostly of iron—therefore these beings like to eat meteors.

Realities (Wirklichkeiten, 1900), Lasswitz's first major collection of essays, is devoted mostly to a popularisation of Kant, but one essay, "On Dreams of the Future," is of special interest to us.

Early in the essay he dismisses static utopias (as Wells was to do in *A Modern Utopia*) because "dissatisfaction and hope" are the motivating forces of human life. He stresses that our efforts

to improve human life are not wasted, although they are per-
petual. For evil never can disappear from this world, since then
our will for progress also would disappear. Religion can make us
disregard the conditions of this world; but only by mastering these
conditions can we make our life on earth any better. Religion and
morality are necessary for progress, but sufficient conditions are
supplied only by human reason. Here we see the effect of Kant in
Lasswitz's insistence that progress be achieved by means proper to
this "reality."

Toward the end, Lasswitz defends the "scientific fairy tale"
that is to result from the "ethical power of technology." (Of
course, our author didn't conceive the evil to which technology
was to be applied.) Once its idealising effects are established,
science can provide the subject-matter of fiction—and this new
literary form will express the writer's own reactions to scientific
knowledge: "It is our task to find a personal form for the new
feeling about nature." Characteristically, Lasswitz didn't discuss
how this relationship is to be expressed—by popularizing science
(as Gernsback was to do) or by transforming, as it were, science
into poetry.[13]

In any case, Lasswitz's is the first explicit justification for
science fiction as we presently conceive it.

His next major work was *Homchen* (1902), a Darwinian
novel printed along with some short stories in a curiously titled
volume, *Never and Ever (Nie und immer)*. Homchen is a marsu-
pial, an ancestor of man, who is braver than the other animals and
also more intelligent, even discovering the use of fire. (Homchen
is a mutant, as we would say now.) But genius is out of place in
this era—the marsupials dreading fire so much that they do not
use it—and Homchen, misunderstood by everyone, lives the rest of
his life alone. A successful genius, as a cynic once remarked, is
somebody who is ahead of his time, but not *too* far ahead. Homchen is so far advanced, however, that his fellow marsupials lose
sight of him; and his feelings of superiority serve to alienate him
still further.

This is a fairy tale (the animals being endowed with human
speech, as is customary in such stories), but a charming one despite
all its philosophising.

The stories of Lasswitz's middle period, starting with *Soap*

Bubbles and ending with *Never and Ever*, are the most rewarding;
his later novels, although ranked highest by himself and some of
his contemporaries, possess today only the limited interest of
period pieces.   *Aspira* (1906), a cloud metamorphosised into a
human being, shows the influence of Gustav Fechner, who believed that all living things are endowed with souls and later[14]
attributed souls even to planets and stars.   *Star Dew (Sternentau,*
1909), Lasswitz's last work[15] concerns intelligent flowers, which
drift in from a moon of Neptune and then depart after observing
the war-like character of humans.   Like *Aspira*, this novel is based
on Fechner, has little characterisation, and contains endless discussions of Fechner and Kant.

4—Summary and Conclusions

Lasswitz's deficiencies are several: his lack of characterisation, his sentimentality, i.e., lack of feeling, and his strong didactic
emphasis.   However,   he   was   didactic   not   about   science   but
about ethics.   His technique of presenting technology was close to
that of modern science fiction.   In *Pictures from the Future* scientific marvels are part of the characters' everyday world; nobody
wonders about them.   In *On Two Planets*, after some initial wonder by humans, technology is accepted as a matter of course.   For
Lasswitz, technology is a means, not an end, its final justification
being the ethical improvement it necessarily brings about.
But despite his two utopian stories Lasswitz had no interest
in society as a whole.   He believed that universal happiness would
ensue if each individual just followed the teachings of Kant and
Schiller.   Thus the utopians of *Apoikis* see "the happiness of a
people . . . not in a large mass . . . of consciousness, but in an
intensive   .   .   .   concentration of consciousness in every single
individual."   Marx and Engels are cited nowhere in his works, and
contemporary social movements are disliked and misunderstood.[16]
In any case, Lasswitz failed to realise in action his philosophical intentions: his perfect characters merely *tell* us at great length
about their ethical principles.   But fiction that contains only characters who are morally perfect, or nearly so, is *not moral*:   it
falsifies   life;   it is untrue, and what is untrue can never be moral.
The moralist succeeds by exhibiting difficulties, by increasing the
potency of life, not by simplifying and castrating it.   Chastity in

eunuchs is no virtue. Lasswitz's humans are never really tempted, and the high moral principles of his Martians fail them when they experience their first real challenge in several hundred thousand years: they behave just like human imperialists. To a sensitive reader these results are far from edifying.

The particular quality of a utopian tale resides mainly in its ideas, which can hold our intellectual interest, not in its characterisation—since utopian individuals, because they are so perfect, are also totally boring. Hence Lasswitz's virtues, his clarity of presentation and lucidity of style, are essentially those of an essayist, not those of a novelist.

Nevertheless, we must acknowledge Lasswitz's basic honesty,[17] and we are entitled to make allowance for the time in which his stories were written. However his satirical short stories deserve unqualified praise, being a close approach to certain types of contemporary Anglo-American speculative fiction.

Even in Germany, Lasswitz never attained the popularity of Wells or Verne in their own countries. Wells, of course, had superior imagination and social insight; while Verne, although not the scientific prophet he is reputed to be (his excerpts from French encyclopedias and textbooks usually becoming obsolete a few years after publication), could write exciting adventure stories, which Lasswitz could not.

But it was chiefly non-literary factors that minimised Lasswitz's influence in his own country. After World War I German science fiction became more and more nationalistic,[18] the "new" Germany, especially after Hitler's ascent, having little use for the pacifistic morality of Lasswitz. And after World War II almost all science fiction written in Germany was a poor imitation of American and British space-opera.

That Lasswitz did not exert his proper influence, therefore, is a result of external circumstances. In America, stories much inferior to his have helped to give science fiction its present orientation.

NOTES

[1]Herbert Schwonke, *Vom Staatsroman zur Science Fiction* (Stuttgart: Ferdinand Enke Verlag, 1957); Hans-Jurgen Krysmanski, *Die utopische*

Methode (Koln & Opladen: Westdeutscher Verlag, 1963).

[2]*Explorers of the Infinite* (New York: World Publishing Co., 1963), 88-105.

[3]Although Lasswitz knew English, it is highly improbable that he ever encountered Hale's short story. And it is still more unlikely that Lasswitz knew of Ziolkowski's "Dreams of the Earth and the Sky," 1895 (reprinted in *The Call of the Cosmos*, Moscow: Foreign Languages Publishing House) in which this author proposed the building of an artificial moon as a way to facilitate space travel.

[4]Lasswitz is free from nationalism or German imperialism: although his main characters are German, he clearly indicates that they are in no way superior to the Englishmen of his book. Kretzman (*op. cit.*, 427) omits the phrase ". . . and we are not any better" in the above passage and interprets it as an example of national prejudice: "It becomes evident that the Martians are really a glorified German race and have the same imperialistic tendencies of that nation."

[5]Lasswitz's "will" is not that emphasised by Nietzsche, but simply the urge to survive, which reason is powerless to govern without some basic "ideal." Neitzsche's *The Birth of Tragedy* and *Unzeitgemasse Betrachtungen* were written in 1872 and 1873-6, respectively, and his *Thus Spake Zarathustra* in 1884-5, whereas the first story from *Bilder aus der Zukunft* (cited by W. H. G. Armytage, *RQ* II, 234) was printed by the *Schlesische Zeitung* in 1871. Hence Nietzsche's influence on Lasswitz is non-existent.

[6]Compare the brain organ to the instrument used by Grosvenor in A. E. van Vogt's *Voyage of the Space Beagle.*

[7]Cf. Jack Vance's "The Enchanted Princess" (*Orbit*, Dec. 1954).

[8]Another aspect of the same problem appears in Lasswitz's short story "In the Universal Library."

[9]I was surprised to learn from H. Bruce Franklin's *Future Perfect* (Oxford University Press, 1966) that excerpts from the book were printed in the June 1890 issue of *The Overland Monthly.*

[10]Lasswitz's first collection of short stories was *Soap Bubbles (Seifenblasen,* 1890), and this was followed by *Never and Ever (Nie und immer),* which also included the novel *Homchen*, and the posthumous volume *Things Felt and Known (Empfundenes und Erkanntes,* 1920). This second book was called *Dream Crystals (Traumkristalle)* when it was published later apart from *Homchen.*

[11]Lasswitz was mathematics professor at the Gymnasium Ernestinium in Gotha from 1878 until 1908; while familiar with the work of Gauss, Riemann, and Lofatschefsky in non-Euclidean spaces he believed they had no physical reality. In his *Souls and Objectives (Seelen und Ziele,* 1908) he explicitly denied that physics would ever be forced to adopt a non-Euclidean theory of space. The main reason for his denial was doubtless his unwillingness to correct Kant's theory of Euclidean space as a form of perception.

[12]As Willy Ley explains in his postscript, this idea—like that of the computer—goes back to the Spanish mathematician, Raimundus Lullus (1235-

1315). Lasswitz, in turn, inspired Jorge Luis Borges' much superior story, "The Library of Babel."

[13]Lasswitz states that "I wouldn't even have touched the aesthetic question if it hadn't been claimed that tales of a technological future are by their very nature poetically useless (*Poetisch unbrauchbar*) and non-literary" (*keine Dichtung*).

[14]Fechner believed that a nervous system wasn't necessary for the development of consciousness and in 1848 he wrote *Nanna, or the Spiritual Life of Plants (Nanna oder des Seelenleben der Pflanzen)*. (In Norse mythology, Nanna was the wife of Baldur, the god of light and spring.) In his *Zend Avesta*—"Zend Avest" being the Hindu phrase for "living word"—Fechner extended his theory by attributing souls to the earth and other celestial bodies.

[15]The short stories in the posthumous *Things Felt and Known* are all slight, being mostly treatments of problems that this author had considered before. In "Those Without Souls" ("Die Unbeseelten") Fechner is presented from the "other side," with violets speculating whether or not men have souls; and in the fairy tale *Frauenaugen* we learn that women's eyes are so bright because they are fallen stars.

[16]E. G., see (p. 10) the attitude toward Socialism expressed in "The Dream Maker."

[17]For example, the Martians of *Auf zwei Planeten* are entirely humanoid. Lasswitz explains that it is a "necessary condition for any poetic effect that we can participate in the feelings of the being depicted. This is wholly impossible if we assume creatures with bodies of incandescent hydrogen or intelligent bacilli procreating and amusing themselves in liquid air. Such beings have to be equipped with quite other senses; they would have emotions that we could never feel; empathy between them and us would be impossible" (*Things Felt and Thought*, 169).

[18]Hans Dominik, the most successful German science fiction writer to date, exemplifies this. Each of his books revolves around a single invention: a new fuel, a means to achieve invisibility, an incredibly strong metal, etc. Around this invention he spins a conventional tale of espionage and intrigue, usually culminating in a great war, either between Germany and America, America and Japan, or the White race against the Yellow race, with the former always winning.

STANISLAW LEM

ROBOTS
IN
SCIENCE FICTION

1.   In the several-times anthologized story, "Compassion Circuit," by John Wyndham, a man is so frightened by his wife's body
having been "androidized," with only her living head remaining on
an artificial torso, that he flees from the hospital and breaks his
neck on the stairs. Now, it has always been possible to break one's
neck, whether or not there were such "head transplants"; but is it
possible that someone could feel such terror in a society where
androids were produced to measure and heads exchanged at will?
Would some one of us be frightened and flee a room if it were
whispered that the old man appearing on the doorstep is alive only
because he carries the heart of a young woman in his breast? Thus,
the unlikely and anti-realistic thing about Wyndham's story is that
it describes an event that couldn't happen under any circumstances. One might reply that he intended only to write a funny
story. But the facts that serve as a premise even in a funny story
must not be absurd: a funny story results when logical conclusions, drawn in a logically correct manner from acceptable
premises, lead to something absurd. Wyndham's method is typical
of a good part of science fiction: into the world of contemporary
conditions, passed off as a future world, the author puts an occurrence which is derived from possible or impossible techniques of
the future, and depicts the reactions of human beings who are

First published in *Quarber Merkur*, no. 21 (November 1969). A somewhat different English language version has been published in the Australian
"fanzine," *The Journal of Omphalistic Epistomology*, no. 3 (January 1970).

307

psychologically as well as sociologically false. The impossible takes the place of the possible.

2.   Literary "mainstream" criticism treats sf occasionally with a sort of good-natured disregard. Authors and aficionados of the genre, on the other hand, often try to prove what a magnificent old tradition it has, extending several centuries into the past: in Greece there existed worthy myths, and sf is a myth of technological civilization. Therefore you have to esteem it highly. But an abominable criticism will not recognize its virtues. Who, then, is right?

3.   The world of the past was stable and without change. What, basically, do all myths say? They are ontological hypotheses about immanent properties of existence. The world of the classical fairy tale is determined ethically in a positive sense: good always remains victorious in its fight against evil. The world of the fairy tale is an ideal homeostasis: "evil destroys the balance, a reaction at least restores the balance," or, more often, the final situation is even better than the original one. Therefore, the laws of the world of the fairy tale are determined by ethics.

The world of the myth is also a homeostasis, although one that doesn't care for the well-being of the citizens of its world. But it isn't an *ordinary* world which one should equate with our world: it is predetermined in such a way that act as one will in it, he can achieve only such purposes as have been determined by that world, over human heads. It is therefore a teleological world; i.e., one directed toward certain goals. But it is subject to laws which, in a self-willed fashion and sometimes with evil intent, transform human destiny into always meaningful patterns, certainly, but more often horrifying patterns. They turn a son into the murderer of his father and the lover of his mother, no matter what he may do to escape such a destiny. That is the ontological structure, the frame of destiny in the mythical world, which in its predestination is similar to the ontology of the fairy tale, but differs in that it has a negative value sign.

4.   The extent to which the anonymous authors of myths and fairy tales intentionally put together the main supporting structures of their works need not concern us here. We simply find such facts when we examine fairy tales and myths. As authors we cannot simply borrow such structures, because they have a specific

meaning. They interpret the world in a very definite, concrete way. We must not repeat mechanically, without understanding, what those writers have said about the immanent nature of things just because we admire them aesthetically. We no longer believe that the world is a homeostasis, directed frontally toward man— that it cares, whether by good or evil intent, for man. In the realistic world described by literature, there exists no predestination and no meaning so long as there is no man. He cannot read the meaning of the stars, the planets, the suns from such works. They contain no hidden meaning; they simply exist.

5.   The concept of an artificially created man is blasphemy in our cultural sphere. Such a creation must be performed by man and is therefore a caricature, an attempt by humans to become equal to God. According to Christian dogma, such audacity cannot succeed; should it happen, it necessarily means that satanic forces were engaged in the work, that hell has helped the creator of the homunculus.

But there exist myths from pre-Christian times which talk about homunculi and do not consider them the result of cooperation between humans and the devil. Those myths arose in pre-Christian times, far from Judaism. A religion can be quite neutral toward the "artifical production of human beings"; only the Mediterranean culture, modified by Christianity, considers the homunculus to be the result of blasphemy. It is for this reason that those "archetypal robots," those literary prototypes from earlier centuries such as the golom, are as a rule evil or at least sinister.

6.   Generally, one can say that the relationship of belief to a special technique is determined by whether or not the belief has dealt dogmatically with the technique. Christian belief has dealt neither positively nor negatively with the automation of sewing; therefore, the sewing machine is an absolutely neutral object—for religious belief. On the other hand, religious thought has dealt with flying insofar as it has spoken of angels; there was a time, therefore, when theologians regarded all attempts to master flight as close to blasphemy. And belief has dealt intensively with the human mind so that the homunculus has become in our civilization a technical product at least partly "determined by the devil."

7.   In science, truth is not a quality of single scientific state-

ments. It depends on the whole system. The same applies for all literature: only for the word "truth" we have to substitute the term "value." The value of objects which are found in a literary work (i.e., which are described in it) is determined by the totality of the work as a meaningful, semantic system. Fantastic literature can have several functions: because of this, any objects found in literary texts can have quite different values. Although the devil appears as part of the plot of Thomas Mann's *Dr. Faustus*, this novel is not a work that would belong to demonology or fantastic literature. The devil in this novel has rather the function of a sign in the semantic sense, and truly he is a subordinate part of a system that belongs to the paradigmatic structure of the Faustian myth. But we do not intend to talk about epic and realistic works, not even when they occasionally include "fantastic beings," be they robots, devils, or werewolves. We shall talk about fantastic literature. How do we recognize it?

Fantastic literature can

a) preach a fictitious philosophy in the sense of a fictitious ontology, as does happen, for instance, in the works of J. L. Borges. The worlds of his stories are not "physical objects." They are semantic objects which embody a fictitious ontology. A fantastic philosophical system in literature is expounded not discursively, but through quasi-physical objects.

b) be a tale which has its origins in the adaptation of paradigmatic structures. Such structures can be derived in two directly opposed ways:

I. The author can hide the "loaned" structure from the reader. He will tell us, for instance, of the decline of a planetary civilization, but uses as the skeleton for his plot the structure of a mystery novel: the question, "Who killed the rich, old civilization of the planet Cygni?" is answered in a way that is really (i.e., structurally) an answer to the question, "Who killed the rich, old aunt?" Or in the novel there appears a being which acts like a blockhead, a catatonic, but which is called a "robot."

II. The author can, on the other hand, as does Cordwainer Smith, tell us clearly and unmistakably which paradigm his story tries to imitate. He then doesn't hide anything from us; he writes a new variation of an old theme; but he also doesn't speak about the real world. He is building an autonomous world within the ontological frame of the myth or the fairy tale and calls it such. The other author (I) tries to obliterate the borderline between the unreal world of myths and the real world which is a multiplicity of physical possibilities.

c)   also deal with real problems: it then chooses for a stage the same world in which we live (i.e., the same ontology, as a set of universal laws).

We have said that the sum of all texts of science fiction consists of two kinds: (1) either science fiction talks about what possibly can occur in the real continuum (in the future) or could have happened (in the past) and then tries to become a branch of realistic literature that follows through its hypotheses; or (2) it is a game, played with autonomous rules which can deviate at will from the rules to which our world is subject. That game can again have two mutually exclusive properties: it is either an "empty" play which has no relationship with the real world—like chess—or it is semantically addressed to the world, in which case we have a parable or an allegory.

9.   Several conclusions follow from what we have said so far. If somebody wants to tell us what horrible consequences technological progress may have, even when only the happiness of mankind is intended, and then proceeds to build a world in which all kinds of work have become automated, we needn't take the "technological parameters" of the robots which inhabit this paradise too seriously. If, on the other hand, somebody wants to tell us which kinds of robots can be constructed and which technological qualities those robots may have, he accepts for his creation the judgment of scientific facts. Between the world of today and the world of yesterday there is this difference: the universe of facts and the universe of all things that were thinkable yesterday formed two separate spaces, hermetically closed to each other. But today the universe of facts and this second one, the universe of all things which can be thought of, form a complicated system. For part of the second number moves in a direction which will collide with the universe of facts in the future, or, to put it differently, those two universes partly overlap, and this overlapping must be considered a function of time. When we read sf, we therefore must

distinguish between those works which are located in the universe of the "for all times impossible" and those works which belong to the set of things that can become fact. The main difference between today and yesterday lies in the movement which every year brings several ideas and things corresponding to them from the realm of the fantastic, empty names into the realm of real things: such as, for example, "the old man with the heart of a young woman."

10. But what, now, of robots? Their description in sf we can consider (a) as an attempt at futurological prediction; we are to be taught what these thinking machines will look like, how they will operate, and of what feats they will be capable. And this can, of course, be described as a social, psychological, or anthropological problem. For the "psychology of robots," or the relationship between robot and human, is a limited problem; the question of the "metaphysical world view" of robots is quite a different problem; and the structure, as well as the social codes of a society which produces robots in quantity, is again a problem of quite a different order.

Or in sf we can consider their description (b) as a work intended to say nothing about the "immanence" of robots or their "existential problems." It can be an allegory, a parable, a fairy tale, a humorous sketch, or something grotesque. Were we intending to think precisely and wholly logically, we should have to say that such sf isn't proper "science fiction," not fiction with a scientific basis.

From the point of view of classification, science fiction must be considered in the same category as the works, for example, of Kafka. But some sort of classificatory laziness has had its effect here and caused the contemporary generic jungle. Kafka's story of the metamorphosis of a human into a bug is not a work of sf; it doesn't say anything about the "futurological perspectives" of such a transformation, and were somebody to claim that Kafka had written a work of "entomological sf," we should have to call that specialist a lunatic. Similarly, Schiller's *Robbers* isn't a mystery play, but were somebody intending to classify all works as to the separate objects and properties depicted in them, he would be forced to the conclusion that Schiller worked in the same genre as Agatha Christie.

11. Let's similarly divulge the sad secret: all robots in science fiction are most uninteresting beings, regardless of whether they are presented as "futurological prognoses" or as "mythic objects." The relationships between robot and human in sf are modelled upon some three or four stereotypes. The objects of imitation are:

a) the relationship between man and machine;
b) the relationship between master and slave;
c) the relationship between man and succubus or incubus;
d) the relationship between man and transcendence (Deity, etc.)

From the first matrix stem the three laws of robotics of Isaac Asimov. It isn't very difficult to prove that they are technically unrealizable. This is a question of logical, not technological, analysis. To be intelligent means to be able to change your hitherto existing programme by conscious acts of the will, according to the goal you set for yourself. A robot, therefore, can remain for all eternity harmless to man, but then he must also be dumb, as it were. Should he be intelligent—be able to act of his own volition—he must have the potentiality of changing his programme at will. In short, what can be thought, can be realized. Of course it would be possible to build into a robot an adequate analogue of the "categorical imperative" without much effort; but when man, as is only too well known, can break the "categorical imperative" without much effort, a robot built on a similar principle would have to be able to do the same. Safeguards can indeed be built into robot brains, but they will only act as governors in a statistical way. He may perhaps kill one human being in a million cases: but it won't be possible to exclude that chance. In addition—and now we speak about a quite different problem—it is possible to do harm unintentionally, as happens when a child kills an animal inadvertently by putting a poisonous substance into its fodder. Here the evil is done without intention. Under the conditions of real life we operate by making decisions without being totally informed about the results of our deeds: and should a constructor build very strong safeguards into a robot so that he will not harm anyone, the robot would often appear to be completely paralyzed. Were he, for instance, to witness several people drowning at the same time, he most probably wouldn't be able to help any one of them, for he would know that any decision of his would diminish the chances of all the other drowning people being saved. Such a robot couldn't be considered a very satisfactory construction. I have forgiven Asimov many things, but not his laws of robotics, for they give a wholly false picture of the real possibilities. Asimov has just inverted the old paradigm: where in myths the homunculi were villains, with demoniac features, Asimov has thought of the robot as the "positive hero" of science fiction, as having been doomed to eternal goodness by engineers. When Norbert Wiener wanted to speak—in *The Human Use of Human Beings*—of the dangers intellectronics may have in store for us, he was unable to find a proper source in the sf field and illustrated the problem with a fantasy story, W. W. Jacob's "The Monkey's Paw."

I do not know of any sf stories in which the robots become the masters and the humans, slaves. Should they exist, they form a very small minority. The subject of the relationship of "master-slave" is used in such a way that it is the humans who become masters of the robots. In such cases the relationship is modelled after the pattern of third-rate structures. For instance, the relationship of the "good white man" and the "good-natured black servant" is used as a paradigm, or the relationship is similar to that of master and dog. What is important about this is that the structure of such relationships is taken not from life, but from one-dimensional fiction which provides handy cliches. Any complex depiction of the psychological (interpersonal) problems cannot be expected from this. Occasionally you'll encounter fictitious technological objects—the Nautilus of Verne, for example—that you'd never mistake for other objects of the same kind from other books. But I do not know even one figure of a robot which has impressed me as a reader in a similar way. As "machine-like" objects, robots therefore are depicted falsely, and as psychological individuals they are depicted dully. When mankind dies off, in the course of a catastrophe, we occasionally find robots as unhappy survivors, as in *Orphans in the Void* by Michael Shaara, for example. The intellectual poverty that becomes apparent there is depressing.

To talk about the relationship between human being and automaton in the sexual sphere is impossible here. Therefore, with utmost brevity: since all sf suffers in the realm of "cosmic sexual life" from Victorianism and puritanism (which are inborn sicknesses that result in a paralysis of thought and imagination), this condition, which moves us to pity, also has its paralyzing consequences in the field of robotics. The situation is made worse by the fact that psychological insight has never been a forte of sf writers. What remains for the created thing when sex is tabooed and the psychologically erotic is unattainable? Only the simplifying grotesque which is arrived at by translating all possible human relationships involving the erotic into the robotic field, as has been done by Fritz Leiber in "The Silver Eggheads." There we have mechanical bordellos with prostitute—androids and, as a special exoticism, the sexual life of robots amongst themselves, with their contacts and plugs. All this appears quite comic, but soon the reader sees through the mechanical principle of such creation; when continued, only boredom sets in. There is something sinister about the paradigmatic relationship between man and incubus, because there he has his most intimate contacts with a creature of hell. That relationship, therefore, has stood in the light of black transcendence. But all thinkable things you can do with an android mistress cannot go beyond acrobatic gymnastics, unless she has a personality in the pyschological sense of the word. Only then is the theme transposed to a new level rich in problems. However, one must determine definitely several parameters to be able to solve the problems concerned. If there are intelligent androids on sale, which can act as secretaries or house-servants, certain social opinions (or biases, if you will) crystallize. Either it is believed in general that there is nothing more common than escapades involving the androids, or they are looked upon with distaste and horror. It could also be that a man who prefers an android to a real woman could be thought of as a ridiculous, effeminate weakling. It cannot be predicted just how the norms of public opinion will develop, not even if all the technical parameters of the robots are known, for such norms in the realm of moral life tend to evolve into unpredictable mass-statistical processes. There exists, therefore, a certain freedom in this field for the writer, but it is remarkable that this theme of the incubus has not been seriously attempted. So, for instance, *La Femme-Modelee* by Luc Vignan, a leading fantasist (as French criticism would have it), is neither pornographic, nor psychologically erotic, nor interesting literature, but superficial nonsense in no way to be compared with *L'Eve Future* by L'Isle-Adam. Yet this latter appeared nearly a century ago!

All themes connected with religion are excluded from the realm of science fiction, and what few exceptions there are only demonstrate this rule. Nothing really good on the attitude of robots toward metaphysics can be found. Asimov's story, "The Last Question," about the Computer who became God after several billion years, is just about the best. The well-known story by Anthony Boucher, "The Quest for Saint Aquin," is marred by a logical error. The monk who has been sent by the Pope to find the corpse of a saint recognizes the dead one as a robot. The robot who is present tempts the papal legate by trying to persuade him to keep secret the true nature of his discovery. The monk is enraged: one cannot help the victory of truth with lies! But it has been said earlier that the holy monk, during his missionary work, pretended to be a human being; indeed, he dies because he refuses to visit a mechanic since such a cure would make apparent his mechanical nature. The holy robot himself has lied to the people to whom he preached the gospel. He kept hidden his true nature and preferred to die rather than make evident that nature. He served truth, therefore, by pretending to be a human being among human beings, and this was a lie.

It is rather simple to write robot stories. First you have to invent a dramatically interesting situation or conflict, and then you call, within this context, one or the other human being a "robot." Or you can promote all characters to the status of robot, as has been done by Harry Harrison in his collection, *War with the Robots*. What do minor clerks, mechanics, executives talk about amongst themselves? That the cost of living is very high, that cures for bilious complaints cost a lot, *et cetera*. And what do Harrison's robots talk about? That replacement parts cost a lot, that a new knee-joint is quite expensive, that the superiors are rascals and exploiters. Very interesting, isn't it? In his volume, Harrison has described a very effective police-robot: but he is really a "mechanized superman" with built-in criminological apparatus. But to return to transcendence. In *I, Robot*, Asimov has written about a robot who—at last!—arrived at the idea that he was created by God who selected human beings as his tools. But then the whole problem of such a consciousness and the self-understanding and existential problems connected with them dissolves into nothing. This robot works effectively, just as he has been programmed to. It is only that he thinks something heterodox. Asimov has skillfully avoided all the depths that began to open, much as in a slalom race. But literature isn't a slalom, for it brings intricate problems into the light of day, whereas sf avoids them. It will be very interesting to hear what theological thinkers claim for the souls of robots. Can a robot have a soul? No? And what if he happens to be smarter, more intelligent than human beings? The future will perhaps see intelligence-amplifiers that surpass the human mind. What about them? Indeed, one can build bionic aggregates, half human and half machine. Should theologians come to the decision that an artifically created automaton hasn't an immortal soul, what, then, is the case of the halflings who have, say, 36% of a natural and 64% of an artificial brain? Has such a bionically-built creature only 36% of a soul? It would be nonsense to maintain any such thing. But a decision has nevertheless to be made when we have the construction of robots. But what does science fiction tell us of those problems which arise from the confrontation of cultural norms and the complex trends of the techno-revolution? It is not malice which makes me ask such questions. One can read about bionic aggregates not only in sf, but also in the futurological books—in Herman Kahn, for instance. How, therefore, will they be regarded once they are here? If science fiction has made any statements about this problem, they remain unknown to me. Regrettably sf is subject to the pressure of strong taboos, and all the talk about their perfect freedom in the realm of all possible hypotheses (about which there was much talk some time ago at a meeting of the sf enthusiasts in the U.S.A.) simply isn't true. A man who has been hypnotized to believe that he is alone in a room will act as if he doesn't notice any of the other beings in the room.

12. It is not always easy to point clearly and unmistakably to the passages in a literary work that cause its aesthetic inferiority. It is much simpler, on the other hand, to point out the logical, as well as factual, consequences of a work. Were we to describe all the sick passages composed badly in the second sense, we should need a whole volume; therefore, we'll give only a few examples of the

nonsense which dominates the robot field in sf.

In Kuttner and Moore's novelette, *There's No Returning Home*, a super-robot is built as a "strategic brain," but goes mad so that humans have to fight it, because under the strain of military decisions the brain of steel has broken down. Its breakdown is explained as the result of a "robot neurosis." That is, a robot cannot bear the burden of responsibility which human beings can bear without difficulty. The implied parallel between the human and the mechanical brain is based on an absurd premise, for while one can compare parameters such as the "hardness" of a steel brain and the "softness" of a biological brain, the hardness or softness of a psychical process has nothing to do with the material from which a brain has been built.

To marvel at the fact that a human being can work smoothly whereas a robot breaks down, though the human consists of "soft albumen" and the robot of "hard steel," is as absurd as if someone wondered that Venus, though a soft goddess of love, consists of hard marble in a statue, while an armed knight, on the other hand, is painted on the "soft linen" of a canvas. The stability of a process of computing information has nothing in common with the substratum of the informative machine: i.e., there is no physical relationship between these parameters.

The falsity of Merliss's novella, *The Stutterer*, lies elsewhere. Mighty robots who have completed their extraterrestrial duties are to be walled in concrete for eternity. One of them secretly comes to earth, to ask man to pardon him and his brothers. After he shows courage and a willingness to be sacrificed, benevolent mankind gives the sign of mercy. Let us imagine a Biafran asking this good mankind for mercy for his tortured country. What help did he get? Not the robot, but humanity is the false part of this melodramatic story.

In one case, therefore, the robot, in another his human environment, is depicted falsely, since it is depicted anti-realistically. Not only specific stories but the entire genre suggests that robots are rather dumb creatures reminding one sometimes of catatonics, while androids are psychically quite human. Why? Do the qualities of the emotional processes of any being depend upon its outward human shape? A psychical life of robots in sf remains nearly non-existent. They are but automatons, similar to enlarged toys.

In *The Instigators* by R. E. Banks, the specialists who deal with the programming of robots form a kind of guild, and the programming is a calling. When the strip of paper that has been perforated in a certain way is inserted into the body of the robot, he begins to waken and does what he has been ordered to do. That's pure nonsense, of course. And even though we disregard the business with the programming, the robots of Banks are automatons in the same sense as the well-known Swiss dolls built a century and a half ago. They cannot adapt to a changed situation.

And when we are, once in a while, told about the spiritual life of such a being, it soon transpires that between the qualities of the consciousness of an artificial and a human being there exist no differences at all, as in Fred Pohl's *The Tunnel Under the World*. The narrator is a robot or an android; he is the copy of a dead human, and his behaviour is that of a human. Now this story is quite good: indeed, one of the best. But as a whole, sf seems quite unable either to describe the "differentia specifica" of technological homunculi, or to suggest it hypothetically as a new psychical quality. The robot is either a blockhead—a dumb bloke—or he is turned into an ordinary being, as if a third alternative were excluded! There do exist several good, even excellent, stories in which robots appear, such as "Short in the Chest" by Idris Seabright, but their value is to be found outside the robot motif.

13. Is there no salvation? Are there no sources that could be examined if one wanted to portray a being which is humanlike and yet simultaneously impresses us as alien? The logical theory of automata tells us that it is necessary to put an "ego-model" into a hierarchically organized automaton: i.e., during the course of his adaptation to his environment, when the automaton models its picture in its interior, he has to set a model of his body against the model of the world, according to the law of logical symmetry. This is the reason for the condition peculiar to all philosophy; namely, that we have an "ego-centered" consciousness. There exists no complete formula for the literary construction of a robot, but that construction has to go through certain stages, all of them in close touch with the accumulated theoretical and empirical material of specialist robot literature. If we disregard this, it is still possible to write interesting, even excellent, works which have nothing to do with the real course of the evolution of automatons.

The aficionado may be content with such texts. Science fiction can also tell us all possible unrealistic things about a robot. I'm not asking for a normative here: *empirically*-based aesthetics in any field of art. But if science fiction doesn't say even a single word about the *real* shape of the developments of the future, which kind of literature is going to enlighten us?

14. So far as we can see, the main directions of the real intellectronic evolution and its reflection in sf are diverging more and more. Intellectronics goes in the direction of the computer, but sf is based mostly on fictitious robots. The theme of the artificial human being, as noted, has had its ancestors in myth. The logical computer, on the other hand, has been created in a mythically empty space. But whereas the further possibilities of the development of robots lead either into a dead end or are stopped by real technological developments, the evolutionary potential of computers remains unlimited, as far as we can tell today. The production of robots leaves us with a fatal dilemma. Should it become possible to build a synthetic being, which nevertheless has all the psychical qualities of a human, it will no longer be possible to *use* such a being as we use a machine. It cannot be sent to a lost cause, it cannot be ordered to do something that will lead to its own destruction, for these would be infamous acts. Should the robot have no way of opposing the order, because of its programming, the result would appear to be an especially infamous proceeding. A being so similar psychically to a human being is, considered ethically, a human being. If we do not murder cripples, degenerates, or retarded people just because they are human, we also cannot treat artificial beings in so murderous a way. What is pragmatically an even more important argument, even should it be possible to build robots as "higher beings"—i.e., as creatures who surpass humans intellectually and morally, for example—it would be nonsense to people the world with such "supermen." Only misfortune for both sides could result. Now we may hear that ethically-based arguments have no power in real life: for even if it were a crime to act as we have suggested, human beings will nevertheless do it when they think it serves their own interests. But the portrait of a world in which all working places have been taken over by automatons with personality is entirely false. The automation of the production process is effected in such a way that these

processes are connected in their physical and informative-regulating parts. In an automated factory there are no two-legged robots, and they aren't likely to be there in the future. Not the moral, but the *technological* directives point so. The picture of a machine guarded by a machine who, perhaps, after work, will exchange a few words with his electronic colleagues and then go home to his electronic wife is pure nonsense. The informative-supervising part of a production-machine will not be separated from the productive-working part. It isn't worth the effort and never will be, economically, to build volitional and intelligent automatons as part of the productive process. Even examples of these processes belonging to the sphere of private life are being automated separately: an automatic clock will never be able to wash dishes, and a mechanical dishwasher will never exchange small talk with a housewife.

Although possible in principle, such products of the robot market as unspecialized as human beings will always cost a lot: in any case a number of automatons doing separate parts of the housework, lacking all psychic characteristics, will be much cheaper than a single robot with a clever electronic head.

This isn't an idyllic picture of the future. Most likely simulcra of human beings will be constructed, especially as guinea-pigs for scientific study. They can be experimented upon in ways that would be considered acts of cruelty today.

As for computers, they have been created, as noted, in a mythically empty space; therefore, one cannot use legends and myths to obtain ready plot structures for them in sf. The science fiction writer has to do his own work there. But the history of mankind is full of examples of the efforts to which human beings have gone in order to avoid having to think of their own accord. Because of this, computers, despite their futurological perspectives, have been much neglected in sf. They appear in it as strategic, counselling, and governing machines. As strategists they generally are dumb; the military plans calculated by such electronic monsters resemble in their degree of difficulty simple school mathematical exercises, as, for example, in Peter George's two novels depicting the end of the world during an atomic war. As rulers they can be equated with quite ordinary psychological testing automatons; they serve as a sieve to separate the loyal members of society from the deviants, as in van Vogt, Sheckley, and countless others. They sometimes are originally conceived of as counsellors, as in Wallace's *Delay in Transit*, in which, the size of a pea, they can be carried around in one's ear. But almost always they are personified. They are, therefore, not computers in the proper sense of the word, but micro-miniaturised robots.

Today we can think of the following roles for computers of the future:

1. They can be an intelligence amplifier of enormous dimensions; i.e., an "intellectronic genius," a wise man. Science fiction does sometimes mention such wise computers which then, sadly, as in the case of Simak, for example, offer the most trivial banality as an intellectual revelation. They may be shown, but never be urged to express themselves, for we can believe in their wisdom only so long as they remain silent.

2. They can be the theme of satirical texts. Then we have an end to all prediction. It is nevertheless very interesting and amusing to read how two strategic computers of inimical sides come to a secret agreement in order to rape this nauseating humanity into peace at last. But when such things are presented as futurological prediction, we have an aberration. Two American authors, MacGowan and Ordway, have written *Intelligence in the Universe*, in which they maintain quite earnestly that such computers, used as strategists, will indeed come to an understanding between themselves, force mankind to keep peace, and govern as severe but just rulers. They also know exactly what will happen later: tired of ruling, such automatons will leave earth in order to find "intellectronic geniuses" of their own kind as "thinking colleagues" in space. Mankind will then put together another automaton ruler who will, in turn, grow tired of the business of government and travel away; and so on, until Judgment Day. It is very pleasing to learn that not only American science fiction writers have remained intellectually childish.

15. But such twaddle has nothing to do with the future of our earth. As you can see, *difficile est satiram non scribere,* even when you try to remain serious.

16. A computer can be the basis for psycho-symbiotic processes; i.e., a basis for close relationship between man and machine. That possibility has never been tried out in literature, because the authors do not seem to understand that then there'll be no

"tandem" work. The human being then has no partner in the psychological sense, but is informatively plugged into the machine as a whole, just as a good driver becomes one with his car. The robot may be similar to a human being, but to humanize the computer only means to exhibit paralysis of one's imagination and one's knowledge. A computer isn't a human being, but a whole universe of possibilities, according to the theorem of Türing concerning his universal automation. It could form the basis of an experimental philosophy, for if there are powerful computers, we will be able to simulate all possible things in them.

For example, sociological processes: it would be possible to model the rise and decline of a civilization, the development of a religious belief, or an economic crisis and the ensuing panic. It would be possible to model autonomous worlds, with properties which the different philosophical systems have attributed to our world—perhaps the strictly deterministic world of Laplace or the monadic world of Leibnitz, with its "pre-stabilized harmony." One could model a being who not only metaphorically but actually could be a "trinity" in the sense of Freud: ego, superego, and id. One could therefore verify hypotheses of an anthropological, futurological, or philosophical nature. One could divide the interior of the computer into the "world" and its "inhabitants" in order to do research into the relationship between object and subject. Yes, indeed, one can write a book about the things one could do with computers (which I have tried to do). Even if it is occasionally impossible to mathematize non-linear processes, they nevertheless can be modelled. One of the most difficult problems of the future is the dilemma of auto-evolution of human beings. Should genetic engineers consider humans only as machines whose parameters are in need of optimization? So-called cyborgisation points in this direction. Considered purely from a technological point of view, the more a machine becomes independent of its environment, the better it is. But there is a dependence of human beings on their environment (such as erotic ties or the ties of friendship) which form autonomous values; i.e., which aren't subordinated to an end. A cyborg who doesn't need to eat, drink, or breathe because he has a built-in atomic source of energy, who can blot out any memory by a simple act of will, becomes a machine which is, as far as function is concerned, more perfect than a human; it cannot feel hunger, thirst, lack of air, anything. But in such a way, step by step, everything which is at the humane core of all our values gets destroyed. Therefore, different projects of auto-evolution could be tested with models, and only then would it be possible to think of the realization of a selected model.

The computer is a universal instrument for the acquisition of knowledge, but it is also a source of danger. The condition in which a society allows itself to be governed by computers may not arrive by way of a common agreement—by a public poll—but can be realized very slowly, creepingly, and continually so that it will be impossible to tell at any point whether or not the "electronic" government has already become a fact. To supervise a single computer whose business it is to see that certain parameters are kept in balance is a task which can be solved relatively easily, but the switching of thousands and thousands of computers into different parts of the social structure can lead to a situation that, as a whole, is quite incomprehensible. For the problem is this: the computer is plugged into the process as a regulator only when a human being is unable to optimize the process, because it completely escapes the comprehension of any human; i.e., is outside the limits of his utmost capabilities. The programme limits the range of decisions which can be made by such a computer, but when a very large number of computers cooperate, whether connected directly or informatively by humans, then their effects are not a factor that can be included in the programme of any one of them, for those effects form a resulting factor. Who shall, in such a situation, guard the computer-net? Who guards the guardian? This task can be too difficult for a human being: the building of a hierarchy of regulators which are strictly one-way directed may prove impossible. In any case, it would be difficult to prove with a hundred per cent certainty that all the relevant parameters of the whole system are under control according to the plan. In real life, for instance, a society which has computerized itself could grow dumb within a few generations because the most intelligent people may pose difficulties for the regulatory work of the computer-net, and the net will then try to eliminate such people, as a nuisance, from the system.

The most important thing about this is that computers never do anything consciously. We cannot attribute to them psychological reasons that would be understandable by way of intuitive feeling: they do not strive for power, they do not know egotism, for they have no ego and no personality. Whether as single units or as nets, they are, considered anthropologically–psychologically, nobody at all. They are but a number of historically new factors, new powers which will co-determine the future course of history. This is a totally new thing in our experience. Something like this hasn't existed in all the civilizations of the past, and therefore the problem posed can be solved only in a way which isn't a repetition of something we already know and have already lived through.

We have simplified this problem—one of a large number—rather brutally. We intended to point out only that it isn't possible to construct a reflection of the condition of the future with cliches. It isn't the archetypes of Jung, nor the structures of the myth, nor irrational nightmares which cause the central problems of the future and determine them. And should the future be full of dangers, those dangers cannot be reduced to the known patterns of the past. They have a unique quality, as a variety of factors of a new type. That is the most important thing for the writer of science fiction. But sf has meanwhile built itself into a jail and imprisoned itself within those walls, because its writers have not seemed to understand that the salvation of the creative imagination cannot be found in mythical, existential, or surrealistic writings— as a new statement about the conditions of existence. By cutting itself off from the stream of scientific facts and hypotheses, science fiction itself has helped to erect the walls of the literary ghetto where it now lives out its piteous life.

Translated by Franz Rottensteiner.

ALEXEI PANSHIN

SCIENCE FICTION
IN
DIMENSION

During the past few years there has been a noisy fight in science fiction between drumbeaters for a supposed "New Wave" and the guardians of all that science fiction is supposed to have been since 1926. The writers of science fiction have been muttering amongst themselves and snarling from the sidelines, but they haven't, for the most part, declared themselves for one party or the other. The actual battlers have been editors and fans, people as central to the creation of science fiction as Judith Merril and John Jeremy Pierce.

It's a murky quarrel. It seems that both sides have chosen up on the emotional strength of the one label or the other, and then found that no one else in their camp agrees on right and proper definitions. Both the New Wavers and the Old have laid claim to the same writers. Roger Zelazny has been split like a wishbone.

Insofar as there is emotional agreement within factions, a biased outsider might say that the New Wave seems to be in favor of literary experimentation, non-linearity and a remergence with the so-called "literary mainstream." And the Old Wave flag-wavers endorse the good-story-well-told, healthy social values, and fiction about science.

Neither package seems entirely worth having. Is science fiction indeed fiction about science, as the assumption has been since Hugo Gernsback founded *Amazing Stories*? It is my feeling that it is not. It is no more reasonable to expect sf to be about science

Originally published in *Fantastic Stories*, 9 (June 1970), 125-130. Reprinted by permission of the author.

than to expect all historical novels to restrict themselves to
military history or the state of the marketplace. On the other
hand, is science fiction actually inferior to the mainstream? In
recent times the apparent movement has been by a "mainstream"
of frustrated social literature that is moving toward science fiction
and fantasy. Barth, Barthelme, Burroughs, Coover, Vonnegut and
Nabokov may point a direction.

The New Wave-Old Wave argument, as its partisans have put
their cases, has been an empty one, but the edginess and bad
temper of the writers has been real. These are uncertain and
often frightening times in science fiction. Things are unclear.
Things are changing. What the shape of science fiction will be in
five years, no one would be confident to say. But some of the
idols of Golden Age science fiction have turned to writing popular
science or other kinds of fiction, and some have stopped writing
altogether in the face of pressure. And among younger writers
there seems to be a sense of a new universe to be opened, though
none of them have yet proved their belief with books.

Joanna Russ has characterized science fiction as the Elizabethan theater after Marlowe, but before Shakespeare. I want to
believe it. I can see the empty Elizabethan theater waiting to be
filled with giant magics—and see science fiction as an unknown
universe impossible to fill. But Joanna's nominations for the part
of Marlowe are Asimov and Heinlein, and I don't think they
qualify. They seem more akin to the morality dramatists who
came twenty years before Shakespeare. In the place of Thomas
Kyd, who was the first versifier, the last of the moralists and the
first of the tragedians, we might name Zelazny or Delany. But
science fiction has still to produce its Marlowe, let alone a
Shakespeare.

Still, the potential of a real rift appears between technicians
content to write formula moralities and melodramas, all in the
same limp gray prose, and experimenters curious to know the true
range of science fiction. The rift is more potential than actual
because the experimenters have yet to fully justify themselves.
Roger Zelazny and Samuel Delany have superseded their predecessors but not surpassed them.

If this were Afterward, and all the possible changes of science
fiction had been rung, this column would be more organized than

I actually expect it is going to be from one issue to the next. Since I think that we actually stand well before science fiction's hour, this column will be a random collection of suggestions, arguments, opinions and dreams. If the New Wave and Old are drum-beaters and flag-wavers, I invite you to see me as the fellow with the piccolo playing "Over the Hills and Far Away."

I have been reading science fiction for twenty years, writing it for ten, and criticizing it for six. My opinions on the subject have been changing all the while, and you can assume that they will continue to change, possibly from one column to the next. What I say is by way of suggestion. It isn't authoritative, objective or final. Treat it accordingly—pick through what I say and accept what you can.

Science fiction has been a literary genre since the founding of *Amazing Stories* in 1926. It has been a naive, insular, uncertain and impolite literature. That's from our side, the inside. The outside has looked on us with righteous contumely.

Sf has been innocent of ordinary literary standards. Since 1950, at least, when Gold and Boucher and McComas set new standards for *Galaxy* and *F&SF*, science fiction has been literate, but even today, most science fiction continues to be written in a dull prose that not only remains much the same from story to story, but even from author to author. Prose that sings or cuts is rare. Variations in prose can distinguish characters, set a tone, produce a range of effect and stimulate a drowsy reader. But most science fiction, among all the musical effects of prose, has been aware only of pace—drone notes set to the beat of a drum.

Sf has primarily been published in pulp magazines and, more recently, in paperback books, and been shaped by their requirements. Among these is that the drum should beat very fast just before the end of the story. Melodrama. Action.

Most science fiction has been short until recently, and even novels have been usually no longer than 60,000 words—which is short. This would seem unnecessarily limiting for a fiction about the unfamiliar.

Science fiction is associated in the popular mind with horror movies, and comic strips, and the worst excesses of scientism. Who among us could say that this is unjustified?

And even after forty years, there still is no generally accepted definition of the field.

Except . . .

Even under deserved criticism and contempt, science fiction has not withered. It has continued to expand its subject, its techniques, and its ideas of its limits. Other popular magazine fiction has almost completely disappeared. But in 1968, science fiction magazines supported by readers—not advertisers, as is the usual case—published three hundred original stories. I think the science fiction short story is an irrelevance that deserves to disappear, but it is a fifteen-year-old fact that science fiction is the present home of the American short story. And *Amazing* is not only still being published after more than forty years, it is the most vigorous present science fiction magazine.

But not only has science fiction proved durable beyond all reasonable expectation, its audience is unusual. Until recently, the audience has been intense, but limited in size and composed mainly of fans, engineers and bright fifteen-year-olds.

However, at any one time, this limited audience supports amateur magazines by the hundreds, and has for forty years. With only a few recent exceptions—college club magazines and the like—these journals have been published without sponsorship, endorsement or subsidy. This is a common fact to us within the sf world, but from the outside it is unique and remarkable.

And every year—again without sponsorship, endorsement or subsidy—science fiction supports conventions by the dozen. In the past few years, the number and size of these conventions has leaped. The first World Science Fiction Convention that I attended was the Seventeenth in Detroit in 1959. The attendance was 371 people. This year there will be any number of regional conventions with that kind of attendance, and the attendance at the Twenty-Seventh World Science Fiction Convention in St. Louis last September was over 1600 people. This makes it one of the largest conventions of any kind in the United States. And all on the basis of voluntary association.

Is it fiction about science that has brought this many people together this strongly? Or is there another more important element that binds?

Until recently, to be published as science fiction meant that a book had an assured limited sale to the traditional narrow but loyal science fiction audience. I used to think it was the general audience that was missing the point, that it was fear and ignorance that kept them from science fiction.

There may have been some truth in this. Science fiction, well ahead of its time, and all that, may only at last have been caught up to by laggard minds. On the other hand, it seems a more likely possibility that what has kept a larger audience away has been the imperfections of science fiction: the melodrama, the crudeness and the insistence upon featuring science to the exclusion of other aspects of life. Whatever the element that has bound the science fiction audience so tightly, is it so foreign to all other readers that the appeals of science fiction must inevitably pass them by? Or is it science fiction that has failed to explore its own possibilities?

There is no question that working in a pulp literature with pulp standards and pulp economies has inhibited science fiction writers from exploring the range of the field. Write a novel longer than 60,000 words? Nonsense—there is no market for such a book. Write a story about daily life in a strange society? The readers would never hold still for it. Write a legitimate tragedy? How? About what? You must be kidding. How?

But now a larger audience has shown an interest. Risk-taking books like *Stranger in a Strange Land* and *Dune* have been published as science fiction, but been seized upon by a new, large, educated, hip, young audience. Are these pure accidents? I don't think so. It certainly isn't predictions about science that have caught these people—it must be some other rarer magic. But the intensity of this new appeal has been as great as it always has been within our limited audience.

And the magic—is it our own secret heart's delight? Is it an accident that Paul Williams of *Crawdaddy* should hand John Lennon *The Three Stigmata of Palmer Eldritch* to read? Is it an accident that the *Whole Earth Catalog,* whose stated purpose begins, "We *are* as gods and might as well get good at it," and which lists appropriate tools, should list *Dune*? Is it an accident that rock music should be about science fiction and rock musicians should read science fiction?

What magic touched the people who saw *2001*?

What would science fiction be like if it regularly and surely engaged this audience, instead of occasionally and erratically?

This is hypothetical, because if someone actually knew the answer he would be writing fiction like nothing any of us has seen before and enchanting us all, science fiction's old audience and its new one. It is this vision of possibility that frightens some writers out of the field and sets others to writing strange experiments.

At the same time, the spectre of respectability and academic acceptance is haunting sf writers with requests for library donations of manuscripts and old laundry lists. ("You have the complete laundry lists of *Robert Silverberg*? That's a thesis for some lucky University of Syracuse doctoral candidate, I would say.") It may mean only the academic hunt for material to analyze is insanely intense, but the degree of interest is enough to make nerves shaky. The Modern Language Association has begun to publish its own fanzine, *Extrapolation*. It has held general meetings on science fiction, and one of the MLA sessions at the just past winter meetings was devoted to John Brunner's *Stand on Zanzibar*. A Science Fiction Research Association for sf bibliographers is being formed. And science fiction writers like Joanna Russ, William Tenn and Jack Williamson teach college courses in science fiction.

It can be frightening. Especially if the safe common sort of science fiction is all you know. Especially if you haven't a clue to an alternative. There are people who would like to see the colleges and the new people go away. Strange to say of science fiction writers, but there is fear of the unknown.

What is science fiction?

In his contribution to the Advent symposium, *The Science Fiction Novel*, Robert Heinlein divided fiction into "the possible" and "the impossible"—Realism and Fantasy. He divided these categories again into past, present and future scene, and found most science fiction under the heading, "Realistic Future-Scene Fiction." And Heinlein in his discussion hinges his "realism" on science. This is the standard ideal of science fiction set by Hugo Gernsback—but it has never strictly been followed.

Science fiction cannot depend for its legitimacy on science. No matter how accurate a story may seem to be, or may prove to be, if it doesn't involve or move readers, it will surely die. And science alone is insufficient to explain a good story.

Cleve Cartmill's story "Deadline," which predicted the atomic bomb in 1944 and brought the FBI out to investigate, is today not much better than a curiosity. Alan Nourse's story "Brightside Crossing," on the other hand, about a Mercury we now know to be impossible, still has the power to move.

In fact, if science fiction did derive its legitimacy from science, last year's science fiction would be thrown on the same rubbish heap as last year's scientific textbooks. Science is a constant corrective procedure. Science fiction based on present science has to be insufficient. Science fiction based on hypothetical science has to be ingenious nonsense.

Science fiction has never done better than pretend to be about science—often to its great cost. L. Sprague de Camp wrote in his *Science-Fiction Handbook*, "The science-fiction magazines persist in publishing stories of strange worlds, the future, marvelous journeys, and utopias with little or no science—no pseudo-science even." Not quite true. Pseudo-science is science fiction's greatest crudity. Gernsback's rules said that science fiction ought to be about science, and the practical result was pseudo-science. De Camp himself was purist enough to try to follow Gernsback— he wouldn't write about faster-than-light travel, for instance, because he didn't believe it was possible. And eventually de Camp gave up writing science fiction for historical novels where the facts more easily stand still.

The quarrel about the relation of science and science fiction is as new as Larry Niven and R. A. Lafferty, and as old as Verne and Wells. Verne said of Wells, "It occurs to me that his stories do not repose on a very scientific basis. No, there is no rapport between his work and mine. I make use of physics. He invents. I go to the moon in a cannon-ball discharged from a cannon. Here there is no invention. He goes to Mars in an air-ship, which he constructs of a metal which does away with the law of gravitation. *Ca, C'est très joli*, but show me this metal. Let him produce it."

But science and the times have abandoned Verne, while Wells, who was never "right," continues to be relevant. Science fiction does not depend on accuracy, which is impossible, but on inner consistency. The subject of science fiction is not the world as it will be, but the limitless world of the imagination.

Science fiction, as a few have always insisted, is fantasy. What we are used to thinking of as fantasy is a conscious recreation of myths and symbols that are no longer believed, but merely expected to entertain. The world is Earth. The spirit is historical and nostalgic. Familiarity is half the appeal. But this is not the only possible fantasy. Fantasy can be disciplined and creative and relevant. It has been crowded out of the last empty spaces on Earth only to find an empty and inexhaustible universe. All time. All space. And that is the world of "science fiction."

For forty years we have been gingerly feeling our way out into this vast emptiness, first exploring our back yard and our neighborhood, and tied to the "realistic" world all the while by the safety line of "science."

Now is the time to cut the line. To sing. To dance. To shout up the dawn. To hurl rainbows. To discover marvels and populate the darkness. And perhaps find ourselves.

"A
CITY OF WHICH
THE
STARS ARE SUBURBS"

The writer is neither a watcher nor a dreamer. Literature does not reflect life, but it doesn't escape or withdraw from life either: it swallows it. And the imagination won't stop until it's swallowed everything. No matter what direction we start off in, the signposts of literature always keep pointing the same way, to a world where nothing is outside the human imagination. If even time, the enemy of all living things, and to poets, at least, the most hated and feared of all tyrants, can be broken down by the imagination, anything can be. We come back to the limit of the imagination that I referred to in my first talk, a universe entirely possessed and occupied by human life, a city of which the stars are suburbs. Nobody can believe in any such universe: literature is not religion, and it doesn't address itself to belief. But if we shut the vision of it completely out of our minds, or insist on its being limited in various ways, something goes dead inside us, perhaps the one thing that it is really important to keep alive.

Northrop Frye,
The Educated Imagination
(1963), p. 33.

If there is a meaning to man, it must be seen and discovered not only in terms of a few years, or a lifetime, or even the rise and fall of generations or empires: the search for the meaning and purpose of man must be extended to the entire lifespan of the race, from the beginning to the end. This entire span is Stapledon's vision in *Last and First Men*. Such an imaginative range, all the while keeping within the realm of the probable, can only be presented today by science-fiction. Like Blake, Stapledon created the images to embody his vision; science fiction provided a ready-made framework for that vision.

Roger Brunet,
The Mystic Vision of Olaf Stapledon
(1968), p. 17.

". . . a universe entirely possessed and occupied by human life, a city of which the stars are suburbs": few works of literature reach toward Northrop Frye's "limit of the imagination" more completely than do Olaf Stapledon's *Last and First Men* and Isaac Asimov's *Foundation Trilogy*, both literally and figuratively. On the former level, they depict man's exploration of physical space and scientific knowledge; Stapledon describes the slow painstaking evolution of man as he spreads throughout the solar system, while Asimov pictures a future in which the entire galaxy is peopled by man. At the latter level, these works explore the universal question of the nature of human history in terms of the future of man.

For both writers, the expression of the human condition is based the same pattern—the slow circular movement of history within a cosmic setting. For Stapledon, the motion is, in fact, an upward and finite spiral; for Asimov, it is, apparently, a closed circle. The basic expression of the former view in Western literature is the Bible, which "presents a gigantic cycle from creation to apocalypse" within which are other cycles:

> individual from birth to salvation; sexual from Adam and Eve to the apocalyptic wedding; social from the giving of the law to the established kingdom of the law . . . [and] the ironic or all too human cycle, the *mere* cycle of human life without redemptive assistance, which goes recurrently through the 'same dull round' in Blake's phrase, from birth to death.[1]

The latter view is that of the Classical epics, in which the basic patterns are "the life and death of the individual, and the slower social rhythm which, in the course of years, brings cities and empires to their rise and fall."[2] Thus in the "low mimetic period of future hopes,"[3] Stapledon presents the full "apocalyptic cadence," from the creation of man, through his attempts to achieve perfection, to his destruction. Asimov deals with the continuous human pattern of life and death within the larger, and apparently unchanging, framework of the rise and fall of societies.

The chief technical device used by each writer is the adoption of the viewpoint and narrative methods of the historian. It requires almost a divine stance to present the creation and destruction of mankind, or even of one society, adequately—not only to comprehend the immense time span involved, but also to see, not isolated events, but a continuing chain of causes and effects. Only from such a position is one able to "look at men, not as living from moment to disappearing moment, but as 'giants immersed in time.' " The closest human approximation of this viewpoint is that of the historian, who, knowing all events, can choose and interpret those which are significant, and which reveal overall trends. In part, the reader is asked to assume this role, to look beyond the wars with Mars or Korell, the death of the Flying Men, or the Mule, to see the overall pattern being formed. But he is primarily aided by the presentation of *Last and First Men* as a chronicle, and of *Foundation Trilogy* as a popular history book.

This historical treatment, while demanded by the scope and theme of the works, has important advantages. Stapledon presents *Last and First Men* as "an authentic message from one of the Last Men," written through the medium of a contemporary author.[5] In this way, he achieves the epic scope required by the action in a plausible manner, since the narrator has been able to travel by telepathy throughout all of human time. He also establishes the necessary detached point of view, since the speaker not only knows all the historical events which lie between our time and his, but can interpret them, and can help the reader "to feel not only the vastness of time and space, but also the vast diversity of mind's possible modes" (p. 17) and in this way begin "to mould our hearts to accept new values." (p. 11) Such a viewpoint inevitably emphasizes the overall pattern of events, since the historian passes over the "ages of quiesence, often of actual stagnation, filled with monotonous problems and toils of countless almost identical lives," and records instead only the "rare moments of racial adventure" which are themselves "but a moment in the life of the stars." (p. 16) From an aesthetic point of view, too, such a presentation helps to create cohesion, interest and suspense, as a "mere sluggish river" (p. 16) of detailed events could not do.

Asimov, too, presents the *Foundation Trilogy* as a factual

account, illustrated by anecdotes, of the rise of the Foundation. The influence of historical writing is obvious; for example, each section of the narrative opens and closes with quotations from the sixteenth edition of an *Encyclopedia Galactica,* begun by Foundation scholars and published in Terminus in 1020 F.E. Thus, the successful establishment of Foundation rule is never in doubt; the anecdotes serve to illustrate significant moments in the history of its development. The theme of the inevitable cycle of the rise and fall of societies is established, while the "historical" presentation ensures the extensive time scale, credibility, and compression necessary to the development of the theme and the story itself. Asimov, like Stapledon, uses the novel's form to present his abstract, general view of history in concrete, understandable terms. First the narrative framework (the impersonal factual accounts) establishes the thematic framework (the cyclic movement of history); then, the abrupt shifts into the point of view of a specific character as well as the lively colloquial tone of the anecdotes help to show that the fate of individuals, as they live, die, and pass into legend, is tied to the social cycle. Again (and more successfully) a human perspective is developed, embodied in vividly-drawn characters with whom the reader may sympathize. Unlike Stapledon's narrator, who, though caught up in the tragedy of his race, is still able to see beyond events and grasp "the eternal form of things" (p. 327), the people of the *Trilogy* live only from "moment to moment"; but their actions form a pattern which reveals itself as the work progresses. In this way, the historical form adopted by Stapledon and Asimov differs but aids them in developing their cosmic theme, enables them to adopt the vast, generalized perspective such a concept requires, and allows them to maintain a recognizable, relevant human dimension in their works.

In the same way, the basic concepts of *Last and First Men* and *Foundation Trilogy* influenced the development of their secondary themes. Though both are in part works of social comment, such concerns are presented in the same perspective as the lives of individuals or races, significant only insofar as they affect the overall thematic framework. Stapledon, for example, deals at length with the immediate future of present-day society, depicting it, not as advancing "steadily towards some kind of Utopia"

(p. 12) but as collapsing due to a combination of accidents with man's inability to achieve the truly human "unification of the race." (p. 31) Stapledon emphasized that *Last and First Men* was "not prophesy" (p. 12); thus his descriptions of the futile, destructive global wars, or the perversion of scientific activity into the "fanatical worship of movement" symbolized by the cult of the Prime Mover Gordelpus are of value as satire; but they are fully meaningful only when seen as illustrations of basic human limitations which prevent man "from living a fully human life." (p. 85) Man's slow progress, which culminates in the ability of the Last Men to overcome these subhuman tendencies, is thus emphasized. Similarly, the fall of the First Man reveals, in microcosm, the fate of all succeeding races which are destroyed by chance, or human folly, or both.   These cycles of racial development and collapse, embodying man's failures and his aspirations, are contained within the overall pattern, and are important only as part of it.

In the same way, Stapledon is concerned with biological experimentation as it affects man's progress. "History is a fragment of biology";[6] and human limitations are, in part, purely physical limitations. For example, the basic ideals of devotion to "truth for its own sake" or loyalty to fate, and "unselfish love of neighbours and of God" or loyalty to man, are first expressed by Socrates and Jesus. Yet "both these ideals demanded of the human brain a degree of vitality and coherence of which the nervous system of the First Men was never really capable." (p. 21)

It is not until two thousand million years later that the Eighteenth Men are able, by their biological superiority, to achieve the "truly human" synthesis of these ideals.

Stapledon uses the modern concept of the artificial creation of a superman to chart the spiral path of man's development. The First Men, ourselves, are destroyed by chance and imperfection. The Second Men, a product of natural evolution, achieve a remarkably high level of civilization, only to be destroyed by their bacterial war with the Martians. The Third Men finally evolve lacking man's "finer mental capacities" (p. 191); they decide to breed "a man who is nothing but man" (p. 208), but the resulting creature of pure intellect is nothing but a monstrous brain, "a bump of curiosity equipped with most cunning hands." (p. 212) Realizing his own limitations, he in turn develops the Fifth Men, whose spiritual development is the highest yet attained. Yet the imminent destruction of the Earth forces this race to migrate to Venus, where it is slowly destroyed and brutalized by harsh conditions and guilt over the murder of the Venusians. The Sixth Men, totally engaged in a struggle for survival, nevertheless create their version of a perfect human—the Flying Men. These, however, inevitably fall because of their own limited natures and a plague of biological defects. The remaining flightless cripples are "strictly pedestrian, mentally and physically" (p. 269); however they, too, are forced to develop a new form of man, one capable of migrating to Neptune to escape the heat of the sun's coming explosion. An unfavourable environment and innate flaws cause a slow brutalization of this race, too; yet eventually the Fourteenth Men emerge, on a level with the First and, like them, destroyed by their inability to "transcend their imperfect spiritual nature." (p. 280) Yet once again, "unaided nature" creates a new race, the equals of the Second Men, whose descendants steadily "advance to full humanity." (p. 281) While Nature was partly responsible for much of the previous evolutionary movements, the triumph of the Eighteenth Men is a triumph of eugenics. The "designers" of the race not only produced a perfect physical type, but developed "distinct and specialized brains" able at last to achieve a true "unity of individual minds." (p. 295) Thus the Racial Awakening and the reconciliation of loyalty to man and loyalty to fate are made possible. Stapledon's twentieth century concern with the future of social and scientific developments is inseparable from his vision of man's future as a slow upward movement to full humanity.

This examination of modern problems in the context of a timeless myth is central to *Foundation Trilogy* as well. In a world of space and arms races the question of the relationship of scientific and technical development to power is crucial; in the eternal pattern of the rise and fall of societies, it is also relevant. The level of scientific development and awareness fluctuates with the state of the society. As the character Seldon points out:

> The sum of human knowing is beyond any one man;
> any thousand men. With the destruction of our social
> fabric, science will be broken into a million pieces. Indivi-

duals will know much of exceedingly tiny facets of what
there is to know. They will be helpless and useless by themselves. The bits of lore, meaningless, will not be passed on.
They will be lost through the generations.[7]

Thus one important function of the Foundation is to be a "scientific refuge" (p. 85), a storehouse of knowledge. But scientific development also affects the social cycle, and is linked to the growth of
power. The very concept of a "galactic empire" is possible only
because of technical advances, especially the discovery of travel
through hyperspace. Thus mental stagnation, a "receding initiative . . . a damming up of curiosity" (p. 29) is both a symptom
and a cause of the Empire's decline. For example, as intergalactic
communication and individual initiative both crumble with the
Empire, science becomes a matter of barren tradition and ritual;
the worlds of the periphery lose the knowledge of atomic power
(p. 46) or, like Siwenna, maintain the power plants in an automatic uncomprehending routine. (p. 198) This decline, in turn,
aids the rise of the Foundation, which, having preserved not only
facts but, more important, the spirit of scientific inquiry, moves
away from the mere "classification of past data" (p. 64) and expands to fill the power vacuum. Fifty years after its establishment, the Foundation gains control over the neighbouring Four
Kingdoms by a combination of diplomacy and technical superiority. Her traders go on to develop a "religion-controlled commercial empire" (p. 127) ruled, not by might, but by humanity's desire for "science, trade, education, scientific medicine"—and atomic refrigerators—wrapped up in a mystical religion whose "priests"
are Foundation-trained scientists. After two hundred years, except for the remnants of the Empire, "the Foundation was the
most powerful state in the Galaxy,"[8] solely as a result of economic
control based on technical supremacy. Her power can be seriously
challenged only by a different form of "weapon"—the emotional
control of the mutant Mule. But even he is defeated by the superior control developed by the Second Foundation's mental scientists. Finally, in the "last battle of consequence during the Inter-
regnum"[9] the Foundation's superior tactics and weapons ensure
victory over Kalgan; after this, no nation can match its development, and the Foundation becomes "absolute master of the gal-

axy." (p. 187) Presumably, it too will finally become stagnant, and decline, while a more vigorous, technically-superior society will develop to change the balance of power again. Just as the contemporary theme of biological development in *Last and First Men* echoed and illustrated the central concept of a spiral movement of history, so the decay of scientific and technical knowledge, and hence power, in the Empire, and the corresponding preservation and development by the Foundation, both reflect and influence the inevitable, endless pattern of the rise and fall of societies.

Despite the modern form, special narrative devices and contemporary themes, however, both writers are basically concerned with the expression of a traditional concept. Stapledon's "essay in myth creation" (p. 11) is, as pointed out above, a secular version of the apocalyptic view of history, a reworking in modern terms of the concept that:

> over cycle of incarnations, human long range goals are supposed to add up to evolution into higher life-forms and planes of consciousness, eventually as disembodied mind, sooner or later to reunite with God/Tao/the Cosmos or call it what you will.[10]

Stapledon sees this progress in spiritual rather than material, social or physical terms. Certainly, science develops, until man can travel in space and control his evolution; men change, until they have a radically different appearance and a life-span of a quarter of a million years; and man's home shifts from Earth to Venus and then to Neptune. But the central development is the slow movement from the time of the First Men, whose post-World-War-I society contains the potential for salvation or self-destruction, through successive strivings towards full humanity, to the achievement of the Racial Awakening and the inescapable destruction of the Last Men.

Within this pattern, individual lives are insignificant. Even races are described only insofar as they succeed or fail to progress spiritually; the Seventh Men, for example, are mentioned because they represent a typical evolutionary dead-end reached by over-specialization, but the races between the Ninth and Fourteenth Men are not even listed. If races are only "movements within a symphony" (p. 187) for Stapledon, individuals are less than notes.

Even the narrator remains an impersonal voice, never identified or developed as a character; the only revelation of his humanity comes when he speaks with anguish, yet acceptance, of man's final destruction. Individuals like the Daughter of Earth and the Last Man do influence moments of history; but they cannot affect the overall pattern, since the first World State inevitably crumbles and the "youngest brother" can only encourage and cheer his fellow men, not avert the final catastrophe. Moreover, the introduction of specific men is rare; for the most part, the scope of the chronicle forces the reader to skim over a broad outline of events, to "fly . . . observing only the broad features of the continent," (p. 17) noting only the most significant incidents in man's progress towards full humanity.

The history of the rise and fall of races is, in *Last and First Men*, the history of man's attempts and failures to achieve total spiritual development, to move beyond the self and "see things whole." The Last Men alone are "flesh wakened into spirituality" (p. 326); they alone find the salvation which accompanies even the secular apocalypse. While other races cannot move beyond selfish personal or ideological concerns, the Eighteenth Men are able not only to subordinate "private cravings to the good of the race, absolutely and without struggle" (p. 297); they are also enabled by their biological superiority to unite with other men as components of a "group-mind." Through the ultimate expression of this unity, the Racial Awakening, they are then able to achieve "ecstacy," the highest state possible to man, defined as "the reconciliation . . . of loyalty to fate and loyalty to man, the two distinct loyalties that man has felt since the beginning of consciousness."[11] The ideal of human existence was, for Stapledon, "an advancement towards ever more penetrating and more comprehensive knowing or awareness, ever more appropriate feeling or willing, ever more creative doing."[12]

These loyalties may be seen as, respectively, goodness and beauty, two ideals which appear irreconcilable. For example, the historical investigations, the dissemination of human sperm, and the mere fact of continued existence are painful, ugly tasks for the Last Men; but they are good, a "supreme religious duty." (p. 325) "Great, and terrible and beautiful is the Whole" the Last Man realizes; but "Is the beauty of the Whole really enhanced by our agony?" (p. 327) The cosmos is destroying man; can its beauty also be good? Though the question is, apparently, unanswerable, the two contraries are at last synthesized in man's acceptance of his inevitable fate, the realization that man "will not be nothing, not as though he had never been; for he is eternally a beauty in the eternal form of things." (p. 327) In the Christian myth, the death of an individual or the destruction of a world is really a cause for rejoicing, because it marks the beginning of eternal life. In the same way, *Last and First Men* ends with an affirmation:

> Man himself, at the very least, is music, a brave theme that makes music also of its vast accompaniment, its matrix of storms and stars. Man himself in his degree is eternally a beauty in the eternal form of things. It is very good to have been man. And so we may go forward together with laughter in our hearts, and peace, thankful for the past, and for our own courage. For we shall make after all a fair conclusion to this brief music that is man. (p. 327)

The spiral ends; man will be destroyed; but he has achieved full spiritual development and hence, in Stapledon's terms, has found racial salvation.

Foundation Trilogy, too, is an "essay in myth"[13] (which develops a vision of man's future within the framework of the classical cyclic pattern of history). The action is circular, and "a circle has no end."[14] The scope of the action is reduced literally to 377 years, and figuratively to a repetition of "the same dull round of things."[15] This pattern is emphasized in part by a constant stress on the inevitability of events.

> The coming destruction of Trantor is not an event in itself, isolated in the scheme of human development. It will be the climax to an intricate drama which was begun centuries ago and which is accelerating in pace continuously . . . The Empire will vanish, and all its good with it . . . A Second Empire will rise, but between it and our civilization will be one thousand generations of suffering humanity.[16]

Thus Seldon, at his trial, maps out the future, with the assurance of a scientist certain of his facts. The psychohistorian's Plan will influence the future, reducing the dark ages to a single millenium; but there is no question of helping or halting the process. Similarly, Seldon tells the leaders of the Foundation that "from now on, and into the centuries, the path you must take is inevitable." (p. 68) The form, too, an account of significant historic events leading to a known conclusion, emphasizes this theme.

But the circular pattern is most clearly developed through specific parallels with past history. Between our time and that of the Foundation, human progress has, apparently, been immense. Men have populated the entire galaxy; the location of the original solar system is lost in tradition. (p. 55) Yet nothing has really changed since 1968. There is still a precarious dependence on atomic power, now fifty thousand years old. (p. 46) People still think and act in the same way—Arcadia Darell could be any contemporary fourteen-year-old. Societies, too, are still organized in the same way. Not only has the basic unit, the family, been maintained, but most important, no one has developed a form of government to replace the rule of states or empires by the most powerful man or nation. No one has succeeded in eradicating conflicts, rivalries and wars, or the human selfishness, greed and stupidity which cause them. This repetition, too, is emphasized by the form; though the *Trilogy* is written as a popular, patriotic history, there is no attempt to disguise or excuse human flaws within the Foundation itself. In fact, it seems, no one has tried. Specific parallels with the fourth century, too, are easy to find. Asimov was, apparently, influenced by Gibbon.[17] "As Trantor becomes more specialized, it becomes more vulnerable, less able to defend itself . . . As the Imperial succession becomes more and more uncertain, and the feuds among the great families more rampant, social responsibility disappears,"[18] says Gaal Dornick, translating mathematical concepts which predict the Empire's fall into words which could describe the last days of Rome. These parallels add another dimension to the *Trilogy*; the Empire-to-Foundation cycle becomes a microcosm of man's entire history, a never-ending circular movement.

Yet individuals have meaning within this cycle, as they do not in the awesome and austere vision of *Last and First Men*. The view that "the action is merely cerebral" and that events are only "the result of the machinations of the prime mover, shifting power elements like pieces on a chess board"[19] is only partially true. Certainly, the fate of some men is the inevitable result of social events. Bel Riose, for example, is a brave and able general, but he is destroyed because ninety years earlier, Hari Seldon had ensured that "a man like Riose would have to fail."[20] But men also influence events. The Seldon Plan itself is the work of one man and his associates; it serves to deflect "the huge onrushing mass of events just a little . . . enough to remove twenty-nine thousand years of misery from human history."[21] The introduction of the Mule, too, is both a plot device needed to create suspense, and an important illustration of the power of individuals to change the pattern of history. The Seldon Plan is "neither complete nor correct";[22] there is always the possibility that "uncalculated for" variables, like the power of a mutant, will bend or destroy it. (p. 93) After the Mule's defeat by Bayta Darell, it still requires fifteen years of effort by the Second Foundation's social scientists, working through another individual, Arcadia Darell, and the sacrifice of "fifty martyrs" to restore the course of the Plan. Thus the cycles of individual life and social change are linked.

These human dimensions, while a vital factor in making the *Trilogy* interesting and relevant, are also important in developing the framework. Asimov's cyclic view of history appears to deny men's hopes of "a progress towards some kind of Utopia, in which beings like themselves live in unmitigated bliss among circumstances perfectly suited to a fixed human nature."[23] Yet this cycle is more than "a pessimistic vision of existence," a "terrifying" repetition of meaningless events.[24] At the very least, the world of the Foundation is no worse than that of today; the human virtues of love, loyalty, intellectual curiosity, courage and self-sacrifice are more important than wars in the rise of the new Empire. Moreover, the growth of the Second Foundation may, in fact, mark a shift to a higher level of human civilization. The development of psychohistory not only enables men to predict the future, and hence influence it, however slightly; it also leads to the development of psychology and a startling advance in man's ability to communicate with others. Before this time, all the suffering that humanity ever knew can be traced to the one fact that no man in the history of the Galaxy, until Hari Seldon, and very few men thereafter, could really understand one another . . . because they did not know one another, and dared not trust one another, and felt from infancy the terrors and insecurity of that ultimate isolation—there was the hunted fear of man for man, the savage rapacity of man toward man.[25]

With this new emotional rapport, comparable to Stapledon's concept of the group-mind, true human understanding is at last possible. Moreover, because in the past man concentrated on the development of physical rather than mental science,

> control of self and society has been left to chance or to the vague groupings of intuitive ethical systems based on inspiration and emotion. As a result, no culture of greater stability than about fifty-five percent has ever existed, and these only as the result of great human misery. (p. 91)

The ultimate aim of the Seldon Plan, however, is to replace these unstable societies with the Second Empire, for which "the First Foundation supplies the physical framework of a single political unit, and the Second Foundation supplies the mental framework of a ready-made ruling class." (p. 92) Man may, in fact, succeed in developing a human Utopia, and the circle of history may have an end.

Thus it may be seen that Stapledon and Asimov, whatever their views on the nature and destiny of man, share a common aim. Both *Last and First Men* and the *Foundation Trilogy* are restatements, in a modern idiom and context, of a vision of life as old as man's imagination itself. In human history, "As one age falls, another rises, different to mortal sight, but to immortals only the same . . . nothing new occurs in identical existence; Accident ever varies, Substance can never suffer change or decay."[26] In literature, too, the mode of expression changes but the cosmic vision remains the same, both the foundation and boundary of the human imagination. It is the attempt to depict, not a single theme or the lives of individual men, but a concept of human life which distinguishes both *Last and First Men* and *Foundation Trilogy*. In this way, both works become explorations of the "limits of the imagination," and maps of the "city of which the stars are suburbs."

NOTES

[1]Frye, *The Anatomy of Criticism*, pp. 316-317.

[2]*Ibid.*, p. 318.

[3]*Ibid.*, p. 321.

[4]Frye, *Educated Imagination*, p. 33.

[5]Stapledon, *Last and First Men* (Penguin, 1963), p. 15. Subsequent references will be to this text.

[6]Will and Ariel Durant, *The Lessons of History* (1968), p. 18.

[7]Isaac Asimov, *Foundation* (Avon, 1966), p. 30. Subsequent references will be to this edition.

[8]Asimov, *Foundation and Empire* (1966), "Prologue," n.p.

[9]Asimov, *Second Foundation* (1964), p. 161.

[10]Walter Breen, "The Blown Mind on Film," *Warhoon*, 24 (August 1968), 23.

[11]Brunet, *The Mystic Vision of Olaf Stapledon* (1968), p. 10.

[12]Stapledon, *Waking World* quoted in Brunet, p. 9.

[13]Stapledon, *Last and First Men*, p. 12.

[14]Asimov, *Second Foundation*, p. 179.

[15]William Blake, "There Is No Natural Religion," in Geoffrey Keynes, ed., *Blake: Complete Writings* (1966), p. 97.

[16]Asimov, *Foundation*, p. 19.

[17]Sam Moskowitz, *Seekers of Tomorrow* (1966), p. 259.

[18]Asimov, *Foundation*, p. 19.

[19]Moskowitz, p. 260.

[20]Asimov, *Foundation and Empire*, p. 81.

[21]Asimov, *Foundation*, pp. 28-29.

[22]Asimov, *Second Foundation*, p. 89.

[23]Stapledon, p. 15.

[24]Mircea Eliade, *The Sacred and the Profane*, translated by Willard Trask (1961), p. 107.

[25]Asimov, *Second Foundation*, p. 86.

[26]Blake, "A Descriptive Catalogue," in Keynes, p. 567.

AWARD-WINNING
SCIENCE FICTION
NOVELS

At present the science fiction community gives two separate, annual awards to writers whose works have been judged the year's finest sf in categories ranging from the short story to the novel. The newer of these, the Nebula Award, is sponsored by the Science Fiction Writers of America, whose membership of 300 or so is limited to those authors who have published at least one story commercially. The other is the Hugo, named of course, for Hugo Gernsback. During the 1950's a third, the International Fantasy Award, was also given but was discontinued after 1957.

Since 1939, with the exception of the period of World War II, editors, writers, and enthusiasts have met each year at the so-called World Convention (Worldcon), held over the Labor Day weekend in the United States and as close as possible to that date abroad. Not, however, until 1953 in Philadelphia did the Convention take official recognition of what it called the Science Fiction Achievement Award. Such may have been the name proposed by the Convention committee, but from the first the members of the convention—fandom—called it the Hugo. Lapsing the next year but re-instated in 1955, it became the Hugo by legislative action in 1958. Since then it has remained a highly coveted prize, for it is granted by popular vote. The procedure and categories have varied; at present there are ten categories, three of which are assigned to the work of amateurs for the best "fanzine," best fan writer, and best fan artist, respectively, once again illustrating how closely knit is the whole of the science fiction community.

The recipients of the Nebula Awards, which date from 1965 shortly after the SFWA became active, are also chosen by ballot, but in this case by the vote of their fellow-writers upon stories published the year previously. Following the example of The Mystery Writers of America, SFWA has published the winning stories and the runners-up (except for the novels) in an anthology series, *Nebula Awards*, edited each year by different members of the organization. Since the Hugo stories are not collected together, this anthology provides what is perhaps the most distinguished sampling of sf available in a single volume annually. It has significant importance, of course, in measuring the temperature and direction of the genre, especially since the selections are made by the writers themselves.

Earliest of any of the official prizes was the International Fantasy Award, first introduced at the British Convention of 1951. Its chief difference from the others lay in that a panel of judges chose the winners, selecting a novel and a non-fiction title in each of the first three years, but only a novel thereafter. Not given in 1956, it was discontinued after 1957.

For the completeness of the following list, I am indebted to both Donald Franson, who has published a small edition of *A History of the Hugo, Nebula, and International Fantasy Award* (1969),* and to Robert Kerins, who prepared an independent report for *Extrapolation*. They have covered all categories in detail, including all nominees, but because of the frequent changes in the classifications, I have chosen to list only the winning novels. Unless otherwise designated, they received a Hugo.

Award-Winning Novels

1951   *Earth Abides* by George R. Stewart (IFA).
1952   *Fancies and Goodnights* by John Collier (IFA).
1953   *City* by Clifford D. Simak (IFA).
        The Demolished Man by Alfred Bester.
1954   *More Than Human* by Theodore Sturgeon (IFA).
1955   *A Mirror for Observers* by Edgar Pangborn (IFA).
        They'd Rather Be Right by Mark Clifton and Frank Riley.
1956   *Double Star* by Robert Heinlein.
1957   *Lord of the Rings Trilogy* by J. R. R. Tolkien (IFA).
1958   *The Big Time* by Fritz Leiber.
1959   *A Case of Conscience* by James Blish.
1960   *Starship Troopers* by Robert Heinlein.

---

*Donald Franson, *A History of the Hugo, Nebula, and International Fantasy Award Listing Nominees and Winners 1951-1969* (Chicago: Sciencefiction Sales, 1969).

1961   *A Canticle for Leibowitz* by Walter M. Miller, Jr.

1962   *Dark Universe* by Daniel F. Galouye.

1963   *The Man in the High Castle* by Philip K. Dick.

1964   *Here Gather the Stars* by Clifford D. Simak.

1965   *The Wanderer* by Fritz Leiber.

1966   *Dune* by Frank Herbert (Nebula).
        (tie) *"And Call Me Conrad"* by Roger Zelazny and *Dune* by
           Frank Herbert

1967   (tie) *Babel 17* by Samuel R. Delany and *Flowers for Algernon*
           by Daniel Keyes (Nebula).
        The Moon Is a Harsh Mistress by Robert A. Heinlein.

1968   *The Einstein Intersection* by Samuel R. Delany (Nebula).
        Lord of Light by Roger Zelazny.

1969   *Rite of Passage* by Alexei Panshin (Nebula).
        Stand on Zanzibar by John Brunner.

1970   *The Left Hand of Darkness* by Ursula LeGuin (Nebula).
        The Left Hand of Darkness by Ursula LeGuin.

1971   *Ringworld* by Larry Niven (Nebula).
        Ringworld by Larry Niven

BIBLIOGRAPHY

For various reasons no brief bibliography can ever be completely satisfactory. The following titles, however, form the core of the critical literature dealing with the genre, most of them having been published in the 1960's.

Amis, Kingsley	*New Maps of Hell* (1960).
Armytage, W. H. G.	*Yesterday's Tomorrows* (1968).
Bailey, J. O.	*Pilgrims Through Space and Time* (1947).
Bergonzi, Bernard	*The Early H. G. Wells: A Study of the Scientific Romances* (1961).
Bleiler, Everett F.	*The Checklist of Fantastic Literature* (1948).
Bretnor, Reginald, ed.	*Modern Science Fiction: Its Meaning and Future* (1953).
Clarke, I. F.	*The Tale of the Future: A Checklist* (1961). *Voices Prophesying War* (1966).
deCamp, L. Sprague	*Science Fiction Handbook* (1953).
Franklin, Bruce	*Future Perfect* (1966).
Gove, Phillip Babcock	*The Imaginary Voyage in Prose Fiction* (1941).
Hay, George, ed.	*The Disappearing Future* (1970).
Hillegas, Mark R.	*The Future as Nightmare* (1967).
Kagarlitski, Julius	*The Life and Thought of H. G. Wells* (1966).
Knight, Damon	*In Search of Wonder* (2nd edn. 1967).
Lovecraft, H. P.	*Supernatural Horror in Fiction* (1945).
Moskowitz, Sam	*Explorers of the Infinite* (1963). *Seekers of Tomorrow* (1966).
Nicolson, Marjorie	*Voyages to the Moon* (1948).
Panshin, Alexei	*Heinlein in Dimension* (1968).
Philmus, Robert W.	*Into the Unknown* (1970).
Plank, Robert	*The Emotional Necessity of Imaginary Beings* (1968).
Walsh, Chad	*From Utopia to Nightmare* (1962).

To name a few from the multitude of amateur magazines ("fanzines") is both to risk omitting titles deserving notice and to incur the displeasure of partisan enthusiasts. Nevertheless, the following merit the attention of scholars and librarians because of the continued high quality of their work, particularly in the areas of book reviews and of columns by active professional writers. In these ways they keep the reader closely informed of the temper of the professional, commercial side of the genre. One, *Luna Monthly*, possesses many of the characteristics of a trade journal.

Journal of the Australian Science Fiction Association. Graham Stone, ed., Box 852, P. O., Canberra City, ACT 2601, Australia.

Luna Monthly. Frank and Ann Dietz, eds. 655 Orchard Street, Oradell, New Jersey 07649.

Quarber Merkur. Franz Rottensteiner, ed. Felsenstrasse 20, 2763 Ortmann, Austria.

Riverside Quarterly. Leland Sapiro, ed. Box 40, Regina, Canada. (*RQ* is included in the annual *PMLA* bibliography).

Science Fiction Review. Richard Geis, ed. Box 3116, Santa Monica, California 90403. (For the past two years *SFR* has won a Hugo).

Science Fiction Times. Hans-Joachim Alpers, ed. 2850 Bremerhaven 1, Weisenburger Strasse 6, West Germany.

Speculation. Peter R. Weston, ed. 31 Pinewall Avenue, Masshouse Lane, Birmingham 30, U. K.

Vector. Dr. R. C. Parkinson, ed. BSFA, Ltd. 10 Lower Church Lane, Bristol BS2 8BA, U. K.

Samuel R. Delany is to edit a new quarterly, *Warp*, published by the New American Library, but as yet it has not appeared though the first number is due sometime during the autumn-winter of 1970-1971. Finally, four individual anthologies should be given attention because of their subject matter:

Moskowitz, Sam. *Science Fiction by Gaslight: A History and Anthology of Science Fiction in the Popular Magazines, 1891-1911* (1968). *Under the Moon of Mars: A History and Anthology of the "Scientific Romance" in the Munsey Magazines, 1911-1920* (1970).

Silverberg, Robert. *The Mirror of Infinity: A Critics' Anthology of Science Fiction* (1970)

Suvin, Darko. *Other Worlds, Other Seas: Science Fiction Stories from Socialist Countries* (1970)

The titles of them all reveal their importance, but it should be underscored that Silverberg's volume marks the first occasion when critics, both from the academic and professional areas, have both chosen the stories and written critical introductions to them.

CONTRIBUTORS

Since 1959, Thomas D. Clareson, Professor of English at the College of Wooster, has edited *Extrapolation: The Newsletter of the MLA Seminar on Science Fiction,* and now serves as the Chairman of the newly formed, international Science Fiction Research Association (SFRA).

He received his doctorate from the University of Pennsylvania and teaches in the fields of American Literature and 19th and 20th century fiction. Previous publications include *Science and Society: Readings at Midcentury* (Harpers, 1960) and *Victorian Essays* (Kent State, 1967), which he edited with Professor Warren D. Anderson. He has also been a member of the Editoral Board of *Victorian Poetry* and published essays on the Victorian novelist, Charles Reade.

SF: The Other Side of Realism is the first of three titles by Clareson to be scheduled for release in 1971-1972. He has done *Science Fiction Criticism: An Annotated Bibliography* (Kent State) and *A Spectrum of Worlds,* an anthology of stories with accompanying critical commentaries (Doubleday).

Now on leave of absence in 1971-1972, Professor Clareson is completing a biography of Charles Reade and hopes to finish at least the necessary research for *Some Kind of Paradise: A History of American Science Fiction to 1926.*

BRIAN ALDISS has been co-editor of *SF Horizons,* the only British journal devoted to the criticism of sf, but he is better known as an sf writer. His recent title, *Barefoot in the Head,* has proved to be one of the most provocative experimental novels in the genre.

MORRIS BEJA is a member of the English Department at Ohio State University. One of his chief interests is the field of popular culture.

BERNARD BERGONZI of the English Department, University of Warwick, Coventry, helped to initiate the new interest in sf with his *The Early H. G. Wells: A Study of the Scientific Romances* (1961). More recently he has published *Heroes' Twilight: A Study of the Literature of the Great War* (1965).

JAMES BLISH plays a double role. He is one of the foremost sf writers with such titles as *Black Easter* and the just-published *And All the Stars A Stage;* and as William Atheling, Jr., he is one of the top critics of the field, both *The Issue at Hand* and *More Issues at Hand* having been published by Advent. In addition, he is co-editor of *Kalki,* the Journal of the Cabell Society.

MICHEL BUTOR, novelist and critic, has written widely, ranging from a study of the *Essays* of Montaigue to critical analyses of the moderns.

PATRICK J. CALLAHAN, Department of English, Notre Dame University, has written critically on Robert Graves and J. R. R. Tolkien and contributes frequently to such journals as *The Blake Newsletter* and *Blake Studies.* He is himself a poet, publishing in the little magazines, most recently *Husson Review,* and in the *1971 Yearbook of Modern Poetry.*

I. F. CLARKE, Professor and Head of the Department of English Studies at Strathclyde University, Glasgow, wrote *Voices Prophesying War,* an historical study of the future-war motif. The second edition of his checklist, *The Tale of the Future,* is now being completed for autumn publication. He has also served as a consultant for B.B.C.

SAMUEL R. DELANY has received four Nebula awards from the Science Fiction Writers of America, the most recent for his novelette "Time Considered as a Helix of Semi-Precious Stones." He is also co-editor of *Quark,* described as a "Quarterly of Speculative Literature and Graphics."

ALEX EISENSTEIN has long been active in fandom, contributing to such "fanzines" as *Trumpet.*

BRUCE FRANKLIN, Department of English, Stanford University, published *The Wake of the Gods: Melville's Mythology* before issuing the critical anthology, *Future Perfect: American Science Fiction in the Nineteenth Century.*

BEN FUSON, Professor of English, Kansas Wesleyan University, is one of the founders of the MLA Seminar on Science Fiction. A bibliophile, he has published *The Centennial Bibliography of Kansas Literature 1854-1961*.

SUSAN WOOD GLICKSOHN now teaches in the English Department at the University of Toronto, where she is completing her doctorate. She is co-editor of the Canadian "fanzine," *Energumen*.

MARK HILLEGAS, Professor of English, Southern Illinois University, taught the first formal course in science fiction at Colgate in the early 1960's. He is author of *From Utopia to Nightmare: H. G. Wells and the Anti-Utopians* and editor of *Shadows of Imagination: The Fantasies of C. S. Lewis, J. R. R. Tolkien*, and *Charles Williams*, which grew out of the MLA Seminar.

JANE HIPOLITO is a member of the Department of English, California State College-Fullerton. She is a collector and has taught a course in sf for several years. Her critical studies of contemporary sf writers have appeared in the U.S. and Britain.

RICHARD M. HODGENS has acted as a film reviewer for *Film Quarterly* and *National Review*. He is now completing an English version of *Orlando Furioso* for publication by Ballantine.

JULIUS KAGARLITSKI is Professor of the History of the European Theatre and Literature at the State Institute of Theatrical Art in Moscow. He edited the Russian edition of the *Works of H. G. Wells*, and is perhaps best known in the West for his *The Life and Thought of H. G. Wells*.

STANISLAW LEM is most widely known as an sf writer, with such titles as *The Star Diaries of Ion Tichy and Solaris*, but he is also one of the leading Eastern European critics of the genre. He is founder of the Polish Astronautic Society and the author of several books on the history of science, as well as *The Philosophy of Chance*, a theory of culture. He is now completing a book on sf and futurology.

WILLIS E. McNELLY, Professor of English, California State College-Fullerton combines his interest in Joyce, Yeats, and Eliot with that in sf. He was one of the contributors to Robert Silverberg's *The Mirror of Infinity: A Critics' Anthology of Science Fiction* and the first academician asked to do the critical introduction for SFWA's annual Nebula award anthology.

MILTON A. MAYS, a member of the English Department of Drury College, has a general interest in 19th century fiction, with specific emphasis upon American fiction, particularly James. He has essays in the current issues of *Texas Studies in Literature* and *American Literature*.

JUDITH MERRIL, long editor of the annual anthology, *The Year's Best*, was among the first to acknowledge the importance of the British experimental sf during the 1960's. She now resides in Toronto, where she acts as one of the curators for the special sf collection held by the Toronto Public Library.

RICHARD D. MULLEN, Professor of English, Indiana State University, is a member of the Executive Committee of the Science Fiction Research Association and Chairman of its Bibliography Committee.

ALEXEI PANSHIN received a Nebual award for his novel *Rite of Passage*. He has emerged as one of the notable popular critics of the genre. His study of contemporary sf, *The World Beyond the Hill*, is now being readied for publication.

ROBERT PLANK holds a dual appointment in the Departments of English and Psychology, Case Western Reserve University. His continuing inquiry into sf culminated in *The Emotional Significance of Imaginary Beings: A Study of the Interaction of Psychopathology, Literature, and Reality in the Modern World.*

FRANZ ROTTENSTEINER has long edited *Quarber-Merkur,* one of the most influential European "fanzines."

RUDOLF B. SCHMERL, Assistant Dean of Research, School of Education, The University of Michigan, has published numerous articles on such writers as Orwell and Huxley.

NORMAN SPINRAD, too infrequently writing as a critic of sf, is one of the leading experimental writers in the genre. His most widely known title is *The Last Hurrah of the Golden Horde.*

LIONEL STEVENSON, Professor of English, Duke University, has written widely on 19th and 20th century fiction. Perhaps his most provocative appraisal of modern fantasy and sf occurs in *The History of the English Novel*, v. 11 : *Yesterday and After.*